Uprising

A Collide Novel
Book Two

SHELLY CRANE

1

Every rebellion implies some kind of unity.
-**The Rebel**

Editing services provided by Jennifer Nunez.
Printed in paperback August 2011 and available in Kindle and E-book format as of June 2011 through Amazon, Create Space and Barnes & Noble.

Printed in the United States

10 9 8 7 6 5 4 3 2 1

You can find the author at her website
http://shellycrane.blogspot.com

   ISBN-10: 1463759347
   ISBN-13: 978-1463759346

Uprising - A Collide Novel - Shelly Crane

This novel is dedicated
to my father, JR. If not for him pushing reruns of Star Trek and Quantum Leap on me when I was a kid, I would never have gotten into the Paranormal and Sci-Fi. Thank you, Dad.

PART 1

Where There's a Will
Chapter 1

Cain and I walked out through the restaurant where he worked. Out of the place I was only supposed to be in for a few minutes to give them a flyer and instead, had been in for who knew how long. And now we were headed to the Jeep where Merrick was waiting for me, but I was bringing a guy along with me. A guy who had just kissed me.

Cain stopped to tell someone he was taking his break.

Merrick looked frazzled, as expected, when we reached the parking lot of the diner. He hopped out of the car and walked swiftly to the passenger side, pulling me up into a hug before even acknowledging Cain. It was a very protective and possessive hug at that. I'd been inside too long and had him worried.

After a bit of macho sizing up on both sides, I conveyed the whole story about meeting Cain in the diner and him taking me in the stock room, explaining that he was not with the Lighters and that he had family for us to meet. I explained everything except the kiss. That little tidbit wouldn't help anyone right then. In fact, I was still boiling from it myself. Then they introduced themselves formally.

"Merrick, Sherry's husband," Merrick said, extending a hand for Cain and he was no longer hostile looking.

"Cain. Nice to meet you," he said sincerely.

"Nice to meet you, too. So, how long do you have left on your shift? I have got to say, I'm pretty excited by all this."

Cain nodded his head in agreement. "Two hours. Come back then and I'll take you to my family. They're going to be ecstatic," Cain said with a wide smile.

Cain went back in to finish his work shift. We would find somewhere to wait for him. He said it would not be wise to go without him as everyone was pretty trigger happy these days. We totally understood that one.

So Merrick drove us to get some lunch at a local burger joint that reminded me of the funny place we first ate at together. We sat overlooking the river, the weather was perfect. The sun was shining bright and the trees gave us some shade, so it was the perfect in between of cool and warm.

It was weird just how normal everything looked and felt out there.

If you were plopped in my seat, you'd be eating a burger and fries with raspberry tea, sitting next to your gorgeous, wonderful husband on the hood of your Jeep, overlooking the never changing river. You'd think this was bliss not hell. In some ways, I guess it still was.

"So, how you are doing lately? I haven't seen you much since I've been spending all my time working down in the hall. Are the new guys ok? Are they treating everyone well?" Merrick asked me as he shoved in a mouthful of Ranch dipped onion rings.

"Yeah, everything is fine. The newbies are great. Miguel is hilarious. Josh is so sweet. Danny is jealous of him, can you believe that? He and Celeste seem to be getting back to their lovey dovey selves. Trudy is acting better now, too."

Mrs. Trudy had been a sort of recluse since her son, Phillip, had tried to force himself on me and then hightailed it out of there with my car a couple weeks ago. We hadn't seen him since. It sucked for her, knowing what he tried to do and then leaving like that.

"Good." He smiled. "You and your hamburgers with extra mayo. You've got some on your lip, cutie," he said and wiped it with his thumb, then put it in his mouth to lick it off.

"Thanks for that," I said with a smirk.

"And you? You're not thinking about things...since Phillip talked to you..."

Although Phillip had left that day he communicated with me once in my mind this morning and Merrick had been extra sensitive about it. We were a little puzzled as to how he did that since he wasn't a Special.

"No, I'm fine. I know it sounds bad but...in all honesty I dealt with so much of Matt's crap and I just feel safe with you. I'm not traumatized. I'm not worried. I'm not scared. He's gone. Ok?"

"Ok. If you can say it then it's true," Merrick said as he pulled me closer to him on the hood of the Jeep.

"I was scared today though. Cain scared the crap out of me! But I am glad we found more of us. Though, where the heck we're going to keep putting these people, I don't know."

I laughed thinking of us all tunneled up under the store like gophers.

"Well, we have Mike now, he is a basement constructor," Merrick said as he rubbed the ring on my finger with a little smile playing at the corner of his lips.

"Yeah, that was wicked lucky."

"Yeah it was and we keep getting all these guys coming in so, we'll have plenty of help with all the work and labor that has to be done. It'll work itself out and be ok."

"Yeah, you're right. You're always right." I smiled against his chest and felt his smile, too. Yes it was possible. "This is so nice, being completely by ourselves.

I know we have our closet, but...this is so much nicer with a way better view than concrete."

"I know. I'm sorry you can't have it your way. And my way. My way, we'd be at our own house right now, on the deck that I helped design and build alongside Jeff, whom we hired. You'd have a garden outside, but it would be up to you what you put it in. I'm assuming because of your parents you'd want flowers not vegetables." He looked sideways at me with a knowing smile and he was right. I didn't want a veggie garden, simply on principal to spite my hippie parents.

I thought he was done, but he wasn't. I continued to listen.

"You'd also have your VW Rabbit back, fully restored by me because I know how much you always loved that hunk of junk. Danny and Celeste would visit and bring our niece and nephew along as well as their dog. Our dog hates their dog and though both are male, they fight like girls."

I burst out laughing as he continued, but he started to get serious. He placed an upside down hand on my collarbone and twirled my curls in his fingers.

"We spend all day Saturdays in bed, only getting up to order take out. You have your own photography business after realizing that Travel Journal was never good enough for you anyway. Everyone loves your work and you are very busy during the week, with all your bookings lined up. Ryan could be your assistant."

"I start my own business with Jeff doing small construction because it's all we Keepers know how to do. We are always home on the weekends, never late to dinner at night, and we never, ever fight. Except...when I'm making you late for work because I can't keep my hands off of you." He nuzzled his face into my neck and kissed my collarbone and throat, pulsing the electricity.

"I'd love that," I said breathlessly, tears threatening.

I wanted to cry to see that Merrick's dream of our life would be the exact mirror of mine if we could have it. I wanted it so badly and it hurt even more to visualize it and know we'd never have it.

Merrick's wandering lips and hand squeezing on my hip pushed any lingering sadness away and replaced it with something else completely. His hand slid lower along my thigh and then...his watch beeped; the timer he set for us to go meet Cain.

I heard and felt the frustrated grunt against my neck as he pulled back and gave me a face. I couldn't help but giggle at him.

"Oh, my pain is funny, huh?" he said with playful eyebrows raised.

He pulled me from the hood and threw me over his shoulder, lapping the Jeep in a blur with me squealing and laughing more than I had in a long while. He patted my bottom, playfully spanking, before putting me down and helping me into the passenger seat. He reached over me to buckle me, then kissed my nose before heading over to his side.

We started toward the coffee shop and I massaged his neck and shoulders for a bit, trying to ease some of his frustration and anxiety mixed together. I knew he liked it because he could barely drive straight, lolling his head back and forth.

Hopefully this meeting would go smoothly, with no incidents. It was just the two of us after all, one of us with extremely back luck, but my protector was here and we were fed, happy and actually had a couple hours all alone and were on our way to meet others to join us.

I was grateful and excited beyond belief.

We followed Cain in his silver extended cab Dodge Dakota up the bend and around the hill a few miles out of town. The Jeep had no problem with the steep hill but I could definitely see what he was talking about when he said no one ever went up there looking for them. Any other car we would have brought would have never made it and we would've had a heck of a walk.

It was secluded and well hidden by a full apple orchard on the hill. It was perfect except for the fact that the cabin couldn't have been more than four hundred square feet, including the front porch. Four people living there together with what couldn't be more than one bathroom and no personal space?

Ouch.

The flower and vegetable garden they had to the side was gorgeous, the whole place was.

There were jasmine vines all over the lattice up the side of the house and huge sunflowers out by the fence and mailbox. I wondered how they grew so well with the crazy weather. A small red barn in the back would have been a perfect spot for the Rabbit to park in. I missed my Rabbit.

I also thought that this could be the little house from Merrick's fantasy. It was perfection in the small, quaint and secluded.

The old man sitting in the rocking chair on the porch didn't move as we pulled in behind Cain. Just kept rocking with his hands in his lap and eyes closed.

Merrick waited for me to come to his side and laced our fingers. As we got closer the old man still didn't move. I saw Cain's mouth open to speak but the man beat him to the punch.

"Cain, we got company, do we?" the old man spoke, eyes still closed.

"Yes, sir, Pap. This nice lady and her husband are part of the *resistance*," Cain said and he emphasized the last word and looked back to wink at us.

"Is that right? Well how 'bout that." His eyes popped open and they were the grayest eyes I'd ever seen that matched his completely gray, almost bald head and full beard. His extreme southern accent blended with the calm country setting and I thought his torn stained jeans and slack attitude were perfect for someone named 'Pap'.

11

"Yes, sir. This is Sherry and I'm sorry, I forgot your name," Cain said and turned to look at Merrick.

"Merrick, sir. It's really nice to meet you." He didn't release my hand but pulled me protectively forward with him so he could shake Pap's hand.

"Nice firm grip, son. That says a lot 'bout a man. And you sure got yourself a pertty little thing, now don't ya? Hello, ma'am. Very nice to meet ya," he said as he leaned forward on the edge of his rocker to take my hand and he actually kissed my bent fingers.

"Uh...thank you. It's very nice to meet you, too, sir," I told him through my slight embarrassment, feeling the blush in my cheeks and down my neck.

"Pap, they have a bunch of people that stay with them out away back from town. They are here to talk to us about maybe joining them," Cain said as he leaned closer and spoke loudly. I saw Pap turning his head to the side as if to hear better.

"Well, son, we are at war. We need all the help we can get. Y'all come on in, now."

He got up and waved for us to follow him inside.

It was blazing hot in the cabin, not for of lack of air conditioning but because of the unnecessary roaring fire in the fireplace in the middle of the day. The sun was actually shining there as well, making it a beautiful and warm day.

The other two men and one woman were sitting at the kitchen table right in the middle of the main room. They didn't seem alarmed at our presence either. The woman was reading a book and the men were playing chess. From my point of view there wasn't a TV or radio or anything else electronic in the place. The only light was the windows and an oil lamp on the table.

"Margaret, Frank, Simon. These here folks are here to ask for our help in the resistance," Pap said as he went over to sit in the rocker by the fire.

The one Pap pointed to as Simon came over to hug Merrick. He had a pile of dark red curly hair and a huge scar across his face. That was about all I saw as I looked away trying not to be rude. I understood that this was traditional between Keepers to hug brotherly with fist pounding backs but everyone else kind of looks a little oddly at it. I remembered that they didn't know Merrick was a Keeper. Then Simon walked back over to resume his game, wordlessly.

I leaned over to whisper to Cain. "Uh...what's with all this resistance talk?"

"Just let him go with it and he'll pretend that he's helping you instead of the other way around. Just get used to it. These type of people have too much pride to accept charity from strangers," he whispered as I nodded my understanding.

"So, Simon is your Keeper?"

"Yeah, but he doesn't talk much, and his body is sixty years old or so, I think, so he's kind of sluggish," he explained. "He's withdrawn. I haven't really

12

needed him much since he's been here. I think he feels useless."

He leaned forward and spoke louder to Margaret.

"Mrs. Maggie, this is Sherry and Merrick," Cain told her and she rose from her chair.

"Well! Goodness gracious! I am so happy to see there is another woman in this world that ain't a zombie!" She cackled. "I was beginning to think I was the only one left wit' sense. Come on in here and sit yourselves down. I'll make you up some sweet tea."

"Margaret, you know good and well she ain't the only woman left in the world now. Don't go exaggerating. Exaggerating is just lying's ugly cousin, now," Pap said as we followed Cain to sit on the couch.

"Now, Pap! I never said she was the only woman left in the world. I said the only one left wit' sense. Don't go putting words in my mouth you old grump. And exaggerating ain't nobody's cousin. You call lying was it is...old coot...dang it all... always trying to..." She kept going even as Pap started his own rant back at her as she made the tea.

It was a battle of wits and volume and it was slightly hilarious and took all I had not to laugh out loud.

Cain leaned over and rolled his eyes to yell over them about how they always did this and just ignore them. They'd been married for 53 years and this was nothing new.

I wondered if they were his grandparents. I also thought his statement must be true because the other two men kept on playing chess as if nothing was going on at all.

We drank our extremely strong and sweet, but delicious iced tea and chatted back and forth with introductions and intentions. I finally got a really good look at Cain as he went to stoke the not needed fire.

He was nice looking, very nice looking. His hair was brown and seriously short and his eyes were blue green like seawater. He looked very much like he was maybe ex-military which was confirmed by the Marines tattoo on his arm.

He was built very nicely under his tan 'Got Coffee?' t-shirt and blue jeans. I was sure that the shirt was his work uniform. I didn't see Cain as the funny t-shirt kind of guy. I was thrilled that I hadn't even noticed how hot he was until now, not even when he kissed me.

I wanted to tell Merrick "See! A hot guy kissed me and I didn't even care because I love you so much!" But then I remembered that probably wasn't a very good idea seeing as how I did want Merrick to like Cain.

As stupid as Cain's kissing diversion was I understood he was trying to keep me and him safe and under the radar. The other guy would've asked me what I was

13

doing in their stock room, I got it. I still didn't like it. However, Cain had been
nothing was polite in a very natural easy way ever since.

As we talked and it began to get darker, I felt I could hold off no longer on
telling them that Merrick was a Keeper, as well as my husband, especially with
their whole honesty and lies and cousins bit from before.

So, I gradually and casually listed the Specials in our group and their gifts,
which they knew nothing about the gifts and were very intrigued, and then I listed
the Keepers.

When I said Merrick's name last Cain's eyes went wide for a second and
then adjusted, but it took the rest of them a minute to catch up. I just smiled and
nodded, hugging Merrick's arm like I always did, and waited for the downpour of
negativity pointed right at us.

Oddly enough, I could see the recognition show on their faces but no one
said anything until Margaret.

"Honey, I completely understand. Anymore you have to look elsewhere's for
a good man. God knows all the men left here on this earth, present company
excluded, ain't worth the price of a wooden nickel in a lumber yard."

A slight pause, then I burst out laughing, my hand over my mouth to try to
stifle it. The others followed me soon after with their own chuckles. I loved this
woman!

They all agreed that we needed to stay together so they went and packed
their things. Merrick told them they only needed to bring one vehicle, as we
already didn't know where we were gonna put them all if this kept up. They piled,
arguing loudly about who was going to sit where, into Cain's Dakota and we were
off.

They followed us through the hills and out to the outskirts of town. They
brought most of their supplies with them, some food, tools and a whole mess of
shotguns, bless them.

Cain said he never stopped working at the coffee shop this whole time since
the invasion. He had a familiar face to the town and must be immune to the
Lighters speak because he had been forced to listen to it daily at the shop and never
fell under the spell.

He said he watched as people's eyes literally glazed over and that was it for
them. After that it was 'Keepers are evil' and 'Crandle will save us'. I remembered
that I never got a chance to talk to him about Crandle. I had a suspicion he was the
Taker I saw that day.

He was certain, as he'd been doing it for months, that he could start doing
the grocery shopping for us if we wanted him to. He could make up some story and

was pretty sure they'd buy it as to why he needed so much. That was until the need warehouses came in about two months. After that, we were all up the creek without a paddle.

Jeff and Miguel pulled in behind the store just as we did. To our surprise, they had someone with them too.

A gorgeous little girl who looked to be about three or four years old. She had the blondest hair in ratty pigtails and the bluest eyes ever. Her baby blue dress was torn on the bottom hem and her white shoes were scuffed and dirty, one sock pulled up higher than the other. She was clinging to Miguel's leg and had a doll in her hand with a missing leg.

My heart immediately jumped and I ran over to see what in the world was going on as Merrick started the introductions with Jeff and the rest of them.

"Hey, Miguel, aren't you going to introduce me to your friend?" I said as I squatted down in front of them to be eye level with the disheveled cutie.

"Sure, Sherry. This is Lily. Lily, this is Sherry. This is the nice lady I was telling you about."

I looked up at Miguel and saw that he had a very strange expression. Something I didn't know him well enough to read yet.

"Well, Lily. Gosh, that's a pretty name. How old are you?"

"Free," she whispered as she tried to lift three fingers together, having to hold down two of them with her other hand, almost dropping her doll in the process.

"Three. Wow! Big girl. What's her name?" I pointed to the mangled doll.

"Miwey. Miwey cuz of my sister wuvs Miwey Cywus...She watches her on...on...TV. She used to," she stammered through her explanation.

"I know who Miley is. That is very neat. Um... Lily? Do you think you might want to come inside with me and get some milk? Maybe we'll ask Mrs. Trudy about putting some chocolate in it too. That's my favorite. What do you think? You want to come with me?"

She looked up at Miguel and he nodded and smiled. She reluctantly let go and grabbed my pinkie and ring finger from my outstretched hand in her little grasp, all the while looking back at Miguel to make sure it was still ok.

I looked back too and he looked at me with that same expression as before and mouthed "later" to me. I nodded and headed inside with the little girl.

Later that night after everyone was getting situated and introductions had been done, Lily had her milk in the kitchen with Mrs. Trudy. Trudy was in an upheaval of emotions over the little girl. First she was excited then distressed as she assessed the little girl's appearance. Then she changed to intrigued at the possibilities, then flabbergasted as to what we were going to do with her.

I peeked out in the commons room and saw that everyone already loved the new people.

Pap and Margaret were a big hit and everyone was rolling laughing at something one of them had said. I could already hear them start to bicker back and forth. I laughed to myself at the amount of entertainment we'd no doubt gain from those two.

Simon and Max were already hunkered down in a corner, telling Keeper stories no doubt. They seemed to be the more serious Keepers of the bunch.

Then I heard Merrick calling my name in my mind, then Jeff. I found them both talking to Miguel and Cain by the stairs.

"Hey, Sherry, I hear you had an exciting day," Jeff said but he sounded so drained and upset, not like Jeff.

"Yeah, we did, but from the looks of it you guys did, too. What happened? You both look terrible. Are you alright?" I said, glancing them over.

"We're fine," Miguel said and Jeff said, "We're ok." Both answered at the same time. Then Jeff again, "Don't worry about us, Sherry."

"What's up with the little girl?"

"I'm not sure I want to tell you. It was pretty..." he swallowed, "...awful." Jeff looked at me with such a look that I knew I better take his word on it.

"Ok, don't tell me, then. So she was alone?"

"No, not alone. She was with... The Lighters can't control babies and small children so...the humans were using her as a fetch girl; getting them drinks and food from the kitchen, cleaning up their messes. That's all I'm going to say about it. Miguel snatched her up and we ran out of there. We did manage to get the food first though."

I tried to keep my expression under control. A 'fetch girl'? Cleaning? What the heck was that? She was only three years old.

"What happened to her parents?" I asked, but regretted it as soon as I said it.

Sherry...don't. You don't want to know this.

Merrick warned me in my mind and I knew that he had seen what Jeff was referring to in his head. He knew I would want no part in knowing about it.

"Those were her parents, Sherry. She had a sister too but..." he stopped, Jeff and Miguel both winced, and then Jeff changed the subject. "And the worst part is she's a Special. I have no idea where her Keeper is."

Jeff stopped and blew an exasperated breath. I thought that they must not have seen much human suffering either as Keepers, always looking after their charges. Miguel stepped in to finish the explanation.

"She was eating out of the trash behind the boozer, the uh club, in town near the grocery. When we found her, she looked worse for wear so I asked her where her parents were and she told me they were out having a blue."

I'd learned from previous conversations with Miguel that a blue meant fight. He continued.

"Anyway, she was so dirty and alone in the alley and there were dead rats and...she said she hadn't eaten anything since yesterday so we-"

"Ok, ok, you're right, don't tell me more. So she's going to stay here with us right? There's nothing else *to* do. We can handle this. We can handle a little girl. She was awfully adorable..." I shook my head and cleared my throat. "So, anyway, I see you've met Cain. He's pretty useful with all his knowledge of the way things are now with the town and things like that. He works at the coffee shop. This here is the guy you need to speak to" I said, mock punching Jeff in the chest. "Jeff's our main brain in this joint."

I was trying in vain to steady my voice, thinking about the little girl...and what would make them wince about her sister. No! Stop thinking about it.

"If you wouldn't mind, Cain, maybe you can tell everyone later of some of the things going on that we might need to know about. Fill us in on the way things work now. Some of us have been locked up down here for quite a while with no idea what's going on anymore," Jeff asked.

"Yeah, sure, no problem. Um...Sherry? Could I talk to you for a minute?" Cain said, immediately grabbing my elbow and pulling me away before I could even answer.

"Sure." He dragged me to the corner of the commons room. "What is it?" I asked, wanting to push his hand off but he looked so serious I couldn't seem to be too agitated.

"Well, first, I wanted to make sure you were ok with everything. With me. About earlier, I'm sorry, I really thought it would work and it did work, but I would have never kissed you had I known you were married."

I gave him an amused look.

"Cain, it's fine, really. We're alive, that's what's important right? I promise. No harm done."

"Ok, good. Well, there's more actually. Um...about that little girl, I know her parents. I've seen them come into the store with her before and believe me, she looks way cleaner and less...um... bruised up now than she usually does."

"What?" I squeaked, the tears in my throat choking out the effort.

I glanced over to see Merrick looking at me, checking to see why I seemed to be so agitated so I just sent him a reassuring smile, half hearted.

"Yeah, and there's still more. The people they're with are big Crandle supporters. Like rally starting, hideout burning, resistance killing kind of people.

You better hope that they didn't recognize your guys or follow them. It would be very, very bad for all of us."

"Ok. I can't believe this. Who would-" I grabbed my chest and blew out an exasperated sigh. "I'll let them know to be on the lookout. And hey...thanks for coming with us and for saving me back there," I said and rolled my eyes at him to show I was joking as I went on. "As awkward as it was, thanks. I know you meant well."

"Anytime. I mean...no problem, Sherry." He was plucking his lip ring with his tongue bashfully, making me want to laugh in spite of myself. "Really, now let's go tell your boys that they better watch their backs next time they head into town."

The Lily of the Valley
Chapter 2

Now days, it was all about Lily. That little girl was toted, tickled, carried piggyback and any other way she preferred, bathed, entertained, kissed, played with, sang to, fed and cooked for, and any which way you put it, it was all about Lily. She was spoiled rotten by the underground resistance non-conformists misfit gophers.

I admit that she is the most precious thing I've ever seen since My Little Pony, but we could hardly even get any work done down there anymore for people wanting to cater to that sweet little face and her every whim.

Trudy had taken the grandmother role and she was serious about it. You had to go through Trudy before you interfered in any way with that child. It was absurdly hilarious!

Lily liked me an awful lot though. I was just likeable I guessed though I never seemed to be that way before. Pre-apocalypse I was an invisible unlikable heap of a mess. Post-apocalypse everyone wanted to be my new friend...or date me, whatever. It was a switch, but it was growing on me.

We gave everyone a couple days to cool off and settle in and then we called a meeting. Lily and I had been pretty much inseparable unless Trudy or someone else was trying to tote her off. She was a talkative little thing, and very smart and articulate for her age.

We settled down for the meeting with Cain. The most fascinating thing to the Keepers was that Cain was a Special, but he was working every day and had no run-ins or problems because of it. Lighters can sense Specials when they're near them and spend a great deal of time to find them, so for Cain to be immune to the Lighter speak and be undetectable was a big deal.

Lily sat in my lap during the meeting with Cain, as he explained all about the new world. I couldn't help but touch and braid her hair as it was so soft and sweet smelling.

I was never much for dolls growing up and even if I had been, mom wouldn't have allowed that one. Barbie was a political conformist with an unhealthy body image, you know.

"Shawwy?" Lily said as she always says my name. "I wish my hair was bwown wike yours. Den we'd match and you could be my new mommy."

Somehow, even though there was talking going on everyone heard her comment and stopped what they were doing to stare at the innocent girl who spoke her mind so freely. My heart wrenched and twisted in my chest. Then she hugged me as she spoke.

"Maybe you could be my mommy because you do things wit me. My wast mommy didn't do things wit me."

I felt her need to feel real love pouring out of her, begging for it. I couldn't help myself while I was wedged in between the couch arm and Trudy with Lily facing me on my lap and nowhere to go with my heart breaking for her. I started to cry, right there in front of everyone.

I hated it, because I could see everyone else wanted to break down the same as me, but her comment hadn't been directed at them, and only a handful of them understood that I would never have kids of my own. I was sterile and I would never hear that word 'mommy' for myself.

I felt Trudy's hand on my back and Merrick's thoughtful eyes on me as Lily spoke again.

"Shawwy, why are you cwying? I cwy when I'm sad, when mommy leaves me alone."

Again with the gut-wrenching. The audacity of people to have children and then treat them this way!

"Lily," I spoke though my tears as Danny handed me a tissue and some of the others began to simulate a sense of business so as not to stare. "I'm sorry that your momma did that to you. That was wrong of her, but you're safe now. Me and Jeff, Trudy, Miguel, Merrick, we won't let them hurt you anymore, ok?"

"Is dat why your cwying? Are you scarwed of dem, Shawwy?"

"No, I'm not scared of them," I said through my sniffles. "It'll be ok. We've got a lot of big strong men down here to keep us safe. Look, you see Mr. Cain's muscles?" I pointed and he made a show of playfully flexing his arms and making faces at her which she laughed whole heartedly at. "See? You'll be safe. Don't worry about those people anymore, ok?"

"Ok, Shawwy, I'll tell Miwey not to be scarwed too."

"Ok, that's a good idea."

She yawned and leaned her head against my chest as, thankfully, Jeff and Cain started the meeting again.

All I could do for the rest of the meeting was lean back with her and try not to cry anymore.

Jeff thought it would be best to give Lily his room, the one next to mine and Merrick's, so he moved down to the new hall and showed all the newbies where everything was down the new 'tunnel' as it was affectionately called.

I tucked Lily in to her new room as she continued to yawn. I wasn't sure if she'd even sleep in her own room by herself, but tonight she didn't put up a fight at all as she seemed exhausted and fell right out. The first night here she slept in Trudy's arms on the couch and the next night my arms on the same couch with Merrick at my feet.

We decided to try it and it worked. We cracked her door and watched for a few minutes like two worried parents of a newborn. It was fantastical. So this was what it was like to be a mommy. Somewhat, a glimpse of it, and it was wonderful.

Merrick didn't speak as we lay down to sleep. I knew what he was thinking but he knew I didn't want to talk about it. There was nothing to talk about really. I'd never have kids and that was that.

He just lay behind me and feathered reassuring kisses over my neck and shoulder as his arms circled me. I was entirely grateful to him for being so perceptive and understanding of what I needed. As his warmth surrounded me I drifted into a sound sleep.

The morning was strange. Everything seemed to be blue. There were no walls, no floor, like a cloud or baby blue water and it was so quiet. Too quiet.

I looked over and Merrick wasn't there. In fact, I wasn't even in our room. I was outside on the grass and the sunshine and clouds were all around me. The grass was green and all the grass I'd seen was dead now.

I looked down as myself and saw I was wearing some kind of odd off white silky nightgown down to my ankles and my hair was braided over my shoulder. As I looked around I saw someone coming. Merrick?

No.

But someone handsome and wearing a white button up shirt with tan khakis and no shoes.

He was somewhat tan and his smile was blinding. His short dark brown hair was spiked to the side stylishly, his green eyes were piercing. The closer he got I realized he looked familiar to me but couldn't place him. He reminded me of a movie I saw when I was younger and I had thought the man would be my dream husband one day. He looked to be about thirty or so.

Then I saw Calvin come out from behind him with a gleaming smile and bouncing around happily. They sat in front of me on the grass.

"Hello, Sherry," the man said deeply as he plucked absently at blades of grass, his long legs stretched out beside me.

Up close I saw Calvin's hair was combed neatly too and he was looking at me expectantly. Oh right, I was supposed to say something.

"Hi. Who are you? Calvin? What's going on?"

21

"Who I am is not important, Sherry. Calvin is here. He is important to you, no?"

"Yes, of course he is."

"I'm here to show you what it can be, Sherry. What you can have. Do you find me attractive?"

"What?"

What the...

"I know that you do. And Calvin? Do you not love him as a son?"

"Of course I love him, but what does this have to do with anything?"

"I want to show you your life with me," he said, then little Lily popped out of nowhere from behind him and jumped in my lap.

"Pwease, Shawwy! Say yes!" Lily squealed, wrapping her arms around my neck.

"Say yes to what, Lily?"

"To our new life, Sherry," the stranger answered for her. "You can be the mother you always dreamed of and be somewhat of a queen as well. A leader. Come and take my hand, be with me. Be with us. Be a mate to me, mother to the children and inspiration to the new world. I can always be this to you, Sherry, look this way if you so chose it. This can be your fantasy come true. Come," he pleaded and extended his hand to me.

For the moment, I ignored it, but...

He was so soothing and everything was calm, and the blue everywhere flexed and swirled around me like wind, but I could see it.

Calvin and Lily looked happy and excited and I was tempted by this man's offer for a split moment, but then remembered where I'd seen him. Though his appearance had been modified some to seem less abrasive I remembered him.

I gasped and as soon as I did it all turned black and the wind whipped, blowing my hair around my face. Everything was black. There was nothing left.

The Taker was in my head yet again and this must be another dream. It wasn't real. Then he appeared before me out of nowhere, inches from my face, back to his longer black haired harsh and choppy, black eyed Lighter self.

"Aww, Sherry. Why oh why must you fight me, love?" he said, very deep and seductive.

"What are you talking about?"

"I'm talking about you. I know all about you, you and your Keeper lover, the children and all the others in your safe home. You humans trying to pull the wool over my eyes. If it's power you want, Sherry, I can give it. If it's children you want, we can have them. If it's love you want," he said as he shifted so fast I didn't even see him move. He swept my hair across my shoulder and licked my neck from behind as I cringed. "I can give you more than you can handle. Come to me,

Sherry. Be with me and let the children live a life more than starving underground, waiting for death."

"What are you talking about? Why do you want me?"

"Calvin is very Special as is Lily. They are both vital to my life force. Pure. Peaceful. Lily with her spirit of peace through tribulation. Oh, I know she's young but she's been through hell. And Calvin's spirit of thoughtfulness and unselfishness. Both are so pure and innocent. And you, my dear. You tie us all together with your spirit of love and forgiveness. You forgive under any circumstance. You've even forgiven Phillip. Yes, yes, I know all about it. You love everyone and everyone can't help but love you, just like your Keeper," he said as he snarled the last word like it was a curse. "I need you, Sherry, to complete my mission."

"That's a pretty lame pick up line...Taker," I said carefully, trying to show him I could stand up to him but not anger him.

"Ah, so you are aware of me. I wasn't sure you remembered me from the store that day. If I had realized who you actually were, and not just an extremely intriguing beautiful human woman, I would have snatched you then. Why don't we go with the pleasantries and you call me Crandle. Hmm?"

He continued to circle around me. I couldn't move, couldn't even see our feet or feel anything under them or around us but the black wind around us and his gaze that never left my face.

"Whatever you say. This isn't real anyway. It's just a dream that I wish I could wake up from."

"No, it is not a dream. This is a visit, of sorts. A visit to your subconscious. It's easier to come to you when you're asleep, but you're not dreaming and I'm afraid this is all *very* real." He came back around to face me closely, and spoke with a low voice. "You see, I am drawn to you, as everyone else is by your love and affection." He grabbed my hips and rubbed his hands up and down in a slow exploration. He pulled me closer and I could feel his breath on my neck as he smelled my hair, but I couldn't move. Physically, I couldn't move. "Even your Keeper mate is so drawn he came to earth to find you. How sickening sweet, but he can't give you what I can. He's weak. It's time to stop playing around and get serious, Sherry. You've seen what I can do, you've seen what I can make. I can always be the image of the man I was before in your eyes, if you prefer that. The handsome, groomed gentleman you find so appealing from your memories. Like your Merrick, or Matt I should say," he said glancing at the scar on my arm and it started to glow red. He smiled like that satisfied him. "I want you and you will come to me and bring the children. This is no coincidence, Sherry. This was meant to be. Come to me and let's be together. I can fulfill every one of your wildest fantasies."

He touched my temple and the scene of him and I in a huge, white covered bed in my head was not one I'd ever mention nor did I want to see again and hopefully, he couldn't tell I was blushing. And why did he keep repeating himself?

"Tempting." Refocus Sherry. "Why do you want Calvin and Lily? Takers want to be daddies, too?"

"I need them. Yes, I would be their father figure so to speak, but I need them to complete me, just as I need you. I need you three to be with me for the balance of good and evil so I can rule. I need them and you will bring them to me." He looked at me so intensely, compelling me in a soothing voice, but in my blurry dream I couldn't completely make out his features.

His voice was calling to something in me. For a split second I considered his offer and then blinked wildly to expel the thought, coming to my senses. I was ashamed and abhorrent. I realized why he kept repeating himself.

"What are you doing?" I narrowed my eyes at him. "You're trying to compel me with your Lighter speak? I'm not bringing myself or the children anywhere. I guess your magic doesn't work on me."

"It would seem not." He pursed his lips. "Not in your dreams anyway. Then we'll have to try another tactic."

As he spoke it all turned to fire and smoke. It blew through me and I felt every lick of every flame. I screamed. The light was so bright it burned and my eyes couldn't physically stay open.

The ground was removed from my feet and I fell, burning into darkness, hearing his words 'YOU WILL FEAR ME AND COME TO ME' bellowed and burned into me like a brand.

My arms flailed and ached and the pin pricks in my shoulder were the most painful they'd ever been. I waited for my feet to hit bottom and crush beneath me.

I caught glimpses of things in the Taker's mind. I remembered Merrick telling me you transfer thoughts when they look into your mind. I saw patience and amusement. He would wait for me, for the right time and he found me...entertaining, silly and intriguing and actually did think I was beautiful. Unfortunately, that little bedroom scene he showed me was only one of many.

Silly? What does that mean? And why did I care? He thought I was silly because I was naïve and trusting. I cared about people so that made me weak. If I had never grown to love the children, he could never have used them as a liability against me is what he was thinking. He wanted me to come to him to balance things out, but what did that mean?

Then I heard Marissa. What was Marissa doing in my dream? She was saying something but I couldn't hear her over the singeing and crackling flames and my own screams which echoed all around me even though I'd stopped.

She was saying 'breathe'. I was breathing, wasn't I? I took a deep breath to test myself and was brought out of my dream into Merrick's arms. Jeff, Marissa, Danny and more stood in my door frame watching me with wide scared eyes.

My throat was sore and I grabbed it reflexively. I was covered in sweat and the scar on my arm was burning and throbbing and glowing red.

"What happened?" I said wheezing and then coughed from the scratchiness.

"You were dreaming," Danny said.

"It was him, wasn't it," Marissa asked, kneeling to sit beside us on the floor, "the Taker. I'm sorry, Sherry, I saw it, but it was too late. He already had you by the time I got here," she told me, seeming almost out of breath.

"You saw him come for me?" I gasped. "That means it was real."

I glanced down to look at my shoulder to check and it was still glowing red, just like when the others were near. Oh no, It was real. Merrick rubbed it with his thumb and frowned.

"It was very real, Sherry, and this isn't the first time you've dreamed of him is it?" she asked but it sounded like she already knew the answer.

I braced myself for the onslaught of unhappy glares from Danny and Merrick at my confession.

"No, it isn't. Once before."

A low grunt from Merrick and I looked to see the worry on his face. He still had me on his lap so I pulled myself further into the shelter of his chest.

"I'm sorry. I didn't think it meant anything. The last one wasn't like this one. This one he tried to...seduce me." Embarrassed, I look up to see everyone looking at me in disbelief.

"What?" Merrick barked.

"Not just sexually-" I started, but Merrick cut me off.

"Not *just* sexually!"

"Not just sexually, but with other things too, like motherhood for one. He claimed he would give me everything I desired if I would come to him. He had Calvin and Lily with him in the dream."

"Sherry...I don't understand. Why would he..." Merrick shook with fury.

I ran my hand up to his scratchy jaw and pulled his face down to look at me.

"Merrick." I forgot about everyone else for a minute and focused on Merrick, who was so full of rage, more than I'd ever seen him. "Baby, look at me. He knows you, well, he knows of you. He knows about all of us somehow. He knows about the bunker, about all the people we have here. He wants Calvin and Lily too. He said we create the balance he needs to be complete? I don't know what that means but... He didn't hurt me, well not until the end. In fact, he seemed jealous...of you. He said the only reason you're here with me is because I'm a magnet for people to love and be loved and you couldn't help yourself. That everyone is attracted to me and that's why he needs me. He was just trying to push my buttons. I knew it was a dream for most of it... Don't worry. He just wants what he doesn't understand. That's all."

"He did hurt you," Merrick said softly, rubbing my glowing shoulder.

"I'm fine, I'm fine," I said it twice, once for him and once for me.

I was still shaking myself.

After we moved into the commons room, I finished telling them the whole dream beginning to end. Knowing I needed to be truthful so we can figure this out, I told them everything, even the extremely embarrassing seduction stuff. Merrick was fuming about that still and at the mention of the bedroom fantasy... let's just say it was all I could do to keep him from dumping me on the floor and going Taker hunting.

Jeff even intervened once with a hand on his shoulder to calm him and I'm sure some silent words were spoken.

Merrick had me on his lap, wrapped in a blanket covering my cami and shorts. Jeff and Marissa threw ideas back and forth and everyone there speculated as to what it all could mean.

Other ideas were also thrown out and not welcomed ideas of when the last time I had touched Marissa had been. That was introduced by Kay. I quickly dispelled that notion as I hadn't touched Marissa but even if I had, she wouldn't do that to me. Not again. In fact she was adamant about helping us and talking and interacting with us lately more than ever.

Marissa guaranteed us that it was real, he was there in my dream and yes, he could hurt me for real if he wanted to, but he wouldn't. She saw that he wouldn't ever hurt me physically.

Well, that was some relief.

Still, everyone seemed to steer clear of Marissa, like she's got a bad case of the plague.

Marissa also saw that the Taker knew so much about Merrick and me from Phillip because Phillip was now a Lighter. They took his body and he had been sharing his memories with the Taker. Luckily, usually the memories, per Merrick's explanation, were only bits and pieces and they shouldn't be able to find us by just seeing them.

The news shocked me when she confessed that she already knew that Phillip was a Lighter and Merrick did, too. I wasn't mad though but they both looked at me like I was going to tear their heads off.

"Why would I be mad that you didn't tell me? I wouldn't want to know that, I still don't. To know that he died and that he suffered like that. I wouldn't wish that on anyone, not even Phillip," I said and meant it.

Maybe this explained what Phillip was talking about that day in my mind and how he was able to do it. Phillip was a lot of things, but no one deserved that end.

In the afternoon that day, I took up the job of cutting everyone's hair. Mainly the massive quantity of guys we had acquired over time that were getting shaggier by the day and in desperate need of attention.

I had clippers in the bathroom, along with a chair, and started with Merrick first. It was a shame really. I was loving his shag, but he insisted he was tired of it so I obliged and took off an inch or two. No matter what I did I just couldn't seem to ruin him. I was pleasantly surprised when I finished to see the Merrick I met in the very beginning.

I was no expert so pretty much everyone was getting some form or variant of a long or short buzz cut. No one complained so I cut away. And cut and cut, for hours. My carpal tunnel was screaming at me to stop and my legs cramped from swaying back and forth.

As Cain took his seat, my final haircut, he asked me about my shoulder scar and why it was glowing and red earlier during my dream.

"It's the Marker's scratch or mark. Long and painful story. Ask Miguel. He was attacked by one too but he's less reluctant to tell the story than I am," I said as I shuddered a little from the memory already popping into my mind.

"Sorry, I'll do that. So...everyone's attracted to you, huh? Even Crandle, the leader of all evil. You are a pretty popular gal," he sang, smiling.

I knew he was trying to joke, to make me feel better.

I also know that Jeff hinted for the haircuts, knowing that I would volunteer to give me something to take my mind of everything, and it worked.

"Ha ha. I've seen Crandle, you know, for real, at the grocery store a while back. Of course, I didn't know who he was then though. I thought he was just a Lighter," I said as I started washing his hair in the sink.

"Wow. I've never met anyone who's seen him in real life or very many who have seen Lighters either. Except those idiot followers of his."

"Well, I've seen both and Markers, none of them were pleasant."

I went on to explain about the Lighter that almost killed Marissa that day and how she compelled him to jump into the ravine. The black Marker skeleton we found. I also told him of the Marker that was here that night when the new recruits showed up.

"Wow," he said after a stunned pause. "My group hasn't had any action this whole time. We've been sitting up in that cabin, twiddling our thumbs, waiting to find others like us. That's terrible, Sherry. I'm sorry. If only we'd found you sooner maybe we could've helped in some way. Pap can't hear worth a dang but he can shoot like nothing I've ever seen."

27

"Well, we're all here together now. Hopefully, they'll be even more of us coming. I don't know what we're gonna do when those need warehouses start," I said, draping the towel around his shoulders and closing it with a hair clamp.

"We'll be ok. We'll just have to learn to conserve and start eating basics. Mrs. Trudy's lasagnas and deserts aren't going to cut it anymore. Pap and I had a garden back at the cabin. There are some vegetables that will grow in winter temps. Carrots, beets, rutabaga, cauliflower, cabbage, broccoli. Like I said, we'd have to get back to basics. Then the few of us that can go to the warehouses without suspicion can go and help supplement what we grow here. They only give you the food you need for the week for yourself so it wouldn't be much." He sputtered at the end with a hair in his mouth.

"Well, we may just have to do that. I really don't see any other choice at this point, but you know, if we seriously stock piled non-perishables, like rice, dried beans and can foods, from now until then, we could last a while before things got really bad."

"Yeah, we should do that. We could fill up a couple empty closets with as much as we can until the time comes. That's a good idea, Sherry. You should tell Merrick. We can go ahead on our first run tomorrow if you want. I'll go too."

"Great. Sounds good," I murmured as I finished up with a razor on his neck.

I thought his hair was already pretty short but he insisted he wanted it topped off and neatened up a bit.

"Alright, all done. Does it look good?"

"It sure does," he said quietly, looking at me in the mirror and smiled genuinely. "Thanks, Sherry."

"You're welcome."

He helped me clean up the horrid amounts of hair and shaving cream. I tried to do it in between cuts but eventually gave up and decided to deal with it all at once.

We added it to the trash by the stairs ready to be taken out and buried along with the rest of it. That was one job I was never privy to and glad of it.

It was raining. It must have been raining pretty hard because we could clearly hear it beating down around us, thunder too. Usually, we couldn't hear it unless it was bad. It was quiet and peaceful in the bunker, except for the storm's white noise.

Merrick, Ryan, Danny, Cain and Jeff are sitting on the floor, letting the women sit on the couches like real gentleman. It was funny that only two of them were human and still they all had such manners.

Celeste was sitting on the couch with Danny in between her knees. Kay and Margo were laughing about something, chatting on the loveseat.

Trudy was sitting next to Marissa with Lily in her lap.

Lily.

I hadn't seen her all day. As soon as she saw me she jumped down and ran to me. It was always the sweetest thing and I wanted to cry again but I couldn't cry every time she did this so I staved off the tears by grabbing her up and not looking at Merrick so I wouldn't see that look on his face.

"Shawwy. Mrs. Twudy said you wouldn't cut my haiwr," she said pouting and furrowing her brow in seriously cute contemplation.

It took all of me to one, not laugh, and two, not give in and give her exactly what she wanted.

"Mmmm, no. Your hair is so pretty already, Lily. We don't need to cut it," I said not being able to resist touching her hair as I spoke.

It was long and wavy, halfway down her back.

She yawned and leaned her head against my shoulder, letting her legs dangle at my sides. I swayed with her even though my arms and legs ached from my haircutting afternoon. It was almost four o'clock. She was overdue a nap. Trudy mouths something to me about taking her. I mouthed back 'not yet'. I missed her fiercely.

Katie, holding Sky, came up to me.

"I know you think Marissa is not dangerous now, but you might want to keep Lily away from her, just in case. She seems very interested in her."

I was a little shocked to say the least. I didn't think Katie was like that, but I guess becoming a mom turned you pretty protective. "It's fine, Katie, but thanks for your concern. I promise you Marissa isn't a threat to us. You guys don't have to be scared of her."

"I know, but it's still scary to think that at any time she could just...make us do whatever she wanted, that's all. I'm sorry, you're right. I shouldn't have said that."

Before I could answer she walked away, swaying the baby. I looked over at Marissa and she was watching me with a small thankful smile. I realized she had heard what Katie said about her. I felt bad.

Everyone was so worried about Marissa turning on us I decided to show my support. I believed in Marissa completely so I took Lily over and we sat right next to Marissa, Lily in my lap.

"Lily, why don't you sit with Marissa for a minute while I go get you some juice, hmm?" I said loudly.

"Ok."

"Tell her all about Miley."

"Ok!" she said happily.

I set her on Marissa's lap and got up to leave them alone on the couch. Some people stared after me like I'd just detonated a bomb. I just smiled and lifted my eyebrows in silent challenge to them but no one said anything.

I stayed gone for a little while, folding a load of laundry first and then I came back with Lily's juice. She ran right to me. I picked her up and ran my hand down her wealth of golden hair and looked at Marissa. She mouthed a 'thank you' to me and I nodded and smiled.

Then I risked a glance at Merrick. He glanced back and forth between me and Jeff with a smile while answering Jeff's question about Calvin. Even though Merrick's smile was dazzling, that comment got my attention.

Trudy took Lily from me at my reluctant request. She said she was going to take a nap with her for a while. It was Marissa's turn to cook so I walked over to the discussion. Merrick reached up to pull me down into his lap.

I stretched out, leaning against his chest with my back and letting my legs fit in between his in length. He wrapped his arms around mine over my chest and I sighed at the feeling of being home, so warm and comfortable.

I listened intently and heard Jeff going on again about Calvin.

"I'm not sure what Crandle, as he calls himself, can want with him. Or Lily for that matter." Jeff's tone was less than pleased. He sounded flat mad. "Why would he want specific Specials and then someone who isn't a Special." He looked over at me apologetically. "Sorry, you know what I mean. I don't know what he would have to gain from it. Unless he absorbs them, but then what does he want with Sherry? I mean, he was human at one point, so maybe he just has the desire to have a...family? I don't understand all of this." He put his head in his hands in defeat, letting the others steer the conversation.

Ryan spoke next. "Well, he told Sherry he needs *her* for balance. Not Calvin and Lily, he just said they were important. Maybe he thinks that by joining with Sherry, his opposite, he can...I don't know, but I think he's just using Lily and Calvin to get to her knowing that she cares about them," Ryan said but his frown made me think maybe he didn't believe any of it.

"In my other dream, he told me to bring him Calvin. He didn't say anything about me being his...mate, last time," I announced remembering that I hadn't brought it up earlier and everyone turned to look at me.

"He did? Well...that might change some things, or nothing at all. I don't know what to think. For right now we need to just be sure we keep Calvin and Lily safe. And you," Merrick tightened his grip on me as he spoke. "We'll need to start rotating with someone to keep watch at night. Someone also needs to sit in the store during the day with Margo and Paul. I'd hate for them to grab them and use them as bait or ransom. Neither Sherry, Lily nor Calvin can leave the bunker anymore," he ordered gruffly.

"Well, about that," I started, looking at Cain. "Cain and I had an idea on how to help out with the food shortage that is coming. Cain, why don't you go ahead and tell them."

He spilled the whole idea, me breaking in to add my two cents every now and then. Once we were done, everyone was nodding their heads in agreement. Except Merrick.

"That's a good plan, Sherry, but you're not going." He held up his hand to stop my protest. "I know you think you have to do this, but he knows who you are and you're wanting to go back to the same spot you saw him in the first place? I don't think so, Sherry. No."

"But there's only a few of us that aren't Specials or Keepers who can go. We need all the hands we can get. At least for tomorrow," I pleaded, knowing his answer but feeling the need to state my case anyway.

I sat up straighter for even more emphasis.

"Honestly. I don't think it even matters anymore, Sherry, about the Specials being out in the open nor the Keepers. We can hide our marks with the makeup you bought. Things are different now."

"Merrick-"

"No, Sherry, I mean it this time. No pouting eyes."

I chuckled humorlessly, which he scowled at.

"But he can already come to me in my dreams any time he wants. Are you not gonna let me sleep either?" I countered.

"Sherry..."

I could tell by his tone that he really meant business, so I surrendered. He was right but I hated being left behind while the others were forced to do all the work.

I concurred with a sigh and rested back against him again. He seemed relieved, like he expected me to fight or pout endlessly until I got my way. I had to smile at that, but then I frowned. Was I really that difficult?

Did I seem like I always got my way or pitched a fit if I didn't? Was I a hissy fit kind of girl? I'd never thought so before.

He peeked around to see me frowning.

I said no pouting.

His tone was sympathetic not demanding.

"I'm not." I bit my lip. "Am I difficult?" I whispered in his ear and I heard him chuckle in my mind and then rubbed my arms to warm me.

No. You're not difficult, I just have this tendency to give you whatever you

31

want and in this case, I just can't do that, honey. I know you want to help, that's just how you are, but I can't let you this time. Thank you for letting it go. Besides, someone's got to be here with Lily and Calvin. You want to be here with them don't you?

I turned my face to him as he pressed a kiss to my temple. I understood that he meant everyone would be leaving tomorrow, leaving me to hold down the fort. I assumed they'd leave someone there to guard us and I was certain that at least one of those would be Merrick. It may not be so bad after all.

Marissa's chicken pot pie was divine. She said it was the only thing she knew how to make completely from scratch. Jeff doted on her for a good while after we finished and Kay and Laura started the dishes. Mrs. Trudy made coffee and I helped her dole it out to those who wanted it.

Some of us were interested in where the others came from, originally. It turned out people were from all over. Aaron was from Utah and was about the only non-Mormon in his home town, he told us. Josh was from Missouri, St. Louis and had been on a full scholarship to play for the Missouri Tigers. In fact, he proudly still sported a different Mizzou t-shirt almost daily.

We learned that Racine found her body in Arizona, which explained the leather skin. Mean, I know, but it wasn't really her body, therefore not her fault that the chick before her had stayed in the sun all day, and I hadn't said it out loud. Then, Mike said he was from all over. He traveled with his job but had been in Missouri when things went bad.

Then Miguel. Oh Miguel. Josh and Danny got him started and he was happy to oblige their millions of questions about Australia.

"So, where are you from?" Danny asked excitedly. "Southern Territory?"

"Heck no, mate. I ain't no crow eater. I'm from a little town in the North, called Humpty Doo," Miguel answered with gusto.

"You're pulling our leg," Danny said, but scooted to the edge of the couch to listen further.

"I've never really understood that expression, but no, I'm not pulling your leg." He laughed. "That's really the name and it's a really small, but nice place with only a few thousand residents, but it had everything we needed. I really miss it there."

"Is that where your parents are?" Josh asked softly.

"Nah. The oldies passed away before I left. That's the reason I came stateside. They died in an accident. A car accident on their anniversary trip. So, I had no other relatives. I was the last of the Walker family left in Humpty Doo and I was an only child. I'd heard that martial arts was big here in the U.S. and I figured

I could come here and make a nice quid."

"What's that?" I asked, loving hearing him talk just as much as the others.

"Quid? It means money, love," he said and winked at me. "So anyway, I met my wife there at the studio I opened. Highway robbery, the commercial rent on Wilshire Boulevard I tell you, only three clicks from Beverly Hills. I'm glad I did it though. I met Rhonda there. She came in for self defense lessons because she'd been mugged a couple weeks before. I didn't offer self defense then because I didn't really have time to add a class for it but one look at her and I gave her a time and posted a signup sheet for a class, just so she'd come back."

He smiled wistfully, remembering and he kind of looked off towards the wall as he spoke.

"She did come back too. And so did twenty five other girls that first night of class." We all laughed. "I completely screwed myself over and had to hire two new instructors to help me with the load and was never home, but like I said, it was worth it. She was beautiful. I got no idea what she saw in a bushy like me." He cleared his throat and looked back at us. "So anyway, that's the story. We left when we realized what was happening. I found Josh there in Missouri, that's as far as my wife and I got by ourselves. He was in a convenience store, stealing power bars. I figured he must be in a bad way, just like we were. We got to talking and sure enough, he took us to the rest of them and here we are."

"Yep, he was one scary dude," Josh said, animated. "I thought he was coming to accost me for stealing and instead he says, "Bog into the peanut butter ones mate, those are the best". He scared the crap out of me."

Josh did a perfect Australian accent for Miguel's quote and we all laughed some more as they bantered back and forth on how it was.

We continued on.

Max's body was from here actually, as were Trudy and Phillip. Jeff had gotten his body from Kentucky where Bobby had been from. Marissa said she was originally from Tennessee and had traveled this way with her Keeper.

She was a high school counselor before this. I found that a little hard to see, but if the shoe fit. Pap, Margaret and Cain were from the town here. Cain moved away to live with his dad in middle school and moved back after he got out of the Marines. Both of his parents were gone.

Danny told everyone our little story. He told them all about how our parents were hippies, about how we grew up and all the funny stuff we were forced to do but left most of the recent details out, for which I was grateful for. Everyone laughed hysterically, but it was hard not to with Danny telling the story.

I'd see Merrick nod or smile or frown at certain parts as he relived them with us.

Trudy was fascinated that I had worked at a tabloid magazine. I tried to explain that it wasn't but she then claimed that she had heard about it and actually read a few copies that she got at the grocery. There was no more denying it. The proof was in the pages.

A little bit later on, Lily sat in my lap on the floor with Calvin to my left and Merrick to my right with coffee in his hand and he actually brought it to his lips to sip it. I turned and smiled at him.

Yeah...it's growing on me.

I chuckled a little and turned back to the movie we were watching in the corner in the second room on our newly acquired portable five inch DVD player, courtesy of the newbies. We were watching a cartoon with toys that talked and were chasing their beloved child across the country.

The kids thought it was hilarious and burst out laughing on more than one occasion. I was just thankful to have even this small sense of normalcy for them.

Calvin got up to take a quick bathroom break and when he returned he sat next to Merrick instead, mimicking Merrick's folded arms and crossed legged position. Merrick and I exchanged an amused glance. I'd never asked or heard anything about Calvin's father. I imagined that it wasn't something they wanted to talk about or they would have so I didn't bring it up.

Later, as the credits rolled, Merrick took Lily from me as even with her small weight it was nearly impossible for me to lift myself off the floor with her. She had fallen asleep at the very end of the movie.

He held her with his arm under her bottom and the other hand behind her head on his shoulder, swaying back and forth. Calvin attempted to help me up in true gentlemanly fashion with a hand out. I swung my arm over his shoulders as we retreated to the commons room. Clock said 8:45pm.

Calvin ran to go find Frank after thanking me for watching a movie with him. I watched Merrick as he eased back carefully out of the Lily's room after laying her down, leaving the door slightly cracked.

I sat by Danny, who rubbed his neck as Merrick went to grab another cup of coffee.

I turned Danny by his shoulders. He already knew what I was doing and smiled gratefully. As I began to squeeze my hands on his neck and massage his shoulder he dropped his head forward. It had been too long since I'd done this for him. Danny was always my biggest customer, or mooch, whatever. He was my biggest bragger too.

As I worked my thumbs into his neck tendons, I listened to their plans for the grocery trip the next morning. They were going to go to several different stop and shops and the grocery store. The Keepers were going to go with them and be van packers and lookouts. Maybe do one more call out to other Keepers since we were getting short on time. Merrick, of course, was staying behind as our bodyguard, along with Ryan.

Later, Trudy and I made a list of the can foods we could think of getting the most of, for the best and more plentiful recipes, along with non food items such as toilet paper. I put on there to get children's Tylenol and Band-Aids, not remembering there being any in the medicine cabinet, just in case.

We had little ones to think of now.

When It Rains It Pours
Chapter 3

The next day, everyone that was supposed to leave left, and I cleaned, did laundry, played Spoons and War with Ryan and Calvin and snuggled with Lily and Merrick.

I made grilled cheese sandwiches for everyone and endured more of Ryan's doting on my cooking. I tried to explain there was no way to mess up grilled cheese, but he wouldn't concede.

Merrick, Lily and I even took a nap together that early afternoon, all spooned together on the big bed in the second room. It was a sweet, perfect, normal day.

While we were still sleeping the others arrived back home and must have called Merrick in his mind to help them. He pushed my hair back and kissed my neck, whispered that they were back and he was going to help, but for me to stay and rest with Lily. Before I knew it, I was out again, waking later to the smell of fried chicken and mashed potatoes.

When I stirred on the bed Lily immediately shot up, feeling my movement, reaching for me. I grabbed her up and we went to see Mrs. Trudy who was cooking up a storm and everyone else was happily and safely sitting in the commons room. Lana signed me a 'good afternoon' greeting in sign language - your flat palm to your mouth and then out, then a hand to your elbow with your other hands straight up, and smiled. I smiled and returned the sign.

Lily and I walked side by side into the commons room. To my surprise and delight as soon as he spotted us Merrick reached for Lily and she went happily to his arms outstretched for her, giggling as he tickled her. My heart flipped with sweetness.

I saw Jeff looking at them, too, with a fascinated and understanding smile on his face. He caught my gaze and our smiles broadened. I shook my head to throw it off.

Sherry?

I froze for a second, not knowing the voice in my mind. The mind voice was different than the Keepers body's voice. I looked around, praying beyond prayer that it wasn't Phillip. Ryan gave me a wave. Ryan had never spoken to me in my mind before so of course I wouldn't know what his voice sounded like. I exhaled and smiled.

It's just me. Sorry I scared you. Uh...do you think you might be able to...give my shoulder a rub? It's bothering me pretty bad after all that unloading and stacking. I've already taken something, a couple white pills Mrs. Trudy gave me, but it doesn't seem to be working.

I nodded and motioned my head toward the kitchen and he followed me in. It must have been pretty bad for a Keeper to ask for something for pain. Mrs. Trudy continued her cooking as Kay helped, looking over her shoulder and listening to the explanation of what she was doing, step by step.

I rubbed his shoulder for a few minutes, working some of the stiffness out. He wasn't kidding. I could feel all his muscles bunched and twitching. He groaned when I pressed in my thumbs and it didn't sound like a good groan.

I grabbed a sock and filled it with rice, threw it in the microwave for half a minute and placed it lightly on Ryan's shoulder over his shirt. He winced.

"Sorry. Keep this here on your shoulder like that for about twenty minutes, then I'll rub it some more for you in a bit, ok? That's not too hot is it?" I asked pressing my hand to it making him wince again.

"It's fine, thanks, Sherry. I feel like such a whiner."

"No, you're not! This body is breakable, Ryan. It takes time to heal and rest is the best thing for it. You'll feel better in no time if you'll let me help you. Just don't wait to ask if you need something, ok?"

He nodded and went back to the commons room. Mrs. Trudy was dishing out portions on plates and Kay put ice in glasses. I helped with silverware and everyone lined up. We ate and then people started to go back into their own rooms.

After checking on Ryan and giving him another quick but deep massage, for which he swore worked wonders, and then replacing the heated rice sock with an ice pack, I caught up with Jeff to see how things went today.

"It went great. No problems or hitches. We got everything on the list and then some. We'll do the same thing next week. It was pretty cold out though, really cold."

Jeff also explained who went with who and where before turning in for the night.

Later that night, I had a steamy encounter with Merrick, which he totally instigated by continually kissing and nipping the nape of my neck. He knew how that drove me crazy.

He was sound asleep and snoring that little barely there, wisp of a snore he did, but I couldn't sleep. I slept too long on my nap and was wide awake. I tried to creep easily out of the covers but Merrick's arm tightened protectively over me. I patted his arm and managed to slide out. I grabbed his shirt and threw it on along with my sleep pants and padded my bare feet to the kitchen.

Cain was already there and made me jump as I saw him move in the shadows, leaning against the counter with his hip. He looked restless. His hair was tousled from a fit with a pillow and his t-shirt and flannel pants were wrinkled.

"Sorry, I didn't mean to scare you," he said, drinking what looked to be a glass of milk.

"It's ok. Can't sleep?" I asked grabbing a glass for myself.

"Nah, I haven't really slept well in years. You either?"

"Well, some of us had nothing to do today, so I slept the day away with Lily," I said laughing.

"Well, that's makes it ok then," he said smiling widely.

"I guess. It just doesn't seem fair that I'm always stuck here being useless."

"The men are supposed to go out and bring home the bacon, right?" he said with a wispy laugh.

"Yeah, but this isn't about women. I mean, Kay and Laura went; it's about me. I'm short and have a tendency to get into trouble so people think I'm gonna break or something and won't let me do anything."

"You should be happy about that," he said softly. "You have people to take care of you, who look after you. A lot of people don't these days."

"True," I sighed. "You're right. How *did* it go today?"

"Great. This crew you got here is a hoot, for sure. Especially Jeff and Miguel, they are a bunch of characters, but they're great."

"Yeah, they are. I love them like my own family," I have no idea why I admitted it to him but I did.

"I can see that. I'm really glad I met you."

His eyes were so sincere I looked away.

"Yeah, me too," I answered softly and fumbled for something else to say.

"Thanks for inviting us to come down here. It'll be good for Pap and Maggie to be around other people. I was beginning to wonder who was gonna shoot who first," he said laughing, making me laugh too.

"No problem. We love it when new people come, it's like Christmas. We spend half our efforts trying to work it out for others to be able to come live with us. I'm sure Jeff showed you the halls. Those are his babies." I laughed but we both stilled at a noise.

A scratching noise. Cain must have heard it, too, because he cocked his head to the side. Then I heard a whimpering. It was muffled, but seemed to be coming from outside. We normally didn't hear much from outside. We looked at each other.

"What is that?" I asked, setting my glass down.

"You hear it, too? Good. I'm not going crazy with sleep deprivation. Sounds like...somebody crying."

"Yeah, it does. Let's go check it out," I said but before I could leave the kitchen he grabbed my arm.

"Hey, hold on. You're not going to check out anything."

Before I could argue it got louder and more desperate. And then we heard the word that set both our feet to motion.

"Help."

Cain released me and ran past me to the staircase. I followed and slipped on my tennis shoes by the wall as he unlatched the door. I wanted to run and get Merrick but thought it might be too late and whoever it was would be gone or worse so I just ran.

Once topside we ventured cautiously to the back door of the store and he eased it open to peek outside. The cold blast of wind hurt my face, but I pushed him forward in anticipation. Our clothing option wasn't a good choice as both of us were wearing pajama pants and t-shirts with tennis shoes. Jeff had been right, it was freezing.

The whimpering continued and we looked across the back yard and somehow in the darkness saw a man standing out in the middle, stiff.

It was then I realized that Cain had grabbed the gun by the door, up over the doorway so the kids couldn't reach. He pointed it at the figure and yelled for him to say something as we continued to make a slow, inching path toward him. Further and further away from the store and closer to the unmoving and unspeaking figure.

"Wait, wait. Something's not right, Cain," I whispered, grabbing his arm to halt him.

"I know, it looks like a trap. Run back, Sherry. Run to the-" he was cut off by something hitting him to the ground from behind. Before I could turn a horrible pain ran through the front of my leg, my shin. It was stabbing and forceful, knocking me over to the ground next to Cain.

We landed hard in the sand and rocks and I immediately turned over to see the man standing over us. How had he gotten behind us so fast? No. There was someone else with him. A Lighter. They were both Lighters.

He continued to stand there looking down at us. Cain put his arm protectively over top me and tried to sit up but the Lighter put his foot in Cain's chest to push him back down.

"Stupid humans," was the figures first words to us. He cocked his head before starting again. "So gullible. That was all it took to get you to come out here?" he said almost sounding as if he wanted to laugh. "I knew there were resisting humans in there. I could smell your stupidity."

All of a sudden he seemed to glow, emitting enough light for us to see his face and him to see ours. He gasped.

"You!" he yelled, looking right at me and pointing a glowing finger. "You belong to Crandle!"

Then his head jerked and he flew backward into the sand. My ears were ringing and the muffled sounds of Cain yelling at me to get up were coming to me. I realized Cain had shot the Lighter and was now pulling me up to run.

We turned to see the other Lighter, glowing as well, and Cain gasped and squinted his eyes before making a distressed grunt, hesitating. I'd have to ask him about that later.

"Cain. How nice to see you again," the Lighter said, dripping with sarcasm.

How did he know Cain's name?

Cain lifted the shotgun steadily and pointed at the Lighter's face, right as he ascended with inhuman speed to stop in front of us.

The trigger pulled and the Lighter flung backward and twisted to land hard with a disgusting thud in the sand. We turned to run back to the store but I couldn't. The pain in my leg made me collapse and then the arm pain took over me even more so than before.

The familiar pin prickles.

I knew what was coming but had to see for myself. As I looked up to the sky towards home I heard the beating of wings and then the familiar screech. Though I couldn't see them in the dark, it sounded like dozens of them.

The more the merrier, the more of them the more intense the pain was and it literally took my breath. I tried again to get up, but at once dropped to my knees, shaking and crying, grabbing my shoulder, writhing in intense spasms. Cain didn't waste time arguing or asking questions, thankfully. He lifted me with ease and threw me over his shoulder as he ran the opposite way of the store, the opposite way of the massive amount of Markers headed for us.

I must have blacked out. I woke up lying on the ground with Cain huddled behind me, rubbing his hand up and down my bare arm to warm me. It was musky, humid and pitch black. My whole body ached and stung and I was so cold my teeth were chattering and my lips and fingers felt numb.

The floor was hard. I blew out a swift breath as realization took me and I remembered what we had just encountered. We were alive, somehow, and Cain had carried me somewhere. He stiffened as he realized I was awake.

"Sherry? Ah, thank God. Are you ok?" he said, sounding way too worried, his teeth chattering.

I turned, even though it hurt so badly, to face him. I couldn't help thinking how highly inappropriate this was, lying on the floor, face to face, bodies pressed together and legs intertwined, his hands running over me.

Sounded romantic, but it was anything but. We were both shaking so violently and his freezing ice cold hand was doing absolutely nothing to warm me, but I figured it made him feel better to try so I didn't say anything. We were too cold to even think about it being a compromising situation. Too close to it being something else way more morbid.

It felt like death; a slow painful death that was swiftly approaching. I finally mustered up the nerve to ask him, though I didn't think I'd like the answer.

"What happened? W-where are w-we?" I chattered, wrapping my arm around his waist, not even asking for permission.

"There's a cliff," he answered wrapping his arms around me too, "and some old caves a w-ways back from the s-store. I ran with you and hid in one. We'll have to w-wait it out until morning." I could feel his jaw shaking on my head as I was tucked under his chin. "You passed out," he continued. "The Lighter must have thrown a rock or something at you. You're leg looks horrible. Might be b-broken."

I remembered the pain in my leg. I also remembered the Lighter recognized me. Crandle must have sent them all the image of me. Merrick was right. It would have been trouble for me to go on the trip with them yesterday.

"I can't even feel it," I stammered. "Too c-cold."

"That's probably the only good thing right now. We c-can't leave. I still hear them out there screeching and yelling every now and then."

"How did you see my leg in here?"

I heard him jingle something from his shirt pocket. He pulled out his key chain and turned on the little keyhole light on the end of the ring. It barely illuminated between us and he quickly turned it off to save it in case we needed it.

"C-Cain. I...I don't know. I feel like I'm dying already. Are we even going to make it until m-morning?"

"I t-tied off your leg with the pull string strap from my pants. If we can just keep as w-warm as possible until then-" As he spoke I immediately pulled him to me even closer as if that would somehow be the answer to our survival.

He wrapped tighter around me too.

"I'm sorry, Sherry, I s-should never have let you come with me," he said like it was a confession.

"It wasn't your fault. I s-should've woken Merrick like I had wanted to but...I was the one who pushed you out the door, remember?"

"Merrick is not going to be happy with me."

I had to chuckle a little at that, despite the situation. "You mean for my getting hurt or for us laying all over each other, lounging around laughing on some romantic w-warm getaway somewhere?" I said, trying to lighten the mood.

I felt him chuckle.

"Either one," he said and then laughed again.

I've heard that you couldn't feel defeated and give up when it looks hopeless. So I joked. You have to fight it; you couldn't give in so I wanted to try to make the most of what little coherency I had left.

We must have fallen asleep somehow after that. When your body gets so cold it starts to shut down. Your heart rate slows and so does your breathing, trying to preserve your energy. It does this against your will, I guessed that was the only reason we fell asleep.

I awoke some time later with a voice in my mind. Merrick!

Sherry?

I waited. Counting the seconds. Then counting minutes.

Sherry? Sherry?! Come on, honey. I'm getting worried.

I was so ecstatic to hear him. He must be looking for me around the bunker. A few more minutes passed and then again, I heard him.

Sherry, I know you can't answer me, but if can hear me, send me a signal of some kind if you can. What happened? What-

I actually heard him mutter a few curses and then say something about his stupid gift only being one way communication.

Sherry, please. I'm dying here, baby. Gah, I wish I knew where you were. I assume that Cain is with you. I hope he is... Unless he's the one who... I'd kill him. I have no idea what happened but don't be scared, honey. If nothing else just hear my voice and know I'm coming for you. We're heading out right now to come look for you two. I love you. Stay out of danger. I'll find you. I promise.

Oh, no! They'll probably head into town instead of back here and crazy Jeff and Merrick's tempers will get them caught. Ah! Merrick was right. This stupid one way communication was useless! Though it was so good to hear his voice.

I realized my teeth weren't chattering nearly as much anymore but it was still insanely cold and dark. I didn't know if it was morning yet or not. I reluctantly tried to wake Cain, not wanting to disturb him if he could still sleep, but we needed to see what time it was.

Merrick must have woken up early and went to look for me when I wasn't there with him. Then woke everyone else when he couldn't find me, and then they must have noticed that Cain was missing, too. Maybe we could head off the search party before they left to get themselves killed.

I scratched Cain's arm lightly to wake him and he stirred, pulling out his keychain light.

"Hey. Are you ok?" he said groggily as he squinted to look at me.

"Yeah, but I can hear Merrick. He says they are going out to look for us."

"Hmmm. I wonder if it's daylight yet. I moved us back far in figuring we'd be safer. Let me go check. Stay here, I'll be right back," he stated as he began to unlock himself from my grasp.

The thought of being left alone in the complete darkness of a cave with no light and no weapon to defend myself, and a hurt leg to boot, was terrifying. I grabbed his arm and clung to him.

"Please, don't leave me alone," I said but felt ashamed of my initial reaction and quickly tried to recover. "I...I know you need to go look but...ok. Ok, I know, just hurry, please," I said as I slowly talked myself into it.

"I won't go if you don't want me to. We can just wait here and see what happens."

The thought of Merrick, Jeff, Ryan or Danny getting hurt or worse because I was afraid to let Cain go signal them was even more unbearable than the silent dark.

"No, it's ok. Just hurry, please," I pleaded breathlessly.

He got up easy and slow, laying my leg back down with ease. Since I had thawed out just a little bit, I was beginning to feel the sting and throb of the wound.

"I'll be right back. I promise." He touched my cheek briefly then I could hear his swift footsteps as he ran with the minuscule light from his key chain making small rings on the ground in front of him.

The cave was total darkness. No sound. I couldn't even hear Cain anymore. The utter silence and darkness was unnerving and everywhere. I tried to keep it together but it was unraveling my self control. I felt the shaking starting again, and not just from being cold with Cain's body heat gone.

Then, my angel.

Sherry, if you can still hear me, listen. We can't come look for you yet. There are Markers everywhere, I've never seen so many in all my years, at least fifty, all in one place. That's just...unheard of. It's still dark. But first thing in the morning, we're coming. It's right at 5:00 so about an hour and a half. Hang on, baby, I'm coming. God I hope you can hear me. I love you.

Miraculously as soon as Merrick finished, Cain's footsteps sounded in my ear and relief swept over me. They both saved me from my panic attack and didn't even know it.

"Still dark," he said gloomily.

"I know. Merrick, he said they'll be leaving in an hour and a half. It's about 5:00 am."

"Ok. Well we'll leave the second the suns hits the horizon and try to catch them," he said, seeming reluctant to sit back down.

I felt around and my hand caught the cave wall above my head. I slid myself up towards it, wanting to sit up and lean. Cain heard me shuffling around and flashed me with his light.

"Wait. Let me help you," he said lifting me under my arms and settling me back against the wall. "How's the leg?" he asked, bending on his haunches down to inspect it.

"I can feel it some now, even though it's still freezing in here."

"You want me to sit with you?" he asked tentatively.

"Please."

He flicked off his light and settled down beside me, pulling me under his arm. He was warm, but nowhere near the warmth of Merrick. He didn't seem to be struggling with the cold as much as me anymore. I wondered if it was because I'd lost so much blood from my leg.

Both of our knees were drawn up with me extending my bad leg and leaning my good leg on his. We huddled there and talked about nothing and everything. Families, famous people we'd met, past girlfriends or boyfriends, anything to keep our minds busy.

He explained that Pap and Maggie were not his real grandparents but since his parents were gone and he had no other family, he took in his old neighbors as his own. He also told me that the Lighter he'd seen outside had been Josh's father. He'd been engaged once but she cheated on him with her boss. The old lawyer and his secretary travesty.

Then I told him about Merrick and me, he especially found it fascinating that Merrick had somehow haphazardly chosen Matt's body. I told him I'd met Arnold Schwarzenegger on an assignment for the paper once. He was an incredibly nice guy but scarily huge. He thought my childhood and parents were by far the most hilarious thing. Hippies.

We sat there passing the time as my teeth started to chatter again, Cain pulling me to him tighter as we waited for dawn to make an appearance.

When we thought enough time had passed, he helped me up and I hobbled while he guided me with his arm. I had heard Merrick a few more times since and he still seemed angry and worried, but always reassured me that he was coming for me.

We made our way through the darkness to the entrance. I could barely see the glow of morning setting in as we peeked out and surveyed the area. Sky was clear of flying menace and the freezing air carried no sound.

I immediately started to shiver as my hair was blown erratically from the high winds. We couldn't see anything near the store, too far, so we decided to go ahead and move that way and hoped we could make it to them in time.

After a few yards I saw the gun that Cain must have dropped in our escape last night. He picked it up, throwing it over his shoulder by the strap and then readjusted me to further lean on his arm. He was mumbling about how there was only two shots left.

All right, Sherry, we're coming. Tell Cain if he's there with you. You two hold tight wherever you are. Love you, honey.

I felt relief course through me. My leg was killing me though with the throbbing. I felt and saw blood oozing out of the makeshift bandage with every step. It must not be broken after all since I could hobble on it but the pain was nothing to snoot about. Before I could even think about complaining I heard a gunshot. I jumped and glanced at Cain. He was looking around to see where it could have come from.

I was trying to focus on Merrick but also look for a shooter and listen to Cain for instructions and deal with the pain in my leg. I saw nothing. We heard another shot, since I wasn't paying attention it sounded far away.

"Oh, no, it's them. They must be already outside looking for us. What the heck are they shooting at?" Cain said agitated as we begin to walk again.

Then a black blur whipped out from behind us to stop about ten feet in our path. Dang it! Could we get a frigging break? At this point a Lighter is a Lighter is a Lighter. I was just sick of them and their horrible timing.

Then a thought. Merrick and the rest of them must have seen a Lighter too, maybe this one, or they wouldn't be shooting.

Cain pulled me behind him and I had to grab the back of his shirt to keep from falling over. I was so weak and tired. I knew if I had to physically fight I was done for even though Miguel's classes seemed to have been helping.

"So, you think you can keep your little mate away from Crandle?" The Lighter smirked at us. "Oh, wait. You're not the Keeper. Hmmm. I wonder, does your Keeper know you are out canoodling with a mere human, Sherry?"

The sound of my name of the Lighters tongue brought bile to my mouth. I held it down but said nothing as there was no point in provoking, especially when I couldn't back it up physically. Cain on the other hand...

"Shut it, Lighter. Move it," he cocked the gun as he barked the order.

"Oh, human, you won't kill me with your blast stick, but even if you could, what I do is for the good of my people, my species. Whether you kill me or not is of no consequence. There will always be another one to take my place, always one to come after you until you surrender. Just give me the girl and I'll let you die quickly instead of slowly."

"Not likely."

"Shame to hear that. For you. For me, I think I'll rather enjoy this." He smiled wickedly as he said it, but I thought Merrick and Jeff said only the Taker could show emotion.

Another gunshot rang out and then in a blur the Lighter was gone. I saw a line of movement and glanced over Cain's shoulder to see my family, almost all of them. The ungifted, the Keepers and the Specials alike were all marching to our rescue, guns, baseball bats, sticks and golf clubs in hands. It was the most beautiful sight I'd ever seen!

Sherry!

Still a football field away, I saw Merrick start to dart in a blur towards us, but he stopped short.

Then all hell broke loose.

Merrick - On The Edge
Chapter 4

I woke that morning to find Sherry gone from the pallet. It wasn't really even morning yet. My watch said 4:30. I wondered what she was doing up. I remembered our long nap and thought maybe she just couldn't sleep. I was tempted to just let myself fall back asleep but something made me need to get up to check on her.

So I got up, throwing on my discarded jeans, but I couldn't find my t-shirt anywhere so I went without. I walked bare foot into the commons room to find it dark and empty except for Max. He was reading a book in the corner under the overhead lamp. I nodded to him and walked into the dark kitchen. I saw two glasses on the counter. Hmm. Sherry would never leave dishes for someone else to do like that.

I checked the bathroom, empty. Stairs and second room, empty. Laundry room, empty. Now I was getting worried.

Sherry?

No answer. There was no adorable woman running around the corner to answer my call. I blurred to Danny's room. She *must* be there. I opened the door to find Danny and Celeste, asleep. At first I thought Celeste was naked and started to turn away, but I realized her sleep shorts were just that short. She must have given Sherry her 'modest' ones.

"Danny," I bent down and whispered, not wanting to disturb Celeste but I remembered what a chore it was to wake this kid up.

Celeste woke first.

"Merrick? Is everything ok?" she creaked, sitting up and looking around.

"Celeste, I can't find Sherry. I thought she might be in here with Danny but..."

She cleared her throat.

"Well, we're just sleeping," she said defensively. "I just sleep in here with him, ok?"

"Celeste, really, it's none of my business."

"But you're his Keeper and I know you try to stop worrying about him but you still do. I know you do. Kay is still a freak about so many things with me." She looked uncomfortable. "Ok, I may not *just* sleep in here but I just wanted you to know, I'm not gonna do anything to hurt him, ok? I would marry him if I could! I love him."

Wow. What a time for a confession.

"Celeste, I appreciate it, really, and I'm happy that you and Danny are making it work but Sherry is missing."

"What?"

"Sherry is-"

"I heard you! Why didn't you say so in the first place?" she asked in a high peeved voice.

"I did," I said exasperatingly and silently cursed sleepy people. "Why else would I come in here?"

"I...whatever," she said and turned to Danny.

I was dreading the long process of waking him. Sherry had to punch and yell and practically abuse him to get him to cooperate. But...as I watched Celeste, I was fascinated. She leaned over him, whispered his name in his ear, then rubbed the back of his neck with her palm in a small massage.

He roused almost instantly.

My mouth gaped open in surprise, and then turned into a scowl as Danny didn't realize I was here and thought Celeste was trying wake him up for...other activities.

She pried his hands from her head and leg, and pushed him back gently.

"Danny, baby, Merrick is here," she said and looked at me with a grin of embarrassment.

"Merrick?" Danny said squinting and sat up with his hair spiked in every direction, rubbing his eyes.

"Sherry's missing. Have you seen her?" I asked getting more impatient by the second.

"What? No. What do you mean missing? There's not a lot of places down here she could go, man."

"I know that but I've checked every place I can think of to look and she's not here," I said standing up and turning to leave.

If he didn't know where she was, then I had to find someone who did.

"Wait, Merrick, where are you going?" Danny yelled to me.

"To find your sister, Danny," I yelled back and tried to call her again in her mind.

Sherry? Sherry! Come on, honey. I'm getting worried.

No answer.

Just as I was about to grab Jeff's door knob, I hesitated and knocked instead. I would want the same courtesy for myself and wouldn't want to find another Danny and Celeste situation. Then I remembered who I was talking about and snorted. Jeff, in bed with someone. A human. Yeah right.

I knocked again and he came and looked surprised to see me.

"Merrick?" he said, coming from his room quickly into the hall and shutting the door with no shirt or shoes on.

"I can't find Sherry."

"What do you-"

"Enough of this. Would I really wake you if she were just in the bathroom? I've looked everywhere and called her. I'm telling you, she's not here."

"Call them, I'll be right back," he insisted quickly and slipped back into his room, shutting the door behind him.

I knew who he meant by 'them'. He wanted me to call all the other Keepers. All I could think about was her in one of the tons of rooms we had and how many men were present in this bunker and the Phillip incident. My anger growled in my throat just thinking about it but I couldn't think of anyone here who would hurt her.

Sherry. I know you can't answer me, but if can hear me, send me a signal of some kind if you can. What happened? What-

I couldn't help but curse and growl at the irony of only being able to talk one way when I so needed her to answer me. I banged my fist on the wall in useless protest of it all. So I called the others.

Get up. I know it's early but Sherry is missing and yes, I've already looked in the normal places. I've called to her with no answer. Can I get you to come and help me look for her? Please, ask your charges if anyone has seen her.

I walked back into the commons room and Max was already up and moving, heading upstairs to the store to check, though I knew Sherry would not be sitting up in the store. Then Simon came through the hall with the behind him.

"Cain is missing too," Simon said and looked about as irritated and distressed as I felt. "I don't know where they are but we've got to go look for them. The only place we haven't looked is...outside. There's got to be a reason for this. Cain wouldn't put Sherry in danger. We need to go topside and look around, see if we can find something."

"Agreed," I say gruffly and quickly relayed to Sherry.

Sherry, please. I'm dying here. Gah, I wish I knew where you were. I assume that Cain is with you. I hope he is... Unless he's the one who... I'd kill him. I have no idea what happened but don't be scared, honey. If nothing else just hear my voice and know I'm coming for you. We're heading out right now to come look for you two. I love you. Stay out of danger. I'll find you. I promise.

I had no idea the where or why of the situation. Why was Cain not here? Where would they have gone? If I were a human man, would I think that they had run off together? But these weren't exactly circumstances to run away together during. He hadn't made any passes at her that I was aware of but every man does fall in love with her to some extent, heck even Miguel and Jeff love her. Gah! It was making me crazy.

"Ok. Let's-" I started, but was interrupted.

"Merrick!" Max intruded, blurring down the stairs. "Markers everywhere."

I ran, I didn't care who was behind me but I felt the bodies blur with mine. When I reached the back door I saw them in the dark. Oh God in heaven! They were at least...fifty, maybe more. Never in my entire existence had I seen such a thing. There was no way we'd make it. Oh, no! No!

"Sherry!" I yelled but heard only beating wings and screeches.

"Merrick, come on, we can't. You know we can't!" Jeff yelled, pulling me back in the door and slamming it behind us. I felt numb. I let him push me back and I fell into the wall. "Merrick, snap out of it!" He knelt in front of me. "Brother?"

He got up and left. I sat there in my trance. I couldn't believe it. She could be out there right then and I'd never reach her. She could be dead already if she went out there. I wanted to move but my body, this human body, just shut down.

Danny came to kneel in front of me in the stock room on the floor where Jeff left me. I barely noticed him. I could still hear them screeching outside, laughing at me and my weakness.

"Merrick," he started, "Sherry needs you, man. You've got to get up. We've got to get ready." I didn't move. He pushed my chest forcefully and grabbed my shirt front. "Merrick. I know, ok! I know how it is. It's Sherry, she's fragile, I get it. I'm worried too. I'm worried sick but we aren't going to get her back by sulking on the floor. Get up," he growled and when I pushed his hands away he continued. "You've been talking to her, I know you have. Tell her. Tell her you're coming to get her as soon as we can."

I looked up to him and saw the determination on his face. He was right.

What was I doing? This wasn't me, I was letting my human grief override my sense. Sitting here would do no good. I nodded and grabbed his shoulder.

"Thanks, Danny. Ok, ok," I answered quickly and closed my eyes for one more try to Sherry.

Sherry, if you can still hear me, listen. We can't come look for you yet. There are Markers everywhere, I've never seen so many in all my years. At least fifty, all in one place. That's just...unheard of. It's still dark. But first thing in the morning, we're coming. It's right at 5:00 so about an hour and a half. Hang on, baby, I'm coming. God I hope you can hear me. I love you.

I could hear my real voice crack and strangle. Danny extended a hand to me on the floor as I opened my eyes. We made our way downstairs to gather with the others. As I descended the stairs I saw a sea of angry and determined faces. Our group was ready for news and ready to do damage. Jeff had filled them in on everything.

"You understand there are Markers. More Markers than you have ever seen before and I have no doubt there will be Lighters, too. You understand how dangerous this is, don't you?" I asked. I needed them to know what we were up against.

"This is Sherry, Merrick, and Cain. There's no question. As soon as the sun comes up, we *are* going after them," Danny answered in a guttural tone and crossed his arms to stop the shaking fury in his hands.

I felt my head start to buzz with that familiar sting at his words. At the thought of him going out to fight and me not protecting him, but I tried to push it down.

"Absolutely," Ryan agreed.

"Well, we've got to do something," Trudy chimed and they all started in on a plan, a course of action but I was afraid there's only one way.

Hand to hand combat. A fist fight with evil.

We waited and plotted and planned. Finally the time came. We took our stakes, irons and bats and whatever else we could find, and ran up the stairs in a procession of Keepers, Specials, and normals who had no idea what to do, but wouldn't be told to stay put, not for Sherry. I wanted to hug them all for their loyalty and then yell at them for their stupidity.

The sun was awake and I looked to the sky, knowing I'd see it empty of Markers and I did. I called to her once more.

All right, Sherry. We're coming. Tell Cain if he's there with you. You two hold tight wherever you are. Love you, honey.

51

Then I noticed something else...Lighters, like I had expected. Two zoomed past, but didn't touch anyone, didn't even really get close. Pap fired off a shot and Jeff yelled at him to conserve his rounds. I wasn't sure what the Lighters were trying to accomplish. Then I scanned the field and saw her.

My heart jumped. She was standing, that was a good sign. I barely saw her outline and Cain's way out past the field and almost to the old caves that are back there that Max told me about before. Aha! I bet that was where they were. But why?

Sherry!

One Small Step For Man
Chapter 5

All at once, a fleet of Lighters took center between us. A quick count showed eight. This was crazy. What were they all doing here? Could Lighters talk to each other the way Keepers did and they had told the others I was there? That we were there? This couldn't be about me. This was about all of us being here. If that was true, why didn't Crandle just come himself? Unless he was scared of a battle. Maybe he *could* be killed like the rest of them could.

They formed a line to expand the gap between Cain and I and our rescuers. Red Rover Red Rover was all I could think about through the burning and throbbing pain in my leg, and wanting desperately to get to Merrick and see Danny safe. I saw him across the expanse of field standing with the others to fight. I swallowed hard at the thought of that, but I knew Merrick would keep him safe, if he could.

The Lighters didn't move. They must have had a plan of some sort because they seemed to have formation and the discipline to stand their ground. They watched, some facing us some facing the others. Then the one in the middle got my attention by waving a few fingers at me in a menacingly friendly wave.

Phillip.

I gasped and recoiled, pulled myself back behind Cain out of instinct, fisting my hands in his shirt back. As much as I thought it didn't bother me- my almost rape- seeing him brought it all back in a flood of glimpses and flashes; images of fists tugging, bruising hands and hard lips.

I started to shake, breathing heavy and closed my eyes trying to block the pictures from my mind. I could actually feel his hot, sticky breath on my neck, the pain in my shoulders from my arms being over extended by his hard grasp, the jolt of flaming nerves in my back from being pushed into the counters edge. His hard uncaring hands wrapped around my arms, bruising me, kissing me and punishing.

It took me a minute of near hyperventilation to regain my composure and to

53

even realize that Phillip's body was really out there, with them, the Lighters. He was no longer one of us...and we were going to have to kill him.

I glanced up to look for Mrs. Trudy, but she wasn't there and I sent up a silent 'thank you' that she wouldn't have to witness the death of her son.

Cain looked back over his shoulder to check on me several times, but hadn't spoken. Probably just thought I was scared of the massive Lighter Battle Royale that was about to ensue, and I was. Scared out of my wits.

Cain had no idea about Phillip, who he was or what he did, and I preferred to keep it that way so I didn't explain. I just let him assume away.

I pushed all that old crap aside, all the uncomfortable feelings and images and put the present right in front of me.

Sherry? Are you ok, honey? Wave to me if you're ok.

I lifted my arm in a couple of long swoops in the air and saw him return it.

This is about to get really bad. I want you to listen. I need you to run like you've never ran before when the fighting starts. Do you hear me? And I mean it, Sherry. No playing hero. Wave if you hear me.

He commanded me firmly and I waved, but I knew I was lying. There would be no running on this leg but there was no way to explain that to him so I lied with a wave and hoped I would get the chance to explain later. I hoped I lived long enough to get yelled at and berated for being so stupid as to come out here in the first place. I hoped Cain didn't die for it, I hoped no one did.

I hoped.

I hoped.

I glanced at Cain and he had a furrowed brow and squinted eyes. Someone was talking to him in his mind too. He looked frustrated.

"What is it?" I asked anxiously.

"Your hubby and Jeff won't stop talking to me at the same time. They are trying to tell me what they have planned. It's a lot of info, especially with Merrick threatening body parts if I don't get you back to him safely." He smiled at me sideways, obviously hoping to help calm me down with his joke.

Surprisingly it worked. I smiled despite our current condition. He continued on to tell me that they were going to let the Keepers go first in a fast, furious wave. Then the rest would come in all at once after a half minute to allow for time of surprise. Hopefully the Lighters would all be engaged and wouldn't be paying attention to the lowly humans.

"I'm going to leave you here, Sherry, when I take off. You just stay here and stay low. I'll be watching to see if anyone comes close to you." He handed me the shotgun and said he'd grab another weapon from one of the others.

I didn't like this idea one bit, especially Cain leaving me with his only weapon, but I wasn't in any position or mood to argue. I nodded to suggest I understood and he waited for Merrick's signal. Then I heard someone else, someone not wanted, and though he was all the way across the field, I could hear him just like he was standing next to me.

"Hello, Sherry. Might I say you are looking ravishing."

The Lighter formerly known as Phillip. I realized that Phillip no longer resided in that body, but it was still too much to have that face staring at me.

"Who is that?" Cain asked, turning a circle to look all around us.

"Lighter," I answered.

"We didn't come here for you but here you are. What a nice surprise. Come on out and meet us in the middle and we'll spare your little friends from a very painful and long death."

Oh, God, help me. He knew me somehow. He knew I'd do it even if I knew I couldn't trust him. I couldn't take the risk, but I knew he was lying.

Come on, Sherry! There are only eight of them and a whole heck of a lot more of us. This would be a piece of cake. Besides, Merrick would freak and lose his focus if you just strolled out there to him and then, get himself killed.

I must have caught him off guard, him thinking I would cave and obey easily and immediately.

"Sherry is actually thinking of saving herself? My, my. I have to say I'm proud of you and thoroughly impressed. Not at all like the sweet, selfless Sherry that was in Phillip's mind. Though I have no use for you personally, you'd make a better ally than I ever thought possible. Crandle is going to be very pleased with your...what do you humans call it? Spunk? You and him can raise those little bastards of yours and live happily. Ever. After."

I flinched at the contempt and disdain dripping in his voice. I pushed back the memories.

"You know him?" Cain asked, but I kept silent.

I kept focused on Merrick and stood my ground, praying I was doing the right thing. If someone was killed because of me, I wouldn't be able to handle that.

They would kill them all anyway.

Then, as quick as that, the blurs of inhuman speed started. I couldn't tell for sure who moved first, Keepers or Lighters. I saw a few figures go down, some not for long, I couldn't tell between them though.

I heard faint yelling, curses and grunts. Then I saw the rest run in, weapons raised. Cain started to move but hesitated and looked back.

"Sherry, shoot anything that comes close. I'll be watchin-"

Before he could finish Phillip was there in a blur, hitting Cain with a rock over the head and pushing him to the ground instead of letting him fall.

He squeezed a cold hand around my neck before I could think or move. He twisted the gun from my grasp, making me cry out from the pain in my wrist and pulled me closer to lick a long stroke up my cheek with his freezing black tongue, from my jaw to my temple.

I shuddered in disgust and tried to pull free but he tightened his grip on me, forcing a choke and grunt from my lips, as he spoke against my ear and tossed the gun aside.

"I only wish we could finish what you and old Phillip started that day, Sherry. Maybe we can remedy that now. Though Crandle probably isn't into sloppy seconds. Or would it be thirds now?"

He continued to nip at me and squeeze my arms and neck, degrading me with his filthy gestures, his sickening sweet breath on my face.

The amount of enjoyment the Lighter was getting out of my fear and pain was enough to make bile come to my mouth. Maybe Phillip's vile and vulgar nature added to the evil in the Lighter that consumed him.

I wondered what the point of it was. What did he gain from breaking my spirit? Was that how Crandle needed me delivered, broken and sobbing? Why didn't he just get it over with and take me to the Taker.

"Oopsy, look at that. Sherry's got a boo, boo," he said, glancing at my leg and smiling widely.

He set me back down to the ground but still held my neck. All of a sudden he reared back a foot with a grunt and brought his boot bottom down square on the wound on my shin.

My leg was broken, I had no doubt. I crumpled and screamed. My ears were ringing as he yanked me back up with his one hand brutally on my neck.

I felt myself shaking and writhing, trying to swallow the sobs that I knew would only satisfy him more. He was holding me only inches above the ground, letting me dangle from his grasp. I felt like I was going to pass out. The sky above turned gray and my eyelids started to flutter.

I reached out in one last attempt to free myself and felt my nails scrape across his face. Light trickled out of the wounds in spurts before his skin could close.

"Ah! You're gonna pay for that you little-" But he stopped mid-sentence and glanced behind him.

Though the noise behind him started to dissipate, I couldn't see around Phillip's body to see what was actually going on. Cain started to stir and just as he got up, he halted, cocked his head like he was listening to something and then lunged forward, snatching me with all his might into his arms, almost throwing us to the ground with his momentum.

There was a bright light that hurt to look at that flashed, and a quick blaze of fire and smoke and a rush of cold wind- which was so strange combined with the flash of lightning that shot up into the sky from the spot where a club went through the Lighter's body. I knew Phillip was gone.

I saw in Phillip's place was Merrick, headless iron golf club in hand.

I could barely breathe as I tried to leap to him, but my leg failed, and I screamed and tumbled. Cain caught me up just in time to pass me to Merrick as he stepped forward to accept me into his arms.

His arm immediately wrapped around my waist to support me while the other hand went to the nape of my neck, tilting my head back with his thumb. He kissed me with such force, roughness and desperation, like he'd never shown me before in all the time I'd known him.

I cried and cried, not able to stop the hot tears of pain, happiness and relief that drenched my cold skin. Some sobs escaped in between breaths, but most Merrick took into his mouth as he continued to hold my lips against his. Tasting the tears as we moved I tried to clear my mind and not think of the pain or what was going on behind us. I could still hear the slight tings of metal hitting. The sand blew furiously around us, but right then, Merrick was there and I was safe.

The brutal kiss turned softer and all the love and protectiveness he had for me was so evident in this kiss. Then it was barely a kiss at all, just him moving his lips over mine, back and forth in a desperate motion. All I could think about was how warm and safe he was and I didn't want him to let go. Ever.

He broke away suddenly and glared at me with his face bright in the orange light of the dawning morning. "Why don't you listen? I told you to run. You never listen! Don't ever do that to me again. You don't know what it's like, to think that I lost you...for real this time," he whispered the last part against my lips, then pulled back to look me over, head to toe. He grunted angrily. "Sherry! What happened to your leg? And your neck?"

I told him that Phillip did it and left it at that. That was why I couldn't run. He could see my leg was broken and that was all that mattered right then. I wasn't about to tell him I was attacked by *three* Lighters, so far.

He looked at me with a broken expression; one of hurt and pain on my behalf. He hated the fact that I was hurt and he wasn't there to stop it. He touched my cheek softly with his hand and pulled back quickly like he hadn't noticed me being cold before when he was kissing me.

"Gah, baby, you're freezing. Here."

He removed the jacket he was wearing and helped me shrug it on. It was so warm from him wearing it that I actually sighed out loud. Merrick didn't feel the hot or cold like we did and I was so grateful that even with all the chaos, he still managed to remember my needs and brought a coat for me.

He lifted and cradled me in his arms against his chest, turning to walk back to the store and the waiting crowd. I didn't speak and neither did he for a few minutes. I buried my face in his warm neck and continued to cry and breathe heavy in pain. He was careful not to jostle my leg, but it still hurt and throbbed, my hiccup crying wasn't helping anything either.

He kissed my hair and rubbed his scruffy chin over it murmuring to me. "I've got you. You're safe with me."

Our peace didn't last for long. Merrick quickly picked up the pace and I refused to lift my eyes and look. My mind and stress level with lack of food and warmth couldn't possibly handle another assault.

He whispered to me. "Hang on. I'm sorry, this is going to hurt."

I know he was about to do the inhuman blur run, which wouldn't feel great on my broken leg, so I gritted my teeth as I felt the wind pick up around us, cold sand blasted my face and bare leg.

Murmurs and shouts, clanging and grunts were heard behind us and around us. I asked Merrick what was going on and he explained that a Lighter could only be killed by being completely run through with light releasing on both sides from inside his body. So the ones we shot didn't die and were now back for more.

A chill ran through me thinking about the Lighters running off to tell the others where we were but they seemed to be hanging around to finish the job instead.

Merrick felt me shivering.

"I'm trying, honey, I'm trying. Almost there," he whispered into my hair.

We reached the middle ground between the cave and the store, then further still in a blur until I felt his slow descent of movement. Merrick pulled us to a stop but didn't release me.

I heard more gunshots and Pap near us, yelling and shouting about 'gettin him some'. It actually sounded like he was enjoying himself, which grated on my nerves.

I could also hear and make out Aaron and Miguel yelling and grunting. I opened my eyes and saw Merrick's warm and blood shot, green eyes watching me wearily. Then I found myself looking into another pair of worried and relief filled eyes.

Jeff's.

"One of these days, Sherry, you're going to give us a heart attack." His words were firm and reprimanding, but neither his eyes nor his mouth could lie to me.

He squeezed my hand before glancing back behind us and ordering Merrick to take me inside. They would finish this he said. I tried to glance back too but Merrick said no.

"Don't look, Sherry, you don't need to see this."

I closed my eyes and pressed my head down, but then I realized that I did want to look. In fact, I *needed* to look, because I caused this. If I hadn't of ran out in the dark after a voice instead of waking someone who could better handle the situation, this wouldn't have happened. Cain could've run faster without having to carry me to safety.

The thought brought tears to my eyes and my throat locked down in a knot of overwhelming regret. I clenched my fists and prepared myself for a vision of slaughter and blood. Whoever was hurt, whoever was dead, whoever was still out there fighting – it was my fault.

I gasped and forced my eyes shut in shame. That quick look over Merrick's shoulder told me more than I ever wanted to know. There were bodies on the ground. Who's? Theirs or ours? The fighting was still going on; blurring figures and then hard slams, fist and legs, swinging makeshift weapons with loud gunshots.

I sobbed, my body refusing to cooperate with my silent internal plea to stop. Merrick didn't speak, just squeezed me tighter. He must have assumed I was crying because I was afraid and in pain. He couldn't know my shame, my embarrassment and guilt for being so stupid and reckless. My conscience was beaten and affecting my coherency.

I knew we were inside, but I couldn't move or speak. I felt the bounce of the stairs, and then the worst thing that could possibly happen, happened.

I heard Merrick's swift intake of breath as he halted his steps. I looked up, then down following his gaze and saw Mrs. Trudy, Lana and Marissa lying on the floor, all three of their faces spotted with blood.

Then the world went black.

Merrick - The Blame Game
Chapter 3

No! They set us up. This was all a set up, a game. They knew someone would hear them and come outside to help. They knew we'd go after them. They knew we'd go after Sherry. They knew we'd take the strong and leave the weaker ones there.

I laid Sherry on the couch; she passed out after seeing Trudy, Lana and Marissa on the floor. I threw an afghan on her and then checked her and the other's pulses. Oh, thank you. They were alive. Where was all this blood coming from?

Immediately I remembered why they had been left down here. To guard Calvin and Lily. I ran to Lily's room- not there. I blurred across the bunker to Trudy's room- no one.

I glanced in Paul and Kate's room, Trudy's old room and somehow both of them and the baby were still asleep on the bed. There must not have been much of a commotion. A quick look in Laura's room and I saw the same, all three asleep. No one was in Lana's room either.

I checked everywhere, our room, Jeff's room, bathroom. I called out their names, out loud and in their minds, though I knew Lily would be scared if she could hear me that way.

Nothing.

It hit me what Crandle told Sherry in her dream. That he wanted her and the children to come to him. I felt the blood drain from my face as my heart slammed painfully in my chest. My vision blurred and doubled from shock

They took Lily and Calvin.

I blurred my way back into the commons room and heard a few others coming back down the stairs from outside already. I grabbed a few towels from the hall and went to see what damage had been done to them. It looked like they'd been hit on the head with something blunt. All three needed stitches. How had they gotten the drop on Marissa? Must have surprised them and hit her before she had a chance to touch them.

I saw a meat mallet in Trudy's hand and a knife next to Lana's. Good girls. They at least tried to put up a fight.

Ryan and Cain were beside me. They said it was over, the Lighters were dead. They asked what they could do to help and what happened? I could see that Cain's head was bleeding too but he insisted he was fine.

I focused through the gasps, questions and chatter to handle what needed to be done. I instructed Ryan to hold the towel to Trudy's head and Cain to do the same to Marissa while I put one under Lana, who seemed to have the worst wound of all. She had a huge gash above her eyebrow and another one in the back. Kay would return soon, I hoped, and she could stitch them up.

I pushed someone aside, Margo I thought, to get back to Sherry. Danny was beside her and must have seen some fury or desperation in my face because even he moved aside when he saw me coming. I just couldn't focus. I couldn't care about anyone's feelings right then. Too many other things mattered. Sherry mattered.

I took her and laid her down in our room to rest in the quiet while we sorted it all out. I wrapped her up in the sleeping bag and zipped it tight leaving on the jacket I put on her. I lit a flashlight on in the corner so she wouldn't wake up alone in the dark.

Making my way back into the commons room I saw that most everyone was back inside now. Jeff and Ryan were tending to everyone best they could. Kay was already working on Trudy with Danny and Cain's help, though Simon was yelling that Cain get his head looked at immediately.

"How's Sherry?" Miguel asked.

He had a bright red and bluish semicircle under his left eye already.

"Her leg's broken."

"I can help. I got half way through an EMT course before I dropped out. Couldn't take all the blood and gore. Where is she?"

I took him to her. I unzipped the sleeping bag and pulled back the blanket. He sucked in a breath through his teeth at a glance at her leg, then left to get medical supplies. We didn't have a splint, I knew. I wondered what he could do for her.

I absentmindedly stroked her hair back from her face. She still hadn't stirred awake yet. I rubbed my thumb over the bruises on her neck...fingerprints.

More of Phillip's fingerprints.

My blood began to boil but I staved it off and prayed that she stayed asleep while Miguel set her break. He returned with an armload of stuff that was anything but medical supplies.

He produced a light wooden shelf board to stint her leg from underneath and the attached 90 degree wall brace for her foot, a roll of duct tape, and an ace bandage to wrap around to keep it in place. Surprisingly, it looked sturdy enough and it just might work. We didn't have much of a choice at that point.

My mind drifted to when Orville Wright broke his leg. Him and his dang flyer, always persistent and never cautious enough. A recipe for stupidity, brilliance and discovery. It reminded me of someone else I knew.

As I looked back down to her I see the faint purple marks under her eyes from the cold and sleepless night that I was sure she endured. She couldn't stand the cold or the dark and she got cold so easily. I didn't know what Cain did but I'd have to thank him for taking care of her and bringing her back to me.

"Hold her down, Merrick," Miguel broke my thoughts with a command and I complied, as unwilling as I was.

I envisioned Danny running in once he heard Sherry's inevitable screams when Miguel set her leg. I shut my eyes and placed my forehead on hers, just like the last time we purposely tortured her after the Markers scratch, where we had to hold her down and burn her to stop the poison. I couldn't watch anymore than she could.

This wasn't the first time I'd intentionally inflicted pain on her. Even though I had her best interest at heart, it killed me to know that fact.

I braced myself, wrapping an arm over Sherry's stomach and arms and applied enough force to keep her still. I heard the crunch of bones as they grinded and snapped back to where they should be.

The high pitched scream was piercing, but she didn't wake. She just screamed a sob, calling my name, not an accusation but a plea. Over and over I whispered that I was here, she was safe, that I was sorry. She couldn't hear me or understand through her sobbing and crying out.

Miguel wrapped it quickly and shoved me some pills he grabbed and insisted I make her take them. She was somehow still asleep but whimpering and her face was a dictionary illustration of painful confusion.

She started shaking again. I still thought it was better that way than her being awake though I couldn't imagine the kind of dream she was having.

Danny ran in as did Ryan and Celeste. Miguel ushered them out, explaining that he had to set her broken leg. Danny and Miguel yelled and went back and forth in the hall as to why Danny wasn't told beforehand that Sherry was hurt, Miguel explaining it was better for him not to see it and he needed the room to work. At this show, a few others started yelling at each other as well.

"Oi! We can't just scream and fight at each other. That'll get us nowhere fast. We've gotta stop blaming each other and focus on what's got to be done now," Miguel barked to get his point across.

Celeste started to cry and Kay dragged her off somewhere out of sight. I blocked them all out and lay next to Sherry, kicking the room door closed with my foot. I hoped that she wasn't having a nightmare and that she knew what was happening to her, that I was here.

Later after her heart settled down and she started to breathe more evenly I slipped out and joined the others. No one had brought up Lily and Calvin yet, assuming they were being cared for elsewhere. My heart ached and pounded as did the blood rushing in my ears. I had to say the words but I just didn't want to. The upset this would cause was worse than some stitches to the head.

Calvin had been a staple member of our core group and a jovial reprise for all of us. He became quite the helper and Lily was sweeter than pie. Everyone was so attached to and protective of her. This would make them want to hunt. This would make them all want to kill.

Maybe this was what we needed, but I had a feeling that Sherry would blame herself for all this. I could already hear her argument in my head of how she caused all this. I knew her completely.

I took hesitant steps to the kitchen to grab a bottle of water. I gulped down half the bottle in one pull, then prepared to speak the dreaded words that would mean war. First, since I knew our conscience didn't work the same on earth, I knew Ryan didn't know yet about Calvin. I had to tell him and I dreaded it, but here went nothing.

Ryan.

He looked at me and I grimaced with what I had to do. I imagined someone telling me this about Danny and how I'd feel. It wasn't fair how our conscience worked on earth. It only buzzed if our human body felt anxious about it. It didn't alert us to danger like it used to.

I'm sorry. I promise you we'll do everything to get him back, but...they took Calvin.

I heard him gasp in my mind. His face paled under his tan and he slumped down on the couch slowly as I proceeded.

"They took Calvin and Lily," I said out loud.

My voice didn't sound like my own. It felt like I barely breathed the words, but somehow everyone heard and were now masking my face of horror and disbelief. There was an explosion of angry rants and questions and rambling ideas.

"Oh no!"

"We have to get them back!"

"We have to go after them!"

"What? How could they do this?"

"How?! Why?!"

"How do you know that?"

"What do they want with them?"

"They can't get away with this!"

Then one statement stopped them all in their tracks. "Oh, no, Sherry."

Everyone turned to see Sherry leaning on the wall on one foot, pale faced and broken looking. It wasn't just her body, but her spirit. The bruises were already very evident around her neck and jaw and her eyes were red from the strain and crying.

How she got up off our pallet with that thing on her leg by herself I'd never know. I didn't hear her make a sound but I wouldn't have over all the racket. Her face told me she heard that the children were missing.

Her chest started to heave with her silent sobs and her eyes closed. I went to her, pushing a few people out of the way to get to her. I grabbed her around the waist just as she started to slump over and held her to me.

She had completely given up, refused to try to stand on her good leg, refused to hold up her head or open her eyes. Just sobbed silently, limp and uncaring of anything. Not like Sherry. My bashful Sherry who didn't want anyone to see her weak. This scared me more than anything, her letting loose right in front of all these people and not caring.

I picked her up in my arms cradling her to me, trying to be careful not to swing her leg too much, but she didn't care about that either. She didn't make a sound other than her steady, deep, soft sobs.

Danny came up beside us and wiped a tear from her face with his thumb. She looked up at him, but before he could speak she did, in a raspy, barely audible voice.

"It's my fault. He got to them because of me."

I couldn't tell if she passed out again or was just closing in on herself but her eyes shut and she didn't respond to anything or anyone after that. Not Danny or Trudy, not Celeste, not Jeff. Not even me.

Jeff came up and spoke to everyone else who was still stunned silent.

"This is no one's fault but the Lighters. I'm sure there is a good explanation. Cain. Why don't you tell us what happened. What were you two doing out there last night?" Jeff asked but was anything but accusatory.

Cain called out from the back near the stairs. The people parted a way so everyone could see him speak.

"We were in the kitchen late, getting a snack, couldn't sleep. We heard someone yelling for help outside. So we ran to see who it was thinking it was someone who saw the flyer maybe. When we got outside there were Markers everywhere and two Lighters. I shot them, but we couldn't turn back and make it and Sherry was screaming because of her arm, the Markers mark. Also her leg, the Lighter hit us with a stone or something. So I picked her up and ran with her to the cave out past the field."

"Cain," I said, stunned, "that cave is almost half a mile away. How did you carry her all that way with Markers and Lighters out there with you?"

"I don't know. I just did. She was freezing and her leg was..." He rubbed his eyes and sighed harshly. "I don't even know how she survived the night."

Cain sounded nothing like his normal cocky self. He was just as beaten and somber as Sherry but all I could think about was that he saved her life. While I slept in my warm room, he carried her through Lighters and Markers, bandaged her leg and kept her alive during the freezing pitch black night in an old cave.

"Cain," I started, but felt a familiar choke in my throat and had to pause to let it pass. The one I felt the night that Phillip tried to...hurt Sherry. "Thank you."

"Don't, Merrick. Don't thank me. I should never have let her follow me out there," his voice cracked when he said 'never'.

"This is Sherry we're talking about, Cain. She's stubborn and doesn't always follow orders very well," I said lightly and tried for a weak smile.

Sherry stopped shaking and was quiet and still so I assumed she had fallen back asleep in my arms. I'd hate for her to hear us talking about her like she wasn't here, but I continued.

"She does what she thinks she needs to do no matter the cost to herself, especially when it comes to these people. Someone was yelling for help and any one of us that had been in that kitchen would have ran to help them too. It's not your fault and it's not Sherry's. I think you both have been through enough to atone for it anyway."

I can't ever repay you enough. Thank you. You don't know what she means to me. She's...everything...

He nodded solemnly and I got a few echoes of my out loud sentiment to Cain along with a few pats on the back and 'well done's. Simon beside him put a hand on his shoulder.

Cain still had blood running down his neck and forehead. His arm was bleeding too. A quick look around showed me he wasn't the only one who took a beating along with Sherry.

There wasn't anyone that was clean and spot free. For the most part it was all minor cuts and scrapes, bruises and I couldn't help but notice one thing. One major thing.

"We didn't lose anyone. Everyone made it. We're alive."

Best Laid Plans
Chapter 4

Merrick placed me down in our pallet. I still refused to open my eyes. Carefully, he shifted me and was so gentle with my leg. He thought I was asleep while they were talking out there. I might as well have been. I couldn't open my eyes and face them. The shame was still too raw. My body just shut itself down and refused to let me participate.

This wonderful group of people who would never blame me or Cain even when we so deserved it. It was my fault more than anyone. I was weak and had no business going out in the dark to help anyone when I couldn't even help myself.

Stupid.

And people paid the price for my ignorance.

Calvin. Just the name made me choke. And Lily.

I knew they all said we'd get them back, but how? Where? When? How could I let them down like this?

Merrick left briefly then returned. I felt him climb in beside me as he rubbed my shoulder lightly.

"Sherry, I brought you some tea. You need to get something in you."

I opened my eyes and looked up at him leaning over me. There was a flashlight in the corner, pointed to the ceiling to illuminate the room. He had a glass of sweet tea and a napkin with a few slices of cheese and rolled ham on it. There was no blame in his eyes, nothing but concern and love.

"Merrick, this is all my fault. I know you'll say that it's not, but it is. I was so stupid. I was so-" A sob choked my plea.

"Stop, Sherry." He framed my face, forcing me to look at him. "Don't do this to yourself, sweetheart. No one blames you because it's not your fault. You tried to help someone. Who could blame you for that? If that were the case then I'd be to blame for what Phillip did to you, the first time."

"What? No! How?"

"Well, he told me how he felt and I gave him the benefit of the doubt. If I hadn't done that and made sure to-"

"That's not the same thing, Merrick."

"Isn't it?"

"Merrick."

"Sherry," he breathed, ordering and begging me to understand and let it drop.

"What do we do now?" I said, my voice cracking.

"You eat and tell me how the hell you survived the night. I stay here with you and keep you warm until you fall asleep. Then tonight, we kill some Lighters and get back our kids."

I had never been more proud of him. My heart wanted to burst from my chest and the annoying tears were coming again. He wrapped his arms around me, laying us back on our backs. I nibbled my cheese and drank my tea through the straw, as ordered.

I told him the whole story; about the Lighter tricking us and then the next one with his filthy talk, about Phillip. Not even leaving out the part where Cain and I had to lay wrapped around each other to keep warm. I knew he wouldn't be jealous of that and I wanted to be completely honest with him.

Always.

So I even spilled about how Cain kissed me in the coffee shop that day, to save me from being discovered and questioned.

"Cain has apologized to me for it so many times," I explained. "I just want to be completely honest with you. I'm sorry I didn't tell you before. It was wrong of me to keep it from you."

"Sherry, the man saved your life, twice, now it seems. I can't be mad at him. Or you. I owe him everything."

He told me how lucky I was. How dumb I was for thinking I could handle things on my own, without him, and he hoped I had learned my lesson this time, that we were a team. Always. Then he whispered that everything would be fine, he was happy I was ok, he was so worried about me, he loved me. I drifted off to sleep somehow at more peace than I ever would have thought imaginable with his soft murmuring of assurances.

We will get them back. We will.

After what I guessed was a couple hours I woke up and Merrick was looking at my leg, rewrapping it with care. He saw me watching him. He finished quickly and lay on his side beside me, leaning on his elbow.

"How do you feel?" he asked.

"I'll feel better when we get on with the plan to get the kids back."

At first I thought he'd argue with me about the word 'we'- me implying I was going too. He didn't. In fact, he reacted as though that was the best news yet.

"Great, let's go warrior," he said smiling and lifted me up in his arms.

He didn't carry me but set me down to my good foot, letting me lean on him. What was up with him? I thought for sure I'd have to fight him to let me keep my dignity and hobble myself in there to meet the others. I looked at him questioningly.

I know you don't want me to carry you out there in front of all of them, do you?

He smiled a knowing smile with a raised eyebrow. A smug he knows-me smile.

Cute.

I realized what he was doing. He was letting me get some of my dignity back from my breakdown earlier. He knew I wouldn't want him to carry me like some broken rag doll. He had already done that more than enough lately when I had no other choice.

Now I did.

Just when you thought you couldn't love someone any more, when you think they couldn't possibly know you more than they already did...

"Nope."

I smiled back and we left our room, hobbling together.

Everyone was already there, either in the kitchen doorway or stacked in the commons room. They looked eager and anxious. Some had coffee in hand, others had biscuits or crackers. Some had all three.

No one seemed to be particularly interested in me but Danny, Ryan, Cain, Miguel and even Josh, who were all watching me the whole time with anxious eyes. Well, I guessed that was a lot.

Everyone else was glued to Jeff, who was giving what I could only describe as a battle decree.

"Thank you. I know how bad you want to pick me up and carry me," I whispered to Merrick as he navigated through scattered people sitting cross-legged on the floor.

Yes, I do, and it's killing me watching you struggle needlessly, but I know you need this. Even if you are just being stubborn. He cut his eyes sideways to peek at me and smiled. *I'm gonna go get you some breakfast. Sit here.*

He moved me beside Danny who took my hand to settle me beside him on the couch. Ryan got up to take the chair arm instead so I could have his seat. Danny patted my leg and gave me a look, like 'how could you keep doing this to me', then propped my leg up on his knee and I was shocked to see how blue, black and swollen my foot was sticking out through the end.

I heard Danny suck in his breath and Celeste gasped beside him. I waved off their concern and tried to focus on what Jeff was saying, but I couldn't. My eyes skimmed the sea of faces, battered, bruised, stitched and bandaged. The wave of guilt came rolling back to me, crashing over me.

Then I saw Lana, refusing to meet anyone's eyes as she stared at the wall. I continued to look at her as if willing her to look at me. When she finally did I immediately regretted it. The pain and confusion in her eyes was too much to look at without wincing.

I signed 'I'm sorry', placing my right hand over my heart in a fist in a circular motion while still mouthing 'sorry'. She nodded and wiped tears but turned back to the wall again. She lost the only person in the world she could talk to. Literally.

Merrick promptly returned with coffee and a cereal bar for me. The brown brew was the perfect balance of sweet and cream.

He crouched down in front of me and we all sat back and absorbed Jeff. He was excited in a furious way, ready to set out and inflict revenge and retaliation on their opposites. The Lighters may have ultimately won the battle - getting the prize - but Jeff was determined to win the war.

"So, the way I see it, with all the gifts that the Specials have acquired here, I don't see any reason that we can't go there and take them back. Josh can see through the walls, Trudy can hear things far off, Danny can plant thoughts, Celeste can find the children by focusing on them and Marissa can compel them to do anything. The Keepers can be the muscle. We can do this."

He went on to tell us the plan in its entirety. We wait until nightfall then send someone out as bait for a Lighter. We knew one would come since they seem to be running rampant. We capture it and bring it down for 'questioning'. He didn't further elaborate on 'questioning' and I didn't want him to.

Everyone was in agreement. No one said, 'hey, it's just a couple of kids, we can't risk our lives for them.' Everyone was in an upheaval and ready to get to the action, to the 'doing and not sitting' part.

Once we captured it we would get what info we need to lead us to where Lily and Calvin were. He would let us know, cooperatively or not, and we'd go and meet them there. It sounded simple enough.

It was decided that Miguel would be the bait. It couldn't be a Keeper or they may not want to attack as easily and we didn't want to chance it taking long because the Lighter was wary. Miguel could fight better than any of us so he volunteered. Oh, boy. It began.

Merrick, Jeff, Kay, Ryan, Josh and Danny - who insisted on helping and Merrick told him he could stand watch at the door - would wait to ambush the Lighter once Miguel lured it out. Then they'd interrogate.

"Now, Sherry, I'll need you for some of the questioning. We'll need to know if it's lying or not about where Calvin and Lily are. Are you going to be ok with that?" Jeff asked, looking me dead in the eye and raising sympathetic eyebrows.

"Of course."

It was all I *could* say.

The meeting ended and some of them took off to get some rest as all of those plans would take place at nightfall. A lot of them stopped to talk to me before heading separate ways. Josh knelt down in front of me and asked me - I counted at least five times - if I was all right in between other adamant questions. I assured him I was just fine before he patted my arm and took off after Miguel, who also asked how my leg was feeling.

After rib crushing hugs from Ryan and Trudy, I asked Merrick to help me with a shower. He did and joined me, insisting it would be easier to hold me up that way. I agreed.

After he helped me get undressed he hopped in with me, adjusting the water to my liking and holding me gently from behind around my ribs with one arm. The water was so hot and good. I hung my head and let it roll down my back while he kneaded my shoulders with his warm hands.

After a freezing, miserable night on the rock hard ground with wounds to boot, I couldn't remember the last time anything felt so good.

I leaned back against him and he feathered some light kisses on my shoulders and neck, sweeping my hair aside. It felt like an eternity since we'd been together like that.

Even though I was black and blue, beaten and broken, I couldn't let this opportunity slip by. It could very well be our last night alive. We were going Lighter hunting, then bringing that Lighter into our home, then setting out into the enemy's camp to save our own people. We might not make it past midnight with those odds.

I coaxed him to let me turn around to face him and wrapped my arms around his neck. He knew what I was up to and immediately went into protective mode.

"Sherry Elizabeth," he said firmly with reprimand. He tried to remove my arms from his neck but I resisted. "Honey, we can't. Your leg," he spoke the words like he was speaking to a child who didn't know any better.

"My leg has nothing to do with *this*," I insisted as I kissed my way up from his neck to his scruffy chin.

I heard him let out the tiniest groan and then shook his head, back to business.

"No, you're hurt and bruised all over. I'll hurt you. No, Sherry. Come on. Let's get you back to our room. You can take a nap and get ready for tonight."

"I don't want a nap, not yet. I want to nap later, with you. Who knows what will happen tonight, Merrick. Be with me. Please." I wasn't giving up and I threw out the serious pout.

I needed this, to not think about Lily and Calvin, about my leg, about the guilt I felt, about everyone else who might not make it tonight.

Merrick would cave, I knew it. I knew him. I felt him shift on his feet as he blew out a breath and I pressed myself to him, pulling him down to kiss me. I tried for my most seductive, pulling out all the tricks, the few I know. I nibbled his bottom lip, fisted his hair, traced his lip with my tongue. He responded just as I knew he would.

He bellowed out a frustrated groan - at himself not me - for his weakness to my ploys. He pushed his arms around my waist tightly and kissed me with all he had. The thrill of victory only fueled me to new heights. He lifted me, pushing me against the wall gently. I could tell he was still trying not to jostle me too much but it was too much. I winced and he immediately noticed, halting his assault.

"It's ok," I started before he could tell me 'I told you so'. "Let's go back to the room. Please."

To my astonishment he complied, with emphasis. I was so confounded about these powers of womanly persuasion I somehow possessed over Merrick, but was grateful for them. He dressed me and himself and carried me to our room. I didn't protest this time. This was no time for hobbling slowness.

Once we reached our room he laid me down, placing a pillow under my hurt leg and kissed me again, bracing himself over me on his elbows. Sweet, long, drugging kisses followed. He played in my now longer hair with his fingers, kissed my bruised neck and collar bone gently, nibbled my lips and chin and fingertips. Drove me crazy is what he did. The already warm room seemed to rise a few more degrees in temperature as he made me – for just a little while - forget my troubles and he undressed me gently in the dark.

We woke up some time later to a knock on our door. Merrick quickly pulled the blanket over us, just in case. Jeff indicated through the door that it was almost time and we should come get some supper.

I was grateful he didn't barge in like some people did. We hadn't dressed after our afternoon...um...rendezvous. I had fallen asleep quickly, completely exhausted after all the things Merrick had done to me and the sweet things he had said to relax and reassure me.

I drifted off to him whispering that we would all be ok tonight, we'd get Lily back, Calvin was fine, for me not to worry, just go to sleep.

But I would worry. A lot. Merrick would be outside with a Lighter, maybe more than one, without me. Though he would probably be relieved about that fact. I seemed to attract trouble as he had once told me, like a magnet, and it was true.

Every time trouble or injuries could seek me out, they did. I would wind up in the way and on his mind with who knew how many more injuries. That would lead him to be distracted and I'd never forgive myself if something happened to him. How did I ever survive without him here before this, literally?

Margaret had laid low with the rest of them during all the excitement, sleeping in the second room. Too aged to really do much good in helping us, but she made us all a big batch of cookies and sweet tea and had been as helpful as could be at her age.

They seemed to be as contemplative of our situation as everyone else, though they were the newest members. I hadn't even heard her and Pap bicker once all day.

Cain made his way over at some point to ask how I was doing as I sat on the couch. I used both hands to pull him down to me and wrapped my arms around his neck as he squatted down to be at my level. I would not be alive were it not for this man.

I squeezed him so tightly, realizing I hadn't even spoken to him since the cave. He rubbed his hand on my back awkwardly at first, probably thinking Merrick would get upset if he saw him hugging me. Probably wondering if I had told Merrick about the caves. Probably wondering if I had even told Merrick about that little diversion kiss in the coffee shop, but he doesn't know Merrick like I do.

"Thank you so much. If it hadn't been for you, I wouldn't have made it. I know it, you saved my life," I said, pulling back just enough to see his face.

"I shouldn't have let you go out there to begin with."

"You tried to stop me," I reminded him.

"Not very well apparently," he said laughing sadly.

"I'm stubborn to a fault, I'm sorry. I think I learned my lesson, though. When people tell me to do things, I'm gonna start listening," I said, my voice cracking with emotion.

"Now don't do that." He rubbed my arms. "No crying, because then I'll cry and be all embarrassed. And you know what? I doubt I would've made it in that cave without you either. You saved my life just as much as I saved yours. You're pretty warm for such a small little thing," he said through a smile.

"Ugh," I groaned, wiping my eyes with both hands, "if that's what you've gotta tell yourself. I know what really happened and I won't forget it. Thank you, Cain."

"Thank *you,* Sherry." He nodded and squeezed my leg before asking me if I needed anything.

When I declined he got up and headed to the kitchen.

Supper was quiet with lots on everyone's mind. I knew there was on mine. If Lily were here, she would have eaten up her spaghetti like a trooper.

The noodles would hang off her chin, so adorably. She'd complain that it was sticky as I wiped them with a warm cloth and then wiped her hands. When she was done she'd go right to Merrick and he would plop her in his lap as she chatted away. Telling him all about what Trudy had made her for a snack that day and how Miguel had showed her how to color using lipstick he'd found in the bathroom which I'd roll my eyes about.

Calvin would be running around with Frank, playing swords with golf clubs. He'd offer to show Lily how to play spoons, again. He'd ask Merrick to help him explain it because Lily just wasn't getting it. Then I'd have to explain that Merrick didn't get it either and we'd all chuckle. Even though the memory made me want to laugh, I couldn't. I looked at Lana, pushing her food around on her plate with her fork and looking back at the wall, like she was looking out a window, waiting for Calvin.

I suddenly realized how much I wanted this for myself. I wanted to have someone to worry about, as painful as it may be. Watching Merrick be a makeshift father made me want him to be a real daddy. He looked so at ease with it and with the task they'd have to do tonight, catching the Lighter.

My heart started to beat a mile a minute as I thought of what life would be like without them. Without *him.* I rubbed my necklace charm in between my fingers absentmindedly, a soothing mechanism.

I couldn't lose him and for the first time since I'd met him, I sincerely feared for his life. I felt the tears stinging my eyes but I held them back. Not just for my sake would I miss Merrick, but for Lily and Calvin's, too.

Merrick had been so good to them both and they would feel the bite of his disappearance as well as I. Just thinking about it made my chest wrench with physical pain and pounding. That was when I decided. I wanted Lily.

I wanted Lily to be ours. Merrick and I could be her parents and she could always sit on his lap and tell him about her day. She could always take naps with me. She could always complain to us about her hair or spaghetti noodles on her chin.

If- I gasped at my thought. WHEN! When Merrick returned tonight, and we got our kids back, I would talk to him about it and see what he thought. Maybe we'd wait a while and see what everyone else thought first. Maybe Miguel wanted to take the parent role as well. Maybe Trudy.

The group that was setting up the trap got ready to go outside and do their thing. I let the tears fall when Merrick hugged me against his chest. It felt so strange to be so totally dependent on someone for safety, yet be so totally worried about that same person's own safety at the same time.

He didn't notice me crying at first but the tears soaked through his shirt and he stiffened. He carried me, still hugging him, back to the wall away from most of the people, then set me down on my good foot.

"Sherry? What's wrong, baby?" he asked me in his most concerned, very husbandly non-Keeper voice.

"I'm just so...worried, Merrick. I feel helpless and useless." I sniffed as he wiped my cheeks with his thumbs. "I don't doubt that you can take care of yourself, but if something were to happen to you-"

"I'll be fine. There's plenty of us to take on one little Lighter."

"But, Merrick, there was more than one little Lighter when Cain and I were out there and plenty of Markers. What if you mean to attract one but you attract more than one?"

"Won't happen, and even if it did, we won't be far from the store. Phillip is gone. He's the one who lead all of them here. We'll be fine. Don't spend the whole time worrying over me. Go sleep for a while, you need the rest. I'll let you know when it's time for you to do your thing." He pressed him forehead to mine. "And you're not useless. We need you later to help us. Everyone's got a job to do."

"Yes, and yours puts you outside with the enemy, while I'm supposed to just stay in here and sleep and relax?" This thought brought a new round of fresh tears and hysteria.

I knew Merrick was completely undone by the sight of me in tears but I just couldn't stop.

"Honey, honey," he crooned, pulling me to his chest and rocking me under his chin. "Please don't. You know I can't stand to see you cry. I don't like you worrying about me. This is what I do, what I've done for a very, very long time. Centuries. Dealing with the Lighters and watching over you is what I was made for. I'll be fine. I'm always fine and always careful. Promise. If there's so much of a scratch anywhere on me...you can spank me later." I felt him smile against my forehead and couldn't help but smile, too, at something so human coming out of his mouth.

"You promise? You'll be safe?" I whispered, biting my trembling lower lip and looking up to him, loving him even more at his constant ability to know exactly how to handle me.

Always with the right amount of humor, caution and concern.

"I promise. Don't worry about anything. I love you so much."

"I love you, too, more than anything."

He leaned down to kiss me gently, but deeply, in front of everyone that would glance our way...so everyone. His hands were on my cheeks, completely stroking all the tears away. I hugged his waist and pushed up on my one good foot to reach even more of him.

Reluctantly, his lips left mine and he carried me to our room, placing me down before kissing me once more on the lips and forehead. He watched me for a second to see how I'd react once he started to move away. Then he turned, shutting the door behind him, with one last peek.

I'll be back in no time. Rest and don't worry about me. That's an order.

I smiled and nodded as the darkness washed over me. My pillow was getting soaked as I continued to wallow in guilt and worry, disregarding Merrick's plea to stop. I wrapped the covers around myself tightly, rubbed my necklace and tried desperately to ignore the excruciating pain in my leg and whispered a pray for Merrick to be right.

Merrick - Another One Bites The Dust
Chapter 5

My human heart was just...breaking. I had to pull to remove her hand from my neck she was gripping so tightly. I bet she didn't even realize she was holding on when I laid her down. It was so painful to watch her cry and know I had to leave, especially over my safety.

My safety.

She has never been upset over me like that, not fearful *for* me. It hurt worse than anything to know that she worried for me, but also, I felt grateful to have it.

She'd been through so much. That poor little body of hers couldn't stand too much more of this kind of life. She'd been bruised and beaten or healing to some degree almost every day since I finally met her, today she looked worse than she ever had.

I painstakingly pushed all that out of my mind and trotted back to Jeff. I needed to get my mind right if I was going to keep my promise to come back to her safely.

What was that look on Jeff's face?

"Aw, brother, she ok?" Jeff asked with genuine concern.

"No, she's not. Let's just get this over with."

"She'll just be that much happier to see you when we get back," he said, slapping my back.

"It's not just that. She's worried about me, about the kids and feels guilty. She's hurting though she's trying to act like she's not. And Phillip's da...the Lighter left fingerprint bruises all over her neck and arm not to mention the broken leg."

"Phillip?" I heard Trudy behind me and cursed myself silently.

We had hoped to save her from this truth and now my stupid mouth had let it slip.

"Mrs. Trudy, I'm sorry," I told her as I turned at look at her.

"What? What about Phillip? He was here?" To my surprise she actually looked horrified instead of happy to see her son again.

"In a way. Trudy, please just let it go. He's gone, he's not here."

"Merrick, he's my son and I'll always love him, but if he has come back here to hurt her again...we can't have that. I won't allow him to hurt my poor Sherry anymore than he already has."

"He's not." Maybe I wouldn't have to tell her.

"Then why did you say Phill-" I saw the recognition hit her eyes and she closed them trying to block the tears. Her fingers covered her lips. "Oh. I see." She opened them again and looked me right in the eye, letting the tears fall. "Well, when you do evil things, evil is bound to find you. Y'all please be careful out there, you hear?"

She hugged me with one of her rib crushers, even Jeff got one, to his astonishment, and she then looked between us both, still holding each of our hands.

"You two have brought all this to us. Wait- that's not what I mean. I mean the good things." Trudy was still crying, letting the tears fall freely as she spoke which wasn't like her. "I never had much of a family and after my husband died, Phillip is the only son who would even speak to me anymore. I have missed being a real family, a happy family that can get through anything together. Y'all gave that back to me. You are more human than most people I've known my entire life. I love you all. Please. Be. Careful."

Dang. I turned to see Jeff, he looked like he might burst out and cry right there, which in any other circumstance would be humorous. We both nodded as she turned away and looked at each other.

This is what you meant. This is the human love you tried to explain to me and I never understood. It actually hurts.

Jeff was rubbing his chest while he spoke and swallowed loudly.

Yes, brother, it does. I smiled in spite of it all. *In the best possible way.*

And Sherry, she loves you even more than Trudy? How do you stand it?

It's easier than it looks.

I smiled at him to convey that it was a joke, but also not. It was easy to let someone love you and to love them back.

We were joined by Simon, Ryan, Kay, Danny, Josh and Miguel by the stairs. Max and Racine came to the stairs as well to bid us good luck.

"Guard you in all your ways, brothers and sisters."

I saw in his mind that Max wasn't just talking to the Keepers. He was talking to us all, a collective unit. A family.

"Thank you, brother," I said in return.

Everyone looked at us, watched us as we moved upstairs and out to set the trap, our one shot to get our kids back.

We all had our weapons, just in case, but our main weapon this time was rope and nets. We took our places strategically placed so Miguel had help from every direction but before that, we went over the plan one more time.

Miguel got into place. I saw him stumbling in the middle of the field. It had been almost an hour.

After what Cain told us, we decided I'd be the designated person to relay instructions to Miguel in his mind so all the keepers weren't yelling at him at the same time.

I could see him perfectly from my spot right on the lid of the barn where the cars were parked. He was trying to walk slowly so as not to get too far away from us. He stopped to tie his shoe and when he did, that was when I saw the Lighter that was standing there, no more than six feet in front of him.

Miguel, don't react, but he's there. About six feet to your front. You shouldn't be able to see him, he's not illuminated, so don't panic yet. We don't want him to know the rest of us are here. He's trying to sneak up on you.

Miguel straightened then walked forward another step, then another. The Lighter just stepped out of the way letting Miguel pass, then turned to attack him from behind.

"Hello," he said menacingly.

Behind you. Now!

Miguel twisted around and grabbed the concealed knife out of his shirt sleeve, popping it out into his palm and swung for whatever he could get a hit on. The Lighter's arm was the lucky winner and while he was distracted, Miguel smashed the Lighter's forehead to his knee.

The Lighter yelled and fell back but wasn't immobile. We rushed in blurs and Jeff and Kay wrapped Trudy's husband's old fishing net around the Lighter, rolling him in the dirt as the rest of us held him down and then tied it all off with the rope.

He was not pleased. He spat dirt, and blinked and yelled. His lip was busted and red dirt was stuck to his lips and face. His face was so plainly evil yet still so plainly human. His dark hair was coated with dust and the more he thrashed, the more flecks fell back into his face and mouth, causing his human body to cough.

We all picked him up together and carried him, wrapped and rolled up. The designated interrogation room was one of the brand new, not quite finished, sleeping rooms. Far away from the entrance and far enough away from everyone else, so as not to hear him scream.

I wrapped a towel that I left hanging on the shelf by the trap door around his head so he couldn't see all the people and so they couldn't see him. We asked the others to try to stay in their rooms but just in case. We made it down the stairs easily enough, without incident.

Danny was cursing the thing. I'd even seen him elbow and knee it a couple times, perhaps subconsciously, maybe not. He was murmuring and muttering about how they think they can hurt his sister and get away with it. That the Lighter better be glad that Celeste wasn't hurt. I felt what he felt. I also felt that Danny definitely couldn't be in the room while we questioned the Lighter.

I knew Danny. He'd go off on him. He would even think he was enjoying hurting the Lighter, but he wouldn't, and later he'd feel guilty about it.

I told Jeff in his mind that only Miguel and us two should be in the room. He agreed that no one else should see this. Even I didn't want to see it, the torturing of a Lighter.

We set him in a rusty old folding chair in the middle of the small room. His hands were still bound behind his back, the net only draped down to his waist, his legs still wrapped in it.

Danny and the others didn't fight us about leaving like I thought they would. In the end, they knew what we would eventually wind up having to do, and if we were all honest, no one wanted to do this. Even to a Lighter. Even to an evil thing.

His black hair was mussed, still dusty, and his head hung though he was awake. Miguel had been slowly bringing in objects; a golf club, paring knife, a book - ironically, a copy of Shakespeare's love sonnets - and a hammer. Trying to intimidate the Lighter, let him know what was coming.

I sent Cain to check on Sherry, but not to wake her. She didn't need to see or hear this yet. Just as I thought about it the Lighter looked up at me. His eyes red with irritation and dust. He laughed. "You think you can keep her from him? Crandle will take what is his. Did you forget I can see your thoughts as you see them, Keeper?" He crescendos the last words for an annoying effect.

I wanted to run him through for even speaking of her. And yes, more irritating is I had forgotten Lighters could read thoughts as we are thinking them.

I sighed slowly. "Quiet, Lighter, or I'll let Miguel get started on you."

I nodded my head toward Miguel who was twirling the hammer in between

80

his two hands for dramatic effect.

Wow. He seemed to know what he was doing. He had the intimidation thing down.

"You think I will tell you anything, Keeper? Especially to your intimidating pet human. I am not as weak as you think."

"We'll see."

I thought purposefully about how I kicked a Lighter's feet from under him and once his head smashed to the ground I drove a broken branch through his neck. I showed him in my mind how Marissa made the Lighter jump off the cliff edge that day like the puppet he was.

I thought of the time I once used a sword, back in the day, to impale a Lighter to a tree trunk and then set his accomplice on fire by torch, setting half the woods on fire and killing who knows how many other Lighters back in a fight in England, in the 1700's.

I also showed him me, stabbing the headless golf club through Phillip's Lighter body just as he was about to take Sherry to their beloved leader. I smiled, though the images made me just as sick as I was sure it did him, and Jeff who was also reading my mind. He winced as did the Lighter. I didn't want to remember either.

"Stop it! You think that affects me, Keeper? I'm not human, fool, not like you have apparently become. You're weak," he repeated shakily, but I could see sweat beading on his forehead. Hmmmm.

Lighters didn't sweat.

Lighters could only read our human mind thoughts, not our Keeper communication. I told Jeff and he agreed with me. We puzzled silently over what in the heck was going on. This should have been harder. He should have only caved after hours of *physical* torture to his human body. That was the only way to break a Lighter; physical pain that they were not used to in their real bodies. I was only trying to show him what would happen to him, not appeal to his emotions.

I wasn't aware that he had any. That he *could* have any. I started to explain to Jeff.

The Taker must be passing his emotions on to the Lighters. It's the only explanation.

Yes, I think you're right. That may make it easier for us later on. With emotions, they won't be as ruthless as they could be.

We'll soon find out. Is nothing ever gonna be the same again? Are all the rules gone out the window?

He shrugged and looked at me, shaking his head in confusion.

We couldn't think about that now. We had to get this done. Time was wasting.

"Alright, Merrick." Miguel stepped forward. "Enough. Let me have some fun with him." He smiled the wickedest smile I'd ever seen on a human as I reluctantly nodded. He looked directly at the Lighter. "Oi," he chirped too cheerfully.

"Screw you, human."

"Where are they?" Miguel asked and didn't need to elaborate on who or what we were talking about.

"Wouldn't you like to know," the Lighter said and then laughed a breath of a laugh.

Miguel stepped forward and smacked the Lighter across the face with the book. The irony of it still with me as the Lighter's head whipped to the side. He blinked rapidly and licked the blood from his lip, looking shocked as he winced and squinted in pain.

"Now, Lighter, tell us where they are? Then I won't have to use the rest of those thingos over there on you," Miguel asked, leaning over him with both arms on the arm rest of the chair.

"Who?" the Lighter asked, spitting his blood on the floor between Miguel and me, then laughed again shakily.

Without a hint of expression, Miguel placed the Lighters fingers of one hand out of the bind and on a cement block. He raised the hammer and smashed it down before anyone could think or say anything. The Lighter yelled and gasped but when we looked Miguel missed.

Or did he?

"Oops. Next time, I guarantee I won't miss." Miguel's voice was so guttural and his eyes were burning with barely checked anger into the Lighter's as he leaned over him. His face was only inches away. "Where are the children? This is your last chance to keep your pretty little fingers."

The Lighter shook, sweating and breathing heavily, the red stain still on his lip.

"What's happening to me?" the Lighter breathed, looking around as if he could find an answer. "What's happening to this body?"

"It's called being human and...weak as you called it. Now. Answer. My. Question."

"I can tell you, but you'd never even make it past the gate. You don't stand a chance. I can tell you because you'd never make it anyway so it doesn't really make me a traitor. I'd pretty much just be delivering you to them." The Lighter kept blubbering, trying to talk himself into it, easing his conscience.

But Lighters didn't have a conscience, or shouldn't.

Jeff was looking at me too, understanding what I was thinking. He was just as puzzled as I was. Why were some of the humans immune to the Lighters speak? Why didn't Phillip's Lighter grab Sherry and run with her instead of torturing her slowly first? Why would the Takers emotions filter down? Why were there so many Markers? Why? Why? So many unanswered questions.

"You think I can't get it out of you because you knock back my efforts?" Miguel yelled at the Lighter.

"I think I don't care anymore," the Lighter said quietly.

"Enough! Answer my question or so help me-" Miguel yelled, raising the hammer in his hand again.

"Wait! No! It's in the city. A...shed! A big green shed, two blocks from the grocery store in town."

"I'll get Sherry," I said leaving immediately, blurring, running all the way down the halls.

Cain and a couple others were in the commons room but I didn't speak to them. When I opened our door she snapped her eyes open and searched, squinting quickly. Once she focused on me the biggest smile lit up her face. I dropped to my knees, yanked back the blanket and pulled her up in my arms, probably squeezing too tightly but I was so happy at how happy she was to *see me*.

"Oh, thank God you're ok," she whispered.

"I told you I would be." I leaned down to kiss her quickly, but she wrapped her arms around my neck, pulling me as close as I could get. After a minute of scorching kisses that almost got her into trouble, I had to pull back.

"Honey, it's time. Are you ready?" I asked as I lifted and cradled her, making my way out of our room.

"As I'll ever be."

Taking One For The Team
Chapter 6

Merrick carried me into the room. The Lighter was there, tied up and dirty. His sweat had made little wet trails down his face in the caked dirt. There was blood on his lip, but he didn't look as bad as I had imagined he would.

I was surprised to find I was actually happy about that. My humanity must still be intact even after all this, though I would have guessed not. I would not wish torture even on the cruelest creature.

Merrick didn't set me down. He cradled me in his lap the whole time as he sat himself on a chair in the corner.

When the Lighter finally looked at me his eyes widened. He sucked in a breath and then coughed, breathing in the dust all over him.

"You," is all he said as he burned a hole in me with his hate filled eyes.

"Me," I answered, trying to be brave.

I was trying not to let it bother me that I was literally three feet from a Lighter. Trying not to let the pain in my leg bring tears that he would misinterpret as fear of him, to my eyes.

"You look just awful, Sherry," he said chipper and then smiled. "You look like you may have been worked over by an associate of mine. Gee, I hope you aren't in *too* much pain."

Then he let out this breathy, evil little giggle, making goose bumps creep up my skin. Merrick tightened his arms around me.

"Watch it, Lighter," Merrick ordered gruffly.

It's ok, honey, he's just trying to scare you. You're doing fine. I'm pretty sure he's lying about where the kids are, just wait it out. We'll get them back, I promise you. Don't let him get to you.

"Now," Miguel started, "tell Sherry where the children are."

84

"I already told you," the Lighter said, dragging out the last syllable and twisting his lips.

"Tell us again, you stupid dill," Miguel growled, making an advance on the Lighter who flinched.

"A large green shed two blocks from the grocery store in the city," the Lighter said almost monotone, refusing to look at me.

"He's lying," I heard my voice say, but I was too sad to put any emphasis behind it.

I was terrified he wouldn't ever tell us where they really were, but I forced that out and trusted in Merrick and Miguel.

"What? No I'm not!" He looked at me with a 'how?' on his face. Why did they believe me and not him? Then he looked back at Miguel. "Ok. Fine. They're in the basement of the grocery store."

"Lies."

I breathed in a frustrated breath.

"Tell her the truth," Miguel angrily spat out the command as he picked up the hammer once more.

The Lighter just sat there staring so Miguel took the Lighter's hand and placed it on the cement block upright by his chair. I swallowed hard and tried not to move.

"Don't watch, Sherry," Miguel told me as he raised his hand with the hammer above his head.

Fine by me. I buried my face in Merrick's neck and waited for the screaming but all I heard was the Lighter yelling 'ok, ok!'.

"Ok! It's a big white gated house. Out beside the radio station at the west end of town. Maple Street. Maple Street!" he yelled it all in a rush of breaths.

Everyone looked at me expectantly.

"Let's go," I nodded vigorously and my voice cracked with relief.

After we all got our gear and the rest of us got dressed. We headed out after Miguel loaded our prisoner in the van. Only a few of them remained, the ones without gifts. The rest of us, even me, made our way to the vehicles and hunkered down for the cold ride to town.

They needed my lie detecting skills, I assumed, otherwise there was no way I'd be going. Or maybe after everything, Merrick was just scared to leave me here without him under any circumstances. Whatever the reason, I was grateful.

Sardined into the three vehicles, we went. No one wanted to ride near the Lighter so he, unfairly, had more room than anyone else.

Celeste and Danny joined Merrick, Jeff and me in the van with the Lighter strapped in the back. We were all cramped up in the middle seat to be as far away from it as possible.

Danny was explaining to Celeste about how they trapped it and took it down to the room to be questioned. How it didn't even put up much of a fight. He still sounded angry to me.

I hadn't even really talked to Danny much lately. Not *really* talked. I missed him. I didn't even know what was going on with him and Celeste anymore. They apparently were still together but what was to come of it? How were things going? Was he happy? Was she happy?

So I asked him. Not just for knowing the answers but also to take my mind off what was coming once we got where we were going.

"So. How are you guys doing?" I asked when I could get a word in.

"Good," Danny answered, not really understanding my question, just small talk.

"No, Danny, how are you guys doing? You and Celeste?"

"I'm good." He looked at Celeste and they both smiled bashfully at each other, Celeste ducking her head. "We're good, really good, considering the circumstances."

"Uhuh. And how's your mom, Celeste?"

"Good. She's a little freaked out by all this stuff, my gift and all. She refuses to speak about it actually but...good," she answered, looking relieved to change the subject.

"That's good. It seems like forever since I've talked to her. So..."

"So..." Danny said with an insisting tone, insisting I drop the subject I so wanted to talk about.

"What? I just miss you guys. We haven't really talked in a long time. I'm your sister...I can be in your business. It's my job."

"Aho, really? Well. In that case," he said playfully elbowing me, then he gave me the dirt I was hoping for, "We're great, really. Margo loves me, of course, and she's the best. I'm the perfect son-in-law that never was. She's happy for us." He smiled. "I mean, we aren't going to go to your extreme to get married but...we would if we could, one day much, much later. Right now, things are just fine like they are." He looked at her and picked her hand up in his lap to play with her fingers and smiled like they'd had this conversation before. "Celeste is working with me on my gift, and I've been working with her some. Her gift is way cooler than mine-"

"Nuhuh, baby," Celeste interrupted him, "your gift is awesome. I just zone in on people, that's nothing, but you can-"

"Nope, nope. You," Danny interrupted her and the nauseating sweetness back and forth continued in spite of the dreary circumstances.

I wondered if this was what Merrick and I looked like to other people? But I was happy for them. They seemed great together and extremely happy.

It was funny how normal things seemed to go on even when everything was so messed up. People could still fall in love, even at the end of the world. If anyone had half of what I had with Merrick, I considered them lucky.

Once we reached the spot the Lighter told us about we stopped two blocks away and across the street. Only then did we realize that there was only one other vehicle behind us.

Jeff reached out to Kay in her mind, he told us as he was trying. Then he got the biggest grin and gave Merrick a look. I knew they were talking and I couldn't help the scowl that raced across my face.

I could hear the Lighter grunting and wiggling in his restraints. It was amazing the things you could use if you just thought. Fish nets for bondage, golf clubs for, what- stakes? Hammers and books as instruments of torture and cooperation.

After a few minutes another set of headlights came into view and then shut off a few hundred feet from us as it coasted to a stop.

Cain jumped out first with something bulky in his arms. He sprinted to us. At first I was alarmed, but then I remembered Jeff's grin after speaking to Kay, so it must not be anything bad.

Merrick opened the side door and pulled me to the edge of the seat. Cain walked up looking pretty smug. I tilted my head trying to figure out what everyone was up to. Cain's hands were off the side, on the other side of the door where I couldn't see them.

"What?" I asked finally, when everyone continued to grin at me.

He produced a pair of crutches, metal and gleaming.

"What? How did you..." I laughed as my eyes filled with grateful tears.

"We thought you could use these. We made a little pit stop. Snagged them from the hospital on the way over here, along with a real walking cast and some other supplies we thought might come in handy, you know, since we were there already," Cain explained grinning and holding them out, ready for me.

Merrick helped me out of the van and I took the crutches from Cain.

"Thank you guys, so much. I can't believe you did this! Believe it or not, I'm a pro at these things. I broke my leg when I was seventeen on a family camping trip. I had to use crutches for four months. Of course, they weren't *stolen* crutches," I said laughing.

"Stolen crutches are better than no crutches," he sang winking.

"True. Thank you, Cain."

"No problem, Sherry. Now, are you ready to get your kids back?"

"Absolutely."

I had to smile at the way he threw ownership on me, like I had rights to claim them for myself.

We gathered around the backside of the van, huddled for protection as much as warmth. It was freezing. We sat alternating Keeper, Special, nobody in order to spread the Keeper warmth around. Merrick's arms were around me of course. I almost felt guilty, but he was mine after all.

Celeste went to work. When she searched for someone in her mind, her eyes turned from green to white, really bright ethereal white. She looked mystical and somehow even more beautiful and fascinating, even though you'd think it not possible.

She searched in her mind for where Lily was so we would know which direction to go or at least how they were doing.

"Ah!" she gasped angrily, making a few of us jump because she'd been quiet for a few minutes. "They've got her tied up and blindfolded. She's lying on a...dirty mattress on the floor. I can't tell where exactly. She's breathing, but very still. Maybe she's asleep. It's dark and it looks like she's alone." She made a small distressed sound. "There's a dead rat on the floor."

A few angry grunts and gasps from the others echoed out. I pushed the knot in my throat back down. I knew this wouldn't be pretty. Merrick's arm tightened around me and I grasped his hand to comfort him as he was comforting me.

Crying would solve nothing so I listened more as she searched for Calvin.

"Ok. He's...the same, tied and blindfolded on the floor, but in a different room. It looks like a bathroom, not as dark. And it looks like he's alone too." She choked out a sob. "He's crying."

Danny pulled her head to his shoulder to soothe her, wrapping his arm around like an anchor. Again I fought the urge to cry and forced myself to focus.

"Ok," Jeff started and cleared his throat. "Now that we know their situations, let's find out where they are and how many Lighters are here waiting for us. Josh."

Josh turned to look at the property. He had to physically be looking at the object to see through it. Nothing seemed to be happening to him, except, his eyes, too, were completely glowing white. His baby face still set perfectly, not twisting or squinting. He panned the house and yard past the gate. There was a lot of tree coverage and blinds.

"I see a group of them...five, right on the inside of the gate. No weapons, just talking."

"Talking," Jeff said, like it was unbelievable.

"Yep, talking."

"Trudy, what are they talking about?"

Trudy stepped up, still with a huge bandage on the back of her neck.

Apparently none of her injuries had affected her extreme hearing.

"They been talking about this Crandle every since we got here, honey. That he is 'magnificent' they called him," she said sarcastically like it was such an outrageous claim. And it was. "The best leader they've ever had. That this was so easy, that they like it here, earth. They are happy that they've practically won and this is almost all over."

Of course. What else would Lighters have to talk about? Everyone took a look around at each other, shaking their heads in disbelief, a few muttering under their breath.

"Ok, Josh, go ahead. Let's finish this," Jeff growled, sounding highly peeved.

Apparently the 'we won' comment wasn't sitting well.

"Ok. Nobody's in the front of the house or any of the front rooms. Kitchen...hall...back bedroom...dark and empty. I'm heading upstairs. Second floor. Bedroom...hall...oh! I found him. I found Calvin! Second floor bathroom. He looks scared. He's sitting in the tub now, blindfold pulled down... He's saying something, but I can't hear. There's a third floor. Wonder who lived here before, this house is jacked. Next bedroom empty... Going upstairs...nothing. It's completely empty. I don't even see any Lighters anywhere."

"That can't be, I saw her. I saw Lily on the floor," Celeste whispered.

"I'm looking, I'm looking...still don't see her," Josh said in frustration.

"Try a basement or something. The pantry or a closet maybe."

"Heading back down stairs... Not in the pantry. I don't see any other...wait, there's a door in the hall... It's a basement. I'm heading down...it's full of...oh, my..." He started gasping and breathing heavy. "It's full of people. They are piled in there so tight they don't even have room to move. They must've been down there for a while. Some of them are...some are dead. Some sitting, some standing. They're scared. I don't think they are under the Lighter speak. I could be wrong. Celeste you said Lily was alone right?"

"Yes, well, at least I didn't see anyone else."

"Ok, I'm heading back up now," Josh said looking green, like he could be sick. "Where else to look, people? Give me something."

"What about an attic? The house is huge, I bet it has one," Danny suggested, his arm still around Celeste.

"Going up...first floor...second floor...third floor...still no Lighters. I see it, the pull string in the ceiling. There. There she is! You were right Danny. She's still lying on the floor. I don't see anyone with her- wait. Oh no. There is someone. He's sitting in the corner, in the dark. I can see his leg kicking."

"It's gotta be Crandle," I announced.

"You're probably right," Jeff said, looking intently at the ground. "Ok. Josh,

Cain, Merrick, Trudy, Celeste, Danny, Marissa and Lana come inside with me. The rest of you go with Simon, Miguel and Kay to stand guard out front and wait for our signal to come in and help us release the people in the basement. Sherry, I'm sorry. I guess you can stay here with him." He nodded his head toward the van...and the Lighter.

"You want me to stay with the Lighter down here by myself?" It came out before I could think and way more whiny than I had intended.

"I don't think so, Jeff, Sherry stays with me," Merrick insisted firmly, shaking his head.

"Merrick, I don't like it either, you know that, but her leg's broken and I'm afraid of what will happened if she comes inside and things go bad." He looked back to me. "Your leg is broken, Sherry, you heard Josh. There are three flights of stairs."

"I'll carry her," Merrick said.

"There's an elevator," Josh butted in before the two could continue, "up to the third floor."

"Good. Besides, Lily will want to be with her," Merrick replied, glancing at me quickly.

"Ok," Jeff relented.

"And, uh, I'm coming with you as well. Calvin's in there," Ryan said firmly, leaving no room for negotiation.

"Of course, Ryan, I'm sorry I didn't think of that. It's settled. Danny. Why don't you tell our friends inside the gate to take a walk," Jeff said, already turning.

"I'll try. I've never done it with more than one before."

He walked forward a ways, stopped and concentrated, cocking his head. I heard Kay and Celeste whispering, going back and forth about Kay wanting to come with Celeste but her insisting she'd be fine. A minute or so later he spoke.

"Ok, I think they listened. I made one of them say they heard a noise at the back of the house. I think they left. Josh, did they?"

"Yes, I don't see them there anymore," Josh answered.

"Ok, let's move," Jeff ordered.

I hobbled behind them on my crutches, but keep up with them down the well lit street. I saw a big, white, extravagant gold bordered sign by the front gate that said 'Mayor Manor'. That explained why the house was so big and guarded.

The house was white with dark green shudders, brick walkways and steps with gold light fixtures and pathway lamps. The gate was already swung open with big letters 'MM' on the front written out on the iron fence. Pretentious much? The landscaping was overgrown but you could tell it was once important and thought out. Bushes and hedges lined the fence and house side. There were no Lighters to be seen.

We continued in silence and then out of nowhere we heard loud thuds. Looking up I saw at least ten Lighters, landing on the street in front of us. We were right in front of the gate, just about to enter.

We froze in our places. We had hoped it was as easy as it looked, waltzing in to take back what was ours without a hitch.

The Lighters took a few steps toward us. Before anyone could act on either side, Cain, who was in front, threw up his hands, pushing them forward and the Lighters went flying backwards, including the car parked by the gate and all the trash cans lining the road and sidewalks.

It exploded with force, a booming noise, bright light and whipping wind. Trash and paper flew around and blew everywhere. The car flipped and slid down the pavement like a toy, sparks shooting, glass breaking and throwing out in all directions. The Lighters flew way up into the air, flipping and turning, some hitting tree branches, parked cars and street lights before slamming back hard to the pavement.

Cain turned to look back at us, just as stunned as we were. More so even. "What the hell was that?" he yelled.

"You're asking us?" Miguel yelled back.

"I don't know! Simon? Jeff?" Cain asked, looking sick.

"I'm not sure but I'm grateful for it. I guess you have a gift after all, Cain. We'll discuss it later. It didn't stop them for long, see." Jeff pointed and sure enough, they were already rising up from the ground. "Someone would have heard the racket. Let's go, break up."

As our group ran into the gate, we saw another Marker skeleton, like the one before in the field, lying black and empty on the ground. The five Lighters who had been there before came rounding the house looking fierce, glowing slightly as the others had before. They produced enough light to see their faces twisted with anger and also anticipation. They were thinking this would be fun.

Marissa ran forward and stopped in front of them. I heard someone tell her to wait and then grunt angrily, but couldn't make out who and they didn't stop her.

"Muse," one of the Lighters said with clear disdain.

I held my breath. What was she doing? She was crazy. Then she leaned forward a bit and whispered something to them. Then she slapped one on the arm and he went running straight into the thick iron pole of the gate, smashing his face into it. He fell down to the ground with an audible thud.

I forgot the Lighters couldn't fight the Muse's wrath. Then she dropped to the ground, just as one was reaching for her and slapped his leg. He too ran for the pole.

Puppets.

Unfortunately, they caught wind of her game and one flipped over her and grabbed her from behind, held her tight as he turned her to face us, pressing her back against his chest, a big smile in place. He made sure not to touch her skin. But just as he was reaching for her turtle necked chin and neck and was about to wrench to break it, he stopped.

His eyes went wide and he started swatting, dropping Marissa who took the opportunity to backhand another Lighter in the confusion, who ran for a pole head first.

The Lighter waved both arms and legs, kicking and screaming, swatting around like there was a bee. A swarm of bees maybe. We didn't see anything. I didn't anyway. The last remaining sane Lighter started towards Marissa and then stopped abruptly, a look of pain on his face. He dropped to the ground like he'd been shot. He held his chest, gasping. Looking at his hands, eyes wide like something was there, blood maybe, but there was nothing.

With a quick look at Danny's satisfied expression my question was answered.

"You did that?" I asked with awe.

"Yep. Let's go before the fake bees leave and this idiot figures out he hasn't been stabbed."

"Wow, baby!" Celeste said, clinging tighter to his arm, in as much awe of Danny as I was.

We left the two Lighters, writhing, shaking and swatting on the ground. The others were still unconscious, but for how long, we had no idea.

We could hear a commotion in the street, Miguel yelling in battle cry. The Lighters had apparently made it back to them. They were fighting. It took everything I had not to want to run and help, but we had our own part of the mission to do. We reached the big wrap-around porch which was gorgeous. Jeff tried the door and it was locked. Dead bolted.

"Ok. Now what?"

"I've got it," Danny said, jumping off the porch. He came back with the 'stabbed' Lighter in tow by his shirt collar.

"Open it," Danny told him.

"I can't," the Lighter said, still clutching his chest and moaning as if in pain.

"Can't or won't?" Danny asked, his voice tight.

"He's telling the truth. For whatever, he can't open it," I explained.

"Why not? Why can't you open it?" Danny said, his face getting redder by the second.

"No key," he said writhing.

"Hmmm. That's sounds like a lie and the truth." I bit my lip, thinking. "You don't have a key, but you know where one is, don't you?" I asked him.

Merrick moved over instinctively to shield me with his arm from the Lighter I was speaking to, as I automatically moved forward to talk to it.

"I...don't know where a key is," the lighter lied, his pitch black hair falling in his face.

"Anyone can see that was a lie, idiot," I muttered, exhaling in frustration.

We were getting nowhere, then Marissa stepped forward.

"Enough. Tell me where the key is," she commanded and then pressed a hard finger to his forehead.

"Under the potted plant by the porch, the rock," he said and as soon as he said it he straightened up and started swinging.

He caught Danny across the chin with a hard blow that sent him flying backwards over the railing into the grass. Marissa ducked but not fast enough. He clipped her temple with his fist and then kneed her in the shoulder as she bent, sending her backwards. Jeff caught her as he blurred up behind her. Merrick swung himself around to stand in front of me in a blur. I didn't even feel him move.

He slammed his fist into the Lighters clothed chest and sent him backwards, falling into the railing as well, rolling and stumbling backwards into the shrubs.

Merrick jumped the rail, using one hand for leverage as he slung himself over it and into the grass with perfect grace and balance, Jeff right behind him. They circled the Lighter, blurring, then slow. The Lighter was spitting out obscenities, hissing mad.

I hobbled over and down the steps along with Celeste to check on Danny who was out cold. Scary. I'd never seen him knocked out before. Marissa was all right, but dazed on the porch swing where Jeff had put her.

Merrick and Jeff were exchanging significant glances, meaning they were talking. Then, Merrick threw himself on the ground in front of Jeff and as the Lighter bent to follow him, Jeff pulled the pointed yard sign stake from the back waistband of his jeans, driving it right through the Lighters neck.

The Lighter fell, the brilliant blinding burst of light and then pounding lighting, flame and smoke taking him with it a split second before he would have landed on Merrick, still on the ground.

"Ok. Someone definitely heard that," Jeff said.

He helped Merrick up and they brushed off as Merrick ran to Danny's side. Danny came around asking what had happened. Why had the Lighter no longer thought he was stabbed?

"He can only be compelled by one command at a time. He would have continued to think he was stabbed but Marissa compelled him to find the key," Jeff explained, brushing his hands off.

"I'm sorry, I didn't know," Marissa said from behind us on the steps, looking upset and wringing her hands. We all turned to look at her. "If something had happened to one of you because of my stupidity-"

Jeff was there in an instant blur, hugging her to him, his hand on her cheek to press her to him, tucking her under his chin.

"No. No, we needed to find the key. I should have warned you about that. It's ok, it's not your fault. It's fine, sweetie," he said, running a hand down her hair.

We all just stood there and gawked like a bunch of idiots as Marissa buried her tear streaked face in Jeff's chest and clung to him. He moved his hands over her like it was nothing - nothing new that is. I had suspected but completely forgotten all about it.

I looked at Merrick. He looked more shocked than anyone. He must've been keeping his part of the promise to stay out of the other Keeper's heads. I grabbed his hand and squeezed to get his attention. He looked at me with a slow, reserved, happy smile spreading crossing his face.

I didn't know about this. Did you?

I shook my head no and he sighed and shook his head too, still smiling.

I can't believe this. I'm so...happy for him. For both of them.

"Me too," I replied smiling, but as we heard a yell from behind us we were jolted back to reality. They were still fighting out there in the street.

"Ok," Jeff said, releasing Marissa, clearing his throat and looking around like he had completely forgotten where he was. "Now we got the key, let's get moving."

He walked over to the porch steps and went right to the plant, by the rock and snatched the key on a long bright red ribbon out from under it. Merrick lifted me in one quick stride to bypass the steps, then set me back down.

Before the door was unlocked, Josh took a quick peek and told us it was all clear. We went in quietly, shuffling slowly. We knew someone was up there with Lily. We wanted to be as quiet as we could until we could no longer hide the fact that we were here.

The elevator was in the hall, past the dining room and sitting room, at the end of the hall. The house was ginormous and *jacked* as Josh had said. Everything was cherry wood and pewter. Paintings and plaques lined the walls. The kitchen appliances were all black, even the cabinets. It looked odd to me and off-putting but I bet in the daylight it looked rich and sophisticated.

The elevator was small, only three could fit at one time so Trudy, Merrick and I took it, waiting until the others were already on the second floor before going up ourselves.

Once Merrick pressed the button and the hum and screech of shifting gears rang out, I knew our presence there would no longer be a secret. It sounded like it hadn't been used in a long time as it jerked to a stop at the second floor and we piled out quickly and quietly.

I was so anxious to see that Calvin was ok, but I would restrain myself. Lana was here and she would be the one to comfort him, to let him know we came for him and didn't leave him here to fend for himself.

As I looked at Lana's face I saw how anxious she was as well. Then I realized she didn't even know that Calvin was there, within her grasp. No one had told her yet and she was just following us. I hadn't spoken to her since I signed at home that the Lighter told us where to go to find them.

I tapped her shoulder and told her as we headed down the hall. I put a 'C' over my heart and point at the door to indicate - Calvin is inside there. She straightened up quickly and rushed forward. Jeff caught her before she could snatch the door open. She struggled and fought him a few seconds while he asked Josh to make sure that Calvin was still alone.

Ryan blurred up and held up a hand to her, to calm and steady her, to indicate to just wait. She stopped squirming.

Josh said Calvin was alone and Jeff released her. She yanked the door open and flicked on the light. We saw Calvin, still sitting in the tub, his eyes squeezed shut and his hands covering his ears. He yelled at us, thinking we were the Lighters and remembering the warnings not to listen.

Good boy.

"I'm not telling you anything! You might as well go on and get out of here. My mom is coming for me. You'll see!"

Lana rushed over and touched his arm and he flinched back further into the tub and yelled louder.

"No! No! I won't tell you!"

Lana touched his arm again and lifted his face with her finger under his chin. He opened his eyes, blinked rapidly like he couldn't believe what he was seeing. Then he leapt up and grabbed Lana around her neck using both of his arms. She pulled him out of the tub and they fell back on the floor in a heap of happy tears and quiet sobs.

It was the most beautiful thing I'd ever seen. Words were overrated. They could say a million words with their embrace. Lana, though she couldn't speak, showed her son she loved him and cared for him and would do anything for him. She braved Lighters for him and he knew she would. He yelled it out before that his mom would come for him.

And she did.

Ryan stood to the side awkwardly. I could tell he was itching to physically make sure Calvin was ok. Calvin quickly turned and hugged Ryan, too. Ryan's eyes went wide with surprise as he beamed and patted Calvin's shoulder.

Marissa and Celeste were both wiping their eyes as we made our way down the hall to the stairs and the elevator. I was still surprised to not see any Lighters in the house or hear anything. I was beginning to wonder if this was a trap or something. It still seemed a little too easy.

Once we were on the third floor and under the attic trap door, Miguel reached up to pull the cord and we heard a voice, a voice I was very familiar with, boom through the house, rattling the hinges of the trap door and the windows.

"STOP!"

We stopped because he commanded it and you couldn't fight the Taker's compulsion; just be still and wait for what was to come.

Then I gasped. It felt like his hands were on my arms, caressing me. His voice was like a caress in my mind as well. Almost...sexual. It made me want to vomit right there.

I rubbed my arms, trying to throw his hands off, but they were nowhere. It was all in my mind. So how do you get someone out of your mind? I raked my hands through my hair. I put the palms of my hands over my eyes. I shook myself, looking around, flinging arms.

His voice was in my mind so loudly, speaking the same things from our dream, the same promises and assurances, letting nothing else in.

I was vaguely aware of yelling and grabbing at me but I couldn't focus on it, only Crandle. Then Merrick was in my mind.

Sherry?

I snapped out of it in an instant with a gasp. I came to and they were watching me with worrisome gazes. Everyone. I was breathing heavy and Merrick was in front of me holding my elbows to keep me from falling, eying me quizzically.

"It's Crandle," I explained breathlessly, shaking my head to unrattle it. "He's...he's up there with her."

"Are you ok?" Merrick asked, looking in my eyes to make sure I told him the truth.

"Yes. Crandle was...never mind. Let's get her out of there and go home, Merrick," I tried to say with conviction but the tears that wanted to fall made me squeak.

Merrick pulled me closer and then we heard the booming voice again.

"Merrick? Sherry's Merrick, I presume."

As soon as the voice stopped, another loud booming. The attic trap door exploded, loudly and violently. Wood chips, splinters and steps along with metal hinges flew, sending us all ducking to the floor for cover.

When I looked up again - over Merrick's shoulder as he'd thrown himself over me - Crandle was standing in front of us, under where the trap door was, a smug smile in place. He was wearing the same attire from the dream. Tan khakis, bare feet, white button up and dazzling smile. I wondered if he only looked that way to me. A glamour to me like before and his true self to everyone else.

"So...this is the one Sherry can't seem to live without. What's so special about you...Keeper?" he asked, only moving to turn his head as if inspecting Merrick.

Crandle didn't seem bothered by the debris he was standing on in bare feet, or the other people in the room with us. He eyed Merrick up and down and then his eyes found me and he locked me in.

Those were the darkest black eyes I'd ever seen, so much deeper in real life. His eyes refused to let me go. It was harder to fight him in person and so different than in my dream. I was instantly ashamed. Shamed beyond shame because whatever powers of persuasion he was using on me were finally working...to a degree.

I wouldn't actually run over and jump in his arms as some inkling of my brain was telling me to do, but I couldn't look away either. He was looking at me like I was the most beautiful human he had ever seen, like he had to have me. Like I was special and he needed to possess me. My mind wanted me to consider his offer, it pleaded with me to.

I felt awkward. Everyone was watching, waiting for something to happen, and I couldn't seem to tear my gaze from him. Then, I felt him caressing my mind again.

His hands on my arms, fingers and breath on my neck, making me shiver and my eyelids flutter. He whispered in my mind that it could always be this way. That he could love me like Merrick, more if I so chose. He'd give me everything, that he was everything Merrick was and more. He was human before, he knew what I needed...all the things he could do to me.

All I had to do was come to him and let him show me how he absorbed a Lighter...

I stared, listening, contemplating. I felt spongy, flimsy, see through. Like I could take anything and it would bounce off. Nothing could hurt me. My lips were parted and dry and I felt my breath going in and out rapidly. His eyes were still so intently focused on mine, his smile was almost contagious. How could anyone with a smile that looked at me that way be evil? He was barefoot for goodness sake! But I could still feel a sense of...wrong.

A flicker of something crept in. A flicker of something right. I turned my head slightly and licked my dry lips, but I was still unable to look away. I knew I was being sucked into something, pulled, drawn into something I wasn't supposed to be but I couldn't quite make it connect...I couldn't seem to focus on what I should be heading towards.

Merrick pulled me behind him and as soon as my gaze was broken from Crandle I was myself again.

Crandle's hands were no longer on me, no longer in my mind. I realized I had no idea how long we'd been standing there like that, gazing at each other. I wasn't aware of any other voices or movements in the room. Was it seconds or minutes? Had Merrick been trying to speak to me?

Instantly, shame and guilt overwhelmed me and a small sob escaped, against my will, and I covered my mouth with my hand. I couldn't contain it any other way.

I replayed the words in my head, the Taker's whispers and promises to me and gasped at my own stupidity and vulnerability.

I grabbed Merrick's shirt back in my fist to keep him in front of me so Crandle couldn't see me, so no one could.

Crandle actually said he wanted me to watch him absorb a Lighter and I didn't revolt! I just stood there and let him touch me with his mind. I was so disgusted with myself, I felt the lump rising in my throat. A couple of hot tears spilled over and I wiped them on Merrick's shirt back. The guilt was a blaze, a fire, even though technically I didn't do...

And then I heard him laughing, out loud. I peeked around Merrick's arm in utter disbelief.

"Oh, Sherry, don't cry, don't distress, and don't be too hard on yourself either, love. No one. No one can resist my persuasion. In fact, you fought it more than anyone *ever* has. That's nothing to snuff at." Then he turned to Merrick. "That's right. I can read your mate's thoughts. Irritating for you isn't it? You want to so badly," he mocked and looked back to me.

I shut my eyes so tightly they hurt, thinking that was how he must have controlled me before.

"No, it's not the eyes, love. It's just you. Humans are weak, mundane things. You remember what I told you before? You can have it you know. Right now. Just tell your mate that you want real power, push his puny protective arm away from you and come to mine. Lily's waiting upstairs for you. Come on. Merrick wouldn't hurt you, even if you betrayed him right now in front of everyone. He wouldn't. Come to me, Sherry."

He was using his compelling voice again and I was worried because I could feel a little part of me wanting to cave.

"I don't think that is going to happen," Merrick said through his teeth and pushed me back behind him further and then spoke to me in my mind.

He's trying to compel you, don't listen. Stay behind me, touching me at all times. I won't let him hurt you. We'll get out of here together, I promise.

Merrick's voice was worried and shaky. They told me before that no one could refuse the Taker's compulsion. The Taker told me that as well. Merrick was worried that he was about to lose me to it, Merrick could tell he was doing it too.

I racked my brain quickly. I had my wits back and I wouldn't be fooled again. Should I pretend to be interested in his proposal? Would that give the others time to do something? Would Merrick know what I was doing, that I was tricking the Taker or would he assume I'd been tricked? What alternative did we have?

Merrick said the Taker couldn't be killed like normal Lighters, so could we fight him here? What could I do once he took me? My leg, I couldn't run. Crap! Think!

Then I remembered, the Taker could read my mind.

I looked over and he was grinning, clearly amused at my inner turmoil. He whispered to me in my head, caressing my arms with his mind.

Even if you come to me only to save your pathetic family, I'll still have you, Sherry. I wouldn't refuse you even if you are trying to trick me. I need you, I want you. It may not be real for you now, but it will be. It can be. Come to me and save them. Save Merrick. Save Danny. Save Calvin. Lily is waiting for you. Come, Sherry.

"Why me? What's so special about *me*?" I asked him out loud without thinking.

He looked taken back that I had spoken to him out right. "Well...you're beautiful," he said sweetly and I actually laughed.

"I doubt the leader of all evil wants me because I'm beautiful. Why?" I asked again with more force.

"Because you're...honest. Pure. Wholesome. Pretty. Meek. Compassionate. Loving." His voice was so...endearing, and then it turned into something else. Mocking laughter. "Short. Shy. Naïve. Weak-minded." I felt Merrick flinch and I held tight to keep him from charging Crandle as he continued. "Puny. Sterile," he dragged out the last word to goad me and I decided to end his long windedness.

"Are you trying to impress me with that list?" I spat out angrily through clenched teeth, pulling Merrick's arm tighter in front of me, needing to feel him there, to anchor me more than anything else.

"It just is. You are puny where I am strong. You are compassionate where I am ruthless. You are weak-minded where I am most definitely am not. You are my opposite in every sense of the word. Altruistic. I cannot exist without you. I searched long for someone like you, someone to complete what we started. If you want to blame someone, blame your Keeper. If he had not come to love you, and I knew that this was a first, I've never heard of such a thing, a Keeper loving a human. Phillip, you remember him, don't you?"

I believe he paid you a little visit a while back in your mind. He warned you I was coming for you, didn't he?

"He let me in on all your little secrets. But I knew...a Keeper could only love you if you were perfectly good. So, one quick glance at your pretty little mind and I knew that it was true. I could find a human worth something in this sea of useless mindless idiots. You were the one that I needed. Once I rid the world of humans, and we," he palmed his chest with both hands, "are all that exist, we need to have you for the balance. There can't only be *evil*, as you put it. There has to be both. Balance. So, in a sense, if I destroy all of you, I destroy myself along with you. I can't have that and your altruism will be the key to your own races destruction. It's the perfect wickedly ironic ending, don't you think?"

"You're delusional. I'm neither perfect nor selfless by any standards, especially not human ones. Merrick doesn't love me because I'm perfect."

"Then ask him why. Why would he risk everything for you if you were not?" he asked but I stayed silent as did Merrick. "If I ask him, he will say that is why. You are quite a sight to behold, Sherry. I wish you could see yourself, so small yet so strong willed. Broken physically," he gestured to my leg, then stretched his arms out to his sides, "yet here you are, in the Lighter's nest ready to strike down anyone who comes between you and your precious Lily."

"Why Lily? Why Calvin?"

"Oh, Sherry, they are nothing to me. Except food," he said laughing maliciously. "Just as those people you saw in the basement will be. I want to absorb them, Sherry, that's all. Children offer so much more...sustenance than Lighters and humans do. They are so pure and clean on the inside. It does wonders for my complexion." He rolled his eyes in fake modesty and then he laughed again, making my stomach turn, but I tried not to show it. "More than anything, they were just my ploy to get you here. And here you are."

You Win Some, You Lose Some
Chapter 7

It was more than strange and embarrassing to have my husband, my brother and my family watch this thing - evil incarnate - sweet talk, seduce and basically try to make me run away with him. It was sick and if he'd stop talking for just a minute, I was sure I'd throw up.

How do we get out of this? What should I do? If I had to sacrifice myself for Lily I would. She had plenty of people who loved her and would take care of her, I'd do it in a heartbeat. But I knew that Crandle wouldn't let them go. Plus, if I went he said he could destroy the world. So...quite a dilemma. It was a trick and I knew it. I also knew he was reading my mind. I wondered if it was everyone or just me.

I saw him raise his eyebrow in amusement to my internal question but he didn't answer it. What would happen if I went with him? What would happen to me?

"You'll become like me," he answered me. "A leader of sorts, depending on your behavior, though I can't let you become a Lighter. I must keep you human. For some reason, we never could make females Lighters. Too weak I guess, but in your case, you could be the closest thing to one, one of a kind and worshipped," Crandle answered and I wondered why he did that when he could speak to me in my mind.

And when I thought back, I *had* only seen male Lighters.

Huh.

"You don't know me half as well as you think you do if you could think that being worshipped is something I would want," I said, but I felt like my arguments were beginning to lose steam.

How long could we sit here and go back and forth like this? Something had to give.

"Oh, I know you pretty well. Every human female wants to be worshipped, especially by men. Have you yourself not thought in your mind that Merrick is at your every female command and pouty whim?" he said looking at Merrick, begging for a reaction.

Interesting.

I *had* thought that but not quite as devious as he laid it out to be. I was being silly and playful, wasn't I?

"Being worshipped by my husband is a bonus, not a requirement for me. I don't need that to be happy. I'm not like other women. I think you've got the wrong girl."

"Oh, I got the right girl. Modest as all get out and naïve as well. You don't see how beautiful you are, how meek. It just makes people want to protect you and love you. You don't use your powers of persuasion anywhere near the level of what you could. Merrick is merely a toy, a play thing. Imagine having a fleet of toys under your every command."

But before I could think of anything to say in response, I saw Trudy in my peripheral. She was already the closest to Crandle on his left, but she inched closer.

"Enough of this rubbish!" she yelled and took her iron rod, ramming it right through Crandle's chest. He fell backward from the force and landed on his back on the floor, banging his head on the hall table. The table fell and the flower vase shattered, spraying water, yellow roses and glass all over the floor.

Cain was under the attic door in seconds, trying to coax Lily, who was now looking down to jump.

"Lily!" he called and then looked back at us to make sure we heard. "She's here. Lily! Come on. Jump down to me."

"No! No! The bad man..." she started and before I could even suggest it Merrick swung into action, instantly heading for the attic.

"Lily, the bad man is gone now. I'm here. Come on, sweetheart. I need you to jump to me. I'll catch you, I promise. Come on, baby. Let's go home," Merrick said pleading.

Merrick was tall with a long reach but it was still a pretty far jump, especially for a toddler, but she must have trusted Merrick completely, like me, because she jumped without a further moment's hesitation. She landed safely in his arms hugging his neck so hard and he hugged her so sweetly in return.

"Mewwick!" she yelled, still hugging him. "Mewwick! Don't make me stay with the bad man! Pwease."

"Never, sweetheart, you belong with us."

She continued to be a trooper, tolerating all the happy crooning and reassuring touches and pats of the others, as I stood in my same spot and observed.

She was happy. Maybe she wouldn't be so happy to see me? She looked as content as could be with everyone else, but when Merrick turned with her in his arms and she saw me, my heart stopped. She practically busted free of his grip to get to me, he had to hold tight to keep her from falling as he strode my way.

"Shawwy!"

She almost strangled me with her petite arms when Merrick reached me. He still held her because of my leg and crutches but she gripped my neck like a vise and I loved every second of it. She was ecstatic, because of me. Seeing me made her happy. That, made *me* happy.

"Oh, Lily bug. I missed you," I told her.

"I wike that name, bug, Shawwy. I wike you to call me dat."

"You do? Well, I'll always call you that then."

I was crying, again. I cried a lot lately, especially when it came to this little girl.

"Shawwy, why you cwying?"

"I'm just so happy to see you, Lily bug. Are you ready to go home?"

She nodded her head vigorously with the cutest little turned up nose and raised eyebrows, but our happy reunion was short lived when I heard a familiar laugh echoing in the halls.

Why wouldn't he just die! Then I remembered that Merrick said Crandle couldn't be killed by running him through, like a Lighter. Only by fire. Oh, no. Merrick wrapped both Lily and me in his arms protectively.

"What a sweet reunion," Crandle mocked, pulling himself up and slowly removing the rod from his chest even slower, with a grimace. White light spurting out of the wound until it healed shut. I hoped that it really did hurt. "Unfortunately, I'm tired of these games and I'm ready to go. Sherry, shall we? Or shall I call the Lighters to deal with your family?"

The ones outside? The ones we already took care of? Others? What do I do? I couldn't go with him. Come on someone, think of something!

"I guess I have your answer then." He took a step forward and shook his head, looking at me. "I'm so disappointed in you Sherry. First I'll call the Lighters to come and kill your 'band of misfits' as you once called them and then I'll take you by force. One way or another, I will have you," Crandle said raising his hands in the air, the rod still in his fist.

His palms started to glow with a faint light, waiting for...lightning or smoke or something, I wasn't sure, but nothing seemed to be happening. What was he waiting for?

Then he blurred forward, moving the few feet to where Trudy was standing. He stabbed her through the back, the rod protruding out of her chest, right where her heart would be.

"No! No!" I heard myself yell but I wasn't the only one.

Trudy gasped and almost fell holding her chest. Crandle held her in one arm while the other hand was placed over her chest. He breathed deeply, taking big breaths and concentrated. His hand started to glow brighter then came a white light from underneath his palm and his eyes glazed over black and dark. Trudy screamed and wrenched to get free, but just as Jeff moved forward to help it was too late.

We saw a ripple go through her entire body, a bright shining light with it that engulfed her and evaporated just a quickly, leaving her skin dull and ashen, and then Crandle dropped her to the floor and walked away.

Jeff, who was close to her already, caught her and helped lower her to the ground. Her eyes were wide and her face pale. Not pale but ash white. She murmured for us not to worry about her, she wouldn't have lived much longer anyway...and then nothing. She stopped breathing and her eyes closed, head rolling to the side and she was gone.

I realized he had just absorbed her. Something I thought I'd never see and never wanted to. I wouldn't have Lily in my arms right that second if it hadn't been for Trudy's sacrifice.

I wanted to cry, scream, hit and beat something, but my need to make him pay was all I could handle at this point.

"Bastard! You bastard!" I heard myself yelling. Cain tried to grab him, but he pushed him away easily in the far wall. Then he was there, right in my face in a blur of a second.

His palm swept forward at the same time to Merrick's chest with a powerful blow, sending him bounding backwards and slamming into a huge aerial picture of the town on the wall. I heard it breaking and shattering to the wood floor behind us.

Crandle was right in our faces. I could feel his sickly sweet breath on my face as I held Lily tighter, and the Taker's arms went around us both like an embrace. Maybe he was going to flee with us this way. Lily spoke before I could.

"You're a bad man!" she yelled with as much force as a three year old girl could muster.

Then she thumped his nose, as innocently as you would thump a bug off your arm.

Crandle's eyes went wide, he looked aghast, how dare she, and then he blinked. He blinked rapidly but then...something else. He started to clear his throat...then choke. He removed his cold arms from us and coughed. He gasped and grabbed his throat. He moved back and doubled over, putting his hands on his knees, still coughing gruffly, and looking up at Lily in angry wonderment.

Merrick returned to my side in a blur and we all looked on, wondering what was going on. Lily had a gift, too. She had just shown us all for the first time, not even knowing she was doing it. As I continued to watch the display, I realized one important thing.

Crandle wasn't expecting us to be prepared.

I pondered whether he knew about the Special's gifts at all. He thought we'd go down admirably and fighting but still go down in the end. He thought he'd win. He was a fool for being so blind and arrogant. I squeezed Lily with pride and then looked at Merrick and saw blood on his sleeve.

"You're hurt!" I yelled and moved to examine it.

He had a gash on his arm. The glass cut through his sleeve and skin on his shoulder but didn't look too deep.

"It's fine, it's nothing," he muttered absently, still watching Crandle.

Crandle continued to cough and hack on his knees on the floor and Jeff decided to use it as an escape opportunity. He motioned for us to head out the hallway. Merrick took Lily from me and I hobbled away but stopped.

"Wait. Trudy?" I asked Jeff, grabbing his sleeve in protest.

"I'm sorry, Sherry. She's gone. We can't save her."

I bit my lower lip to hold back the sob and nodded as Merrick pushed me, urging me down the hall. Lana and Calvin were behind us. Everyone else was in front.

Then I heard breaking glass, doors slamming and pounding footsteps. I realized the reinforcements had been called in.

Theirs.

More Lighters were here. Merrick shoved Lily and me on the elevator and hopped in with us quickly. The moment the doors opened on the first floor, I saw them, waiting for us all.

Some of us, Jeff and Ryan I could tell, had made it downstairs and were fighting already. Merrick blurred us through the commotion to the front door, putting us in the shadowed corner of the foyer.

"Stay," he commanded and kissed me quickly.

I would stay this time. I had so much to lose now, precious cargo in my arms. The rest of them took their stand as the fighting continued in the main hall, a huge room with an obscene gold and crystal chandelier hanging right over the center, right above the fight.

Jeff and someone else snuck off, I saw them go. He saw me watching and I must have look frightened because he reached out to my mind, which he didn't do often.

We're headed to the basement, Sherry, to let those people out before they all get killed. Hopefully, they'll all be too scared to care if we're Keepers or not. Stay right there with Lily. Don't move.

I nodded. As soon as he rounded the corner out of sight, the lights flickered

105

and a clanking sound resounded. Rattling glass. I glanced up to see where the noise was coming from. I screamed.

I yelled for everyone to move. As they too looked up, I heard gasps and yells. Even the Lighters stopped and looked, and then ran. Everyone scrambled and scattered in all directions as the massive chandelier came down. It shattered and smashed in the middle of the room sending pieces of glass everywhere. The boom from the crash was enormous and I felt it rattle the floor when it hit.

I shielded Lily and when I looked back, thankfully, no one was hurt. Merrick and Danny were safely by the staircase.

Crandle appeared, falling, jumping down all the flights of stairs, down the middle to land gracefully on the rug and glass in front of us.

"Going somewhere?" he bellowed, laughing deeply.

The Lighters were flanked behind him and our crew retreated some towards the door, towards Lily and me. The Lighters looked fiercer every time I saw them.

This couldn't be how it ended? After all this, we die here, in evil's house, right on the brink of our escape?

Crandle continued to laugh, reading our thoughts, at least my thoughts of defeat. I wasn't giving up. I was just accepting the way it was. Crandle would kill them all and then take me away with him for God knew what purpose.

He stepped forward and motioned with both arms moving forward in a push movement for the Lighters to attack. I braced myself, smothering my face in Lily's hair and murmuring for her not to look, it would be over soon.

But then I heard Calvin yelling, pulling our attention. He stepped out from behind Lana towards the Lighters. I heard the glass crunching under his feet.

"You killed Mrs. Trudy," he accused and yelled as Lana held his shirt sleeve to restrain him and I could hear the tears in his voice.

When Crandle threw back his head and laughed again he started all the Lighters in a laughing frenzy. Calvin's hands and arms started to glow a faint red. His breathing accelerated. His arms pulsed with each breath and then he threw his hands forward, all I could see was a blazing swirl of red, orange and black.

I could feel the heat and my eyes wanted to squint from the bright light. Calvin was spouting fire from his hands and arms and fingers. I recoiled with Lily on instinct into the doorjamb and covered her ears and eyes from the sight and sound of them burning.

Crandle and the other Lighters screamed and screeched, pulling at their flesh, faces and clothes as the licking flames consumed them. Yelling, cursing, running, and falling.

I looked away not wanting to see death. Not wanting to remember. Then I felt Merrick touch my arm and as I looked up, I saw Jeff coming around the corner with a mass of dirty, thin, some bleeding, frightened people behind him.

106

The burning Lighters were running around, touching and bumping things in the chaos, not purposely, but just trying to put out the flames on themselves. Small spurts of light where their skin was burned away escaped from them.

The Taker came forward, engulfed in flames and looked at us so disdainfully as he burned. His face was stoic and surreal. He knew what was happening. He also knew he'd come back as another Taker, this wasn't over.

Then he threw his head back and his body exploded in a burst of cold air and light. It was strange to see the fire all around us and yet feel the cold wind we always felt when one of them died. There was lightning like with the others but it was raging in every direction, not just up. It was quick, a few seconds and he was reduced to nothing.

The curtains caught fire in the big room by the front window first, and then the cloth table runner and huge fake flower arrangement on the hall table went up in the blaze.

Merrick and Jeff started ushering all of us out, including the basement people, who looked too scared to care who helped them, just happy to be alive. Jeff was right.

I saw cops and ambulances already outside, probably because of our earlier encounter in the street with the Lighters.

"Oh, no, how are we gonna get past them?" I asked, still shielding Lily but not moving since I couldn't walk with crutches and carry her too.

"Blend," Merrick answered and pulled his arm around me, taking Lily first.

By this time we were all dirty with soot and coughing, we looked like everyone else as we made our way down the porch and through the yard to the street. I didn't see any of our group out and about other than the ones that were in the house.

No one stopped us.

No one looked at us.

No one cared.

We casually walked, spread out to the van and other vehicles further down the street.

We hobbled over and made it at last. The part of our group who was supposed to stay behind and fight the Lighters was there already, packed into the vehicle, hiding and looking grim. Hoping to come out of this unscathed was a fool's hope. We lost Trudy and as Miguel explained, they lost Mike. I guessed, all things considered, we should be grateful for *only* losing two.

"So what do we do with it?" Miguel asked, referring to the Lighter still tied up in the van.

"Well, it can't give us any more information. I suppose we should kill it," Jeff advised matter-of-factly.

"Kill it? But it's defenseless," Celeste announced in a shrill panic, like we didn't know that it was tied up.

"It's not defenseless, Celeste. It would kill you the first chance it got. Should I let it go first then wait for it to try to kill me before I strike it?" Jeff's response was calm, but I could tell he was tired, agitated, and ready to go home and be done with this day.

"Well no, but...I'm sorry. I know you're right it just feels...wrong," she whispered, looking at the ground.

All I could think right then was that I was freezing, my leg was throbbing, Lily was tired and traumatized as was Calvin. I was ready to take what was left of my family home.

"Enough," Miguel said bitterly. "One of those bloody things killed Mike and I'm not letting it go. I'll handle it. Everyone else get in the cars and go home. We'll stop somewhere out of the way in the van and take care of him. We'll meet you at the store."

We drove a while. Merrick, Miguel, Jeff, Danny and Celeste, Lily and the Lighter, in the van. We were driving slowly; Miguel said he was looking for a good spot. Good spot for what? Just do it already if that's what we had to do.

I didn't want to be responsible for the death of anything, but if we left him alive, what of the ones he'd hurt later as I knew he would. Could I actually condone this? Or could I say it was for the greater good to be rid of one more evil thing?

I was just ready to go home. I couldn't take another freezing uncomfortable night. Lily was sleeping soundly on Merrick's lap. He was warmer than me. He didn't even argue with me about it. Lily was to sit on his lap and that was that. I sat next to him, his arm around me instead, as it should be.

At least I knew this night couldn't get any worse. We'd dealt with more Lighters, Takers and Markers in the past day than we had in all the other months combined. If I never saw another one of any of them, it'd be too soon. But I knew I would.

No sooner had I thought that, I heard a strange sound. A warped gunshot almost, muffled or silenced. Glass flew everywhere, pelting my head and back, my hands flying up instinctively for protection. Merrick, tucked Lily and me under his arm.

I felt the van jostling and jerking. Miguel had lost control and I saw him hunched over the steering wheel, a blood spot on his shirt in the back growing bigger.

Oh, no! We were heading right for the bridge. Would the control fence keep us from going over?

The question was answered and the answer was no.

We busted through the side and careened over the edge. All I saw through the windshield as we went over and down was dark water and nowhere else to go as the van plunged into the river.

This was it.

The force from crashing into the water sent us banging into the back of the front seat. The Lighter flew over our heads, slamming all the way into the front windshield, still tied up. Its head smashed against it with a loud thud and I heard Lily screaming.

I didn't see what happened to Danny and Celeste in all the commotion. My vision blurred and the sounds were muffled. Then I slowly began to come back into my own consciousness and regained my composure. I saw that Celeste was unconscious and that Danny's head was bleeding.

Water started to pour into the broken back window. That was when I realized with finality what had happened. Miguel, still passed out on the steering wheel, thank God he was wearing his seatbelt, had been shot. He had a bullet hole in his shirt, that was why we lost control. But who shot him out in the middle of nowhere? Lighters didn't use guns.

Merrick started to panic. He was shaking. His arms squeezed us so tightly. His eyes were wide with fear. Lily whimpered softly against my chest.

Sherry... I don't know how to swim.

"Babe..."

I started to explain the mechanics of swimming and that I'd help him but I remembered about my leg and make shift wooden cast. I didn't even know how I was going to get myself to the top let alone Lily and him. As if he was reading my mind, Danny came to the rescue.

"Sherry, if you're sure you can make it, I'll take Lily."

"What about Celeste?"

"I'll...hold Lily and pull Celeste behind me," he said, but he heard how impossible that would be and frowned.

Oh God help us.

"Jeff?"

"I can't swim either, Sherry." His voice shook and he didn't look much better than Merrick did.

How were we going to do this? Two panicky Keepers who couldn't swim, a toddler, an unconscious women, an injured man and a cripple with only one good swimmer?

The van was half full of water and we had to get out. Now. It was my turn to panic.

"Just go, Danny, take Celeste. I can help Merrick with Lily. We'll be fine. No time! Go!" The water continued to rise and it was at my stomach. "I mean it! Go."

"What about you-"

"Mewwick, I'm scarwed," Lily cried, fighting to get higher on his chest.

"Don't be scared, Lily bug. We've got you. Danny, go! No time to argue. You know I'm a good swimmer. I'll be fine! Go! Now!" I yelled and if I could compel like Muses or Lighters I'd have used it right then to make him go without another word.

He grunted in frustration and looked reluctant, but pulled Celeste toward the back, taking a deep breath, and he was out of the window under the water level and up towards the surface.

"Merrick, Jeff, listen. Merrick, I need you to help me with Lily. Jeff, you're going to have to try to get Miguel out and to the surface. All this is going to be is holding your breath and kicking until you reach the surface, ok? You can do this. I know you can. I believe in you both. Let's go!"

Merrick grabbed Lily and me, and we headed for the window.

"Ok, Lily, Merrick, when I say three, take a deep breath and hold it in and grab on tight to me ok. Jeff, just follow us the same way out. Kick with all you've got, ok. I love you." And the tears choked my words, but I had to finish them. "I love you both. I love you, too, Lily."

"I love you, honey." Merrick kissed my forehead. "We'll be ok. I'll kick with all I've got," he spoke, but he didn't look convinced. In fact, he looked like this was goodbye, but I couldn't even think about that.

The water was up to my chin.

"Don't do that, no goodbyes. Now let's go. I'll see you at the top, both of you." I looked at Jeff and then back. "Ready, Lily? Hold your breath. One...two...three," I shouted and we plunged under the water and squeezed ourselves through the window as we tried to make an impossible attempt to the surface.

Water Under The Bridge
Chapter 8

I kicked with my one good leg, holding tight to Lily. She stopped moving and my lungs were burning. I couldn't see how I was still alive, but somehow I pressed on. My leg protested, not so silently. I would keep on going until I lost consciousness.

Merrick was still grasping my arm, helping me hold Lily and kicking as well. I couldn't see through the murky, dark, freezing water, but I felt his jerky movements. The only light was the headlights from the van below us. I felt something pulling me from consciousness.

Death.

It was coming. The last few seconds before the final darkness. My eyes were begging to close and surrender to it. My face twitched, my lungs burned and ached. I strained with everything in me, kicked with the last effort I could muster. Kick! Kick!

My lungs couldn't possibly hold another second but somehow I pressed on and on and then...and then...

Then, finally, I broke through the surface and the icy cold breath, though stinging and painful as it was, filled my lungs and I was alive.

"Oh, thank you, God!" Danny yelled as we struggled to catch our breaths. "I was coming to get you. I had to wake Celeste." He ran to me in the water and pushed my hair back so he could see my face. "Are you ok?"

I nodded as I sputtered and coughed.

"Then, I'm going after Jeff." He plunged back into the water.

I could see again, the blurriness went away enough for me to focus with the small amount of light from the streetlamp. Merrick was on his knees in the water beside me, gasping and coughing. Lily was in my arms, not moving.

"Lily!"

I crawled to the shallow bank as quickly as I could, painfully. My leg throbbed; somehow the dang splint was still intact. I was so out of breath and exhausted but I had to push through that. I laid her head across Merrick's lap and tilted her neck back and gave one good blow in her mouth.

She automatically spat and sputtered and coughed. She was crying loudly and screaming, scared to death, and shaking violently from fright and cold.

"Lily," I said soothingly, my teeth chattering. Relief flooded me.

"Lily, sweetheart, open your eyes," Merrick said, leaning over her, rubbing his hand over her forehead and hair to smooth it and soothe her.

She obeyed and though she still whimpered, she calmed down enough to pick up. I rocked her in my lap. Merrick's arms were around us both as we knelt in the murky water and mud.

I heard splashing behind us and looked up to see Danny hauling Miguel, who was now awake and yelping in pain, out of the water and Jeff wasn't far behind him.

Yes! Thank you! They made it.

Merrick helped Jeff to the bank and we all sort of caught our breath and listened to Miguel's colorful cursing and yelling in pain and confusion.

Then Merrick and I hauled Lily to where the others were. I hugged Danny so tight, tighter than I was sure I ever had. We all huddled there in a circle for a minute, calming our heartbeats and settling our breathing.

I couldn't believe how bad my chest hurt from the lack of air and then freezing air. It made my heart ache for poor Lily, so tiny and fragile. She must have felt ten times worse. She was so quiet, awake, but very still.

Celeste passed back out but woke up after a few pats on the cheek from Danny. We made sure everyone was ok, taking turns it seemed asking each other, all of us worried about the other. Miguel was the worse off, but still the same Miguel. After a quick explanation of what happened, he checked his wound and claimed "he would live".

Jeff decided it was best to go up the embankment towards the road again and wait. Merrick had to carry me. Danny carried Lily. Jeff helped Miguel up the steep hill and over the railing. Celeste dragged herself, barely. We were a pretty sad bunch.

Once we were all up on the road and looking around we saw another van, parked on the side by the ditch. Its lights were on.

"There. Those are the ones who bloody shot me. But why? Why would they..." Miguel asked wincing and swaying as Jeff pulled his arm around him and set him to the ground.

The lights flashed at us and all the doors opened to reveal a band of armed Crandle fans. One of them was even wearing a t-shirt that said 'Why buy the cow when Crandle will give you the milk for free'.

I had no idea what type of guns they were carrying, but who cared. I was so exhausted and cold I could barely focus or even register to care. But I did care. And I was sick of everything that could go wrong, did go wrong. Murphy's Law could stick it. I was just done.

"Well, hello there," one of the men in the center spoke, his voice deep, really deep. "You're still alive I see. That's a shame. It would've been much easier for you if you'd just died in the crash."

"Wait, Jack, look. They've got Lily," a female voice announced, sounding entirely too annoyed to be referring to the precious thing Danny was holding in his arms as she stepped up to cling to the man's arm.

My heart clenched in my chest painfully. This was what death felt like I would imagine. I thought I was dying in the cave and then the water, but no, that was cake compared to this. Compared to watching Lily freeze with fear, her glazed eyes too big for her face, her tiny little fist bunching Danny's collar like she was hanging on for dear life and her lips quivering.

Those people seemed like they were going to attempt to get her from us. Over my dead body. And it may just come to that.

"Lily?" the man, Jack, barked with authority, hooding his eyes with his hands and focusing on her.

"Danny, bring her to Merrick," I said low so he could hear, but the others couldn't.

He did and Merrick wrapped her up in his warm arms.

"Lily! Come to your momma!" Jack ordered again.

"Pwease don't make me go. He's a bad man," Lily whispered with tears in her eyes, looking right into Merrick's face.

It must be breaking his heart as it was mine because he looked sick. Sick that this little girl had to go through so much and yet he was thrilled that she wanted to stay with us without even a second thought.

"Of course not, sweetheart," Merrick told her, readjusting her to his right arm so his left could support me better. What I wouldn't give for those stolen crutches right about now. "You don't ever have to go to them again if you don't want to."

"Lily. It's momma. Come on now. Get down from there and come to your momma," the female voice said, sweeter this time, coaxing.

"Enough," I said through my clenched teeth to keep them from chattering. "You can't have her. Now get on with it. You shot at our van. Shot Miguel. Why?"

"Uhoh! We got ourselves a big mouth. Ignorant woman. We were called in when you attacked the house. You stupid fools! You really thought that you could not only defy the authority of the leader, but also go to his home, attack him and get away with it? Bold but stupid. No wonder if you've got this little...pathetic excuse for a women leading your outfit," Jack said with clear disbelief in his voice.

Merrick growled deep in his throat beside me.

"We went to get Lily back, seeing as how he kidnapped her," I snapped back.

I could only make them out slightly in the yellow glow since my eyes had adjusted. The men behind the female and Jack held lantern flashlights and that was helping too. The women rolled her eyes and made a 'who cares' face, her hands going to her hips but the man stood firm and completely still.

"If that's true he had a reason. He always has a reason. You think I care about that? We sacrifice everything for Crandle. Even her. Nobody or nothing is worth more than the savior of the world. This is war, darling, or hasn't anybody told you?" the man spouted with a tone of disbelief, like how could we be so stupid as not to believe it already.

Lily, clinging to Merrick, buried her face in his neck. I knew she didn't really understand the words he was saying, but she understood the ramifications at least. They didn't want her as a daughter. They didn't really want her at all except to do bidding for Crandle.

I wished I could comfort her with words, but what could you say to someone who was hearing from their own father's mouth that they didn't want you? Especially the words of a delusional psycho and his blindly adoring, idiotic wife.

"Ok, whatever, let's get on with this. You don't want her, fine. We do." Merrick and I looked at each other and despite the situation smiled knowingly. I continued. "Now what?"

They all pulled guns from the backs of their belts simultaneously, like it was some plan or choreographed cheesy action movie stunt. Ugh. I was at my breaking point. I was slap happy. They had guns pointed at us and all I wanted to do was laugh at the cliché.

"She won't save you. If she won't come to us then I have no problem with sending her to hell with the rest of you," Jack said with gun pointed, taking one small step forward.

We stand off, them on one side of the street with guns pointed and us on the other, injuries a plenty and weaponless. I could hear Danny whisper to me from behind me.

"I can make one of them drop the gun, but not all six of them at the same time, the others will just shoot us before I can get them all down."

"I know, Danny, I know," I said knowingly, not defeated.

I look back at all of them. Jeff was standing in front of Miguel as he lay on the ground. Celeste was standing with Danny, their arms around each other.

I didn't want to die and I didn't want them to die, but fate hadn't exactly been a very nice ally lately.

I'd been almost killed more times than I could count on one hand in the past day. I was tired, drained and achy but the sun was slowly coming up. I had Lily, Merrick and Danny there beside me.

We did what we set out to do. Get Lily and Calvin back. Calvin was safe with Lana and as harsh as it might be to say it, I'd rather Lily be here with us, even to die, than to live a life of abuse and God knows what else with Crandle or these lunatics. If this has to be it, the end, I guess being in the arms of the ones you loved was a better way to go.

I closed my eyes and hugged Merrick and Lily to me. Merrick must have understood, too. He pulled us tighter and rested his forehead on mine. I tried to block out the fact that Lily's lips were blue and we were all still shaking uncontrollably, except Merrick, who had desperately been trying to cover us with his warmth.

We stood there together and I felt Danny's and other shivering arms surround behind me, Celeste probably, but I didn't really care who. They were all my family now. I wrapped one arm around to touch them.

I heard Celeste crying, but I just whispered to Lily.

"I love you, Lily, so much it hurts." I told her, not caring if the gun men heard us or care what they did anymore. I just wanted her to know that someone really and truly loved her.

I heard a gasp and whispers. I glanced up to see what they were waiting for. Following their gaze I saw a vehicle coming down the road.

We all stared, glancing back and forth between the oncoming truck and the evildoers gunning us down, wondering what they were going to do. Maybe this truck was with them.

The truck began to slow down as it neared us. The sun was barely casting a glow over the horizon, a brilliant orange and yellow haze over the land and sky. Wow, a whole night outside without Markers. I had forgotten to even think about the possibility of Markers in the mix, that would have definitely have made things way more...interesting.

As grateful as that revelation made me I pulled myself back to the freezing cold reality of standing road side, about to die and wondering what the truck was...Wait! I knew that truck!

Cain!

Cain's silver Dakota was making a slow ascent up to us on the hill where the demolished bridge side was. I tried to keep my excitement to myself and not show it on my face so the others across the street wouldn't know.

I elbowed Merrick behind Lily slightly.

I see him.

I glanced quickly at Danny and he had already noticed, too. Then I heard a shout; a deep, manly, bellowed scream. Turning my attention back to the ones with guns, one of the men in the back had taken off running through the brush and dirt behind them holding his gun over his head, knees drawing up high as he sprinted away.

Danny.

I sighed in relief. Danny willed him to run. It was too much confusion for them, the truck and now their man leaving them. They glanced around to each other in confusion. Another one of their men took off running and yelling. Jack yelled at him to 'Get back here idiot', but he didn't stop. He couldn't.

The truck had almost come to a stop, barely rolling about twenty five feet from us. Jack and his wife were restless. He lifted his gun and Cain or whoever was driving gunned it. Tires squealed and smoked as he accelerated quickly towards us.

Merrick pulled Lily and me down to the ground behind him, throwing himself over us. Danny and the rest of them got down, too, afraid of Jack and his trigger-happy finger.

I turned my head in time to see a blaze of fire coming from the truck side and at first I was horrified thinking that the truck was on fire, but then I see Jack, his wife and the rest of the gun men running and yelling.

I heard the woman yell "devil". I sat up and saw the stopped truck just as Cain, Calvin, Simon and Ryan jump out of the now open side door. Calvin. Calvin and his fire hands saved us. He got the fire from his fingertips he always wanted after all.

My heart jumped up into my throat with pure joy.

"You were right, Sherry, if there is trouble, you will definitely find it," Cain said jokingly, helping me up.

I threw my arms around him for support but also for a very tight hug that I desperately needed. I couldn't stop the tears and didn't want to. He hugged me too, for real this time, and I was grateful. He finally got it. We were family, completely stuck with each other and I wouldn't have it any other way.

He leaned back a little, but still held me up.

"Are you ok? I see you got rid of the perfectly good crutches I got you." He smiled but still looked concerned. Then looked around scowling. "Where is the van?"

"With my crutches...at the bottom of the river."

He looked us all over, as Miguel and Jeff were helped up by Ryan who also came with them to find us. He took in our wet clothes and blue lips.

"Oh, no. You were in the van when it went over the bridge." He paled, whispering, not a question, but a statement. "How? How did you get out?"

"Well...it was pretty tricky," I squeaked through my tears and almost collapsed from the relief.

I was sure we weren't going to make it this time. I was positive that was it. How we made it out alive, I still couldn't wrap my head around it. It just didn't add up. The odds were stacked against us so high, I couldn't see over it.

I started to sway and Cain grabbed me up under my knees and behind my back and carried me to the van - the enemies van parked on the side of the road. The van they left with the keys inside. Convenient.

I didn't fight him as I normally might because I hated to be weak. I couldn't fight anymore. Exhaustion and relief took me over and all I could do was let him carry me. He placed me in the middle seat, carefully and with such ease as to not jostle my leg, which somehow was still wrapped up in that dang bandage and shelf brace.

Just amazing.

Merrick was right behind us with Lily and the rest followed. Ryan drove the van for us and Simon grabbed shotgun as we were all clearly incapacitated and laid out in the back seats. Cain and Calvin followed us in his truck.

There were a few blankets in the van in the back and Jeff grabbed them and spread them around.

I was warm, alive, back with my family, my head on Merrick's shoulder and Lily's now warm hand in mine.

Heaven.

If only Mrs. Trudy's hot biscuits were at home waiting for us. Then I remembered that there never would be again. She was gone. I closed my eyes. I wasn't ready physically or mentally to deal with that yet.

I looked back to see Celeste and Danny huddled in the back corner. They always found a back corner. He was running his hand down her muddy hair, murmuring, and then he kissed her and she clung to his neck. I looked away to give them some semblance of privacy.

Jeff was checking out Miguel's wound on his shoulder. With the amount of blood soaked through his white t-shirt, I couldn't believe he was still awake. But he was and he was not happy.

I looked up to Merrick's face. He was watching me. I just stared at him for who knew how long. Who cared, he was mine. He looked just as worn out and beat as I did as Lily slept on our laps.

Soundly. Safely. Ours.

I stared at him. I didn't really want to know what I looked like but Merrick's black hair was all disheveled. There was a shadow of scruffiness from not shaving for a couple days across his chin, circles of gray under his eyes from lack of sleeping and too much worrying. His gray t-shirt was torn and bloody in a couple spots, his eyelids heavy and dark...and there was a smile a mile long on his face, just for me.

He couldn't be more gorgeous.

He cupped my cheek with his palm and brought my face slowly up to his, his other arm around me for warmth. His lips barely grazed mine at first, and then he kissed me for real, wrapping his hand around the nape of my neck and in my hair.

Already I was breathless, and for a split second I was embarrassed that we weren't alone, but it didn't last long. We were alive and gratefulness was wrapping itself around me like silk. I reached my arm around his neck as best as I could with Lily on our laps.

The electricity was definitely turned on. My lips tingled and the more he kissed me the more I wished we were in our closet. The irony made me giggle a little under my breath. I actually *wanted* and couldn't wait to get back to our closet. Who would have ever thought?

He pulled back, resting his forehead on mine, our lips barely apart and we practically shared breath.

Something funny, Mrs. Finch?

I heard his laughter in my mind and I laughed again.

"Irony," I whispered. "How in the world we keep surviving, I'll never know. I'm sorry you got stuck with someone so utterly attracted to trouble. I'll try to tone it down from now on."

"Don't worry about it. We'll always be together, that's why we'll always survive. Besides, it certainly makes things exciting," he whispered smiling.

"Sounds like a plan to me, Finch."

"A good one."

"I love you."

"I love you. Now kiss me, wife, before I can't contain myself anymore."

"Yes, sir." I saluted and complied, laughing.

We finished our ride home that way. Lips and tongues locked, breathless and tingling. Grateful kisses. Lily slept the entire way. As for the rest of them, I didn't know, my entire focus was elsewhere.

We pulled into the store and under the shed with our newly acquired van. We'd have to hide this for sure, probably paint it as well if we intended to use it.

I was carried in by Merrick and Danny carried Lily, while Ryan and Jeff helped Miguel. Calvin was so happy, bouncing around on his toes and skipping as he circled around us.

The second we opened the hatch door there was an explosion, a huge blow of sighs, yells and excited screeches. Everyone was waiting for us. I was patted and touched and squeezed as we receive our welcome and tried to move past so the rest could come down.

Merrick set me on the couch and knelt in between my knees, but I saw Marissa waiting back away from everyone else by the kitchen entrance and it grabbed my attention. The second Jeff came down she lit up and fidgeted, wringing her hands and swaying her weight on her feet. It was almost like she wanted to run to him, but was afraid that he may not want her to.

As soon as he saw her, he pushed through everyone to run to her, picking her up in his arms and kissing her. She wrapped her arms around his neck, crying and smiling at the same time. He kissed her so forcefully and long that I felt like I should blush and look away.

Then he released her - not really, just put her feet down to the ground and grabbed her face in between his big dark hands that made her eggshell color look extra bright and white. He looked at her thoughtfully for a moment then his eyes moved around the room, to survey how much damage he'd just done. He saw Merrick and me watching, maybe a few others, but most were caught up in their own reunions.

He took her hand and walked over to where we were.

"I know, I know," Jeff said to Merrick, putting his hands up in surrender, still holding her hand in his.

Marissa bent down to me, telling me she was glad we were ok. Merrick and Jeff did the manly Keeper hug thing. They looked at each other for a few moments. I knew they were talking silently so I looked back to Marissa.

"I'm so happy for you," I said, and I meant it, grabbing her other hand. "You could have told me."

"We...we just weren't sure how everyone would feel so... I mean, Jeff practically hated me when we first met. I just didn't want to cause him any more problems," Marissa said sheepishly.

"Hey, I know how it is. If you remember, Merrick and I are the original freak shows," I said laughing and trying to wipe dried mud from my arms and hands.

"Yes, I remember. I wanted to tell you and Merrick, but Jeff thought...you'd be angry. Because he gave you guys so much flack about it before."

"I knew. I saw you guys before once, I just tried not to make a big deal out of it, but I guess I should have said something. I knew Jeff would feel that way." I felt Jeff and Merrick looking at us. "Though why he would," I said and smacked Jeff's leg, "is beyond me. Come on, Jeff, you had to know we'd be happy for you."

"This is all new to me, Sherry," Jeff said softly, shrugging.

"I've heard that before," I said smiling, looking at Merrick, then back to Jeff. "Jeff, you saved my life," I said vehemently. "You're mine and Merrick's family and I love you. I want you to be happy. I'm so happy for you if you are."

I pushed myself up to hug him.

"I'm glad you think so. I...you're the closest thing to a real sister I'll ever have," he said, clearing his throat and pulling me tighter to him.

"That sounds awfully human of you." I tried not to laugh, but I couldn't keep the smile from my face as I pulled back to look at him.

"I hope so," he said laughing, "because I'm not going anywhere," he said sweetly, looking over at Marissa and smiling.

Miguel was brought in to lay on the couch as he instructed Kay what to do for him. He was pale, compared to his normal coffee tan skin, making him look really bad off but he was still Miguel. Loud, boisterous and yelling at Kay.

"Just get the bloody thing out before I cark it!"

She tweezed the piece of metal out as Miguel squinted in pain and threw out more amusing language. Then she plopped the small hunk of metal on the towel beside them on the end table.

"Well, I'll be stuffed," Miguel said and then laid his head back in exhaustion and fell asleep quickly. Or passed out. Whichever made him seem more manly.

I hobbled a step over to Merrick who accepted me with the biggest smile. Miguel was ok, the kids were back, and Jeff and Marissa were out as a couple and happy. How could so much good come out of such a rotten day?

Merrick folded his arms around my waist and kissed me. As I started to put my arms around his neck I felt a slight tug on pants leg.

We pulled apart and looked down to see a halo of golden hair, two hands pulling on each of our pants to get our attention. We laughed and she looked up. Merrick scooped her up and held her in between us. She was pushing her hair out of her face with her palms feverishly, so cute. Her poor little outfit was destroyed, muddy and torn.

"I'm hungry, Mewwick," she said sweetly, matter-of-factly.

"Is that right?" he said playfully, about two octaves too high. "Well we can't have that now can we," he replied as he kissed the corner of my mouth and then lifted her in his hands like an airplane, flying her into the kitchen.

Her laughter and squeals of delight the whole way filled the rooms.

The End of the Beginning
Chapter 8

"Mewwick! I gotta go potty!" Lily squealed, wiggling on Merrick's lap.

"Uh...well."

Merrick looked around franticly for someone to help him.

"I'll take her Merrick," Marissa volunteered.

"Oh, thank you," he answered graciously.

"Sorry," I said, "I'll be back on my feet soon and then you won't have to endure all the girly stuff."

It had been three weeks since that awful day. The day we all almost died. The day I made a stupid mistake. The day Lily and Calvin were taken from us and returned. The day we lost Mike. The day we lost Trudy.

We had a memorial service for both of them. No bodies of course but we buried some things for them; things that reminded us of them like Trudy's apron. We put two big rocks over that with their names written on them.

They were out back past the store on the other side of the shed near the tree line. Nobody would see them back there, but we all would know where they were.

Shockingly, no one had mentioned anything on the news about Crandle's death. They were still business as usual. Keepers are evil, Crandle is a God. Blah blah. Jeff and Merrick believed that was because they want to wait until the new Taker comes. They don't want to seem leaderless and weak.

We all watched the news from then on. For one reason or another we discovered that we were all immune to the Lighter speak, which was great, no more worrying about that when we went on food runs. Merrick and Jeff speculate it was because we'd been aware of them too fully and too long so they could no longer control us like they could before. Maybe up close, but not over the T.V.

The need warehouses were still going up as planned, only a few weeks before they took effect. Things were going to get rough around here, but we had some ideas. And some good minds and bodies behind those ideas. I had faith in this group. We'd be ok, we have to be.

And Miguel, he had to be the fastest healing man ever. He only wore the makeshift arm sling Kay made him for a week. Within another half week, he was right back to normal. Teaching his karate lessons and on me about resting my leg constantly.

He was a freak of nature.

Lost in thought I heard someone saying my name. I snapped out of it and giggled a little in embarrassment. Cain was knelt down in front of me, his hands on my knees for support with an amused face.

"Sherry?" he said smiling at my daydreaming stupor.

"Sorry," I laughed. "What's up, Cain?"

"I just wanted to tell you guys about the store trip in the morning. Explain how it was going to go down and make sure everyone is ok with that. Miguel, Jeff and I have got it all planned out but I need a list of things from you since...you know, Trudy's not here."

Yes, I knew.

"Ok, no problem. I'll get on it."

"Are you doing alright? How's the leg?"

"Lot's better. It actually doesn't hurt at all anymore but Miguel insists I wear this stupid thing for a few more weeks," I said the last line loudly so Miguel would hear.

He did. He looked over and rolled his eyes, laughing.

"Well good, someone needs to make you listen around here." He laughed squeezing my good knee. "How's Lily today? Been busy and haven't seen her much lately."

"Perfect," I said and I couldn't keep the smile from my face.

"Wow. It's funny, you know. How so much bad can happen to us and yet people still find some good. If you look hard enough...you can *always* find the good. It's just amazing to watch the human condition take a hold of people and wrestle us to the ground in submission of it. All of us, from all walks of life, some not even from this world. You can't fight it, but...even if you could, why would you want to?"

I just stared at him in utter disbelief and awe. I just loved him. I loved these people. And he was utterly and incomprehensively correct. Why fight it?

He continued and I listened.

"Lily has a better life than she ever did. And Jeff and Marissa, Danny and Celeste...you and Merrick. You all found each other, despite all this," he said opening his arms to prove his point.

All this was everything. Cain's sincerity was breathtaking. I'd cry if I didn't start the jokes. So I did.

"Well...we'll find you a good resistance girl soon enough, Cain. Don't worry, it's my next mission."

"Oh no." He lifted his hands. "If Sherry puts her mind to it... I'm thinking I should probably be worried. Kidnapping a girl for me is still against the law, you do know that, right?" He smiled and quirked an eyebrow.

"I know...but what's a little jail time compared to true love, huh? Don't worry about it, I've got you covered, Cainy boy."

"Now I *am* worried. And you know, you are the only one I will ever let call me 'Cainy boy', right?"

He smiled again and squeezed my knee.

"Yeah, I know," I said with satisfaction.

He laughed, shaking his head as he chucked my chin softly and retreated to the kitchen.

Merrick had completely grown into the father role for Lily, whole heartedly and willingly. She loved him with a fierceness only rivaled by my own. They did everything together and he spoiled her like any human father would but better. Of course, we still had to fight for her attention. Though Mrs. Trudy was gone, there were plenty of people to divide her time between.

She started Karate lessons with Miguel. He loved it even more than she did. His face when he watched her mimic him was priceless, you just couldn't look at her without awe and protectiveness.

And Marissa reads to her a lot, even taught her to read a few words by herself, pretty good for a kid who had never even been read a book to until now.

And Cain, Jeff and Danny all act like uncles in the truest since of the word. They play and chase and give piggyback rides and color and watch the same old cartoon movie over and over with her. She squealed with satisfaction and glee as though she had no idea what to do with herself. Like she didn't know what this felt like.

Being loved.

And me, I cook with her, bathe her, put her down for her naps, brush and braid her hair, let her sweet talk me into just about anything. Everything a mother would do.

Because that is what I was.

She may not call me mommy and I would never ask her to, but it was how I felt. Everyone even asked me for permission before doing anything with her or giving her snacks and such. The first few times I cracked up thinking why on earth they thought I had more rights than them to make a decision about her.

However, everyone started doing it. Everyone considered Merrick and I her guardians. I mean, I guess it was no secret we wanted the job and Lily certainly wasn't complaining.

And Calvin, Oh, Calvin.

He was just a handsome, healthy, happy young guy. He was growing and becoming a little man, taking care of business. He took an extra interest in his mother since she rescued him. His love and affection for her grew that day as well as his respect.

He made sure to include her in his conversations and relayed what our meetings were about. He was a sweet perfect son who was growing up way too fast. It happened. Adversity waited for no man...or child. He had to grow up. His youth had been beguiled from him, but what other choice did you have in these situations?

He wasn't bitter one bit though. Maybe he just hadn't figured out that he had a right to be yet. I hoped that day never came. I hoped he continued to think that this was just what was and some things you couldn't change. But that was ok. Some things weren't meant to be changed. All things happened for a reason, one reason or another.

The past three weeks were peaceful; calm, quiet, blissfully danger free. Both children survived and suffered no nightmares or trauma remarkably.

Not only Lily's parental figure but also another role had been handed to me, against my will in more ways than one, but you had to do what you had to do.

I was the new Trudy.

I made all the kitchen shopping list and dinner menus. I did a fair amount of the cooking though we still rotated with the other ladies.

Everyone just kind of started asking me things and making me responsible for Trudy type situations. At first I completely rebelled in body and spirit. I was grieving and it just made it harder but so was everyone else. So I took the job and have handled things every since. It was kinda funny considering I was one of the youngest in the bunch and I had been hefted such responsibility in such a trustworthy fashion over so many people.

In a way, I was flattered. My crew of misfits trusted me fully to do it and do it well. And I would.

As for Merrick and I, things couldn't be better. After a few days of resting and recouping things pretty much got back to normal. Except for the fact that Merrick was even more determined now to watch me closer than ever.

His whole 'you are not safe without me' theory had panned out more than once, so I let him do what he felt like he needed to without giving him any flack. If it made him happy to watch me like a hawk every minute of every day, so be it. My personal secret service. A gorgeous and persistent secret service who forbade me to leave the bunker under any circumstances.

He constantly asked me if I needed help with anything, how was my leg, could he do some laundry since it was hard for me with crutches. And did I complain? No! What other guy in my life has done these things for me? Zero!

And Lily only made things better. We spent our time with our new family during the day and played with our new charge, as I affectionately called her.

Then the nights were just for Merrick and me and things just got better and better once we entered that little room and closed the door.

Even with all the bad stuff that was happening, I still considered myself the luckiest girl this side of the hemisphere.

Amazing guy, amazing family, amazing love.

It was a Tuesday...I think. We were hanging around the commons room after a dinner of Mrs. Trudy's famous pancake recipe that I made from memory. Miguel finally informed me I could use a walking brace. Yeah! So I did and was making the most of it.

Marissa and I doled out coffee. I saw her out of the corner of my eye as she bent down to kiss Jeff quickly before giving him his usual, six sugars and lots of cream. It still made me smile to see them and know that, these days, just about anything was possible.

Merrick took his coffee cup from my grasp, letting our fingers slide slowly against each other as he always did, giving me that I-can't-wait-until-tonight look, which still sent chills down my spine. I smiled knowingly and bit my lip.

How did he still have the ability to drive me so crazy after all this time? It felt like it did when we just met. The butterflies and tingles hadn't relented.

After our coffee and chat I put myself down on Merrick's lap, exhausted from pancake flipping. Can you guess how many pancakes have to be cooked for a crew this size? Yeah...

"You look tired," Merrick said sympathetically.

"I am tired," I whispered, putting my head on his warm chest.

"Ready for bed?"

"No, can't make it. Too tired, must sleep," I muttered with my eyes closed.

He leaned down and nuzzled my neck whispering, "I could carry you, if it wouldn't hurt your pride."

"Are you in some hurry to get into that room, mister?" I sang playfully, popping open my eyes and lifting an eyebrow.

"Oh, yeah," he breathed, his breath blowing the curls around my neck, making me shiver.

I gazed into his green eyes, utterly baffled by his love for me. Maybe one day I'd accept it completely, but today...still baffled. His slow spreading, knowing smile brightened the room like he knew what I was thinking, something he had always wanted to do. Then he asked me his usual fatherly line of questioning.

"Did Lily go down for bed alright?"

"Yep, she didn't even ask for a song tonight. She was pretty tired. I think Uncle Danny chased her over every inch of this bunker today."

"He is so great with her. I always knew he would be good with kids, but..."

"Never have any of his own? Yeah, I know. He makes a great uncle. Wind them up, spoil them rotten, then send them back to mommy and daddy," I said laughing and Merrick laughed too.

It was true. I doubted that Danny would have kids of his own or that he would've even without the end of the world. He just never seemed interested, but now...I didn't know.

Danny and Celeste were probably the most blatant couple in the bunker. They made out in every corner, they canoodled in every hallway and dark corner.

It was wonderful! I was so happy for them and glad they found other. There was not a smidge left of my original wariness.

Granted, Marissa and Jeff had been known to smooch in the public eye as did Merrick and me, but some things were better left in private. But right now, with Merrick's lips mere inches from mine, his fingers rubbing the ring on my finger and his soapy clean smell all around me, all I wanted to do was kiss him.

And I did.

Pulling him to me, he resisted like a toddler resists a tootsie roll. He chuckled under his breath as I captured his lips with mine. One arm went around my back and the other rubbed in the hair hanging around my neck. I heard murmurs, and the radio and a card game around us, but all I could feel as I ran my hand through his hair was him and his deep breaths against my cheek and neck.

You're making me insane.

I gasped at his groaned words. I'd never heard him speak to me in my mind while we were kissing before. It was strange...and oddly enjoyable. My Merrick had my full attention and right then, all I could think about was how I was suddenly very ready for bed. I whispered something along those lines in his ear, feeling his grin on my cheek.

"It's about time, woman. You can't just strut around in that apron, flipping your pancakes. You *know* what it does to me," he whispered jokingly.

I giggled and bit my lip, but before I could respond we all heard something that silenced us all.

"Hello? Everyone awake?" a voice yelled from the stairwell.

Margo.

She was supposed to be closing up the store.

We all turned and watched the stairs to see what she was yelling about, fearing the worst. Things had been good for too long.

I heard a lot more footsteps, more than Margo could produce by herself. Then my breath became non-existent as I lifted myself from Merrick's arms and hobbled to the entrance way of the commons room. Chills ran over my arms as I saw a flood of faces I thought I'd never see again come down into our safe haven with weary and anticipatory expressions.

One face in particular out in front I was more than happy to see.

"Lillian!"

PART 2
DAWN OF A NEW DAY

The New Kid In Town
Chapter 1 - The Taker

I woke up with a rag in my mouth. A moist rag from my heavy breathing, saliva and what tasted metallic, like blood as well. Human blood, my human blood.

I didn't feel right.

I felt...good.

Great even. Much better than dead, which is where I was headed the last time I remembered anything other than now.

I heard distant whispers but couldn't comprehend them and didn't care. I marveled at my body, the way it vibrated with life. Hummed and pulsed with my heartbeat, now so much stronger than before. My blood felt potent and important. I tried to wiggle, to sit up but-

A sharp pain stabbed my temples, sending me crashing back down the little progress I'd made, back to the hard cold floor. I tried to grab it to brace myself, but my hands were bound. What? Why?

I was furious but something was settling in my mind, expanding the nerves and vessels. Something vague and foggy. I remembered...others.

I remembered...pain and confusion and commands. My commands. I told them to bound and gag me. Well, the old me did, the previous one, before me. That's right. This wasn't my body, I mean it was, but with other's life in me. My life now, my blood, my vitality.

I opened my eyes for the first time and saw the ones chatting in the corner. I had no idea what their names were nor if they realized I was awake. I was sure not, seeing as how I specified to be untied and un-gagged before I woke. I didn't want anyone to hear my cries of pain or hurt my new body. The process of incarnation was so different than just absorbing another life force.

How did I know all this? And my nose was itching like I'd never felt before in my lives and if I couldn't scratch it soon, so help me...someone would pay.

I blinked and squinted to focus. My eyes were crusted and sore. I wondered how long I'd been changing. I mumbled through the gag to get their attention.

"Mmmmfmpm."

The taller one had the smarts to gasp and look shocked at least as he sprinted towards me.

"My Lord, I'm sorry, we thought you had more time," he sputtered as he pulled a knife from his pocket and began to cut what I could only assume was rope binding my hands and feet.

Once free of the gag I coughed and licked my too dry lips.

"Don't call me 'My Lord'." I wiped my mouth and scratched my nose groaning with the pleasure of finally reaching it. "Wasn't this discussed with you? Get me loose, fool."

"Sorry my...sir. Our last Taker preferred us to call him that."

"I'm not anything like your last Taker," I scolded with certainty.

"I can see that, sir. What would you prefer me to call you?"

"Right now, my driver. It's daylight is it not?"

"Yes sir," he said and double checked his watch twice while the other idiot, the short rounder one, stood in the corner, frozen like the prey he was.

"Then I can't fly right now, can I? Call my driver and then you may call me Malachi from now on. Do you know what Malachi means?"

He extended an arm to help lift my body from the floor and I swatted it away in annoyance. Did he not know who I was?

"No, sir, I'm afraid not."

"Yes, you need be afraid. Malachi means messenger. And I mean to deliver a message. Would you care to know what that message is...before anyone else?"

I watched his eyes get bright with excitement and his lips part in anticipation at the promise of being special and enlightened. He leaned forward and looked side to side, as if I would whisper it to him.

"Yes. Please, sir, yes."

"I'm taking over this world, not unlike your last Taker, pathetic as he was, but I mean to succeed. And I will. How you ask? I'll show you." Before he could move another inch I grabbed him and held him to me, like an embrace, placing my palm over his chest and watching the tell-tell light of essence spring forth, filling the room and illuminating my preys companion with enough light to see his round face go rounder and his eyes bulge in fright. "By taking no prisoners and showing absolutely no mercy," I spat out at his life filled me.

Oh yes...I remembered this. It was like a drug. Their expressions and the scent of fear wafting off them like a spring bouquet. I couldn't get enough and the humans were even better at sating me, but unfortunately for these two, there were no humans here.

His power and life floated and zinged through my veins to my arm then my shoulder, through my chest to my heart, where I needed it most. I couldn't stop the sigh that sprung forth. I groaned at the numbing sweet sensation that I got through my whole body. No human or Lighter experience could compare to the utter annihilation of inhibition and personal suffering. I almost forgot how good this felt. Man, it was good to be back.

And right then, absorbing this fool and anticipating his friend being next...there was nothing but pleasure.

And So, We Meet Again...
Chapter 2 - Sherry

The high pitch, girly squeals and peals of delight and wonderment were all that could be heard in the concrete block of a home, and I was a little embarrassed to be the guilty party.

I still wasn't getting around the best on my foot and almost tripped trying to leap across the couch to get to Lillian. Merrick caught me before further embarrassment was had and I hobbled to her as quickly as I could. I heard murmurs and greetings behind us, but couldn't concentrate on them.

Even though Lillian wasn't even that close of a friend and I'd only known her for a short four weeks before we parted ways from our first hideout, the basement of the warehouse, I was sure I'd never see them again. I'd always wondered if they made it or not and where they were, how they were faring.

I felt Lillian's tears on my neck and glanced up to look at her. Oh, my. I hadn't noticed before.

She looked destroyed. As I looked around, they all did. Matted and dirty, bruised, injured and broken. Even though she was glad to see me I sensed something different about her. She was stronger, physically; I could feel her hard arms that used to be soft and feminine around me, but also spiritually stronger.

The sweet, innocent gleam that once was in her eyes was no longer present. It had been replaced with fierceness and her jaw was set in a determined way that told me it must've stayed that way a lot. It made me wonder what they have been through.

I framed her face with my hands and felt her rough, dirty skin and the small scars on her cheeks.

"Lillian, I thought I'd never see you again. I can't believe you're here. How did you find us?"

"We didn't," she said, placing her hands on top of mine, "I mean, we did but we didn't know it was you. Word about your flyer got out and we made our way here for shelter. There were others we'd found but they thought the flyer was a trick but we had to try. We came down the hatch and there you were," she croaked and started to sob, placing her head on my shoulder again.

"Lillian, don't cry, you're safe here with us." I tried to placate her with my soft reassurances but she continued to cling to me.

I looked around the room and saw other members clinging as well. Piper.

Piper, the Keeper who hated and resented me for Merrick's love for me, was clinging to him just as much if not more so than Lillian was doing with me. A wave of hot jealousy blared through me. I felt guilty instantly but still...jealous.

Merrick catches my gaze and as I looked closer he wasn't even hugging her back. In fact he was trying to extricate her. He pleaded with his eyes, begging me to rescue him and I felt the sting leave my stomach. Of course Merrick didn't want her hugging him, not after knowing how she felt about him.

I walked Lillian to the couch and set her down.

"I'll go get you a glass of water, ok? Be right back," I told her but made a small pit stop.

"Merrick, I need you in the kitchen. We need to make them some sandwiches or something. I'm sure they are all hungry and thirsty." I turned to Piper and smiled my sweetest grin. "Hey, Piper, I'm glad you're here. Is everyone alright?"

She pulled back enough to finally glare at me, her fists still knotted in Merrick shirtfront, her face streaked with tears and dirt, but I felt no sympathy. She was giving me one of the most hateful looks I had ever been on the receiving end of.

"Of course, Sherry. I should have known you'd still be stringing Merrick along," she all but spat.

"Piper," Merrick warned.

"Not at all, Piper, but we can talk about that later. Right now I need my husband to come and help me. Excuse us."

I was satisfied to hear her gasp and I grabbed Merrick's arm with a determination to yank if need be but she let go freely with a surprised look on her face. He put his arm under mine to help me to the kitchen and then turned to me.

"Thanks."

"No problem, on my part anyway. What's with her?" I asked, glancing over his shoulder to see her still glaring.

"I don't know. I would have thought she'd been in my brain the second she saw me, like she used to, but she didn't. They must be exhausted. She was genuinely surprised by the husband remark," he said smirking.

"Yeah, I saw. I'm sorry I threw it out there like that, but I figured that be the fastest way to deal with it."

Piper was still by far the strangest Keeper I'd met. She had feelings of jealousy and hate even back when I first met her. That didn't seem right considering that Keeper's themselves didn't harbor those feelings.

"Don't apologize. I'm glad you did. We have too many other things to deal with right now that to worry about...things like that."

I nodded and pulled him down for a quick kiss. He bent willingly even wrapping his arms around me and pulling my feet from the floor. I didn't know if he was doing it for me or for her to see but I didn't care. I didn't open my eyes as I didn't want her to think I was taunting her because I wasn't. There were plenty of available men, even other Keepers, to suppress her Merrick-appetite. I just hoped she realized that soon.

I pulled back and looked up at him to saw his green eyes bright and burning.

"I really do need to make something for them. They don't look so good. You can help if you want but I'm sure you'd rather be catching up with the other Keepers."

He shook his head.

"Nope. There's nowhere else I'd rather be. Besides, you need me. Admit it, wife," he said playfully.

"I need you," I whispered, rolling my eyes and smiling at his sweet consideration.

He kissed me again and we set to the task of making a bagillion sandwiches. I was stealing cute Calvin's word of course. Everything was so over exaggerated with him. In his eyes it took a hundred hours to get through a day of boredom, there were a million cards all over the floor when we played fifty-two card pickup. And when we made sandwiches for a crew this size, it took a bagillion of them.

After we got done, with Kay, Lana and Marissa's help, we passed the ham sandwiches out along with bottles of water. While they ate, Jeff filled everyone in on what we'd been doing since we parted ways.

I saw familiar faces and new ones. We still had Piper and Polly though. Yay...

Also Susan and Frank with his Keeper Kathy, then of course Lillian and her husband Michael's Keeper Mitchell. Where was Michael? Oh, no. And Sam and Lavonne and the others? Is that why Lillian looked so broken?

There were two new faces. Mitchell introduced them to us as Kenny and Alec. They were both about thirty or forty years old, hard to tell with so much dirt on them. Both were ordinary nobodies like me, not Special and not a Keeper. They seemed nice enough, but quiet.

I wondered why the bell didn't ring. We installed a door bell up in the stock room of the store. If we had new visitors or a problem up top, you rang the bell to signal us down below to be alert. I know, top notch technology, right? It was all we had to work with and it was efficient. Maybe Margo just didn't ring it because she brought them down herself. I hope it wasn't broken.

Jeff began to introduce us and it took a while, which was a good thing. I hoped one day we'd have so many, you couldn't keep track anymore. He smiled a huge smile and winked at Marissa when he said her name. When he got to Merrick and me, he left his script behind and improvised.

I loved Jeff.

"And most of you know Merrick and Sherry from the basement, but what you don't know is that they got married since we've been down here and they adopted an adorable little girl, Lily, who's napping right now."

Then he went on, leaving no one time for anyone to say anything to us or dwell in their negativity. I didn't have to even look at Piper, though I did, to feel her glare on me. I also got some smiles and a surprised and amused, yet sad, look from Lillian.

Merrick pulled me closer into his chest from where we sat on the floor, leaning on the wall and kissed my temple. I smiled thinking how Jeff said we adopted Lily. It wasn't said or talked about. It wasn't confirmed. Everyone just took it as it was. She was ours.

I realized I was avoiding Lillian, to some degree. I knew I'd have to ask about Michael and I wasn't ready yet. Poor Lillian. I couldn't imagine loosing Merrick. I remembered how she loved Michael, talked about their future and the kids she wanted with him. It broke my heart to have to ask her.

Cain was on one side and Merrick on the other when Lillian came to kneel in front of me while we heard the chatter from other's getting acquainted.

"I know you're wondering about Michael," she said bluntly. "He died a week after we left you guys. It was hard to find a place to hide for a while. It actually didn't have anything to do with *them,* the Lighters, ironically. He was electrocuted when he entered an abandoned house that we were scoping out to see if it was safe to stay there, for a while. Somebody had rigged the house for intruders. They were dead already but the trap was still set there. We've just been bouncing around, house to house for so long, never feeling safe, never getting a full night's sleep. Never knowing which one of us is next..."

She finished and just sat there, looking at the wall behind my head. She started to sway on her knees and her bottom lip started to quiver. I knew she was about to lose it. I left Merrick's grasp and reached up to hug her, both of us on our knees.

I held her for a minute, feeling the pressure of Merrick's warm hand on my back. Then I heard an exasperated sigh and a tapping. I look over Lillian's shoulder to see Polly, watching us and tapping her annoyingly small foot. Her arms crossed and a less than tolerant smile on her lips.

"Oh, no, not this again. Sherry, just leave her alone. She starts this all the time. I mean, how many months has it been for goodness sakes? Michael died a long time ago and he wasn't even killed by a Lighter or whatever those flying things are, he was killed the normal way. At least you should be grateful for that Lillian. He died a human death, some of us aren't so lucky."

It took all my power not to throw Lillian to the side and charge Polly with all my puny strength. I felt my eyes go wide and my breath heave in a heavy long intake. Everyone stayed silent, watching the interlude. Lillian didn't even turn around.

"I mean," Polly continued, "why does she get to be the one to complain all the time? None of the rest of us get our way either. Poor Lillian, poor Michael, poor sweet innocent blonde Lillian. I'm sick of it!"

I wouldn't have any more of it.

Polly opened her mouth to speak again and I stopped her.

"Enough Polly! Like you haven't lost anybody. This isn't just about Michael if you had been listening to her. You have no idea what you're talking about," I all but yelled.

I must have surprised a few because everyone's eyes gravitated to me and I saw they were wide. Even Cain beside me took a swift intake of breath in shock. I refused to feel bad. No one was sticking up for Lillian.

"Sherry, I see you haven't changed. Still chasing Merrick, still yelling at me, telling everyone what else what to do. I have to say, I didn't miss you."

"Ditto," I answered.

"Enough is right, Polly. You are always on Lillian about something. Enough," Susan snapped and then sent a small smile to me.

Jeff intervened.

"Alright, alright, everyone is tired and needs some rest, I'm sure. Let's just get your rooms ready and everyone can hit the sack for a while, huh?" Jeff said, motioning for Miguel to join him down the hall with the others trailing behind him.

I released Lillian as Marissa came and asked her if she could help her find a room.

"Thank you. We'll talk later," she said and left.

I sat back and watched them go.

"What the heck was that, Sherry? I've never heard you yell at anyone before," Cain asked, looking more amused than upset.

"She always pressed my buttons, everyone's buttons, back in the basement before. She has no regard for anybody's feelings. Who's to tell Lillian how long she can mourn her husband? What she can and can't be upset about?"

"No, I agree. I'm just surprised it was you that said it," he said smiling and chucked my chin.

I smiled back and then laughed as he gasped and flinched. Lily snuck up on him and jumped in his lap when he was looking at me.

"Lily bug. Did you sleep good?" Cain asked her, settling her better in his lap.

"Yep, Uncle Cain, I did. I was dweaming about pancakes," she said matter-of-factly like it was completely normal.

Us that were left in the commons room all laughed.

"Me, too. I dream about them all the time. Sherry makes good ones doesn't she?"

"Yep," Lily answered, twisting her doll's hair.

I smiled and turned to Merrick, but he was lost in thought, staring into nowhere.

"You ok, babe?" I asked rubbing his arm.

He turned and smiled, pulling me into his lap. "Yeah, I'm great, actually. I hate to say that I was worried about them, but I was. I hated it when we had to split up back at the basement. I can't believe they found us. It's just bizarre. Small world," he mused.

"It is, isn't it? That's all? Nothing's wrong?"

"Nope," he pulled my forehead down to his, "I'm fine. Just thinking. I'm proud of you too. Polly shouldn't get away with that crap."

I smiled at his now often use of slang words. He never used to do that. He kissed me and we'd barely touched lips.

"Eew!" Lily and Cain both groaned.

I made a fake jump to tickle her and she bolted, laughing and squealing.

"So what's up with Lillian?" Cain asked, stretching his legs back out and flexing them.

"What do you mean?" I asked.

"I mean, what's up? Kids? The husband, I know of. She seemed sweet. And she's cute, in a dirty ragamuffin sort of way."

"Cain! She just got here!"

"I know, but you *did* promise me a girl, remember?" he said smiling.

"A promise is a promise, Sherry," Merrick mocked, laughing while Cain bumped his fist.

"Jeez! Give her a minute! She might not even like you, ya know. Her husband, Michael, was a pretty great guy."

"Yeah," he said and sobered, "I'm sorry. I probably shouldn't be joking about this right now, should I?"

"I don't think it's that, Cain. She's not pining over him. I think it's just that she hasn't had time to stop since we split up. It sounded like it was pretty bad for them. She probably hasn't even had time to grieve properly, especially with Polly yelling at her about it. Just give her some time. Besides, you're cute enough I guess."

"Cute enough?" he said and grabbed his chest in mock hurt. "I'm taking my wounded pride to the hall to see if they need help down there."

I pushed his shoulder playfully as he got up.

Merrick and I sat there for a while, me enjoying his warmth and his shoulder. I dozed off after and woke up to see him asleep too, with Piper watching us through hooded eyes from across the room.

Cleansing Waters
Chapter 3 - Cain

"Dang it," I heard myself mutter as I stubbed my toe on a frigging ugly bag someone left in the hallway.

I kicked it to the wall and immediately regretted it as I saw the tall and strange, dark haired girl from before, who was blasting Lillian for crying, come out of a room and lock me in a heinously wicked gaze.

"Sorry," I muttered but keep walking.

What I wanted to say is, 'You left your bag in the way and you deserve more than just having your bag kicked you hateful Amazon'. But I didn't say that and never would.

I'm seeking out Lillian of course. Not just because I was joking with Sherry about her but because she did seem sweet, but she also seemed like she could use some help. She had that broken and fragile thing going on. I liked to feel needed and useful.

I found her with little problem as I saw Marissa leaving her room after getting her settled. She went straight to Jeff and whispered in his ear then bit her lip, playing the innocent seductress nicely. He smiled and laughed, pulling her into his room a couple doors down across the hall and shut the door.

I shook my head. Those two are almost as bad as Merrick and Sherry, who seem to be touching or talking to or about each other every waking minute of every day. Which would be fine except for one thing.

I am absolutely in love with her.

I know, I have to get over it. For one she was only nineteen. Seven years didn't usually make much difference but for someone that young it did. She didn't act young, that was the thing, but it still mattered. But number two and most important, she was married.

I would never ever act on it. I would never ever say anything to her about it. Merrick's the best, like a brother to me. I couldn't do that to him, plus the fact that Sherry loved him and didn't love me.

I wasn't really fine with it all but I'd find a way to be.

I'd busy my time with something other than Sherry, which what with us being trapped together and almost dying, then worrying about her all these weeks as she has hobbled around trying to take care of everybody had been hard.

The first time I knew she was gonna be trouble for me was the coffee shop. Yes, way back then, the very first time I saw her. She came in with her long brown curly hair pulled across one shoulder, leaving one side of her neck exposed. I immediately busied myself behind the counter so as not to draw attention with my staring. I wiped a circle into the counter the full minute she looked around the shop, watching people.

I thought it was such a waste for a cute pretty thing like her to be enthralled by evil but she wasn't watching the TV. She was watching the people. It was interesting because the Lighters speak drew you right to it so I figured I'd bust out the question that would make or break her story once she finally made her way to the counter.

I knew right off something wasn't right but I thought it was too good to be true. After the whole kissing-to-save-us incident, which was a good idea, I then learned she was married and I remembered thinking, crap. I could still remember exactly what her lips felt like, the way the soft skin of her wrists felt as I held her arms above her head.

Of course, I had thought to myself, of course, she's taken. Then I met Merrick and realized how he could get her. He was a beefy tall dark guy with a fierce protective streak for Sherry. Then I learned he was a Keeper and knew why.

139

I have tried every since then to stop loving her. Us getting trapped in the cave together did nothing to help the situation and her constant willingness to be her sweet smiling touchy self didn't help either. But I tried, really. I'm still trying.

But now, I have distractions. The new guys...and girls, or girl I should say. Lillian. The others seemed a little too young and hell bent on revenge for my taste. Lillian was really cute. She looked a little young to be married, but then again so did Sherry.

"Hey, Lillian is it?" I asked tentatively, tapping on the door slightly. "Need some help in here?"

She looked up at me and I saw her better. She was a mess. A pretty mess but a mess just the same. Her eyes were red from crying, her hair matted and she had dirt on her arms and face. Her eyes, though, were clear and a deep bright blue and fastened to mine instantly.

Man, the bluest eyes I'd ever seen.

"Um, I don't think so. I didn't bring a lot with me," she said softly and chuckled sadly.

"Yeah, I guess not. Well if you need anything, let me know. I'm Cain." I reached out to shake her hand.

"Oh!" She made a big show of wiping her hands on her pants legs, even dirtier than her hands. "I'm sorry, I'm such a mess. Nice to meet you."

She extended her hand, but I knew she didn't want to and was just being polite. I took it anyway.

"You, too. It's ok, Lillian," I said grasping her hand, surprisingly soft for someone in her appearance, "I'm not sure what happened to you guys but you're not the first new people to come in here. We know it's rough out there. Like I said, if you need anything, I'm two doors down, that way," I told her and point further down toward the hall.

"Thank you, Cain. Actually, if you could show me to the bathroom, I'd like nothing better than a shower before everyone starts fighting over it."

"Sure thing, follow me."

She did and we parted our way through the hordes of people crammed into the hall and doorways looking for rooms. She was getting pushed around a bit and wasn't in any shape to force her way through so I reached back and took her arm, pulling her in front of me until we got out of the hall.

I decided to take her to the less crowded bathroom on the other end. We entered the commons room and no surprise, Merrick and Sherry were murmuring and smooching on the floor, as were Celeste and Danny in their usual corner.

To be perfectly honest, and to my dismay, I'd never seen happier people.

Lillian stopped and turned to me.

"So, Sherry and Merrick got married?"

"Yep. That's what I'm told. It happened before I got here."

"Huh. That's strange. I wonder when that started. But Jeff and Marissa too? I saw them before in the hall."

"Yep. Not married though, just, I don't even know what you'd call it these days. Dating doesn't seem to fit does it?"

"No, it doesn't. So how did you come to be here?" she asked, her eyes drifting back to mine.

"Uh, Sherry came into the diner I work in. She helped me get my family, and then they brought us here."

"You sound very fond of her."

"Do I?" I shrugged. "I am. That little gal and me have been through a lot together since then."

I looked away remembering it all. The cave where we almost froze to death, Sherry's broken leg, the Markers and Lighters. The Taker. Their van going over the bridge into the river. Lily's parents. The list of blunders could go on for miles.

"She does seem very Mother Hennish doesn't she?"

I glanced over and saw that Lillian was looking at Sherry like a sister would with a smile to boot.

"Yeah, that's a good description. Even more so now, I'm sure, than she was back then. She's taken on a few more responsibilities lately."

"Yes, I heard. Wow, so they found a little girl somewhere?"

"Jeff and Miguel did and we all sort of adopted her, but Sherry and Merrick are...I don't know, her guardians. She loves them like parents and they love her, too. She's the cutest thing you've ever seen. Two feet of blonde, bubbly and gorgeous."

"I can't wait. I always wanted kids. I guess that's not possible now," she muttered quietly.

I looked at her, she must have seen something there, sympathy maybe, because she quickly went into a spat of recants.

"I don't mean because of my husband being gone, I just meant because, who would bring a child into the world like this you know? I mean, that'd be pretty selfish. Wait... I don't mean that. Crap. I don't even know what I'm saying anymore," she said, scrubbing her hands over her face in exasperation, or maybe it was embarrassment.

Either way, it was pretty cute. I couldn't help but chuckle at her which she smiled and blushed at before she finished her explanation.

"I'm sorry, I'm a mumbler."

"It's ok. It's refreshing actually. No need to hide how you really feel. We're all friends here. Well, most of us."

She must've got my meaning about the Amazon woman and giggled, pushing her dirty hair behind her ear with her fingers. As we passed each room I motioned and pointed, telling her what each one was used for. We reached the bathroom door. I leaned against the doorframe with my shoulder and put my hands in my pockets.

"Thanks, Cain, and thanks for the tour. I'll do my best to remember everything, but no guarantees."

"No problem. I'll just have to keep showing you until you learn it. I'll leave you to it."

She smiled at me, a real smile, as I walked away and I returned it. Nice girl. I wondered how old she was, what she looked like not caked in dirt, was she really as sweet as she seemed, would she be able to get over her husband, would she be the one able to replace Sherry in my thoughts. Gah, I hoped so.

That night after everyone showered and the ladies slaved over making dinner for everyone, we traded stories. Everyone piled in the commons room, wall to wall, some people had to sit in the hall and on the stairs. I found my usual spot. Next to Sherry on the back wall. Ahem.

But oh, wow.

When I saw Lillian emerge from the hall all scrubbed clean and hair brushed, I knew I must have done some kind of girly gasp. I couldn't believe my eyes. I almost asked Sherry who the creature was before it hit me. Her hair was seriously blonde where before it had been dingy and almost brown from mud.

Her skin was a sharp pale making her blue eyes very bright and blue, the thing you had to look at first when you see her. It looked like she was wearing some of Sherry's clean clothes.

I also saw that I wasn't the only one looking. Miguel, Josh, even Ryan and that new Keeper were looking as well, just as in awe. Hmmm. And she didn't notice one of us.

She came to sit herself cross-legged on the floor in front of Sherry, sort of half turned to focus on us and whoever was speaking. I wanted to say something to show the others that I was closest to her. Something childish like "Nana, nana boo, boo", but I kept it to myself.

I tried to focus on Susan, who was speaking at the time. Everyone told their own story if they had one. Pap told our sad little pathetic story of before we got there. Maggie joined in of course to correct and yell at him about changing things to make them sound worse than they were.

Everyone laughed and it was light conversation mostly. No one went into great gory detail about the things that had happened. Lillian didn't speak and no one else spoke of her husband. Sherry whispered to Merrick and he smiled at her, then she whispered to Lillian and she smiled to. Then Sherry got up, wobbly on her cast. I extended a quick hand which she took, she always took it. But she wouldn't if she found out how I felt, so that was one of my main reasons to keep quiet. I was wondering what she was whispering about when she turned to me.

"I'm going to go get Lily, Cainy boy," she whispered to me.

Gosh, I loved it when she called me that. I had no idea why. It was a stupid, childish name, but oh man how I loved it. And she never spoke it where anyone else could hear it.

None of the new ones had seen Lily between her naps and baths and such. Sherry was apparently excited to make a debut of her.

Lily had been detained in the kitchen with Marissa and Kay for the stories as they finished the dishes. Sherry wasn't sure if they'd be too gory or upset her. I was just as excited as her. I knew everyone would fall in love with her just like we did.

She came back carrying the girl in her arms, on her hip, her tiny frame barely able to handle even Lily. It was quite comical to look at. I glanced around to get the reactions which were comical as well.

You couldn't resist all that blonde hair and bashful smiles. They gasped and oohed and ahhed. Lillian's was by far the best reaction. The sweet womanly tears started to gather in her eyes but she dammed them back and smiled widely.

"Lily, this is the new people that are gonna live with us," Sherry started and went around the room with the introductions.

Lily was a perfect little specimen. She smiled and waved her fingers at them and tucked her face shyly into Sherry's neck when someone cooed at her. Our own little Shirley Temple. Since she'd been taken care of and Sherry brushed her hair regularly, which she wasn't getting before, her hair has started to curl at the ends making her even more precious and doll looking.

Sherry put her down and she ran right to Merrick's arms, outstretched for her. After Sherry sat back down I decided to go get ready for work. I still worked at the diner/coffee shop. It was a good cover to get things from the grocery store and be seen out in public. Soon the convenience store we lived under would no longer be used or needed.

We started tilling the ground for our garden. We decided to put it under a tarp cover with holes cut in the top for sunlight. It was the only way to keep prying eyes from the sky from seeing the garden and coming to investigate but still let it get rain and sunshine through.

It was the end of the week and that was how it went these days. For the past few weeks we'd been doing the end of the week store runs, preparing for when the need warehouses come and it'd be a lot harder to shop.

I told Jeff and Miguel as much before I left that another run needed to be done. We agreed that all the ones that could go would go in the morning. So far we had three sleeping rooms full of food. It wouldn't be near enough but it was a start.

I glanced back to survey the crowd before I went up the stairs and saw Lillian throwing back her head and laughing at Lily. I smiled and decided that I was happy with our new guest.

Breaking New Ground
Chapter 4 - Lillian

I lay in the dark, in a new place, in my new room, alone. It was late, but I heard talking in the hall. It was so quiet in this place. You could hear everything. And it was hot and too dark and way too small.

It was perfect.

What luck to find them, Sherry and Merrick and the rest. If I could see the ceiling I'd be staring at it. I wondered if it too was concrete, just like everything else.

I decided I had laid there long enough. I should have fallen right out but I just couldn't. My mind wouldn't be still so I climbed out of my pallet. I wore Sherry's t-shirt that she loaned me though the sleep pants were a little short. I cracked my door open.

The people I heard talking were still in the hall. Jeff and Miguel. At least I thought that was their names. They saw me peeking and the severely handsome one spoke.

"Hey, sorry, did we wake you? Lillian, right?"

"Yes. No, you didn't wake me, I couldn't sleep anyway."

Marissa popped her head out of a door, grabbing Jeff's arm.

"Miguel, that's enough planning for one night. Please let Jeff come back to bed now," she said pleadingly, even as she pulled Jeff towards her through the door.

Miguel chuckled.

"Ok. Ok, I guess I need my own Sheila so I can have someone to jerk me from my duties too!" Miguel yelled as Jeff laughed and slipped in the door, shutting it behind him without looking back.

Miguel rolled his eyes and turned back to me.

"Want to rock up to the kitchen for a bit? I make a mean cup of hot tea," Miguel said and I was fairly certain I understood what he was saying so I nodded and followed him down the hall.

Miguel wasn't very handsome, nice looking but too rugged and sharp to be 'handsome'. Not that I cared what people looked like. He seemed really nice though and has a nice smile.

"So, I heard the bloke say you guys have been living in an abandoned house?"

"Yeah, we found a three bedroom we've been staying at for about two weeks. We usually can't stay somewhere for very long. Things haven't been too bad until we started seeing those things all the time. The flying things?"

"Markers."

I decided I was totally in love with his accent.

"Yeah, those. Then one night a Lighter showed up so we figured we better move since Mitchell didn't get a chance to kill it. That's when we headed this direction." Then I thought about what I just said and felt my face pale. "Oh, God. I can't believe I just said that. How cold of me."

"No it's not, it's a Lighter. They aren't human anymore, love. Well, I guess that doesn't matter. They don't have humanity anymore is more like it. Like the Keepers do. Most of the Keepers have more humanity than most humans I know."

"Yeah, Mitchell is really great, for sure."

"Did I hear my name?"

I turned to see Mitchell, he saw us right as we rounded the corner into the commons room, as everyone called it.

"Yes, actually," I said surprised at my relief to see him.

I had barely seen Mitchell since we'd been here. He kind of took over the protector role of me since his charge and my husband died. I wasn't sure how I felt about that. I thought Keepers didn't love, that they couldn't. But now, seeing Merrick and Jeff so happy and even intense in their relationships, it was making me question Mitchell's intentions.

What if his being so nice and sweet, all the touching and consideration had to do with more than being Keeperly?

"Hey, Lillian, how are you setting up?" Mitchell asked and came to stand beside me.

"Ok. This place is great. A nice hideout."

I wasn't sure what to say. I still felt out of it.

"Yeah, it is," Miguel agreed. "All we got are little rooms and swag beds, but it'll do, right? Me and my crew came here because of the flyer too, a few months back," he said then poked his hand out to Mitchell. "Name's Miguel. We didn't get a chance to introduce ourselves earlier."

"I'm Mitchell, nice to meet you. I'm Lillian's Keeper. Well..."

"It's ok, Mitchell. He was my husband's Keeper. He died," I explained.

"I see, I'm sorry. I lost my wife a year ago as well. I know how it is."

"Oh, I'm sorry. Yes, it's rough."

146

I didn't know what else to say then either.

"Well, I'll be in the kitchen if you still want that tea," he said winking and smiled, already walking to the kitchen.

"Thank you."

"So how are you really? You cleaned up nicely," Mitchell said, looking me over.

He'd always been sensitive to my moods, always there for me. It was a good thing he wasn't in the room earlier when Polly went off on me. He would have let her have it as he'd done on many occasions for my sake. I just couldn't fight her, not on that. Not over Michael. It seemed so contradictory and I just let her do it to me every time.

"I'm ok. I'm just so tired and wasn't able to sleep."

"Come here," he said, grabbing my hand and pulling me to the couch.

I went willingly. I knew what he was gonna do as he sat and pulled me down next to him, putting my head in his lap to scratch my head.

"How are *you*?" I asked after I got situated.

"I'm fine. It's weird being here, especially finding Merrick and Jeff and the rest of them."

"Yeah. Weird is a good word for all this. It's a nice place though. Perfect for what we need it for."

"Yeah. I hear they've had some trouble, but things are better here than they were for us. We made the right choice coming here. Don't worry. Everything's going to be ok now."

"I know." I decided to go ahead and bring up the subject we were avoiding, about Keepers...uh, dating. "So can you believe Merrick and Sherry? I wonder if they had something going on back at the warehouse."

"Merrick used to watch Sherry. He wasn't supposed to. We're only supposed to watch our charge, but...anyway. He was struggling with it all back then. I guess it worked out for him."

"Looks like it. They look happy. It's nice that people can still find each other, even with all this going on." I winced at my words and wished I could take them back.

I wasn't trying to provoke him into a confession, but it looked like I was. I tried to hurry and change the subject.

"So, I overheard they're making a store run in the morning. I think I should go with them."

"Lillian, you know how I feel about that. I don't like you going places where I can't...keep an eye on you."

"I know, but, Mitchell, you aren't my Keeper. I'm not a Special. Besides I won't be by myself. Cain and a few of the others are going. I need to do what I can to help."

He stopped scratching and started to run his fingers through my hair and on my neck, almost absentmindedly. He'd done this so many times to soothe me, it felt like second nature.

"I know I'm not your Keeper, but I still feel responsible for you. I also know you. You won't feel good until you've done something to make yourself useful. I'm not...in a position to make you stay so..." He sighed, giving in. "Please be careful."

"I will. Thanks for looking out for me, I appreciate it but you don't have to. I've told you this before. I don't want to be a burden to you just because Michael's gone."

"That's not what you are to me." He was silent for so long, I wondered if he'd say more or leave it. Eventually he spoke again. "You may not be a Special, but you are special. Don't forget that. I will always be here for you, not because I have to, because I want to."

"Thanks, Mitch," I said and squeezed his knee.

"You're very welcome, Lil. Now sleep," he said as he resumed scratching my head.

And I did.

The next morning, everyone was bustling around getting ready for the store trip. I had fallen asleep on the couch, on Mitchell's lap, for the whole night. My neck stung with a kink, but I pulled myself up slowly so as not to wake him.

He was so sweet. We both fell asleep last night and he'd stayed with me. I could see how uncomfortable it was. His head rested back awkwardly on the back of the couch and I smiled and silently thanked him for always thinking of me.

I turned after throwing the afghan on Mitchell and ran right into Miguel. He grabbed my arm to keep me from falling.

"Oh! I'm sorry."

"That's alright, I've got no qualms about catching the pretty ones," Miguel said and winked, releasing my arm.

"Thanks." I looked around. "So, everyone is going on the run?"

"Just about, everyone that can go, at least. We got a lot of stocking up to do before the need warehouses screw it all up for us."

"Yeah..." We slowly walked to the hallway together. "Well, I can go, I guess. If you need me."

"You don't sound so sure."

"Well, Mitchell doesn't want me to," I admitted softly.

"Well, then, I wouldn't go. Those Keepers seem to know what they're talking about. If he doesn't want you to, he must have a reason."

"Hmm. Ok, that makes sense."

"So," he leaned on the wall beside me, "you're pretty young, ay?" he said, his Australian accent more prominent for some reason.

"Yeah." I ducked my head and tucked my hair behind my ear to cover my blush. My age had always been a sore spot for me, since I had been married so young so I tried to joke. "But I can legally drink and rent a car."

He laughed and nodded. "True. So, coming with? Jeff and I could always use another pair of hands." He looked at me expectantly.

"Um." I glanced at the couch where Mitchell still slept and then spotted my sweet tour guide, Cain, in my peripheral, coming from his room in the hall. He smiled at me and punched Miguel's arm as he walked by. "I don't think so. Next time, definitely."

"Ok. Maybe, uh, we can talk more later? When I get back?"

"Sure," I said and smiled. You couldn't deny how nice he was.

"Alrighty, then. See you later, Lillian," he tipped his head to me playfully.

"Miguel," I said and did the same.

He laughed as he walked away. I turned and caught Cain's gaze from the stairs as him and Merrick made their way out. He smiled at me again and even from that far, I could tell just how blue green his eyes were.

Merrick eventually pushed him forward and he disappeared along with the rest of them making their way out of the bunker. I kind of felt bad for not going, but for some reason, I felt like I needed this time off. Just this one time to let someone else do what needed to be done. I needed this to show Mitchell that I cared about what he thought.

I saw Sherry bouncing around in the kitchen in a mad dash to organize some breakfast before the others woke up. I smiled and saw her reaching for something on the shelf - the shelf she had no way of reaching - so I made my way to her. We had some catching up to do anyway.

The Need For Speed
Chapter 5 - Merrick

These runs got worse and worse, sitting in the van, waiting for Cain to exit the store so we could pack the vehicle quickly and head back home. I'd never felt so useless in all my life. But what else was there to do?

I flicked the radio from one station to another. It was what I did. I started going along with them a few weeks back since we had more people to go into the stores and more vehicles to take, they needed more packers.

This new development did not thrill Sherry in the least. It took much convincing that I would be safe and she even cried a little the first time I left and when I returned.

I had once made a vow to always keep her with me, at all times, and we stuck to that rule for some time. But after we started making weekly store trips to stockpile supplies, I thought it was better for her to stay at the bunker instead of coming with us. Marissa was there with her and Danny, and both used compulsion and could thwart an enemy if need be. We'd added a few precautions to the trap door and such. As much as I hated leaving her- I mean hated it- and I'd never tell her that, she was safer there. Had it not been for Lily, I wasn't sure I could've convinced her to stay.

Nothing was the same since what happened that day, with the fight with the Lighters. She worries about me and she never seemed to so that before. She thought I was invincible or something. Now that she has seen the death first hand...she worries.

She realized that we all break the same.

I stopped the radio on a station blaring some rock tune that I'd never heard before. I just needed to stay awake at this point. I closed my eyes for a minute and wondered where Cain was as he was taking a long time. I tried to hurry him along with some encouragement in his mind.

For the love of all, Cain. If I had a grandmother, she'd be faster than you.

Cain taught me many things these past couple months, sarcasm being the main thing. I really only use it on him. He was like a brother to me, almost catching up to Danny, which was saying something. He saved Sherry's life and has been there for us both more times than I could count. He still put himself in danger every day to work at the diner, but that would soon change when the need warehouses came.

Regardless, I was probably the most at ease with him than I was with any other human male other than Danny. I laughed and joked, and could say just about anything I wanted and he just rolled with it. Sherry, him and I wound up spending a lot of time together.

I startled as I heard a tap on the window and looked up at a human face I didn't recognize. He had dark sunglasses on, though the sun wasn't out, and he tapped the window with a club of some sort, a night stick.

Ah crap.

I rolled the window down lazily and nonchalantly in hopes of seeming uninterested.

"Yes?" I asked.

"You can't sleep here. You need to remove your vehicle from the premises."

"I'm waiting for someone. He's in the store."

"Why are you waiting out here in the cold? Why didn't you go in as well?"

I practiced the story we made up.

"I'm sick, not feeling well. I just came along to help him load it all once he gets done. He's a whiner, my roommate. If I don't at least drive him, he complains to no end," I stated and rolled my eyes for dramatic effect.

"I see."

He paused. I wondered if he bought it. He seemed to have.

"Alright, well, this is really against the rules...no manned vehicles and no loitering. I guess I can let you slide this time but the next time, you have to go in with him or stay home. Got it?"

"Yes, sir. Got it."

He began to walk away, but then turned back. "Where do you live, son?"

I found it comical that his body couldn't be more than five years older than mine but he referred to me as son, as some kind of degrading show of authority, I was sure.

"Out off the interstate," I answered.

"Where off the interstate."

"Way out, off I-70. Near the Casey exit," I told the most truth I could without telling it all.

"What are you doing in Effingham? Just shopping?"

"Yes, sir."

"You boys go to school? College?"

"No, sir." I rubbed my eyes with my fingers and yawned, trying to look bored and uninterested.

"What do you do then?"

"My roommate works in town. I don't do much of anything."

"You don't have a job?"

"No, sir."

"No wonder he's on your case, boy," he said laughing and shifted from one foot to the other.

"I guess."

"Your friend sure is taking a long time."

"Mmhhmm."

"Why don't you go in and check on him."

What the..? What's up with the third degree?

"If it's ok with you, sir, I'll just wait. Like I said, I feel like crap. He should be out anytime. I'm fine waiting here, really."

He continued to look at me or I assumed he was. I couldn't tell because of the dark of his glasses where his eyes were actually looking. He leaned back to glance in the van and saw all the seats had been removed. He stilled.

Crap. Crap. Crap.

He returned back to me slowly.

"Expecting a big load, son? How much stuff can two kids need?"

"We don't need much," I lied. "We use the van for other purposes, if you know what I mean."

I had no idea what I was saying. I hoped he bought it. I knew human males said things like that, macho stupid things about nonchalant sex and other extracurricular activities.

"Hmmm. Well, I know what you mean. You need to be careful with things like that. A boy could get himself into trouble."

Just as I was about to agree I saw Cain, loaded down with two huge mounded shopping carts full.

Crap.

"What's this?" the man asked suspiciously, as I knew he would. "This your roommate? You lying to me boy? What's going on here? What do you need all this stuff for?"

As Cain approached, looking weary, I jumped out, grabbed the man while he was distracted and placed him in a head lock, pressing my thumb into the pressure point on his neck. He passed out quickly and I placed him in the van. Cain was less than pleased.

"What the hell?" Cain asked as he began to frantically unload the carts.

"He made us, I had to do something. Let's hurry before he wakes up. We'll drop him off somewhere like last time."

"Dang, Merrick, I can't leave you alone for five minutes," he teased.

Unfortunately, this wasn't the first human I'd had to drop on one of our trips to town. Of course, no one knew that but Cain and me. And I'd prefer it to stay that way. Times were getting desperate and I didn't want Sherry or anyone else to freak out when we were so close to the need warehouse deadline and needed these trips now more than ever.

"That was quite a bit longer than twenty minutes, pal. What happened?"

"I had a problem with the credit cards. Most of them are empty now or don't have enough to cover this amount of stuff. Took me a while to find one that would go through and they were starting to wonder about me. This was a tricky trip, that's for sure," he said as he pushed the man's legs further in to start loading the bigger boxes of toilet paper and rice. "Oh, and by the way, if you had a grandma, there's still no way she could beat Margaret, ok."

I chuckled. "I'm sure. Well, it's almost over. Coming to town won't be necessary at all anymore, for me anyway."

"Yeah, I don't know what I'm going to do when I can't work. I've worked every day since I was fifteen. That's eleven years, in case your Keeper mind can't keep up."

"Well, I've worked every day for six thousand years. All day, every day, no sleep. So stop whining."

"So, you're an old man, that's what you're saying?"

He lifted an eyebrow at me so I threw a bag of rice at him and he laughed as it hit him in the stomach, making him 'oof'.

We got everything loaded and I started the van. A while later I pulled the van over behind an old house on our way out of town to drop off the nosy man. I laid him out comfortably in the grass, though it was yellow and scratchy and I was sure it provided him no real comfort.

We left him there, with his sunglasses still intact and on his face. As I pulled back onto the road Cain began to question me about Lillian which I was grateful for. I always hated this long ride and welcomed the distraction.

"So, I came home last night from work and Lillian was asleep on the couch. Her head was in Mitchell's lap," he scoffed.

"So?"

"So? He had his hands on her," he said like he was disgusted, "in her hair and on her back. He was asleep too. They looked a little more than cozy."

"Mitchell was Michael's Keeper. She's close to him, it's not uncommon."

"Yeah, like you and Sherry? That's what I'm worried about. All these women are jumping on the Keeper wagon. What about the ones of us who are left, huh? What about me?"

"Well, they can't help it. They can just see how wonderful we are. It's just pulls them in like a fish on a rod," I said grinning at him.

I loved to goad him. Even though he knew I was doing it, he'd take the bait every time.

"Bite me. And I saw her talking to Miguel in the hall this morning. I wanted to punch the stupid grin right off his face."

"You really like her? You just met her yesterday."

"I like her, I'm not saying I want to elope," he said and gave me a look that said 'like you'.

"Well...I don't know. She hasn't said anything to Sherry about either of them. I wouldn't be too worried yet. Like I said, it's not uncommon for humans to have close relationships with their Keepers. Most of them are different, special in a different way. He lost his charge and she lost her protector. It's natural that they would team together and become friends, they had no one else."

"I know, I'm being shallow, but I can't help it. I feel like I'm in a fish tank and all the food is slowly being gobbled up by the other fish. Man, she was hot though, wasn't she? When she came out of the shower...ah, I thought I was having a heart attack. Gorgeous."

"She's alright."

"Oh, come on, I won't tell Sherry if you say another woman is hot."

"I think she's pretty, yes, I might agree with gorgeous, but it's not the same gorgeous you're thinking of."

"You want to explain that to me further, mister vague."

"Well, I have Sherry, so I don't care what other women look like because I have everything I need. When someone is completely in love with you, it just blocks everything else out. Sherry is like...a creature from my dreams. Like she was made for me."

Cain stayed quiet for a minute. I assumed he was pondering over what we'd said. I bet that he was thinking about if he was being shallow with Lillian or he really liked her.

"Well, I hope I know what that feels like someday," he said quietly looking out his window.

Cain told me about his fiancé once, the woman he was engaged to before all this happened. She had an affair, cheated on him with her boss, a lawyer from some big time national firm. She was enthralled with him because he'd been in a commercial and she talked non-stop about it while she was at home. Apparently, she'd been more enthralled than Cain had realized. He caught them in the act of not working, in her office...on her desk.

I wondered if that was what he was thinking about, if I said the wrong thing.

We were almost home and we stayed quiet the rest of the way. I thought about Lily and what she was doing right now; probably trying to talk Sherry into something like a snack of pickles and syrup. And Sherry. Sweet Sherry had such a hard time resisting. It was adorable, all of it. I couldn't believe it was *mine*.

I glanced in the back and did a double take. I saw something I'd never seen on these runs before. Actually, I'd never seen one in real life before either.

"Cain, what in the worlds is that doing in here?"

He glanced back and smiled. "A surprise."

"Lily is going to freak," I said happily, smiling too.

"I know. I can't wait."

Little White Lies
Chapter 6 - Sherry

"Lillian, you don't have to do that. You just go back in there and rest a little bit. It's ok, I can do it. I don't mind," I insisted for the fifth time.

"I want to. I need something to keep my hands busy. Besides, I have nothing else to do, since I didn't go on the run today." Lillian was being stubborn and insisting on washing hers and mine and Merrick's clothes as payment for borrowing clothes to sleep in last night.

"Ugh! Fine, but I'm helping."

We had been going at it for almost ten minutes about it. Lily was napping soundly in her cute room. We let her color on the walls with whatever we could find. She drew ponies, rainbows and butterflies, typical little girl stuff, except for the watermelon. She loved watermelon. She asked me to help, too, so I drew a little girl with a doll.

Merrick got Cain to pick her up a new doll on one of their runs and Miley was now sitting on the shelf in the commons room. She couldn't bear to part with it for good so we stored it for later. She loved the new doll even more and she aptly named it Joy.

Cain also picked her up some crayons and coloring books along with Calvin and Frank some more puzzles and an electronic handheld game with rechargeable batteries. Cain was our go-to guy for whatever you needed. He could get you just about anything.

So Lily's room was littered with pictures and drawings and full of color. Especially purple, her favorite color. Calvin and Franklin started bunking together to give their parents some privacy and they took their makeshift tent from the second room and placed it in their new room together. Miguel showed them how to make it camouflage with some permanent markers.

It took forever! But they finally got it done and were so proud of themselves. Miguel and Ryan even helped them rig it to stay more securely to the walls and ceiling. They were ecstatic and we barely saw them out of their room for two whole days.

"Well, you can help if you like, but it's only fair if I pull my weight around here. I don't need any special treatment."

"I'm not doing that. There's nothing wrong with you just taking a day or two to recuperate. I know it's rough out there with everything that's going on."

"No need, but thank you. You know, I missed you, Sherry."

We walked back into the laundry room with our last armloads of clothes. Lillian grabbed Mitchell's clothes, who was in with Max going over some Keeper stuff, from his room to wash as well. Hmmm...that was sweet.

"I missed you, too. I hated us having to separate before. It didn't seem right."

"I know. I never had any brothers, sisters or even cousins growing up. My family was really small and private. We stayed home a lot and I went to a small private school so... It was neat to me, for us to all be piled in that basement together, like now I guess. I know y'all probably hate it, but it's nice to have so many people to talk to."

"I like it. I mean, the circumstances suck, but I didn't have a big family either. I have one now." I smiled thinking about it. "This is a really great group. You couldn't ask for better people. I think you're going to like it here," I said as we began to place the clothes in the suds in the big utility sink.

So, total, we had Lillian's, mine, Merrick's, Lily's, Mitchell's and Cain's clothes to wash. Cain worked so much and went on every run and trip there was to do, so I always did his laundry for him. It only seemed fair. When the heck would he have the time to anyway?

"I think so, too. Everyone's been really helpful and considerate."

"I saw you talking to Cain yesterday," I threw out very casually, hoping she wouldn't catch any undertones.

"Yeah, he showed me around. He's really nice."

"Yeah, he is."

"You two seem close. He said you both had been through some stuff together."

"He saved my life."

"Really?" she said, her hands stopping. "What happened?"

"Long story. Short version, Cain and I we were tricked by Lighters into going outside to help someone, got trapped in a cave out behind the store, almost froze to death and we faced a battalion of Lighters, Markers and the Taker himself after he kidnapped Lily and Calvin."

"Uh...whoa."

"Yeah. Anyway, Cain carried me when I broke my leg." I motioned to my walking cast. "He also found the cave we stayed in. Then later on that day, he rescued us after our van went in the river."

She blew out a long loud breath. "Mitchell said you guys had had some excitement but I had no idea. That sounds terrible. It doesn't look like you had much more luck than us after all."

"We have, but well, unfortunately, all that happened within a one day time span. So...Mitchell. How's he? You two seem to be kind of close."

She rubbed the shirt up and down the grate but stared up at the vents with the clothes blowing in the wind as they dried. Her mind was off somewhere else but she still answered my question. I wondered if where she was in her head was good or bad.

"He's great. He has been a Godsend since Michael died. He was upset, like me when it happened, Michael being a Special, his Special and all. He has kind of taken back up the Keeper thing with me. He watches out for me. It's nice."

"I see, and now you're doing his clothes for him."

Her eyes snapped back to attention, then focused on me. "Well, yeah. He's busy and I'm just sitting here so... It doesn't mean anything, Sherry, honestly, he's my friend and I just like doing things for him."

"Are you sure?"

"Positive. Besides, aren't you doing Cain's laundry? I promise you, we are just friends."

Mitchell took that opportunity, unbeknownst to him that he was being talked about, to walk in. "Hey, Lil. What are you ladies- Ahh. You didn't have to do that. Thank you, though," he said as his spied his shirt in her hands.

"It's fine, I was already doing mine anyway. I know you're busy with Keeper stuff."

"Not really. There really isn't any Keeper stuff anymore. Max was just showing me how they schedule their runs and things like that. Maybe I can help them next time."

"Or me."

"I already thought you were going today. What happened?"

"Well... I just didn't feel like going."

Lies and Mitchell could tell as well.

"Lil," he chastised softly.

Mitchell began again and I suddenly realized I might as well have not even been in the room. They were about a foot apart and he was looking down at her and I saw it as all too familiar. I stood still and quiet and let them finish while Mitchell continued. "You didn't go because of me, right? Because of what I said?"

"Well..."

"Lil." He leaned a little closer and placed his palms on her upper arms. "I wasn't trying to make decisions for you. I just knew I'd worry about you while you were gone. I'm sorry if you thought I'd be upset with you."

"It's not that, I just didn't... If you didn't want me to go, I knew there was a good reason so...I trust you. That's all."

Awkward. I wished I could slip out of the room, but I knew I'd break the spell. His eyes were fiercely and affectionately locked on hers and his thumbs moved back and forth over her bare shoulders. She looked endearingly oblivious to what was really going on with Mitchell. Did she know how he really felt? How could she not see it?

I tried to tiptoe out, but Lillian was brought back down to earth by my movement.

"Oh, Sherry. I'm sorry. Uh...Mitchell, remember, this is Sherry. Sherry, Mitchell."

"I remember," Mitchell said, reluctantly releasing Lillian's arm and extending a warm hand to me. "I can't tell you how great it is to see you again. All of you. You all have quite the set up here."

This was the first time I'd gotten a really good look at Mitchell. His body was about thirty eight or thirty nine I guessed. Quite a bit older than Lillian, who if I remembered correctly, was only twenty two or three. He had brown hair, was taller than Lillian, who was taller than me. He was pretty slim but nice looking with brown eyes. He looked very easy going with his beard stubble and somewhat shaggy hair.

"Yeah, we do. Unfortunately, the people who let us stay here with them are no longer here, except Max. They both died, recently."

"I heard about that. I'm sorry." It sounded like he really meant it. "Well, I wasn't trying to interfere with your work or butt in. I just wanted to check on Lil," he looked back at her and his eyes stayed there, "and uh, you know, see how things were going. You don't have to do my laundry, but thank you. I appreciate it."

"Mitch, after all you've done for me, it's the least I can do for you," Lillian said softly.

"Well, thank you." He cleared his throat. "Nice to see you again, Sherry. The guys are about to be back, Max said, so I'm gonna help them get all the vehicles unloaded, but uh, maybe we can talk some later, Lil, after dinner maybe?"

"Yeah, sure," she said and picked up another batch of clothes to start scrubbing, it was a shirt I'd never seen and could only assume it was also Mitchell's.

"Ok, great, see ya later."

He left, but peeked at her once more at the door way before heading into the hall. Wow. That Keeper had it bad.

"Lil? Mitch?" I asked her with a coy smile.

"Yeah. It's what we call- What?" she said incredulously, seeing my expression.

"Uhuh. Well, Lil, I think it can safely be said that that Keeper is definitely

159

more than your friend. Or at least he wants to be."

"Really, you think so? You see, this whole time I just thought he was being nice because of Michael, but when we got here and I saw you and Jeff and Marissa. Well, now I'm starting to wonder if maybe...there was something more there. He is a little touchy feely. I don't know what I'm thinking..." She threw the clothes down in the water, splashing suds everywhere which just seemed to exasperate her more. "Sorry," she muttered.

"It's ok. This isn't about Michael is it?"

"Shouldn't it be?" she said, her voice shrill.

"Why do you say that?"

"Well, he was my husband. He's only been dead not even a year yet and I'm...I'm entertaining the idea of someone else having feelings for me? It's not right. It's not right, Sherry."

"Lillian, there's no time table that tells us when our grieving can end. That's up to you. It doesn't mean you didn't love him if you move on."

"It does though, doesn't it? Especially if I move on with his Keeper. It just feels..."

"Wrong?"

"No, it feels right. That's why it scares me. Not with Mitchell, per say, but...moving on feels right. It has to mean something was wrong with Michael and me, and I just didn't notice it or...I don't know." She ran her hands through her hair. "I'm so confused. Mitchell has never made a pass at me, never tried anything so, maybe I'm misunderstanding the whole thing."

"Michael would want you to be happy so, no, I don't think that's what it means and uh, no. I witnessed Mitchell in all his googly eyed glory just now. That Keeper feels something for you."

"You think so? Really?"

"Really."

Her lips twitched as she tried not to smile, but I saw and we both burst out laughing. We finished our laundry and talked about something entirely different. Anything we could think of that didn't involve googly eyed Keepers.

Max was right, all the store trip pairs started to get back within a half an hour. I always hated this part. Waiting to see when Merrick would come in, if at all. I didn't like thinking like that, but I worried so much about him. Merrick and Cain always went out together, which was the one thing that made me happy. The same teams always worked together, so that they knew how the other worked and handled things.

Cain and Merrick made a good team. They got along great at home, better than great actually. Other than me, Merrick was closer to Cain than anyone else, even Danny lately. They hung out and goofed off all the time.

Team after team came home. I unloaded the stuff in the kitchen as they brought it in, but most of it went into the hall for future use. I tried hard not to think the worst when Merrick and Cain continued to not be the ones coming through the door. Finally, they were the only ones left out who hadn't returned yet.

It was time to start dinner already. I got Lily up from her nap and Pap and Maggie, along with Lillian, entertained her while I started to cook with Marissa and Kay to help me. My nerves were making my stomach knot. They'd been last home before but not long after everyone else. The last team came home twenty two minutes ago. Twenty two minutes. Was I being nuts? Was I worrying needlessly?

I boiled the water for the pasta and brewed the tea.

Thirty five minutes past.

I set out the silverware and folded paper towels. Marissa said they'd be here soon, for me to stop pacing, they'd be fine.

Forty seven minutes past.

I mixed the cheese in with the pasta, got out plates and helped Marissa put ice in glasses.

One hour and thirteen minutes past.

We called everyone to start the line to fill their plates and I settled Lily in with a bowl.

Jeff hugged me sideways around my shoulders at the sink and told me not to worry, that they probably got hung up or a flat tire. Nothing they couldn't handle.

One hour and twenty eight minutes past.

Then, blessedly, I heard the familiar squeak of the trap door being lifted and raced to the stairs from the kitchen. As soon as I turned the corner I saw Merrick looking around. When he saw me, he grinned and opened his arms to me. I jumped up into them without hesitation and exhaled all my worries and stress.

Those stupid all day store run trips just killed me. I couldn't handle the stress of it and in fact, I would be glad to be rid of them.

He kissed me forcefully and I was glad to see I wasn't the only one that was still glad to see the other. He held me up to him and I heard the others behind me. I even heard some 'ahh's and 'finally's. I was horrible at hiding my worry; everyone knew I was freaking out. Then I heard something a little bit more annoying.

"Ahem."

We both parted, reluctantly, but he still held me up and we looked over to see Jeff.

"Thank goodness you're back. I thought I was going to have to tie Sherry to a chair to keep her from ruining the floor with her pacing," Jeff said smiling.

"My Sherry? Worried?" Merrick looked at me playfully and put my feet back to the floor. "Impossible." He kissed my nose. "Now, Jeff, if you'll excuse us,

I have some business with my wife," he said, never taking his eyes from mine.

Then he grabbed my hand and began to tow me to our room amid all the people smiling and trying not to giggle at us.

"Business, huh?" Jeff said laughing. "Is that what they're calling it now?" he called after us but we didn't stop.

As soon as we entered our little room, his lips were on me. I was still upset and curious as to what made him and Cain so late but it would have to wait. And I wasn't complaining.

His eager hands were in my hair where I loved them. His hot breath hitched and skipped across my neck as he kissed warm flutters on my jaw and collarbone. That was one thing that hadn't changed. His body temperature was still incredibly hot. One more reason we were so perfectly matched, because I was constantly cold. But not right then as I felt the heat rise in the room.

Clothes flew away with incredible ease, lips and hands claiming skin. He urged me gently to be quiet as he sometimes had to do.

Afterwards, he silently continued to kiss and caress me as we lay on our sides, facing each other. Maybe he understood how scared I'd been and wanted to completely reassure and comfort me before we talked about it.

"I'm sorry we were so late," he finally said. "Cain ran into credit card trouble, but he handled it. It just took a little bit longer than normal. I'm sorry. I hate it when you worry."

"It's ok. I know sometimes things happen, but I just can't stand not knowing what's happening with you out there. My mind runs wild with-"

"I know." He kissed the tip of my nose. "I'm sorry." He kissed my cheek. "I'll make sure that little jerk gets his act together for next time." My jaw. "Please forgive me." My forehead. "I missed you like crazy." Then he kissed that little spot behind my ear, making me groan and giggle and bite my lip.

"It's ok, Merrick. You're forgiven." I laughed as he continued to kiss all sorts of places in his plea for forgiveness. "You're forgiven! I missed you, too, I always do. I'll be so glad when this is over. I'd rather you be a farmer than a shopper."

"Me, too, but we need this right now. A couple more runs, that's all we need to help get things started good for us, that's all we can do really anyway. Then I'm home free and you won't be able to get rid of me."

"Good. I can't wait."

"Mmmm, I really missed you. Cain's not half as cute as you are," he said, skimming his fingers down my arm.

I laughed which I did an awful lot lately, especially with Merrick. He was a pro at knowing exactly what to say to me in whatever situation. Whether I was happy or sad or mad or worried, he still knew me completely.

"I hope not! So other than that, how'd it go?"

"Fine," he said quickly.

It was a one word lie. I froze.

Merrick just told me a flat out lie.

A Little Slice Of Heaven
Chapter 7 - Sherry

Oh, no. I swallowed hard. Merrick hadn't just flat out lied to me since we'd been at the warehouse basement and it had all been silly relationship stuff, never anything important. Should I call him on it? He knew that I knew.

"Fine?" I asked again softly.

"Yeah, fine," he said moving his hand to play with my fingers on my belly, but not looking at my face.

My heart flipped in disappointment. He wouldn't lie unless it was something important, something he really didn't want me to know, for my own good. I bit my lip while I contemplated how to handle it but then he groaned and put his face down on my belly.

"I'm sorry, I'm sorry. I can't do it. I can't lie to you," he said muffled into my skin. He raised his head and looked me in the eye. They were full of regret and something else. Fear. He thought I would be furious with him. "I'm so sorry, baby. I thought I could just say it was fine and you wouldn't question it, but I knew you could tell. I was trying to protect you...but I shouldn't have to lie to do it. I'm sorry."

"What happened that you thought you had to lie about it?" I asked softly.

"Can you just trust me to handle it? It wasn't anything too terrible. I just don't want to worry you over it, ok? It's over."

"Now I am worried,"   I said and sat up.

He groaned again.

"Don't be, baby, you know me." He sat up too and framed my face with his hands. "I'm not gonna do anything stupid or reckless."

I continued to look at him, worry etched all my face. He spilled.

"Ok, ok." He let his hands fall to mine and he laced and unlaced our fingers. "There was a man, he questioned me. End result, I had to put him to sleep and we dropped him off somewhere to wake up later," he rushed through the words so fast

I barely heard him.

"Who was he?" I asked.

"One of the new human enforcers."

I gasped.

The enforcers were a human task force, not unlike police officers, whose main job and goal was Keeper and resistance hunting out and the new Taker laws enforcement. The new laws were put into place to keep people like us from cheating their system. There was to be no one in the stores without being checked behind the ear, no loitering in any parking lots, no home or small business deliveries of any kind, no television programming allowed, but the local news, etc.

"Merrick!" I pulled back in shock. "That's not a little thing. The enforcers answer directly to the Lighters and city officials. You could have been taken right then!"

"This is why I didn't want to tell you. We handled it. We'd done it once before-"

"You what?" I covered my mouth with my hand in shock, then put it back down to my lap. "Once before? Merrick!"

I was so upset. All I could see were visions of Merrick being brought before the Lighters and being dismembered or worse, tortured slowly for information about the rest of us. Them poking and prodding through his brain for thoughts of us and our whereabouts.

"Honey, listen." He moved closer and framed my shaking face with his hands once more. "There is nothing to worry about. Cain and I can handle ourselves against one human man. I won't ever do anything that will make it so I can't come home to see your pretty face again." He kissed me when I snorted, then became serious again. "I will always come back to you. Do you hear me? Always together, remember?"

"Merrick, I don't know what I'd do if something were to happen to you," I creaked.

"You'll never have to find out."

"You can't be certain-"

"I am. Trust me, I'll always come back to you," he said firmly, then plastered another smile that I could feel against my cheek that still after all this time made my heart flutter. "Now, that you've drained me of all my energy..." He pulled me back to the circle of his arms and kissed me deep and long, probably trying to distract me. What did it say about me that it worked? "Can you please feed me now? I'm starving and I thought I smelled your scrumptious macaroni and cheese earlier."

"Flattery will get you everywhere," I said wryly and couldn't help but laugh.

He helped me dress in the dark and once everything was back in place and he stole a few more kisses, we went out for our walk of shame.

That wasn't really an appropriate title since we were married, but it seemed like this was a common occurrence for us. Every week he came home from the store run, every week we made a spectacle of ourselves with kisses and hugs at the stairs and every week he shamelessly dragged me to our room, unable to wait another second. Ok, he didn't have to drag me, I practically ran down the hall with him, but you know. We were newlyweds for goodness sake!

Then we come out some time later and he could care less what everyone thought as we walked hand in hand like nothing happened, but I couldn't be that way. I saw their silly looks and grin. I knew it was all in good fun but still... Oh, well. I should be happy that Merrick was so confidant and secure about us and it wasn't like I'd have it another way.

As soon as we reached the commons room Lily jumped from Marissa's lap and sprinted to Merrick. He nabbed her up and she squeezed his neck.

"Lily bug."

"Mewwick! I missed you. I had to take a nap all by myself today."

"Really? That's terrible," he said mockingly as he toted her into the kitchen, with me on his heels.

He started to make himself a plate, while carrying Lily, but I told him I'd get it. He sat down at the table with Lily on his lap with Cain there already, a plate of his own in front of him.

"So, what else did you do today?" he asked her.

"Shawwy let me help make bwownies today."

"Brownies? Wow. Well, where are they?"

"Well, Uncle Danny and Uncle Wyan ate dem all."

Cain tried to stifle a laugh but choked on his tea instead. Merrick chuckled but didn't seem too surprised.

"Did you at least get one first?"

"Yep. I got two."

"Oh, good then."

"Come on, sweetie," I said, setting Merrick's plate down in front of him and reaching for Lily's hand, "let Merrick eat, ok."

"Why can't I call Mewwick Daddy?"

The stunned silence that followed could have lasted for hours for all I knew. That was the absolute last thing I expected to pop out of her innocent mouth. Cain and Merrick were just as stunned and stilled, except they both looked at me like I had the answer.

Merrick looked on the verge of extreme happiness and throwing up at the same time.

166

"Do you want to call Merrick Daddy?" I asked softly, sitting in the seat beside them.

"Frankwin has a daddy. He said Daddy is someone who takes cawe of you. I wike Mewwick. He's not mean wike that other Daddy."

Merrick locked eyes with me over her golden halo of hair. I could see how much he wanted it, to hear those words for himself. I nodded to him in encouragement. If anyone was going to tell her she could call him that, it would be him.

"You can call me anything you want to, sweetheart," he said softly.

"Ok!" she yelled happily, kissed his cheek, jumped down from his lap and ran off to play elsewhere.

We all sat there in silence for a minute then Cain resumed eating. I turned full on to face Merrick.

"Well, that was interesting."

"Yeah," he croaked and cleared his throat. That was all he said before taking his first bite. "This is really good, babe." He kissed my cheek but didn't look up at me.

"Thanks."

"It *is* good," Cain stated.

"Thanks," I repeated. "So...you were going to hide the fact that you two ran into an enforcer...twice?" I asked Cain but kept my tone playful though the situation was anything but funny to me.

"Ah, come on! You told her?" Cain asked Merrick, looking disappointed.

"Of course I did," Merrick said firmly. "She's my wife. Sherry can handle it."

"It's not just Sherry *handling* it I'm thinking about," Cain whispered.

"I won't tell anyone else so they won't freak out, but you shouldn't want to keep it from me," I said with a slight bit of hurt in my voice.

"You freak out more than anyone," Cain said looking right at me.

"I worry more than anyone. It's different."

"Not to a guy. It sucks when women freak out and worry, especially when there's nothing we can do to change it. Sometimes things have to be done that aren't fun or even safe. But it's gotta be done to keep this group here alive and there's no point in you sitting here pulling your hair out the whole time, sick with worry, when there's no other solution."

I felt wide eyed and remorseful. That's what my worrying did? Made them feel that way?

"I'm sorry, I don't mean to be-" I started but Merrick interrupted me.

"Don't you apologize," he said softly and looked from me to Cain. "Enough ok, it's fine. Only a couple more weeks and we'll be through with all of it, for good."

"Yeah, ok. I didn't mean anything by it, Sherry, you know that right?"

"I know," I answered.

A long pause. "Ok. Well-" Cain said and started to get up.

"How's work?" I asked to keep Cain from leaving. I didn't want him to leave just because it was awkward.

"It's ok. It's kind of boring lately, what with less people coming in. There's only two weeks until the warehouses go up and people are already acting like they can't buy anything from anywhere else."

"Really. Well what-"

"Crap! Sorry, I totally forgot something!" Cain yelled making me jump. "I heard people talking about the new Taker yesterday in the shop."

"What?" That got Merrick's attention.

"Yeah. Supposedly now there's a new one, named Mal... Mali something."

"Malachi," Merrick answered, letting his fork drop to his plate with a loud clank.

"Yeah, that's it. How did you know that?" Cain asked but instead of answering Merrick sat with a concentrative look.

"Yeah?" Jeff said as he in came quickly and I realized Merrick had called him in his mind.

"Malachi's the new Taker," Merrick told him giving him a look.

"What? No. Maybe the name's a coincidence."

"With our luck? Doubtful. It's him Jeff, I know it." Before I could ask what was going on Merrick filled us in. "Takers are usually new. Human souls or maybe their spirit hanging around the body after they die, who absorb the Lighter instead of the Lighter absorbing him, but there is always a part of the Takers before him, inside. He knows exactly how to do everything any Taker has done before him, he knows all about it. But Malachi has already been the Taker. Instead of some twisted form of reincarnation it's...re-reincarnation."

"Hmm. Well, they're having a big party/dance/rally thing Friday night for him to introduce him to the world and they are giving a speech and all. I was thinking I could go, see what's up. Maybe Sherry could go with me...as my date," Cain said and turned to me with lifted eyebrows and a smile.

"I agree. That sounds like a good idea," Merrick said stunning me, but then he continued, "but I don't want Sherry in town."

Even though I knew what his answer would be, I still slumped a little in disappointment. The prospect of having something else to do other than domestic chores was thrilling for about three seconds, then reality hit.

"Oh, yeah, the Taker, I forgot. Well, he won't be there himself. I don't think anyways."

Every since the Taker tried to get me to go with him and be his, uh, mate or whatever, Merrick had forbid me to leave the bunker under any circumstances.

"It doesn't matter. I don't want Sherry in town, especially not without me," Merrick said with finality.

"Well I still think you should go. You're immune to the Lighter speak and they can't sense you're a Special," Jeff said. "If you want to, that is. I don't want to put you in danger but you'll know a lot of these people right?"

"Yep, mostly. Ok, well, maybe Lillian could come with me. Or Marissa. No not Marissa, they can tell she's a Muse. Dang it. Well, I'm not going clubbing by myself."

Jeff said he needed to think and left. Merrick grabbed my hand under the table.

You understand why you can't go, don't you? Please don't pout. I can only take so much of your disappointment in me in one day.

"I'm not. I understand why." I smiled sweetly at him and answered him aloud because there was no other way to.

"Good," he said and smiled back and returned to finish his pasta.

The previous Taker tried to make me run away with him. He said he had plans to destroy mankind and needed one altruistic human to remain to order to keep the balance and not destroy everything they had worked hard to accomplish- in other words, taking over the world. I thought the whole idea was ridiculous, but he based his whole existence on it so I guessed he must have really believed it.

That Taker was killed by Calvin and his fire fingers. We knew a new Taker would be along eventually but this was pretty quick.

Cain looked at us for a moment, realizing Merrick had been speaking only to me and then shrugged, sensing the conversation over. He took his plate to the sink and refilled his tea glass. Leaning on the counter with his hip he turned back to us.

"I'm really gonna miss sweet tea," he said and sipped it smiling sadly.

It wasn't just the tea. The tea represented everything that we were about to lose. All the simple things we'd been taking for granted. Once we ran out of normal things like tea, there wouldn't be much of it anymore after that. We would use most of the small rations they gave us at the need warehouses in a day with a bunch like this.

We already haven't had a lot of fruits and vegetables in over a year. The weather was making it impossible for most things to grow and everything was scarce at the grocery store.

"Me, too," I agreed, "and eggs. Eggs I'll miss the most."

"Oh! That reminds me," Cain said and smiled hugely.

He walked over to the fridge and reached inside. I looked at Merrick and he was grinning too. Cain then produced a big green ball from the bottom drawer and plopped it gently on the counter.

I heard my breath catch.

It was a watermelon!

A real watermelon!

Lily's absolute favorite thing to eat we learned and she even drew pictures of them. I personally hadn't had watermelon in years.

"Lily!" I yelled loudly knowing exactly why Cain had gotten it.

Lily skipped in nonchalantly, as did Marissa with her, hand in hand. When she saw Cain next to the counter she stopped dead in her tracks. You'd think it was the most precious of diamonds and gold but no, our Lily has simple taste.

She screamed, she squealed, she ran and jumped to Cain. This brought another round of onlookers to see what the fuss was about. Everyone was in awe. As I said, it had been a long time since we'd had real fruit.

Cain and Lily nuzzled and smooched as she thanked him before he passed her to me and took a long serrated knife from the drawer and began to make small slices. The first one went to Lily and she devoured it. I refused a piece as badly as I wanted one. There was too many people and too little watermelon to go around.

Cain gave me a knowing smile.

"You are the sweetest, Cain," I whispered and kissed him on the cheek before taking Lily away to finish her slice.

He looked slightly taken aback, but smiled, maybe even pinked in the cheeks a little which amused me, and continued to slice and hand out to eager hands waiting their turn for a piece of momentary heaven disguised at sticky red sweet watermelon.

Keeping Up Appearances
Chapter 8 - Cain

I tried to hold myself together, perfectly still, though I could have taken her right then and kissed those lips that taunted me right off that pretty face.

Oh, man, that was so close. *So* close. Her lips touched me, not even an inch from my mouth. They were so freaking soft and - whew, boy. I had to stop this.

I heard someone speaking, interrupting my internal tirade.

Lillian.

"How on earth did you get a watermelon?" she asked softly and genuinely impressed.

Everyone else that wanted one had gotten their pieces and left the kitchen, it was just her and me now. And one small slice of watermelon.

"Well, it was tricky. First, I had to fight an old lady for it, seeing as how things like this don't last long anymore. Then, I had to put down a down payment just to get the thing out the door."

She laughed. Really laughed. It was awesome to see her still smiling when she looked back up at me. She again tucked her hair behind her ear and I determined that it was probably a self-conscious notion of hers.

"Well, however you got it, I'm glad. I haven't seen so many smiles in a very long time."

"Well, there's one piece left. It's all yours."

"No," she shook her head and waved her hand, "you're the one who fought old ladies for it. You deserve it."

"I'll split it with you," I said as I turned to slice the rind once more down the middle.

"Deal."

"Technically, I should lose points, not gain them, for fighting old ladies by the way," I joked.

"True," she said smiling and reached for two plates, when she turned back she had the cutest amused look on her face. "Did you really fight an old lady?"

171

"Nah." I almost seemed ashamed to admit it. "In fact, we would have had two watermelons had the old lady not shown up."

"That's more like it," she said looking pleased and cut up the slices with a fork and dealt the pieces between the two plates. Her eyes drifted to the rod in my lip and she bit hers before looking away.

She put salt on her watermelon which I thought was disgusting but after a little coaxing, she got me to try a bite and I was pleasantly surprised at the delicious mixture of salty and sweet.

"Wow, I thought I couldn't be surprised anymore," I observed as I cleaned up all the sticky counter mess.

"I'm still surprised every day."

"Really? Well-"

"Lil?" Mitchell interrupted, though I didn't think he meant to. "Oh. Sorry. Didn't mean to interrupt."

Yep. Like I thought.

"No, you're fine. We were just discussing...watermelon philosophy," Lillian said looking at me and smiling.

"Ooookay," Mitchell said and I could tell he had no idea what we were talking about but loved to see her laugh. Mitchell was one of the guys I saw looking at Lillian like she was a Goddess when she came out of the shower the other day. And he called her Lil? What's up with that? "Well, like I said, I didn't mean to interrupt. I just wanted to talk to you about something when you get a chance."

"Ok. I can talk now," she said and then looked back to me. "Thank you. That was really sweet," she laughed, "you and the watermelon."

"No problem."

Then she followed Mitchell out, tucking her hair behind her ear.

Crap.

So, after I cleaned up the kitchen like the man I am, I went back into the commons room and remembered that I forgot to talk to Lillian about Friday night. But it would be rude to go butt in when Mitchell just came and got her from me, right?

Besides, as much as I might like Lillian, I didn't know her. I knew there would be no way that Merrick would have let Sherry go but I'd much rather her go instead, just because I think she knew how to handle herself if something were to happen. Not for my own reasons of the thought of dancing the night away with Sherry.

No, definitely not that.

I may get my chance anyway. Upon entering the commons room I see they had cranked up the record player. Katie and Paul, always Katie and Paul instigated these dance offs, were all over each other, bending and spinning. Little Sky was in her bounce seat, jumping up and down, beating some poor stuffed worm senseless.

A discreet Keeper meeting was going on in the corner and I decide to join, since I was sure I knew what it was about.

"Hey, ho, I didn't mean to spoil everyone's fun," I said to the group. "I would never have said anything about the new Taker if I knew it was gonna make everyone so sullen."

"We've got to talk about it, Cain, and we all agree with you about going to the meeting if you're up for it," Jeff answered.

"Oh, I'm up for it. I just got to get myself a hot date."

"Yes, we definitely don't want you to go alone."

"Agreed. Excuse me. You can get back to your Keeper lingo now," I said and walked over to where Sherry and Merrick were sitting.

I was in the mood for a little self-inflicted torture.

"May I have this dance, milady?" I asked in my best English accent and extended my hand to Sherry on the floor.

She laughed and took my hand, letting me pull her up.

"How can I refuse an offer like that?"

"You can't, it's best just not to fight it." I turned to Merrick. "You mind?"

"Of course not. Just make sure you bring her back," he said and winked at us.

"Sure thing."

I held her hand as I pulled her further away where there was room. Her fingers were short, cool and soft. Then I placed her arms around my neck, her hands really because she was so short, and rested mine on her upper waist, very gentlemanly.

"I'm not very good at this. Merrick taught me everything I know," she said looking bashful, watching our feet like she was waiting for disaster.

"Really? Where'd he learn it? Keeper academy?" I said low in her ear and she laughed.

"No, Mrs. Trudy. She taught quite a few of our men how to move. She was a little obsessed with making sure the couples here knew how to dance for some reason."

"Aha. Well, you seem to be doing a fine job to me, very graceful."

"Thanks, but you don't have to make up anything for me. I know the truth, Cainy boy."

My heart flipped. She had to know what she was doing to me. She *had* to. It had to be so viciously all over my face. I tried to cover with some fancy moves

173

because if she looked in my eyes, she'd see, I knew it. I twirled her under my arm and then took her left hand in mine this time instead of letting her return it to my shoulder. It was so small and dainty with cold fingers. Always cold.

"I wouldn't dare, Miss lie detector. So, you're gonna let me go Friday night all by my lonesome, huh?"

"Cain, you know I can't go. Even if the Taker hadn't caused all that...drama, Merrick still wouldn't let me go and you know it. As much as I'd love to."

"We could sneak off, runaway together. Or only run to the party, whichever you prefer."

"Oh, yeah?" She snorted and giggled. "Why don't you try some of that charm on someone who can fight it, huh? You keep this up and I'll crumble for sure and break Merrick's poor heart," she said in a hilarious flurry of mixed together facial expressions and accents.

If only that were true.

Wait...No, I didn't want that. Did I?

"Ah, well, there's not a lot of girls to resist anymore, I'm afraid. Especially if the Keepers keep turning on their charm."

"Aha. So you know about Lillian and Mitchell then? I was going to talk to you about that today."

"So it's true? Jeez," I groaned.

"Not officially, but if he had his way..."

"Yeah, I can see that. So, she's taken then. Just come with me. Come on! We'll talk Merrick into it. We'll get Danny to compel him."

"Cain!" She laughed out loud and the Keepers in the huddle looked our way curiously. "Tempting as that is, you know why I can't. The new Taker would know me in a second. He would know I wasn't a supporter. Even if that wasn't the case I doubt I could fake dancing all night. This is seriously bad," she said laughing, looking at our feet again.

"You're doing fine." I leaned in to whisper in her ear, "And Merrick is just being a stick in the mud."

"He just worries about me."

"He's not the only one. I worry about you dying of sheer boredom stuck in this bunker all day."

"Yeah right!" she laughed and playfully pushed my chest. "You're real worried about me! Wanting to bring me right to the Lighter's table."

"I do worry, but I also know you can handle yourself. I really do wish you could go. I trust you. We make a good team."

The way I said it must have revealed something because the look she gave me was strange. Her laughing eyes softened and she studied my face.

"We do. I wish I could go too. Be careful, ok. Please?"

174

"I always am."

"No, I mean it. Don't be your usual cocky self. Please, be careful and make sure you come home. Promise?"

I let my mind run for just a few seconds, that she was telling me to come home because she loved me and wanted me.

"I will, I promise." Then I lifted her hand to kiss it, feeling like it would be a perfect opportunity to, and saw something that brought me screeching back to reality.

Her bright, shiny, little silver ring on her *I'm taken* finger. The ring indicating not only that she belonged to someone else, but my best friend. Not only that, but they were crazy in love with each other and according to the story had risked a lot to get married. Merrick had wanted her to have it all exactly like she had dreamed, risking his own life to put that ring on her finger the proper way, in the church and official.

My chest hurt with an ache of shame as I realized how far I'd let this fantasy go on.

I released her hand without kissing it as the song ended. She could see a change come over me and crinkled her forehead like she does in worry.

"Are you ok?"

Sweet Sherry. She would never expect anything but chivalry from me. She had no idea the devious, sinister things I'd thought and fantasized about.

"I'm fine, just tired."

And as I walked away, I knew she could tell that I was lying.

But I didn't stop.

The Long Kiss Goodnight
Chapter 9 - Lillian

Mitchell took me to the laundry room, turning over some crates for us to sit on. I could hear the music coming from the commons rooms as we navigated the hallway.

He pulled two soda cans from the shelf and handed one to me as we took our seats.

"Wow, Mitch. You always think of everything," I said, laughing as mine spewed a little on the concrete floor.

"I try. I found these stashed on the back of the shelf. They're not cold but..."

"It's perfect." I took a sip. "Mmmm, hot, flat cola. It's almost as good as watermelon." I elbowed him playfully. "Thank you."

"Doubtful, but you're welcome. Um, so I heard that Cain is going to a rally Friday night for the new Taker at some club in town."

"Really?"

"Yeah. They, the Keepers, are going to ask you to go with him. You're the only not Special female that hasn't been compromised so...but that doesn't mean that you have to. I want you to know you don't have to do this."

"Well. I don't know. I might have to. Mitchell, they've helped us so much. If they need me-"

"That doesn't mean you have to do this. You'll be mixed in with Lighters and rallyers. I know you're immune to the Lighter speak but that doesn't make it any less dangerous."

"Well, maybe I should wait for them to ask me first. Maybe they were just talking."

He took a long drink of his soda then put the can down on the floor beside him. I put mine down, too. He turned to look full on me.

"I don't think so. I didn't bring you here just so they could try to send you out or you could send yourself out on every mission out of guilt or responsibility," he said low, but harshly.

"But that's not why I would be doing it. We can't just think about ourselves here."

"I'm not! I'm thinking about you!" he all but yelled.

"Mitch, what has come over you?" I stared at him. He never yelled or raised his voice to anyone but Polly in defense of me.

He took my hands, not like usual. This time he laced our fingers and he stared at them for a moment, and then looked up to me.

"What's come over me is you. I care about you and I don't want to see you hurt."

"I care about you, too. That's why I'd do it. We need all the information we can get to help us. All of us."

"You care about me?" he asked, but refused to look up to my eyes, just watched our hands with odd fascination.

"Of course I do."

What did he want me to say? Was he wanting me to confess my feelings? I didn't want to hurt him. I liked him, but did I like him the same way? I couldn't lose him, too. I needed my best friend.

"Do you? Really?" He met my gaze and held it. His thumbs caressed the insides of my wrists sending embarrassing shivers through me. "I'm not sure it's the same kind of care as I feel for you."

"What kind of care do you feel? I know you're protective. Michael would appreciate it, as I do, but like I said, I don't want you to feel obligated."

"And like I said, I'm here because I want to be. I care for you very much, and not just as a Keeper."

"You've been very good to me," I said and it came out way softer than I intended, so I looked away.

"And I'll keep being good to you. I want to always be here for you, keeping you safe, as close as you'll let me be." He turned me back to face him with a finger under my chin. "I know you miss Michael and I would never try to replace him...and..." he cleared his throat, "I know I'm not human, but I'm here. Whenever you need me, whatever you need, I'm here, Lil."

The close proximity was affecting my breathing. I let the words sink in and tried to find hidden meanings. Or maybe they weren't hidden. Maybe he was trying to tell me exactly what he was saying.

I couldn't process a response. I was so beyond confused. I did miss Michael, but as I told Sherry, I couldn't help but feel something for Mitchell. What exactly that was, I didn't know yet. Or was it just hero worship because he was so protective of me? What should I do?

My body seemed to respond without my permission, making up my mind for me. I leaned forward, which wasn't far to go because we were already so close. I placed my hands on his knees to steady me and let our lips touch.

His hands immediately came up to frame my face and I was thrilled that he didn't push me away, so I hadn't misinterpreted. Now I just had to decide if I liked kissing him or not. I pressed my lips to his harder, opened my lips against his and felt him do the same. It'd been so long since I'd kissed anyone, and I realized, he never had.

He was breathing heavy with deep needed breaths. Our knees interlaced as we sat and turned toward each other on our crates. He smelled of the soap I used to clean his shirt this morning. His lips were hard but gentle and his five o'clock shadow scratched my cheeks.

I had no idea how long we kissed before I broke off. He didn't release my face but put his forehead on mine. There weren't fireworks, but it was nice all the same.

"You don't know how long I've wanted to do that," he said breathlessly.

"Then why didn't you."

"For one thing, this body is almost twice your age. And another, I didn't think you wanted me to. You've always been so content with just being my friend."

"I don't care about your age. I was confused about Michael and everything else going on. Confused about you. I had no idea that you felt anything more than obligation to me," I said and pulled back a little to look at him. "I was scared. I still am."

"You don't have to be scared with me. I'm not going to pressure you into anything. I know this is a situation to be careful with. I just want to be here for you."

"I know, and I'm grateful, but..."

"But what?"

"Maybe I'm ready for you to not be so careful with me anymore," I said, shocking even myself and I heard his breath hitch.

He eyed me intensely with some wonder and sympathy mixed in. His fingers wiped at my cheeks. That was when I realized I was crying.

"Are you? I'm not going to rush-"

I cut him off with another kiss. That was when I knew I was ready to move on. I wasn't in love with Mitchell, I knew that, but I was in *like* with him. This wasn't something I'd jumped into. I had thought about this and now I was ready. Ready to leave Michael in the past as the sweet memory he was and start something new because who knew how much time we had left to live anyway.

Mitchell didn't hesitate. He pulled me closer and kissed me back with enthusiasm. This time his arms went around my waist and mine went around his neck.

Once again, time went away from me. At some point we pulled away reluctantly, realizing the music had stopped and things had gotten quiet again. It wasn't the best kiss ever, but it was good. I still wasn't sure what I felt for him. I already knew that Miguel, with that accent - ah - was attracted. I'd seen him follow me with his eyes around the room. And Cain was being super sweet to me, too, and incredibly charming and his sea green eyes...but I just wanted to kiss Mitchell to see that I still could.

Mitchell pulled me up from the crate.

"It's late. We should get to bed," Mitchell said then paled. "I mean, by ourselves. I wasn't implying-"

"Mitch, I know." I laughed because it *was* funny. "It's ok. I know what you meant. I am really tired, but I need to talk to Sherry first."

"Ok. I'll walk you, if that's ok."

"Of course it is," I insisted.

He seemed pretty happy and satisfied as he walked me back to the commons room, holding my hand and left me with Sherry before heading to his room for the night.

Sherry eyed me with a mixture of amusement and I-told-you-so. I smiled at her and squatted down in front of her.

"You were right, I'm ready. Thank you." That was all I said before heading over to Cain, who looked to be sulking on the staircase. His head in his hands, his elbows on his knees. "Cain?"

He looked up and immediately pasted on a horribly sad excuse for a smile. "Hey, there."

"About Friday night? I'm in. I'll go with you. Let me know what time you want to leave and what you need me to do and I'll be ready. G'night."

And I left before anyone could talk me out of it.

The next morning, I woke up late. I pressed my fingers into my aching eyes and then stretched my legs, flexing my toes. I half expected to run into warm flesh, another body beside me. It was still weird to sleep by myself, without Michael.

Before this we'd been sleeping wherever we could find a place, mostly not beds of any kind, so it was hitting me hard then just how things had changed. And how much I missed sleeping next to someone.

I decided to stop feeling sorry for myself, or I'd be a sloth there all day, and changed my clothes to leave the room. The hall was deserted as was the commons room. I saw Cain heading up the steps, out of the bunker. I wondered what it was he did out there. No one else ever went outside. It was kind of forbidden, I guess you'd say.

So, naturally, being the bored and curious girl I was, I decided I'd follow him.

 I lifted the hatch door, a heavy, wooden, creaky beast. I remembered the stock room from the other day when that woman had brought us through there. We'd showed up here because of a flyer someone saw at a truck stop. He didn't want to stay he'd said but knew the Lighters were bull crap so he stored the info for later. And then told us where to go when he happened to spot us wandering around.

I placed the door back quietly and looked around at the high shelves...and bumped right into Cain.

"Oh!" I cried and silently cursed my always bumping into people lately. I tried to think of something to say as he stood and looked down at me with cocked head and amused face. "Busted?"

He laughed a deep ember of a laugh and it was wonderful. It sent a wave of nerves through me. His face, which had been tight with concern or something, even in his jest, released and now looked five years younger. He seemed stressed and maybe even trying to cover up unhappiness. I didn't blame him. I probably was, too.

"Yeah, I'd say 'busted' fits here nicely. What are you doing?"

"Following you, being bored, wanting to be useful. Take your pick."

"Well," smiled again, "I'm really the only one allowed out. We try to keep everyone inside to ward off any suspicions. If someone saw a bunch of people running around outside...you know?"

"Yes, I know. I assumed as much, but really, I'm going stir crazy. I have to do something. What are you doing out here? Maybe I can help?"

"Well, Lillian, it's your lucky day." He leaned in to whisper conspiratorially. "I don't follow the rules either."

He grinned and placed a hand on my back to guide me out the back door. The sun hit my face and I wanted to gasp at the feel of it. You never knew when the sun would be out or it would be snowing or raining. It was a treat for it to be so mild outside and I soaked it in.

We walked to a small shed in the back. Behind it I saw a garden covered with high tarps. I couldn't tell what they were growing. There were barely green sprouts sticking out. They'd made a little sort of green house with all these tarps and I was impressed.

"So, what's all this?" I asked, looking back at him.

"Our garden. Sherry and I came up with it. See, once the need warehouses come, we won't be able to get enough food to feed everyone anymore, so, we're gonna try to grow a majority of it. Right now we're stock piling. That's why so many of us go on store runs every week."

"Need warehouse? What's that?"

He chuckled at some personal joke.

"Where you been?" he asked and then proceeded to tell me all about them and what had been Crandle's plans. When he was through, I couldn't help but shiver and think that the Lighters seemed to think of everything.

He walked me around a little more and told me all the vegetables they were planting. How certain ones can grow in harsh conditions. I asked a few questions and he answered them.

I was trying to decide if I should go back inside when a strong gust of wind shot through the yard. It was so strong that I had to grab Cain's arm to keep from falling over.

"This is another reason no one comes out here," he yelled over the howl of the wind and tried to shield me a little with his body, but it didn't work too well. "It gets pretty wicked sometimes."

"I see that."

Once it died down, I started to walk back to the store but was yanked back by my hair. I cried out at the pain and shock. At first I thought Cain had done it but it was so hard and hurtful, surely he wouldn't have. I looked up and back. Sure enough, it wasn't him but he saw what was happening the same time I did.

The wind had wrapped and knotted my hair around one of the poles that kept the tarp over the garden. But with all the ties and twists and rope around the pole to keep everything together and tight, it was snarled within the mess of it and as I started to try to free it I realized it was stuck. Really stuck.

I started to panic a little. Cain tried to help as we pulled at and tried to separate pieces of my very long blonde hair, it was well past my shoulder blades now, it wasn't working, in fact, it seemed to make it worse.

"Uh, Lillian, I may have to go get some scissors," he suggested.

"No! Please," I cried. "Look, I know it's stupid and silly, but I- I love my hair. I don't want to cut it, ok." We kept trying. We kept not getting it untangled. "Dang it! Just dang it."

I was losing my hope of not cutting my hair.

"Lillian," he said softly, "I promise you, you will look just as gorgeous with shorter hair. I think we have to cut it."

"It's not about my looks, Cain." I wanted to cry. And that thought made me want to cry harder. I was seriously about to cry over something as vain, girly and silly as hair. In the end of the world. But he didn't understand. "Cain, I just...I need my hair, ok? Michael always-" I stopped abruptly and wished I could leave, but couldn't.

"Your husband. He loved your hair, is that it?"

"Yes," I admitted. "I just feel like I..."

"Ok. Let me look around and see what I can find, ok? Stay here," he said and gave me a cocky grin.

"Ha ha," I said and couldn't help smile, too.

He came back a few minutes later with some kind of black grease. I didn't ask what it was, I didn't want to know, as long as I got free.

He rubbed it all over and around the ends of my hair and the pole and slowly started to pull and separate the pieces. Sometimes he had to yank slightly, holding the other side of the strand so as not to hurt me. It worked!

We pulled it all free and I tried to run my fingers through it, but it was impossible. I couldn't imagine the mess I must have looked with black grease all in my snarled hair nest. Right then I didn't care because I still had it for it to be a mess. I jumped right to Cain and wrapped my arms around his neck.

"Thank you so much. I know you think it's silly, but..." I pulled back to look at him, but didn't let him go. "I don't have anything. I have like five possessions to my name. Everyone has always loved my hair; my parents, Michael. I just couldn't...get rid of it," I admitted and wanted to cringe.

There was no way to explain it without sounding stupid.

"It's ok, I understand, really." I hadn't realized his hands were still on my waist until then. His fingers flexed a little and I felt a flutter in my stomach. His face was inches from mine. "I understand better than you think. Being in this place that isn't ours, with hardly anything that belongs to us, just trying to survive. I understand."

"Thanks, Cain, really."

"Ok," he said awkwardly and stepped back like he just realized how close we were. He cleared his throat. "Uh, how about we go back inside. We'll see if we can get you cleaned up."

"Yes, agreed."

We walked to the hatch door and he started to lift it, but stopped. "Lillian," he turned to me, "I'm really sorry about your husband."

I was a little taken back by his sincerity. He looked straight at me and I stared back into a sea of blue green.

"Thanks. I'm ok, really. We weren't even married that long and didn't know each other very long before that. I miss him, but in a way, I'm almost glad he's not here to see all this."

He knew exactly what I was talking about, 'this' was everything. He nodded.

"Maybe you can come with me again this week and I can show you how we do things, plant some carrots with me. What do you say?"

"Sure, I'd love to help."

"Ok, but uh, Lillian." He came to stand right in front of me and wrapped a strand of my hair around his fingers. "Your hair is pretty gorgeous. Why don't you wear it up next time, huh?"

He chuckled as if to soften the flirting he was doing, but I wasn't buying it. And man did I like it. I swore my hair was tingling. "I think that's a good idea. Thanks for the quick thinking out there. Most guys would have just said I was being stupid and gotten the scissors...or worse, a pocketknife."

He laughed and continued to rub and examine that same strand of hair. "No problem. Let's get you inside and see if Celeste can help you with..." he waved his hands in front of me, "all this."

"Hey, now. Is it that bad?"

"Define 'that bad'?"

I groaned and he laughed. "I'm half joking," he said and laughed again at my furious attempt to produce order to my locks, grabbing my hands and bringing them to our sides. "Come on. Celeste can help if anyone can, I guarantee it."

I followed him down to the bottom of the stairs. He looked around and saw Max sitting in his favorite chair. "Hey, Max, will you call Celeste for me?"

"Sure," he said and went right back to reading his book.

Celeste bounded in within a few seconds. "You know, Max, it's one thing for my own Keeper to be in my head, I don't need... Oh my...Lillian! What happened to you!"

"That's why we called you," Cain said. "We had a little debacle. Can you help?"

"Of course I can. Come with me, Lillian. It hurts to look at you."

"Ok, just a second." I turned back to Cain. "Thanks again, I mean it."

"No problem, I mean it," he said smiling. He winked at me and toyed with his lip ring with his tongue.

"So, you'll come let me know when you go outside tomorrow?"

"Yep, if you still want to."

"I do."

"Then, I will. Me, you, carrots. It's a date."

I laughed and saw Celeste raise her brow and quirk her lips. I bit my lip. "Ok, sounds great. Bye."

"Bye, Lillian," he said, almost crooned, and his deep voice just wrapped around my name perfectly.

As I walked away, following Celeste who was whispering that she knew just what to do for my hair, I looked over my shoulder once more and saw that Cain hadn't moved yet. He was still smiling and he was watching me go.

Pipe Down
Chapter 10 - Merrick

"Something is definitely up with Cain," Sherry said Wednesday morning as we sat on the floor, leaning on the wall.

"What do you mean?"

"I don't know. He's just not acting right lately. He's moping once second then smiling the next. He's...fickle. Cain is never fickle."

"He's fine. He's just upset about Lillian and Mitchell. He mentioned her on the run."

"How do you know about them? I didn't say anything to you," she asked, looking at me mysteriously.

"Well, I may have caught a glimpse of Mitchell's mind here and there, by accident."

She gasped.

"Merrick!"

"Hey, I'm not perfect. It's hard to break old habits sometimes. I only saw a glimpse but it was enough," I said and smiled, looking at her sideways.

"Merrick! I can't believe you." She smacked my arm playfully. "Shameful, after you've told them so many times to stay out of *your* head." She paused and I waited, knowing what was coming. "So...what *did* you see?" she asked and bit her lip.

I laughed, hard. She was so cute and predictable. "Just a kiss," I said through a yawn.

"Aww, Lillian. I'm so happy for her."

"Me, too. Now. Enough about other Keeper's love lives. I'm so tired from working the garden I can barely think. Tell me about your day. What did you and Lily bug do?" I asked with my eyes closed as I put my arm around her and pulled her into my side.

"Well, not much to tell if I can't talk about that. Lillian and I chatted forever about it the past few days. She feels like she's betraying Michael."

"I'm sure Michael would want her to move on and be happy."

"That's what I said."

"Well, aren't you smart," I said and touched the end of her nose with my finger.

"Yeah." She grinned.

"And Lily?"

"Lily took her nap and did her schoolwork with Marissa. She's really loving it and doing so well. Then she did her lessons with Miguel and Kay later on. She ate two huge bowls of macaroni and cheese. I had to pull her from the trough, like somebody else I know," she said grinning and poked my ribs.

Marissa and Lana had taken teacher roles and schooled Lily, Calvin and Franklin for a few hours during the day.

"Hey, it's hard work taking care of you girls. I need my strength. It wouldn't be a problem if you weren't such a good cook."

"Hmmm...you know, it-"

I didn't get to find out what 'it' was because I heard a crash. A very large crash and breaking glass clinking on the tile floor with a scream that followed.

"Stay put," I told Sherry firmly as I got up.

I and many other Keepers blurred into the hallway where the commotion was coming from.

Polly was standing in the bathroom, her arm still extended towards Susan. The vanity mirror above the sink was shattered. Shards of dingy, reflective glass were all over the tile floor around Susan's feet and the sink bowl. A hard plastic black case lay on the floor as well. It was, I suspected, the culprit of being the thrown object.

Piper was standing in the hall as well, observing, nothing more. Susan was yelling and now that all was quiet, we could hear what she was saying.

"You're crazy! Crazy! Get out of here!" Susan screeched and backed away from Polly until her back hit the wall by the sink.

"*You're* crazy!" Polly shouted. "You think you can just use my razor without asking?"

"Polly, why would I take your razor? I have my own. You're crazy! That's just a little too unsanitary for my taste anyway. Now if you'll excuse me, young lady, I'm trying to shower. Leave."

"I'm not going anywhere until you give me my razor, hag."

"I will do no such thing. This is mine. Now get out!"

"Ladies," Jeff broke in harshly. "What in the worlds is going on here?"

They both started yelling at the same time.

"She stole my-"

"She threw it at me-"

"Why would I lie-"

"It's so gross-"

"She just barged in-"

"Ok! Ok! Ok! Enough!" Jeff yelled and threw up his hands to draw attention. "I think we can-"

"Now hold on," someone interrupted Jeff.

Piper.

"We can't have people just taking things and it being alright to do so," she continued.

"I never said it was Piper," Jeff retorted and motioned for them to follow him. "Let's get away from all this glass."

Piper, Polly, Susan, him and I went to the kitchen.

"Now. It's not ok to take things that aren't yours but it's also not ok to throw things at other people, let alone break things," Jeff explained, looking between the two.

Everyone still looked to Jeff to be whatever form of mediator/leader/instigator/level-headed one that we needed him for at the time being. Right then, it seemed to be all four.

"If she hadn't stolen the razor, I wouldn't have thrown the makeup case," Polly insisted.

"Even if I had stolen it, it still doesn't warrant breaking a mirror just by my head, let alone throwing things at me," Susan claimed.

"That sounds like an admission to me," Polly said crossing her arms in triumphant to which Susan gasped, but Jeff cut them both off before they could continue.

"Alright! No more, ladies. We haven't had any trouble or drama between the members of the group until you two and I'm not about to have it now."

"That's not true," Piper chimed almost happily. "From what I hear, Sherry had caused her own set of problems."

"Piper, I'm gonna stop you right there," Jeff said holding up his hand. "Don't. Sherry has been through plenty and none of it was her fault."

"Well, I'd say leading men on and then complaining when they act on it is causing plenty-"

I snapped.

"Don't you say another word about Sherry!" I yelled and Jeff grabbed my arm.

I realized I had taken a step towards her though I wasn't sure what I planned to do.

"Merrick. My goodness, so defensive," she said and even smiled smugly.

"You don't know what you're talking about," I growled.

"Don't I? She flirted with that poor man, then he kissed her and she cries rape? What more is there to know? Like I said, she's causing problems that weren't necessary."

"Enough, Piper!" Jeff yelled.

"It's still true, Merrick. Nothing has changed. She'll never be good for you. Humans and our kind don't mix that way. You deserve better than this mundane life that's been chosen for you by that little-."

"Get over it, Piper. There will never be anything different for me. I chose my own fate and am plenty happy with the results. It's none of your business, end of discussion," I said with as much conviction I could throw out.

I didn't want to embarrass her. Even after all she'd said I still didn't want to call her out for her interest in me in front of everyone but that was what was next on my tongue if she didn't shut up. Plus, she had to know that she was referring to Jeff as well. Marissa was still human even though she was a Muse.

"I dare say this is far from the end, Merrick, if I have anything to say about it," Piper said flipping her hair sideways as she cocked her head in flippancy.

Before I could retaliate I saw something beyond Piper's shoulder in the doorway to the kitchen.

Sherry.

She heard everything and stood there, leaning against the doorframe with her arms crossed looking pensive. Pensive and hurt.

"We are done here," I said, enunciating each word and pulling my arm free from Jeff.

"We'll see," Piper countered and I heard Jeff start in on her behind me.

"Piper, you have no idea what you're talking about. Just be quiet. I won't have all this hostility. Polly, you broke the mirror, I suggest you go clean the mess," he continued but I blocked him out.

"Sherry-"

"It's ok, Merrick. There's no law that says everyone has to like me, right?" Sherry said and smiled weakly but I could see how much she hated it.

"Come on." I grabbed her hand and began to pull her with me. "Don't worry about her. She's just..."

"Jealous? I can tell. I have to say, I've never seen such a, uh...unlikable Keeper before."

"Me either. I remember thinking that about her before. She's definitely one of a kind. And not in a good way."

"How can she act like that? I thought you were all made to be civil and easy going."

"Free will, honey. We can choose just like you can. She would never have had to deal with rejection or adversity had we not come here. This is where we are...tested, so to speak. This is where we'll see how we choose to react to situations. For whatever reason, even from the beginning, she chose to act..." I trailed off searching for a word that wouldn't be offensive to Sherry's ears.

"Crazy?" she suggested and smiled up at me.

"That's a good one."

"I feel sorry for her," she said softly and I rolled my eyes at her but couldn't help smiling too.

Sherry always reacted this way, always forgiving, always worrisome, faithful and understanding. It wouldn't be so bad if it didn't always happen that Sherry was the one that had to be so self sacrificing.

"Let's go take a nap and I'll make you forget all about it," I suggested in a low voice and pulled her to me, nipping her chin which she loved.

"I already have," she said laughing. "You are really good at that, you know, making me feel better, no matter what?"

"Well, good then. In that case, you want to see what Danny and Celeste are up to? I need to speak with him about some things anyway."

"Sure. Marissa already came and got Lily for her classes so, we're free."

Danny?

"In the second room!" Danny called out his location in response to me asking him in his mind.

Cain and Lillian, who were sitting facing each other on the couch, looked up curiously at the sudden burst of unprovoked information, but returned to their conversation and inched closer as Lillian smiled and laughed at whatever Cain was saying.

Before we went further I turned back to Piper and saw that yes, she was watching with a decided determination in her set jaw, so I decided she needed a little convincing. I would protect Sherry from anyone, even another Keeper, even from the petty thoughts of a Keeper trapped in a body she couldn't control the chemical emotions for.

I looked back down at Sherry and smiled at her, then tipped her head back bringing my mouth to hers, wrapping my arms around her. I closed my eyes, but could feel Piper's hateful gaze on us.

With every passing second Sherry was getting more breathless; clinging, with my shirt bunched in her fist like she always did. I heard her whimper so I decided I best end it. I released her and she gazed at me and bit her lip in cute glazed-over confusion and passion. But then she smiled up at me and I couldn't help but feel loved and wanted, the best thing in the universe. It was still a little crazy that all this was mine.

I wrapped my arm around her shoulder and pulled her to me to kiss her forehead as we walked towards Danny. Her petite cool arm around my waist the only thing keeping me on the ground.

This Life Is More Than Just A Read Through
Chapter 11 - Sherry

We found Danny and Celeste in the second room, where Danny said they were. The second room, as we called it, was the old bedroom of Phillip; the man who originally let us stay here and kept this huge room all to himself though we were all packed in the rest of them like sardines. Not to mention, he was the one who almost raped me, had Jeff not come to my rescue.

"Hey, sis, what's up? Are you ok? You look a little, I don't know, red?"

Merrick and I looked at each other and laughed a little, smiling knowingly.

"It's nothing. What are you guys doing in here?"

They were both sitting on the little hideous pink loveseat on the wall. Celeste's legs were in Danny's lap. Normally they sat in the commons room in the corner on the floor.

"Oh, nothing," Celeste answered, looking at the ends of a few strands of hair and grimacing. "It's just getting so crowded in there. Dang it! Look at my hair! Split ends everywhere."

"Well, it's a good thing that it's so crowded, Celeste," Danny said, trying to hide a smile at Celeste's obvious misfortune.

"I know, I know," she said letting the hair go and looking back up to him. "It's just crowded that's all. I'm glad they're here, though. Don't get me wrong."

We weren't the only ones in the second room, but we were spread out enough to not be on top of each other. We had taken down most of Phillips decorations, if you want to call them that. His posters of questionable taste were burned or buried along with the other trash. The lamps, stereo and fan stayed.

The stereo was playing a CD and I could hear some song quietly. Red Hot Chili Peppers. Yeah, that sounded about right for Phillip's collection. There was a stack of no less than two hundred CDs on display on the wall shelf. It was there the whole time and we never knew.

I saw Danny mouthing the words to "Can't Stop". 'Knocked out but boy you better come to. Don't die you know the truth as some do. Go write your message on the pavement, burn so bright I wonder what the wave meant. White heat is screaming in the jungle.'

"Well, I wanted to come see you, ask you how the lessons are going. Kay's not working you too much is she?" Merrick asked.

We both sat down on the floor in front of them. Kay had been one of the Keepers giving lessons or classes on how to control the new Specials gifts. They practiced their gifts on each other, sometimes for hours at a time, trying to learn to control them at will and in complete focus.

"Nah, she's great. It's Miguel that's the freaking Nazi!" Danny said and laughed. "He's a slave driver, for sure. He's been showing us how to use our gifts while training with the Karate and self defense lessons. At the same time. It makes me feel all Chuck Norris inside."

"Yeah, it's awesome," chimed Celeste, just as animated as Danny had been, talking with her hands. "Like Danny will tell someone to duck in their mind at the same time that he knees them in the face or...like, Calvin can torch someone while Danny tells them to freeze or, Cain can blast them with his sonic boom hand thingy and then while they're down, we all run over and stomp them. It's awesome. The old stock room is totally trashed now."

"Well, that sounds interesting," Merrick said looking amused. "So everything's going good then? I know it's fun, but you are making progress, right? Learning something?"

"Oh, yeah," Danny assured. "I'm not saying I want to invite the Lighters to a tea party, but...if we ran into one, I think we could probably take them."

"Danny," I chided, "don't get cocky."

"I'm not. I meant all of us, not me by myself. I'm not that dumb. But you know what, you should see Lily."

"Yeah, she's so stinking cute," Celeste sang.

"I came to watch a few times when I had a minute. Why do you guys have to practice right before dinner, huh? I'm always in the kitchen and miss everything," I said and felt a pang of guilt.

Everyone had their job and that was mine. Someone had to take over for Mrs. Trudy.

"I know, little sister," Danny sympathized as he always joked with me that way. I'm his big sister, but by looking at how short I was, you'd never tell it. 'Little sister' had always been his endearment for me. "It sucks, but it's the only time when everyone is together and all the other stuff is done. Plus, we get to eat right after instead of raiding the kitchen when we get done for snacks. I am always famished when we get done," he said and then remembered what we were talking about and sat up straighter. "But Lily is so focused. Miguel works really good with her, knows exactly what to say to get her riled up. So far, the only thing she can do is make the person she touches choke, but hey, that's better than nothing. She did it to me once in practice. It really does feels like you're choking. It was wicked."

"Is it safe? To do that I mean. Calvin's gift isn't some minor thing, it's serious. What if you hurt each other practicing, by accident?" I asked, picturing Danny choking and wondering if they had panicked or not.

"It's ok," Merrick said, sensing my anxiety. He pulled me closer to him and laced our fingers. "Calvin only practices after everyone else has left the room. Miguel is there and he's trained as an EMT. Plus, they *have* to practice so they know how to control it. They are being very careful, even with Lily. Miguel told me that he only let's her practice on him now, just in case. It's alright."

"I'm not just talking about Calvin and Lily though," I said softly. "I mean, like Celeste, no offense, but your gift isn't proactive is it? It's a means for missions and spying and definitely an asset but how do you practice with the others? Are you always the target instead?"

"Don't be silly, Sherry. I am the target sometimes, but I practice my gift too. See, I can only see a person by focusing on them so it's not as cool a gift as I'd like, but I can alert the others to danger and things like that while they are fighting. I'm more of a scout. I'd be the lead on a mission so, it's ok. It's fun anyway. We all have our purpose."

I sat in stunned puddle of her profoundness and cool demeanor. I thought for sure she'd get all up in a tizzy with me about the 'your gift isn't proactive' thing.

"Well, then, I just don't want to see anyone get hurt, that's all, least of all you, Calvin or Lily."

"I know, but believe me, Lily can take care of herself. She's got the deadly choke fingers and that total blond babe thing going for her, plus the rosy cheeks." She pinched her cheeks to demonstrate. "If they got past us and she was somehow compromised, just when they thought they had her she'd make them choke on their own stupidity and leave them lying on the ground like the heap-of-a-loser they were. She's going to be blonde *frigging* awesome someday."

"Uh, baby? You're blonde," Danny said to Celeste, thoroughly enjoying the conversation.

We all loved to get Celeste riled up. It was quite entertaining.

"Yeah, but not *that* kind of blond. She's in a whole other class of blond. Babe blonde," she spouted while her hands were animated and her pointer finger wild as she explained.

I rolled my eyes as Danny laughed out loud at her logic.

"Please don't refer to her as a 'babe' just yet, ok? She's four," I said and felt Merrick chuckling next to me.

"Hey, a babe's a babe. She's gonna be a heartbreaker. My miniscule ability to fool with the opposite sex will be nothing compared to that girl," Celeste said it like it was the truth, she actually believed this stuff.

"Ok," Merrick butted in, trying to stifle his laughter, "well, I'm glad everything is working out. Speaking of babes. Sherry," he chided, "Miguel said you've missed the last three lessons."

"I have. Katie's been sick this week and Kay is busy with the lessons and sweet Maggie tries to help in the kitchen but doesn't get very far before she's breathing hard. There's not a lot of people left to do the cooking."

"Well, Lillian's here now. You can alternate or something. Everyone needs to take their turn with chores and get in their training and lessons," Merrick suggested and gave me a firm look.

"Yeah," Danny said as he got up to change the CD, "and also the rest of the new ones aren't doing much of anything either. I don't think any chores have been assigned to them yet. What about Polly and Piper?"

"No, thanks. I'd rather slave alone than be put to that punishment," I spouted quickly.

"Oh, yeah. Forgot about you and Polly's little tiff," Danny said as he sat back down.

Now, Ok Go's 'Here It Goes Again' played behind us.

"Yeah. That," I said and cleared my throat uncomfortably looking at Merrick. He smiled at me and quirked his mouth in a half smile - half sympathetic look. "I just wanted everyone to get settled in and comfortable first before I started dishing out rules and jobs. You know?" I sighed. "I'll get Lillian and Susan to help in the kitchen with the cooking. Polly and Piper can be...dish duty I guess, though I'm not sure how many dishes we'd have left if they helped."

"Why don't you let me handle them," Merrick suggested thankfully. "Piper can help Cain with the new garden and store trip stuff and Polly can be on...uh, cleaning duty?"

"Ha! Like that'll go over!"

"I can tell her she's in charge of it on Mondays and Wednesdays."

"But...our cleaning days are Tuesdays and Thursdays."

"I know, but this way she'll be out of everyone's hair. At least the place will be really clean," he said and smiled.

"You're a genius sometimes, you know that," I said and his face lit with amusement.

"Yeah," Celeste said, looking at her nails. "She'll definitely do it if she thinks she's in charge. She's a little nuts."

"A little?" I said and we all laughed. "Ok. Thank you, Merrick. I'll let Lillian and Susan know and I'll be at practice, I promise."

"Good, I'll tell Miguel and I'll join you. I haven't had my butt kicked in a while." He grinned at me and I glared at him for making fun of me. "What are we having for dinner tonight?" A subject change no doubt.

"Rice, baby! Rice and beans and more rice and beans," I answered with fake enthusiasm.

"Yuck," Danny answered while Celeste chimed, "Gross" at the same time.

"Welcome to the apocalypse you two," Merrick said and stood up. He reached his hand to me to help me up as well. "Who has lunch duty today?"

"Uh, Laura and Margo. Why?"

"Come on, wife. There's a little matter we need to discuss."

"Is there?" I stopped in my tracks, thought real hard, trying to think if I'd be in trouble for something.

"Yes. I heard Calvin's birthday is in eight days. Ryan said he'd like to do something for it."

"That's a great idea!" Celeste said and turned to place her feet on the floor.

"Well, we can try. It won't be much of a birthday I'm afraid," I said feeling glum about even attempting to pull off something like that.

It must have stunk to be turning twelve in an underground bunker. Also we had realized earlier that we had no idea when Lily's birthday was but already talked about it and figured she was probably four by now. Maybe we should make up a day for her and celebrate then.

"Calvin won't care. We'll all make a fuss over him and he'll love it," Merrick said, and he was right.

I knew he was. Calvin wasn't shallow.

"You're right. That sounds good. I'll see if we still have the stuff to make a cake or cookies or something."

"Good, it's settled. I'll let everyone else know. The ones who want to participate can. Lana will be pleased, I think."

"Yeah, she will. I'll get her to help me. I want her to feel included in it too, you know."

Merrick looked down at me and grabbed my face between his big warm hands. He smiled.

"My sweet Sherry, always thinking about everybody else. Your sister is a real saint, you know that, Danny?" he said, but never took his eyes off of me.

"Uh, yeah, I do. Come on, Celeste. We're heading outta this love fest," Danny said and Celeste giggled as he grabbed her hand and towed her away.

"That's one way to get rid of him," Merrick said laughing and then brushed his lips against mine before taking them completely.

When he finally stopped the slow delicious torture that was the kiss I spoke to him again.

"Did I ever tell you how much I love it when you call me 'wife'?"

"Nope, but I knew you would." He leaned closer and spoke in a loud whisper, like it was a secret. "I know everything there is to know about you."

And to prove his point he nipped that little spot behind my ear that I love, making me shiver and giggle.

"I see. So you know just how to torture me," I murmured.

"So, wife," he said smirking, "you're ok with Piper and all that mess, right? You know there's nothing to worry about with her. She's just bitter about being here and she'll get over it."

"No, I'm not worried about her. After all, I got you in the end, didn't I?"

"Nuhuh, I got you," he whispered in my ear.

And then he kissed me again.

Big Bold Black Letters
Chapter 12 - Cain

"So, is that not the best PB& J you've ever had, or what?" I asked Lillian as we leaned on the kitchen counter, biding our time until tonight. We'd just come from the garden and I decided to make us a snack.

"It was. Thank you." She finished her last bite and licked her finger. "I didn't think you could really make peanut butter and jelly better, but you sure proved me wrong."

"Are you cracking on me?" I asked and raised an eyebrow at her in jest.

"No way, I wouldn't do that."

"Are you sure? Because it sounds like you're cracking on me."

She stifled a giggle with her hand. "Ok, maybe a little bit, but it was a pretty darn good sandwich."

"Ha ha." I bumped her shoulder with mine. "So, are you ready for tonight?"

"Yes. Eighty six percent sure that I'm ready."

"Only eighty six? Not maybe say...ninety two?"

She laughed again and touched my arm across the kitchen island, making me smile even wider. It felt like forever since I'd genuinely smiled wide and true because I was actually happy about something and not just pretending. But I'd been doing that a lot this week with Lillian.

We'd spent every day together in the garden and lots of time sitting and talking together inside, not always by ourselves, but still.

"Ok, maybe ninety two. I guess I need to go get a shower. Thanks for letting me help and for the sandwich. I haven't had enough fun lately."

"Well, don't worry, tonight will be great."

"You're not worried at all?"

"Me? Nope. Everything will be fine."

"Ok, see you in a bit."

"Can't wait."

And she walked away backwards before turning, tucking her hair behind her

197

ear and smiling.

In a few minutes, Lillian and I would be walking out the door for town. I was not really looking forward to it. I was, but I was just as *not* looking forward to it, too. I told Lillian it was fine earlier, but I got to thinking. I mean, I had her to worry about instead of just myself. What if something happened? What if I blew my cover at the diner? What if Lillian freaked? There were a million *what ifs*, but we needed this. We needed the information.

And *I* needed to freaking get out and have some fun.

This whole week I worked in the garden or at the diner, trying to keep busy and stay away from Sherry as much as possible. I'd barely seen a single soul all week except Lillian. We talked a lot. She told me about how much trouble they'd had trying to find a place to stay and some about her husband. I felt pretty good about her. She seemed to be pretty happy to see me most days.

But then, Miguel danced with her one night as Paul had cranked up the record player and she seemed pretty happy then too.

He was into her, I could tell. She laughed and smiled, but she did with me too. I didn't know what to think. She seemed mostly oblivious to us all and our affections. She was just genuinely sweet.

And now, Mitchell was waiting at the stairs with me. Waiting *for Lillian*. Ugh. I could see it all over his smug Keeper face. Merrick, Jeff and Simon were here with me as well, Merrick spouting pointers but I couldn't seem to focus tonight. I was trying but was too worked up, too edgy.

Then we saw Sherry, then Celeste, then Lillian.

Holy canoly.

Lillian was a vision in jeans and a blue top that matched her eyes. We knew the girls were getting her ready as she had to look nice and look like she dressed up to go out. They had been scrounging for nice clothes and makeup and such to see what they could put together. And boy, did they put something together. She was hot.

"Wow." I heard Mitchell muttered and I wanted to punch him for stealing my line.

"Yeah, wow," I said thinking how ordinary I looked in jeans and a black sweater.

Lame.

"Thanks. Celeste had something I could wear so..."

"She does look amazing," Celeste said, boasting her own skills.

"Well, are you ready? Let's get this thing on the road," I asked, holding out my hand to her.

I was glad they left her hair down with big curls at the ends. I loved long hair, especially the hair I helped to save, down and swinging when they turned their heads, you know. I especially loved it down when girls danced, which I planned to do tonight. For research purposes, of course.

"Yes, let's. Do we have everything?" she said and took my hand and I realized she was shaking a little. "There's nothing else we should remember?" she said, looking around to everyone standing around us.

"Just don't talk too long to any one person. It would give you a better chance to say too much or the wrong thing if you did. Also, don't think about the bunker remember? Don't think about us," Jeff advised.

"And don't leave each other's side. That way, you won't have to worry about what the other has said to someone else. Plus, it's just safer to stay together." Merrick turned to look at me. "Don't let anyone else dance with her if you can help it. Even if she goes to the bathroom, Cain, walk her to the door. Got it?" Merrick stared at me for confirmation.

"Got it," I said, I realized I was still holding Lillian's shaking hand so I squeezed it to soothe her.

I had to fight a smile when she squeezed back.

"And don't leave too early. You have to seem like you want to be there. Drink, dance, have fun, do whatever everyone else is doing, but remember to look around and listen while you're doing it," Simon, my Keeper, chimed in. "And be cautious, Cain. Stay safe."

"No problem."

"And if they have flyers or material, make sure you take some," Mitchell said and I nodded to him. Then he stepped closer to Lillian and framed her pale face with his tan hands, the contrast shocking. "Please, be careful," he said softly and I thought he might kiss her, right there in front of all of us, but he reluctantly released her and stepped back.

"We will. I promise," Lillian said and I liked how she said 'we'.

I started to tug her towards the stairs and shouted down to them as we walked out.

"We'll be back by 2:00 a.m. Have fun, kids."

"Be careful, Cain," Sherry yelled, and I couldn't stop myself.

I turned to smile at her as I shut the trap door behind me.

I put Lillian in the passenger seat of my truck, climbed in the driver side and clicked my seat belt. The radio blared when I cranked the truck and I fumbled to turn it down quickly. It was my Incubus CD blaring 'Anna Molly'.

"Sorry," I muttered.

"It's ok, I like Incubus."

"Really?" I said, surprised that she knew who they were. "How old are you?"

"Twenty one."

This shocked me a little.

"Really?"

"Yeah. Why so shocked?" she asked but looked amused.

"Uh, you just seem older, I guess. And you were married so, I just thought you were...older," I tried to explain as I pulled out onto the highway.

"I got married young. I'm a homemaker and somewhat of a homebody, too. I never was interested in the party scene. Tonight, you'll have to coax me into remembering this is supposed to be dancing and looking like we're having fun."

"We will have fun, no coaxing or intervention needed. I promise."

"Huh," she said and covered his lips with her fingertips to stifle a laugh, "you're sure about this?"

"Yes. Why?" I kept glancing at her sideways as I drove.

"I just don't know you that well and you don't know me. What if I hated dancing? What if I hated music? What would you do with me then?"

If my ears weren't deceiving me...it sounded like she was flirting with me. "Let me worry about that. I promise you'll have fun, no matter what. I'll make it my mission, you know, besides our other mission."

She laughed out loud which made me smile and commit the bouncy sound to memory.

"Ok. I place myself in your capable hands."

Hell, she was killing me.

I was pleasantly surprised to feel that inkling of ache I experienced whenever I left the bunker - left Sherry - slowly drift to a dull pound.

Once we arrived, I parked and went to her side of the truck. I could hear the thump of the bass from the club but couldn't make out the song. She was applying lip gloss in the mirror when I opened the door.

"Thanks," she said and took the hand I offered her to help her out of the truck, "I haven't had to get dressed up to go somewhere in a very long time. I feel kind of strange."

"Well, you look awesome." I winced at my words. "I mean, you look very pretty."

"Thanks," she said shyly and tucked hair behind her ear.

"So...rule number one of a night on the town. Smile, don't stop smiling."

"Smile. Got it," she said smiling and I was happy she was playing along.

"Rule number two, we listen to the Keeper's advice. No dancing with anyone but me and you have to dance every time I ask you to. I hope you're wearing good shoes."

She chuckled and scoffed, "I don't remember them saying I had to dance every time you commanded it."

"Oh, I guess you just weren't paying attention," I jested. "Rule number three. If you're not having fun, tell me and I'll fix it."

"How?"

"I'll think of something. I'm pretty crafty."

She grinned and nodded her head. "Ok. Those rules sound reasonable enough. Do I get any rules of my own?"

"Sure."

"First. If *you're* not having fun, tell me and I'll..." She shrugged. "I'm not sure, but I'll try my best."

"Ok," I said with a grin.

"Second, I don't care if you drink, but please don't get drunk," she said and looked like she thought I was gonna bite her head off.

"I never do. Not my style anymore. Anything else?"

"Third, don't do anything crazy, like dance on the bar and make me have to hurt you in front of everyone."

I laughed out loud. "I'd almost like to see you try."

She laughed too and pushed my arm playfully. "Oh! Don't test me, Cain! I am vicious when it comes to public humiliation."

"Ok, ok. I promise no table dances. Is there more?"

"Last..." She took a deep breath. "Don't think about Sherry," she said softly. I felt all my breath leave me. "What?" I breathed.

"You don't think about Sherry and I won't think about Mitchell or Michael."

I tried to gauge my tone and words carefully. "Why do you think I'd think about Sherry?"

"I've seen the way you look at her and the way you try not to. If I'm wrong I'm sorry, but I don't think I am."

"You're not," I admitted quietly.

There was no point in lying when she flat called me out on it. She stopped me with a hand on my arm.

"I'm not judging you, Cain. I just want to have fun tonight, completely let go, with no obligations, guilt or awkwardness. Even though I don't know you that well, I've had a lot of fun with you this week. Let's just pretend, that we're really good friends who've done this tons of times together. I know I'm being extremely forward but... I need this night out so bad." She sounded on the verge of tears. "I need to not have to think for just a little while. I can't take living like we have been, so scared all the time and looking over my shoulder. Please, Cain. Let's both just forget our problems and have fun, for the one night we have to just be normal again." She paused and looked embarrassed. "I'm sorry, I'm not usually so-"

What could I say? I felt the same way.

"Yes," I interrupted her, "you're right, I need this, too. I promised you a good time and I meant it. Ready to get to it, friend?" I offered her my hand.

She smiled gratefully and took it.

"Absolutely."

We finished the distance through the parking lot, which was packed, and then we reached the doorman.

"Marks," was all he said and I turned to show him behind my ears, which he smeared and rubbed with his thumb to make sure it wasn't covered up. Then Lillian lifted her hair and he did the same to her. "Ok. Cover is ten for both."

I paid him then held the door open as Lillian entered the club.

A waft of smoke and the smell of beer and sweaty dance floor bombarded us as I took the lead and pulled her behind me with her soft, warm, long fingers in mine. I have a serious thing with hands. I'm a hand and hair man.

"Do you want a beer or something?" I asked when we stopped at the bar and I pulled her close to speak into her ear.

The music was so loud, I doubted she could hear me, but she answered me.

"Um, whatever you're having."

I heard the tone. I dated enough in my day to know it. "You've never have a beer before have you?" I asked.

"No," she admitted and started to look embarrassed. Then she perked up and smiled brightly at me. "I mean, yes. Lots of times, Cain, you know this. You know everything about me! Now get me my usual and stop playing around. I'm ready to dance!" she yelled and at first I was baffled, then I remembered our agreement in the parking lot.

The agreement about pretending to be old, good friends who partied together often and were completely cool with each other and ready to have fun.

"I was just making sure you were paying attention," I said winking at her and then tapped the bar to call the bartender. "Two lime and tonics, please."

"Coming up." He made them with astonishing quickness and pushed them forward on the bar for me to catch them. "That'll be six dollars. No tab tonight."

"That's fine, here you go." I handed him a ten.

"No beer?" Lillian asked when I turned back around.

"Not for me, not anymore," I answered.

We grabbed our drinks and sliced through the masses to a less crowded part in a corner. She followed me and I was surprised we made it without spilling drink all over us.

"So, how you do like this place? Not as hopping as our usual spot is it?" I asked, playing along with the game.

"No, but it'll do. This is non-alcoholic?" I nodded and she took a small sip of her drink, letting the rim barely touch her lips. "Ugh! I mean, mmmm."

I had to laugh at her. She was pretty cute and we practically had out heads together to be able to hear over the noise.

"You can't sip it daintily my adorable Lillian. Tonic has to be swigged."

"Oh?" She swigged. I mean swigged big time. "Oh! It does make it better! You were right!" She took another gulp and then set it down on the railing overlooking the crowd in the pit, licking her lips. "So what else is on the agenda for tonight, handsome?"

"There isn't one, gorgeous. We'll wing it like we always do."

"Sounds good to me," she said smiling and looked up at me for a moment too long to be considered casual. "Thanks, Cain."

"You're welcome. Now, finish your drink while we look around a little and then you are mine...on the dance floor."

"Yay!" She clapped rapidly and excitedly. "I can't wait. But sugar lips, no Macarena this time." She lifted her hands as if to halt my protest. "I know you love it but I just can't stomach it another night."

"Dang, baby! Come on! The Macarena is my thing!"

"I know! I know! I'm sorry. Next time, I promise." She laughed and patted my arm.

"Oh, alright. No Macarena but I get to choose the last dance so you better be nice to me."

She smiled and lifted her drink to her lips to sip but then remembered my advice and took another big swig. I loved watching her. She was bright and happy looking and really looked like she could be truly happy just about anywhere; easy going and easy to please. The fact that she was devastatingly gorgeous and didn't know it, helped some, too.

But I peeled my eyes from her and looked around like I was supposed to. There were posters, t-shirts and propaganda vendors lining the walls with the new Taker's face on them, along with some Anti-Keeper stuff as well. I didn't dwell on that because it wasn't important.

I looked towards the stage and saw what I could only assume was the instigators of this shindig. A huddled group of enforcers and city folks massed together and looked to be getting ready for the speech.

There was a huge banner above the stage in big bold back letters that said "What would this world be without its leadership? Welcome our new savior, Malachi!" and cheesy balloons everywhere.

I could think of quite a few things the world would be without their leadership, but I kept them to myself. Nothing seemed to be out of the ordinary. No Lighters were present yet that I saw except two who were guarding the back stage door. There were no enforcers, except those by the stage, unless they were out of uniform.

I turned back to Lillian to find her looking around as well. Her glass was empty. Then one of the many promoters stopped in front of us. "Having a good time?" he asked.

"We are, thank you," I said politely.

"You know who to thank for all this is our savior, Malachi, who unfortunately won't be here tonight but please stay for the rally and speech, then make sure to take some promotional items on your way out. We have t-shirt, cups, posters. Even baby bibs."

"Wow, a plethora of goodies. Thank you, we'll be sure to do that."

He nodded to me, then gave Lillian the once over and smiled a little too long before he moved on to the next suckers down the line from us. I turned to her, feeling the need to stake a claim to her or something, though I knew that was ludicrous.

"What do you say, hotness? Ready to boogie?"

"Yep." She hiccupped and covered her mouth giggling. "Oh! Sorry." She smiled bashfully. "Yes, I'm ready. Let's boogie, as you say."

To my astonishment, she actually towed me out to the dance floor with our interlaced hands over her head. Once we hit a clear spot she turned around and stopped dead in front of me. She looked unsure. She leaned forward and whispered as loud as she could in my ear.

"I've never really danced before, except playing around. I want to, but could you show me?"

I answered by taking her arms and putting them around my neck, my hands on her hips. I started swaying us swiftly with the upbeat music.

The song was 'Kids' by MGMT.

She seemed to like it and was receptive to me leading her. One of her hands even went up into my barely there hair once when we were jostled by another dancer and she turned to apologize to them. I could have died right then and been a happy man. I loved it when girls rubbed my head.

I followed her, as I had been instructed to do - though I would have anyway - to the bathroom and stood outside the door. A couple of other completely wasted girls came out before Lillian. One of them pulled her friend to a stop in front of me by her arm. She was typical hot girl type; long jet black hair, tight, red v-neck tank with a generous show of cleavage - no doubt paid for by Daddy's money - and a short skirt leaving nothing to the imagination.

"Hey, there," she said.

"Hello, ladies."

"Waiting for someone?"

"'Fraid so."

"Aww. It's just not fair." She made huge pout lips. "I'm looking for someone to play with."

Back in the day, I would have jumped on that faster than you could say 'go'. Not that this girl was anything spectacular, but I had low standards. Pretty much any invitation was honored as acceptable but now, I was ashamed of the way I used to behave. When on leave from the Marines, and sometimes during my deployment, I was a bit of a skeeze when it came to women. I was a partier, a clubber, an anything where there were girls and beer, kind of guy. Drowning my sorrows from the loss of my mom, early in the year that I signed up, and the subsequent mental descent of my dad.

I hated that about myself. I hated that that was who I used to be, who I became to escape my problems. If the Lighters hadn't come and shaken everything up, I had no doubt I'd still be that person.

"Sorry, girls, I'm all taken," I answered her back and saw the familiar challenge in her glassy gaze.

"Are you sure," she asked and let her finger drift down my chest, "because I can be really persuasive," she said and tried for seductive, but she wobbled on her heels.

"Sorry, not gonna happen," I said as I removed her finger.

She hmmphed and was promptly carted away by her friend before she could embarrass herself even more, to which I was grateful. Lillian came out mere seconds after the girls left.

"I heard that, you know," she said, smirking.

"Did you?"

"Yep. I'm sorry if I'm ruining your game," she said and looked like she was trying not to laugh.

"No way, that's not possible. I'm always on my game. Besides, I don't go for girls like that anymore."

"What? Pretty girls?"

"She was not pretty. She was...fake. She could be pretty, but you shouldn't have to work so hard at it, I think."

"Aww, that poor girl probably spent hours putting on that garb just to have you turn her down."

"She's not my type. Just so you know, I'm one of those cliché guys that prefer blondes," I said, leaning in to whisper.

She smiled up at me, rolled her eyes playfully at my obvious line, and tucked her hair behind her ear. I took her hand and eagerly towed her back to the dance floor.

"So, how do you like this thing called dancing?" I asked after a couple songs.

To my dismay, they were now playing Katy Perry's 'California Gurls'.

"I love it! It's fun even if you hate the song!"

Ah, my dream girl.

"Yep. Told you you'd have fun with no intervention needed."

"You were right. Why I ever doubted you, sugar puss, I'll never know!" she said and laughed as I swung her around in a tight circle once, pulling her tighter to me.

"Sugar puss?" I quirked a brow at her.

"Yeah, sugar puss. You don't like it? How about sugar daddy? No, that one's no good. That will ruin your reputation and mine." I laughed but she kept going. "Hmm, how about sweetie pie? Is that good enough for your manliness to handle?"

"I like sweetie pie just fine. And you, you will be my lovely."

"I like it. It's sweet and true all at the same time," she joked.

I laughed and laughed at that woman. She had definitely come out of her shell and the tonic and smoke filled air weren't to blame. She was just happy to feel human again. I realized, so was I.

One Fine Day
Chapter 13 - Sherry

"Rice and beans," I said to answer the question for the fifth time today about what we were having for dinner. Again.

People were getting anxious about meals, since they knew things were about to get scarce. Our garden was coming along, but still, it was worthy of some worry I guess. It could definitely be a problem if the garden took a turn for the worse. I hated to think about it actually.

We finished with making supper, and most everyone was done with their lessons, so I started to hand out bowls – bowls of rice and beans which people were not enthused about. What else was I supposed to do? We couldn't eat like kings every night. We had to start eating more basic protein and filler meals. Even Merrick agreed with me that I was doing the right thing and of course Cain always went with whatever I said. It was his and my idea in the first place.

Merrick had Lily at the table with Calvin and Franklin. I took Margaret and Pap a bowl each since they were not getting around so good these days.

"Thank ya, Sherry, honey. You sure are a sweet girl to an old lady," she said.

"Oh, come on now. I don't see any old ladies here," I said and she smiled at me warmly.

"Well, well. Rice and beans. Hot dog!" Pap shouted and took the bowl from me eagerly.

At least someone around here was excited about supper.

I turned to return to the kitchen but before I made it, a piercing noise cut through the bunker making everyone jump and be still, stunned.

A doorbell.

I ran to the stairs out of instinct, but Jeff already blurred there and beat me to it.

"No, Sherry, stay here. We'll go check it out."

207

Merrick, Simon, Max and Mitchell were there too in a flash.

"Us five will go," he shouted louder. "Everyone else stay put, we'll be right back."

They picked up their pointy weapon of choice from the bin on their way out. Merrick passed me on his way up the stairs and touched my cheek.

Stay here, Sherry, I mean it.

"Of course. Since when do I disobey orders?"
He cocked a brow at me and smiled.

Love ya, honey.

"Love you. Be careful, promise?"

Always.

Then he was gone with the rest of them. Hmmm. Who was working the store? It wasn't Margo, it wasn't her turn. It was...Susan's. She had asked to alternate that job since she didn't like being in the bunker with Polly nor Piper.

We were still selling off our old inventory. We weren't allowed to purchase anything else to add to it and once it was gone, you were through. The new law enforcement had passed that decree along, sealing our fate. The need warehouses were so close to opening, and then our store cover story would really be over with.

But how did Susan know about the doorbell? I guess they taught her about that when they showed her how to run the store.

When I looked around though I see her, sitting with Frank by the record player. So, who was up there? I kept looking around and there was no Margo in sight. Huh. I guess she was in the store after all.

I began my worrisome pace.

I hated it. I hated it when they went out, especially for something like this. I decided my pace could be used to pick up dishes instead of doing nothing so I did that, too.

"What happened?" I turned to see Marissa, scowl firmly in place.

"The bell rang. They went to check it out."

"By 'they' you mean Merrick and Jeff. They always do this. Why can't they take turns running this place like everybody else? Someone else can take suicide duty for a while," she said flirting with bitterness.

"Everyone looks up to them. I know it's not fun for us, but these people need someone to look to when things happen or it'll be chaos around here. Besides.

Merrick has that look he does, and you know Jeff has that commanding voice. You just have to do what he says."

"Thanks, Sherry," she said and smiled sadly. "I know you don't like it anymore than I do, but thanks for trying to make me feel better anyway."

"Come on, pace with me."

She laughed as I laced our arms and we walked back and forth and around the furniture, picking up dishes and cups everyone had left in their haste of the doorbell incident.

"All we can do is wait for them to come back. Hey, who was in the store?"

"Margo. Margo's always in the store," she said and rolled her eyes.

"But I thought it was Susan or Paul's turn?" I ask.

"It was but Susan wasn't feeling well and Paul...I'm not sure what happened with that. I just know that Margo was working it today."

"She works too much."

"Yeah, but she likes it. She's still a little freaked out by all this stuff. You know she doesn't allow Celeste to talk to her about her gift? If you pay attention, she doesn't even like to be alone with the Keepers either. Heck, she refuses to be alone with me, though I guess she has good reason."

Marissa's face showed she thinking of the time she used her Muse's Wrath to compel me to find Katie, Paul and her sister's family. It led to excruciating pain and complete drainage of my energy for a few days.

"Oh, no, it can't be that bad. She loves Kay. They talk all the time."

"Yeah but that's only because Kay saved their life. Kay is Celeste's Keeper. The rest of them, she's never talked to. Think about it."

As I did think about it I realized she was right. Maybe she was scared of them.

"That's sad. Why does she feel the need to be that way?"

"I think she just doesn't like that others have more power. We could hurt people and no one could stop us, you know. Some people can't handle that they aren't in control of their own lives anymore."

"I can see that, but the Keepers are here to help and you all have risked your lives for us. The Keepers came all the way here from their perfect home to be right here with us during all this."

"Hey, you're preaching to the choir."

We rounded up all the dishes and piled them up in the kitchen sink. It wasn't our turn to do them and I was beat and worried so, for once, I left them where they were and went back to worrying over my husband.

They had been out there for almost half an hour and no one had come or gone from the bunker since. I wanted so badly to wrench open that door and peek out the back.

All of a sudden Kay shot up out of her chair looking stricken. She blurred to the trap door, followed by Ryan who came blurring out of the back room. As if he sensed us watching, he turned quickly before heading up.

"Don't come up, Sherry. Stay here."

Why does everyone always say that to me? Then he blurred up the stairs after grabbing a golf club out of the bin.

Then it hit me, what must be happening. The Keepers outside called to them in their minds and told them they needed help. Oh, no. Suddenly Kathy - Franks Keeper, Ann - Katie's Keeper, and Patrick - Laura's Keeper - came rushing to the stairs and stood there conversing silently. Then Patrick rushed up and outside while the other two, slammed the trap door shut, locked it, and stood as if to take guard.

I gasped as I realized with conviction that something horrible was going on outside. I ran up to question Kathy.

"What? What's happening?" Others had noticed the commotion and were crowding around, too.

"I need you all to go to the back room, the storage room, and lock the door. Now," Kathy tried to speak with authority but her voice cracked with emotion, giving her away.

Susan stepped forward. "Kathy, tell us."

"You don't need to know. It would just upset you."

"Don't say that, it just makes it worse! Tell us, please," I begged.

She sighed and then spoke. "It's bad outside. From what I can see in the others minds, the Lighters lured them into a trap. They are everywhere. I was told to stay and guard you. Now go to the stock-"

"No!" I yelled at the same time that Marissa yelled, "No way!"

"You'll be safest in the stock room. Now go."

"Like hell I will! That's our family out there!" Marissa yelled and went to shove Kathy out of the way.

"I was told to-" Kathy tried again and blocked the way.

"I don't care! We do things differently around here. I'm not your Special and you have no authority over me. Now move. Jeff is out there. I'm going to him and you can't stop me."

"Me, too. Danny!" I yelled knowing he'd want to help us. Merrick was out there. Our family was out there and Kathy was still hung up on the 'protect the Specials at all cost' bit?

He came running around from the kitchen and I quickly filled him in. Everyone else was there too and Miguel practically lifted Kathy and placed her to the side as we all grabbed whatever we could find as a weapon and ran up the stairs.

But of course, I didn't make it far. "Sherry, no," Miguel said and placed a hand on my shoulder to stop me as everyone else ran by us.

"Not you, too!" I yelled. I couldn't help it. "Miguel, that's my family out there!"

"I know, mine too, but that's also your family in there." He nodded towards the trap door. "Lily and the rest of them that can't come, they need you to stay here with them, not to mention the fact that you're still in a walking cast. I promise you, I'll bring them back."

I knew who he meant by 'them' and I knew he was right about someone needing to stay and I felt a ping of guilt for forgetting Lily was napping and Calvin and others were still oblivious to the drama from their back rooms.

I let out a frustrated groan and sighed as I fought back angry tears.

"Ok," I grabbed his shirt collar, "bring them back. And bring yourself back, too."

"I will. Go and lock the door."

I slinked my way quickly back down the trap door and stairs, slamming the door and bolting it home.

Then I walked backwards until my back hit the wall. I slid down until I sat on the floor, drawing up my legs and buried my face in my hands on my knees to wait; wait for someone to come to that door and knock, wanting back in.

Or wait for no one to knock and know that all my family was dead.

Love = Battlefield
Chapter 14 - Merrick

How it happened was a little too much coincidence, too much precision. I wondered if they caught on to us because of the flyer or maybe the extra traffic coming our way. Whatever the reason, they came and they brought an army.

A fleet of only, from what I counted, ten Lighters, but at least twenty Markers were hovering, plotting, waiting for us when we exited the store. Somehow, they tricked Margo into ringing the bell.

She was too freaked and locked herself in the bathroom of the store and wouldn't come out, not even for us.

We came out into the dark and saw them, lined up and ready, waiting for us. It wasn't until we'd gotten closer that we felt the presence of the Markers above us. It was eerily a copy of that day that we went to save Sherry and Cain from the caves. Except this time, there was no prize to collect. This was just a hunting party and they were looking to kill.

Once we got into the thick of it and realized we were in trouble, I called the other Keepers to come and some to stay and guard the others, but it was too late. The Markers descended on us and chaos came in a fury.

Amazingly, after twenty minutes of fighting we still hadn't lost anyone but we were wearing down and they were just getting started. I started to feel the burn of fear and dread. I wanted Sherry. I wanted her like nothing ever before, just to touch her one more time. Could I remember exactly what her hair felt like in between my fingers? I didn't know for sure. But I didn't want to die without knowing.

I didn't want to die period but here it came.

I staked a Marker who swooped and tried to claw my back, then turned and was punched in the jaw by a Lighter. A smug Lighter who took pleasure in sacrificing his Marker brother for his own diversion.

As he peeked in my mind I saw his as well, as we went round and round. I saw that they had no idea we were here. It was just chance that they came upon the store. When Margo was questioned she looked them in the eye and couldn't keep her thoughts blank. She tried, I saw that, but she couldn't and told them all about us in her mind.

That was why she was in the bathroom. She knew what she did and felt responsible. The Lighter who questioned her let her go ring the bell instead of kill her then because he knew it would alert us. Then he called the others and the rest of the story was playing out right in front of me.

Even if we died, as long as we killed them off, they wouldn't know the rest of them were here. They'd be safe.

No sooner I thought that, I heard a commotion behind us, yelling and screaming coming from the store. I turned in horror, thinking the Lighters had gotten into the bunker, but no.

It was them; the Specials and not specials coming to our rescue, weapons drawn and battle faces plastered. A couple, Celeste and someone else I couldn't see, positioned themselves with spotlights beamed our way by the door.

Immediately the rest of them started using their gifts and I could see what genius Miguel was thinking by letting them use their gifts and defense lessons at the same time.

The Lighter I was fighting was so lost in awe at the crowd of people running towards us that I stabbed him before he could recover.

I turned to see Danny.

No!

That was my first thought, my conscience screamed in agony for my charge, but then I remembered Danny wasn't little Danny anymore. Danny was a Special with gifts and he was using them. He would duck and concentrate and kick, all at the same time and the amazing thing was...he was bringing them down. He'd already brought down two Lighters in the minute he'd been out here, all by himself.

I searched for Sherry, knowing I'd see her stubborn behind out there too, because everyone we knew seemed to come out of that door, but no, I didn't see her and I was truly thankful.

We battled and continued to. It was really late and we raged on. Lighters went down with astonishing ease but Markers were worse for fighting, harder to get a handle on.

Miguel and I worked together on a Lighter, him coming at it from behind. I worked my stake through his neck, strikingly close to Miguel's face but he didn't seem to be worried. He trusted me. I turned to see the others working together, the Specials and Keepers fighting beside each other. Kay was keeping the Lighters away from the door and Celeste. Also, Racine was guarding Josh as they worked together, circling back to back.

Even though we all watched and looked out for each other now, looking after your own personal Special was still a hard habit to break. Shockingly hard. I even found myself glancing to and inching towards Danny every five seconds as if my feet moved on their own accord.

And when I turned back, I saw it. I saw it before it happened, as it was happening. I yelled to him, Mitchell, in his mind but it was too late.

The Marker grabbed Mitchell by his pant leg and lifted him in the air, him flailing upside down. I ran towards them, followed them as they flew. I tripped over something and when I looked down...

It was a body.

Aaron.

The man who punched me when they came that first night and thought I was hurting Sherry in this very back yard and at dark too. As much as it hurt to see him there I climbed back up and kept running to Mitchell, but as I looked up I saw how high they were...and then the Marker dropped him. A planned strategy.

There was no way he could survive. No way.

As I blurred I heard the sickening thud his body made as he crunched and slammed to the ground just as I made it, too late. His body visibly bounced on the hard dirt before settling still and lifeless.

I reached for him to check his body for a pulse and was not surprised when I found none. When I touched him his neck moved unnaturally to the side, twisting sickly, showing me that it was broken and there was no more life in his body. Ah, Mitchell. He would never have a human life. There would be no After for him either.

Mitchell was dead.

Uprising - A Collide Novel - Shelly Crane

We Got A Hot One
Chapter 15 - Lillian

"Ok, folks. It's time for 'Kissed or Dissed'. You have one minute," the DJ said over the loud speaker.

"What does that mean?" I asked Cain.

"Well, this club does this thing where when they give you the signal you have one minute to find someone to kiss. Whoever, when the minute is over, doesn't have someone has to get up on stage and sing."

"That sounds so juvenile."

"It is, but it's tradition," he joked. "Besides, don't worry. You have someone to kiss."

I gasped slightly involuntarily. "What?"

"Are you gonna sing? Cause I sure ain't."

"Ten seconds," the DJ yelled. "Judges, get ready to be on the lookout."

"Ok, ok, I'm not singing either. I just want you to know how stupid this is," I said even as he came closer.

"Stupid or not, if we want to stay and get what we need, we've gotta play along. Besides, lovely, we kiss drunk all the time anyway, right?"

I smiled at his willingness to play my game. "Right, sweetie-"

He cut me off as the DJ yelled time with his lips on mine. I wasn't sure of the rules of the game, if it was supposed to be a peck or if it was timed but Cain was not taking chances. Or maybe he was just enjoying himself.

His lips were warm and commanding and he kissed me long and hard and good; more deeply than Mitchell had and more skillfully than Michael ever had. His hands were on my waist, pulling me toward him, closer. Then one came up to snag the nape of my neck so he could have complete control.

Fireworks.

As cliché and girly and silly as that sounded, that was how it felt. It was everything I hadn't felt with Mitchell that I had wanted to. I was on fire, burning from the inside out, anxiously anticipating his next move.

His lips gently parted mine and that was all it took to completely shatter any lingering resistance. My hands were somehow around his neck, but I couldn't remember putting them there. I didn't remember pulling him closer either, but there I was doing it. He had the most fascinating tongue that flicked instead of caressed against mine and I loved it.

For a second I felt cheap. I'd just kissed Mitchell a week ago. I mean, it was not like we were committed or anything, but still... It was all so confusing.

Feelings.

I liked Cain, too. Jeez. I was a feelings prostitute!

Then, after what was only actually mere seconds he pulled back slightly and looked down at me. His eyes were bright and locked onto mine, his breaths were uneven and slightly ragged.

"Well." He cleared his throat. "Wow, that was...uh..."

I wondered if he had felt what I felt.

"Yeah," I said licking my lips, but regretted it when I saw his eyes follow it then shoot back up to mine. "So, is that it? Contest over?"

He smiled cockily. "Yeah, I'd say we held out long enough."

"Oh, well, good." I saw them drag some poor drunk-out-of-her-mind girl up on stage to be humiliated because her boyfriend was in the bathroom. "Do you want to get another drink.?I don't particularly want to see this."

"Yes. Let's," he said and grabbed my hand to pull me behind him to the bar.

I was starting to question and doubt everything. I'd spent some time with Mitchell this week, just talking. He hadn't tried anything and honestly, I hadn't felt compelled to either. But. How could I have been so blind to Mitchell's feelings for me? How come I liked him but not as much as he did me? How come the age thing didn't bother me? Is it because I didn't actually think it would go anywhere? How come I'd known Mitchell for months and Cain only for a week but my feelings for him were so intense already? How could I have feelings for two people at the same time? How come Cain's kisses were so electric?

"So, you're still having fun then?" he asked me once we reached the bar.

He held up two fingers to the bartender to tell him two more.

"Yes, a lot. I have to say, I love dancing. It's a shame Michael and I never-" I stopped myself but it was too late. "Oh, I'm sorry. I didn't mean to bring up... I'm sorry."

I felt so terrible, not only for bringing up my dead husband, but also for thinking about him and Mitchell as well. Cain wasn't thinking about Sherry was he? Or maybe... Was that why he kissed me like that?

He pulled me back to look at him with a finger under my chin. "Hey, it's ok. I can't really be mad at you for thinking about your husband. Besides, you were going to say you wished you done this with him, right? There's nothing wrong with that. Happy remembrance is ok, it's sad pining that we are against tonight."

"Thanks." I had to ask. "So, you're not thinking about Sherry, then?"

He looked at me thoughtfully for a few moments, cocking his head slightly. Then the bartender slid us our drinks and I followed him away from the bar once more. Once we were settled against the wall somewhere he returned to my question without my prompting.

"You think I kissed you, pretending you were Sherry," he said and once again stared at me with a thoughtful gaze.

I decided to be truthful. "Yes."

"No." He took my glass from me, setting it somewhere behind him and then turned me to look at him full on, his hands still on my shoulders. "For one thing, your kissing stands on its own without any help from my fantasies. Believe me."

"Ok," I answered, not sure if I believed him yet or where he was going with it.

"Second thing, you are a gorgeous creature. I was lucky to be the one kissing you in here tonight."

I wanted to roll my eyes at him, but he was dead serious.

"Third." I realized he had a penchant for numbered list. "I have to get over Sherry, I know that. What better way to do that than be here with you and only you." He must have seen my brow crinkle because he held up his hand and continued. "I'm not saying we're an item or anything. Don't run for the door, honey, all right? I'm just saying...you're sweet and fun and beautiful. I want to get to know you more, that's all."

I relaxed at his words. "That sounds perfect," I said.

He smiled, then I smiled and I even welcomed the tentative hand on my waist he used to steady himself as he leaned back to get our drinks from the table.

Then we heard the PA system blare a sharp whistle and all went silent as the conversations halted. Cain whispered that the rally must be about to start.

I took a flyer from a cute, young, blonde, teenage girl passing them out. Cain didn't even glance up at her, which gave me a boost of confidence. I read the flyer and it stated the same thing as the flyer above the stage basically. That we would be nowhere without our leadership and needed to bow down to the new Taker. Of course they didn't call him that, they called him Savior.

Sickening.

It said his name was Malachi and he would be residing in the former Mayor's house not far from here. I showed it to Cain and he read it over my shoulder.

"Dang," he whispered. "That's the same place the last once lived, or headquartered anyway. That's where we had to go to get Lily and Calvin."

I remembered the story and gasped."Why is he here, so close? What's here that would make him stay here out of all places?"

"I'm afraid to ask. Sherry probably."

"Oh, no, I forgot about that. You think?"

"I don't know any other reason. Maybe because they have such a big following here. It's huge here compared to other areas."

"Hmm."

I thought about what he said. I looked around and watched the others. I could see a Lighter - no, two Lighters in the back - and it made my skin scrawl to think about them being so close. How hard was it for them to be here in a room full of humans and not want to kill us? Course, they probably did want to.

A man took the stage. He must be an enforcer or something. I'd never seen one before. I listened intently, as did Cain.

"Welcome! Welcome! We are so pleased that you could come tonight. I know you are enjoying yourself and we'll let you get back to it, but first, we want to make sure you understand and know who to thank, not only for this party, but for your freedom as well. Malachi is not only a savior but he's a leader. A leader who has suffered just like the rest of us but had now has the political power to end our suffering. The Keepers may hold our moon hostage, but they will not hold us!"

His crescendo was perfect for the full effect and let the crowd scream in acceptance. They gave people who had testimonies a chance to speak. And they did, by the piles. We stood there for almost forty five minutes just listening to their stories.

Finally the man was escorted away by the Lighters and the rally ended. They cranked the music back up and the dance floor filled quickly. I glanced at my watch, it was 12:45.

"We're gonna have to leave soon," I stated and bit my lip.

"Yep. I was just thinking that. But you owe me a last dance, remember?"

"Yes, I do. And I'm happy to do it. I've had a lot of fun. So much more than I thought possible in the circumstances. I know I won't get to do this again so... thanks, Cain."

"It was my pleasure, lovely," he said and kissed the backs of my fingers before taking me to the dance floor.

Keane was playing. I couldn't remember the name of the song but pretty soon it didn't matter. Cain had been waiting for a slow song to come on so he could play the 'last song' card on me. I knew it. He knew I knew it. It still didn't matter.

He once again wrapped my arms around his neck and placed his hands on my hips. He swayed me slowly and I let him lead me easily. The song was sweet and melodious. He was an incredible dancer and a great lead. He didn't jostle me around; he pushed and pulled with the right amount of force to smoothly transition in the steps and sways.

219

"You really got the hang of this tonight," he said, his breath on my ear and neck as he talked over the music.

"Thanks, you're a good lead."

"What?" he asked and I had to lean in more.

"I said you're a good lead."

"Oh. Thanks. My mom made me take lessons when I was in middle school."

"Really? Aww, how cute," I said and smiled to goad him jokingly.

"Ah no. Not cute, torturous. But I guess it paid off in the end. I got you to dance with me," he said and winked.

I felt myself blush and tried to breathe it off. "Yep, definitely paid off. I think she'd be proud if she were here."

I meant it as a joke, but my voice dropped to almost a whisper when I said it. He looked at me for a moment then spoke. I didn't know where his family was or what happened to them.

"I doubt that. She wanted me to be a lawyer. Fight crime from the inside not with guns. She wasn't exactly happy with me for joining the military."

"Really? Did you have a good relationship with her before that?"

"Yeah- well, no. But she uh..." He looked uncomfortable and cleared his throat. "She killed herself when my dad left her and I joined up. Then my dad kind of got a little...messed up after that. He died the next year."

I understood what the undercurrent meant. "It wasn't your fault."

"I know, I guess. It just sucks not being there for her. She thought we abandoned her. I couldn't leave Afghanistan, and my dad... Well, I won't poison those delicate ears of yours with foul language, so let's just call him an ass...as in a donkey."

I laughed and he seemed like he was in a lighter mood and I was glad. I was sorry to bring up a sore subject. "Well, thanks for the consideration."

"So, anyway, now I work at a diner." He laughed. "My mom's whole ambition was for me to be some rich lawyer and I serve coffee to truckers and townies."

"Well, a diner is kind of like a courtroom," I teased.

"Ha, ha, ha." He tickled my ribs, as I was so ticklish, and grabbed me up when I squirmed laughing into his shoulder. "You're a funny girl."

"Well, my mom wanted me to be a preacher so, you get no sympathy from me. She was very disappointed in my homemaker lifestyle."

"Wow. Well, you got me beat on that one. Why did she want that?"

"My dad was a preacher." He looked slightly shocked so I changed the subject. "So, how old are you anyway?"

"Twenty six."

"That's not too bad. Mitchell is thirty nine, you know."

"What? That's ancient! And you're twenty one? He's a grandpa!"

"No he's-" I stopped. "We aren't supposed to be talking about them." I made a motion of zipping my lips. "You'll have to keep reminding me."

"I got no problem with that, lovely. Now how exactly should I keep your mind off of it?" he asked and ran a finger down my cheek. "Man, you're skin is so soft," he whispered against my other cheek.

I was frozen in his arms as he continued to sway us even though I stayed silent.

All too soon the song ended and he reluctantly released me and stepped back. "Ready to get out of here?" he asked.

"Not really. But yeah," I answered.

We grabbed two of everything that was free on our way out. We had t-shirts, mugs, stickers, posters, hand held fans, buttons, even car air fresheners, everything with the Taker on them. Not like we'd use it but we needed to look enthusiastic and also, these things might come in handy for future scouting and spying.

We drove home and talked about nothing and everything. The best part was that he didn't once mention Sherry and I didn't once think about Michael. Not Mitchell either.

Maybe I should have thought about him though, as Cain played with my fingers on the middle seat between us, I wasn't bold enough to scoot myself to the middle, and we chatted about past jobs and favorite bands. He told me all about his military stint.

Whatever happened, I refused to feel guilty. I was young and the world was ending. I should have a few inches of running room.

As we pulled into the store parking lot, seven minutes until 2:00 a.m., he parked us under the awning at the back shed. It was so dark out and I was a little freaked. I looked around warily.

He grabbed a big black flashlight from behind the seat and pulled me out of the driver's side behind him and then shut the door. We didn't walk yet. He was looking at me in an intense way that made me forget all about being scared of the dark.

"Lillian? Would you mind if, since we aren't inside yet, technically we're still party friends, right?"

"Uh, yeah."

"And you had fun being old friends tonight, right?"

"Yeah, absolutely."

"And drunken party friends can still kiss, right?"

His voice was low and rumbling and I heard my breath catch as I fought to steady my voice. "We're not drunk, Cain."

"You didn't answer my question," he breathed.

I licked my lips again subconsciously and once again regretted it as I saw his eyes watching me intently. He probably thought I was doing it on purpose to taunt him. "Um."

He didn't give me a chance to answer, but I didn't push him away. Oh, goodness... He was so good at this.

This kiss was even more skillful, if possible, than the first. More intent was involved. He pushed me gently against the truck side and pressed me there, under the cover of the shed. His hand moved in my hair, massaging the back of my scalp and playing with and rubbing the curls that had turned flat from Celeste's earlier makeover.

My hands had nowhere to go but his hips, which were extremely lean compared to his muscular shoulders. He was gentle, but I could tell he wanted more. He was probably used to *getting* more from girls back in his day, before all this.

I let him kiss me for as long as I could take it. When I felt my breaths coming so shallow it was unbearable I pulled back and gasped out my breaths. He laid his forehead on mine and sighed. "I'm sorry," he whispered, "my lovely, you are just too incredible to resist."

"Well," I chuckled breathlessly, "I think we better go inside before I don't ever want to go back."

He laughed and looked up at me ruefully. "If only that were true."

"It kind of is. I had fun. Thank you. Anytime you need another accomplice, you know where to find me."

"You got it, babe," he said softly and my heart flipped so big and loud, I was sure he could tell, but he just watched me with a look of...what? Wonder? Amazement? Maybe he thought I had been too far gone with Mitchell already and now...

"Alright, you. Ready?" he asked as he pushed off the truck and me.

"Ready."

He held my hand as we walked back. Our fingers laced, his other hand holding the flashlight, guiding our path. As we got closer to the back door, I started to see some dark spots in the tan sand that we stepped on.

"Cain, what is that?" We looked closely. The sand had footprints everywhere and those dark spots. I gasped.

"It's blood," he growled anxiously.

He pulled me faster to the door and locked it behind us. He knocked and when they let us in I knew something was really wrong.

Sherry was still up. Everyone was up. What in the world? They were crying, some were furious.

"Lillian," Sherry started then stopped to take a breath and stifle what looked like tears about to come. "Lillian, Mitchell..."

Cain still had my hand and was standing next to me. I felt his fingers tighten on mine.

"What is it, Sherry?" he asked her, but stayed where he was.

I thought for sure with the way she was so distraught he would have gone to her immediately, but he stayed by me and held my hand tight.

"Aaron and Mitchell. They..." she tried again, but stopped again.

Merrick came up behind her and placed his hands on her shoulders. "Lillian," Merrick said to me, "we had a run in tonight. Mitchell... Mitchell's dead. I'm very sorry."

Sherry pulled herself away from Merrick and hugged me tightly.

"I'm so sorry, Lillian," she said and pulled back quickly to retreat to Merrick's arms.

"Honey, Lily's up," he said glancing over his shoulder and rubbing her back. "Lillian, I'm sorry," he said softly and glanced quickly at Cain before leading Sherry away.

Cain immediately turned to hug me to him, pressing my face into his neck and whispering in my ear while his arms encircled me, but I could only make out half of what he said.

"Lillian, I'm so sorry...let me take you to...some rest...we'll talk...get you some water...sweetheart, talk to...be alright?"

Then I couldn't hear him anymore. I was numb and frozen.

Mitchell, my best friend, was dead.

I was out partying and kissing another guy, knowing how he felt about me, and he was here, dying.

Mitchell was dead.

Only In Dreams
Chapter 17 - Sherry

I picked Lily up and hugged her to me as she ran from her room in her long t-shirt with pink and purple hearts. Everyone was upset and she woke up in all the commotion.

"Shawwy, what's wong? Why you cwying?"

I didn't realize I was.

"It's ok, baby, let's get you back to bed."

As I slipped her through the crowd, holding her head to my shoulder so she didn't see the bloodied and bruised people all around, I turned just once to look at Lillian.

Cain was just then sweeping her up off her feet into his arms and taking her towards her hall. She lay limp in his arms and his grim gaze met mine for a few seconds before I passed into Lily's room.

"Lily, we have a lot of work to do tonight. You might hear some noises but everything is ok. I want you to stay in bed, ok? Promise me."

"I pwomise," she said as she swiped her hair back from her face.

I pulled the hair band I had on my wrist off. I had forgotten to put her hair up before bed. I twisted up a quick ponytail for her and she laid down, searching sleepily for her doll. I put Joy in her grasp and slid out quietly.

Then I practically ran to Lillian's hall, I knew her room was on it somewhere, though I still didn't know exactly which one.

I found Cain in the hall creeping out of a room closing the door.

"Cain," I whispered.

He straightened and immediately pulled me in for a tight hug and spoke into my hair.

"Are you alright? What the- What happened, Sherry?"

I explained everything to him, just as Merrick had told me what happened when they finally came back down that hatch.

"The Lighters were here. They tricked Margo into ringing the bell and sending some of the Keepers out. They were outnumbered." I started to cry again and we slumped to the floor in the hall.

My heart ached for my gruff rescuer, Aaron, who thought he saved me from Merrick that day in the yard, and poor Mitchell.

"Go on, Sherry, what happened?" Cain said as he rubbed my arm.

"It was just like that day, when we went to the cave. Markers were everywhere. They called the other Keepers to come help and left one to stay with us and told us to hide in the storage room. That's when we knew it was bad," I choked on a sob. "So we ran out to help, all of us, well- all of them. Of course I wasn't allowed to go. I never am," I said and could practically taste the bitterness, but I knew it was just the anger talking. "So, Danny and the rest of them ran out to help but the Lighters took Aaron out first thing and a Marker got Mitchell not long after. They eventually cut all the Lighters down and either killed or ran off the Markers. They were out there for an eternity it felt like. Everyone else is ok just a little...banged up. Margo is still locked in the bathroom in the store. She refuses to come out. Celeste has been up there with her since they got back in, trying to coax her out."

"Oh, man. If I'd been here, I could have helped," Cain said and leaned his head back on the wall.

"No, you would've just gotten hurt, too. How's Lillian?"

"She's in shock. She won't talk."

"It's got to be hard on her to lose two people she cared about back to back like that."

"Yeah," he said gruffly. "I'll stay with her."

"Ok, I've got to go check on people. A few need stitches and stuff like that, including Merrick."

"I'm glad Merrick made it, and Danny. I'm glad they're ok."

"Thanks. I'm glad you weren't here though. And I'm glad Lillian wasn't here either. This will probably sound stupid after all that but...how did it go tonight? Find anything useful?"

"It was fine. We got some things to give the Keepers to look at. Everything went fine," he said softly and sat staring at the wall in front of us.

"Are you ok?" I asked, knowing none of us were.

"Yes. No. I don't know, I feel guilty."

"Cain, you couldn't have-"

"I was having fun, Sherry." He cut me off briskly and pinched the bridge of his nose. "We danced, we were laughing, we talked, we kis-" he tried to cut it off but it was too late.

"You kissed?" I asked softly, thinking back to what Lillian had said about liking Mitchell and feeling some confusion.

He hesitated then looked at me. "Yes. We kissed. While you were here

225

fighting, we were out there dancing and kissing," he said like it was disgusting.

I grabbed his face within my hands. "Enough, Cain. Everyone tries to take the blame for everything around here. This is not your fault. This is their fault, those filthy Lighters, and I'm sick of it. I'm sick of them making us feel like we didn't do enough or we haven't sacrificed enough already. We have sacrificed everything. All of us. Don't feel guilty over a couple hours of fun when it wouldn't have changed the outcome, even if you had been here," I scolded firmly never letting him break my gaze.

"If you say so."

"I do."

"Sherry," he breathed, "you're too good to be true, you know that?"

"So I've been told," I joked and pulled him in to hug me.

He squeezed me tightly around my waist and pressed his face into the crook of my neck as I sat on my knees in the hall with him. He smelled like a bar - smoke, beer and sweat - but surprisingly it kind of smelled good on him.

I felt him nuzzle my neck a little closer. I thought he was just getting more comfortable, but then he rubbed his face on my throat and I felt him inhale deeply, his arms tightening on my waist. I panicked for just a second, thinking he was drunk or grief stricken and about to do something he shouldn't so I pulled back and asked questions instead.

"So, did Lillian enjoy herself at least? She needed a night out more than anyone I think."

He cleared his throat and sat back, crossing his arms.

"Yeah, she seemed to."

"So, did you kiss her or did she kiss you?"

He startled at my question and looked at the floor. "I guess it was me. It was a game we had to play at the club. Look, do you really want to talk to me about this?"

"Why not? Lillian won't be any shape to tell me about it for a while and you've piqued my interest," I smiled but he didn't.

"I don't really want to talk about kissing girls with you, Sherry."

"Why not?"

"Because...I just don't."

"Are you sure you're ok? Can I get you something?"

"I'm ok. I'm gonna go in and sit with Lillian, make sure she's ok before hitting the sack."

"I've got to go, too. I'm surprised Merrick hasn't come looking for me yet. I need to find Danny." I started to get up but looked back at him. He looked awfully sad or - I don't know - something strange. "You're sure you don't need anything?"

"No, sweet girl, I don't need anything," he said and smiled sadly as he helped me from the floor.

"Ok." I hugged him once more, because he looked like he really needed it. "You know I love you, Cain, right? I'm glad you were safe tonight."

He blew out a long breath, blowing the hair at my neck. "I love you, too, Sherry." He released me and stepped back. "G'night."

He pushed her door open and went in without looking at me again, so I turned and swiftly made my way down the hall to the rest of my family. I still hadn't seen Danny. Merrick told me he saw him go to the store with Celeste and that he was safe but he hadn't been down yet and I so needed to physically touch him and know he was ok.

I saw Merrick leaning over Ryan so I walked over and put my hand on his back to let him know I was there.

"Piper! Enough!" he bit out and turned with a look of red hot fury, then noticed me and immediately backpedaled his anger, softening his face a little. "Oh, Sherry, I thought... Never mind. Can you help me here?"

"Sure, what do you need?" I said and looked down at Ryan. "You ok, Ryan?"

"It's just a scratch," he said and I stopped dead in my tracks.

"A scratch? What kind of scratch?" I absently rubbed my shoulder.

"Not that kind. I can't be poisoned by them, Sherry."

He knew I was talking about the Marker's mark, when they scratch you to mark you so the Lighters can find you. If the mark isn't burned you go into a coma. It was extremely painful, even now.

"Oh, good." I turned back to Merrick. "What do you need me to do, babe?"

"Can you wrap this?" He handed me a gauze pack and pointed to Ryan's leg, where they was a huge gash.

Not a scratch.

"Sure. Are you ok? You need to have your arm looked at."

I noticed his shoulder was still bleeding and his shirt torn and red in more than one place.

"I'm fine. I'll fix my arm in a minute. First Ryan. Then...you and I, we'll talk later," he said softly before heading off to someone else.

Before he walked off he turned and looked me pointedly in the eye and said something to me in my mind.

We'll talk about Piper. And we'll talk about you and Cain.

I jolted at what he said as he turned to walk away. Me and Cain? What did that mean? Piper? What did we have to talk about her for? And why did he bite my head off thinking I was her touching his back.

There was one Keeper who keeps causing problems around here and I'm about ready to stomp some black haired, nosy, interfering and careless Keeper behind.

I wrapped Ryan's leg as instructed and he was a good, very non-whiny patient as always. The best kind.

I told him as much which he still apologized and tried to make it seem like he was being a baby to which I dutifully informed him that he was not.

After that I turned to survey the rest of them. Everyone was helping others or bandaging themselves or gone to bed by then, entirely exhausted, frustrated and sad.

Mike gone.

Trudy gone.

Aaron gone.

Mitchell gone.

A multitude of others, gone.

Though most didn't know Mitchell that well yet, it still hurt to see others hurting over him. It sucked to lose people, especially so senselessly. What purpose did it serve? I wasn't downplaying his sacrifice, absolutely not. He died trying to protect us and that was what I meant.

If this enemy, this nuisance in black and darkness, would just head home and stop this undeserved takeover of our planet, then Mitchell wouldn't have felt the need to die for us. I was sick of it all.

In fact I began to wonder if 'sweet Sherry' was getting a little bitter. A little too much acid on my tongue, a little too many tears trailing out against my will, a little too much worrying and scrounging for some semblance of humanity and understanding. What if the next thing was the last straw? What if I couldn't take it?

What if the final step was now and I was forever scarred, bitter and pissed?

I couldn't think about that, as another woman who fought against a nonsensical takeover, Scarlett O'Hara, would say, I'll think about that tomorrow.

Finally, *finally,* after my internal debate over my level of resentment was over, I saw Danny coming down the stairs. He was dirty, but otherwise intact and towing a tear streaked Celeste behind him.

"Danny," I heard myself say and he looked up to meet my gaze.

I made quick strides to him and he engulfed me in his free arm.

"Danny! Why didn't you come tell me you were alright? I've been worried sick about both of you!"

"I've been with Celeste up in the store. I asked Merrick to-"

"He did but hearing is not the same as seeing," I chided and then turned to Celeste. "Is she ok? Margo?"

"She's still refusing to come out," Celeste said indignantly, wiping her eyes with her forefinger. "She's being ridiculous and now I'll get no sleep at all worrying about her."

"Ah, she'll be ok. Guilt is a big thing to handle."

"She didn't do anything wrong! She had nothing to be guilty about!" she yelled.

Celeste never raised her voice to me or anyone that I could remember. Sweet, easy going, prim, blonde, adorable Celeste just practically screamed at me, right there in front of everyone.

"Celeste," I said softly and Danny started to say something, it looked like in my defense, but I cut him off with a hand up and spoke softer. "Sweetie, I know she didn't do anything wrong, that's what I'm saying. The guilt over something you think you did, but didn't actually have any control over, is almost worse than if you *had* done it on purpose. I know."

I was thinking, of course, about that day Cain and I got lured outside by the Lighter and tricked. Our family came to our rescue and by the end of the day, two of them had died. I was right there with Margo in the bathroom, feeling her guilt and shame. Not wanting to face anyone and see their looks of blame but worst of all, not wanting to see their looks of pity or absolution.

Celeste blanched ay my words, her blue eyes so bright against her pale skin and the angry red of her cheeks, her eyes rimmed and gleaming with frustrated tears.

She knew exactly what I was referring to. I could see it written all over her face. She glanced around self consciously at the faces who were watching us, watching her outburst.

"Sherry." The tears fell again and she reached to hug me, jerking herself free from Danny's grasp. She squeezed me tightly and her voice was muffled in my hair. "I'm so sorry. I didn't mean to yell at you. All you ever try to do is help I just...she's being so stubborn and I don't know what to do. I'm so sorry. Please forgive me."

"There's nothing to forgive. You're upset, we all are. It's been a bad day." I pulled Danny to me with a hand on his arm and spoke quietly to them both as we huddled there. "I'm so glad you're both ok. I was worried about you out there. I wish I could be more help, but... You're safe now, that's what matters. I love you guys so much. I don't know what I'd do without you."

It was kind of comical. Me, short little me, being the motherly figure of this scenario, giving the 'I'm so glad you're home safe' speech to two kids who had almost a foot of height on me. It was also ironic that before I would have gotten snorts and sarcasm from my brother but now...

"I love you, too, sis. I'm glad you always get stuck inside, that way, I don't have to worry about you, too."

He glanced at Celeste for a second and she gave him a little 'we've talked about this' look. I had wondered how he felt about her rushing out to the front lines, now I guess I knew. And I was proud of him for at least trying to protect her.

Celeste turned to hug me again.

"I love you too, Sherry. I'm sorry, again." She rubbed her hands over her face and through her hair. "I'm not gonna sleep a wink. I'm going to get a pillow and head back up to sit by the door with her. Bye, Sherry. Thank you."

"No problem."

"I'm going to go with her," Danny said quickly.

"You should. That's what good boyfriends do."

He smiled at me and rolled his eyes, tweaking my nose before he ran to catch up.

Merrick found me later in the kitchen. I was getting some things ready for the next day, food wise, chopping onions and measuring rice for soup.

Most everyone had turned in. It was incredibly late, or incredibly early I should say, almost five in the morning. I couldn't go to bed by myself and didn't want to look for Merrick, for some strange misplaced fear of what he wanted to talk about. Plus, I didn't want to interfere with his duties of helping the others.

"Hey," he said and stopped in the doorframe.

"Hey. How is everyone?" I asked as I wiped my hands on the dishtowel.

"Asleep finally. I went to our room but you weren't there."

"No, I didn't want to go without you. I hoped you'd come get me when you were done."

"Well, I'm done."

"Ok. Let me just-"

"Sherry." He waited for me to turn and look, and took a deep breath before he spoke again. "What's going on with you and Cain?"

What? What did he mean? "I'm sorry?"

"You're sorry you didn't understand what I said, or you're apologizing because you got caught?"

I felt my lips part in surprise and my eyes go wide. "What?"

"Just tell me. I'm a big boy, Sherry, I can take it. Just tell me why," he said a little snidely and I almost choked on my answer.

"What?" I repeated.

"Why? Why would you do that? After everything we've been through, why this? Why now?"

"What?" I repeated because no other word would come to mind.

"You heard me, Sherry," he growled and it was all I could do to not burst in tears right there from just hearing his tone alone.

He had never raised his voice or spoken to me with anything but love and concern. It seemed a lot of us were going through a raised-voice spurt these days. But this? He sounded cold and hurt. But I really had no idea what he was talking about. As I thought about it, the more I stayed silent the guiltier I looked, so I hurriedly spoke.

"Merrick, I really have no idea what you're talking about."

"Yes, you do. I saw you," he said tightly.

"You saw me? You saw me what?"

"Kissing Cain in the hall earlier."

"What! I *was* in the hall with Cain earlier, but I absolutely was not kissing him!"

"I saw you!" he yelled back.

I ran through my mind; me sitting with Cain, then hugging Cain, Cain smelling my hair in drunken stupefied arousal. Maybe that looked like kissing from the back side of me. It was all I could come up with.

"I hugged Cain in the hall, like I always do. He was really upset for Lillian and feeling guilty for not being here. Maybe it looked like something it wasn't from behind me, but-"

"I saw you! With my own eyes, not some skewed view of you. You and him. Kissing and wrapped around each other and about to do plenty more for everyone that came looking to see."

"Merrick," I squeaked. Was I drugged? Did I and just didn't remember? Was Merrick drugged? "I didn't! I promise you, I have no idea how you could have seen me do that. I didn't kiss him!"

He stepped forward slightly, pushing off the wall, clenching his fist. I'd never ever seen him direct any anger of any kind at me and I was...terrified. Not that he'd physically hurt me, but that he could not want me anymore. For some reason, that thought had never crossed my mind until then.

"Enough. There's no point in lying about it anymore," he spurted loudly and then pushed me slightly, forcing me backwards by holding my arms until my back touched the wall.

He braced his hands on the wall by my head, caging me in, and I was wondering if I needed to retract the 'not that he would physically hurt me' thought. I was scared. I scrambled for a reasonable reply as the tears started to fall.

"Am I lying? Can't you tell?" I replied softly.

He wavered for a second. I saw that maybe he could tell I wasn't lying but wasn't ready to give up yet. Somehow, he was convinced I had kissed Cain, and as human eyes went, you believed what you saw.

"I said, enough. I wasn't the only one to witness it. Piper and Polly came and got me, said there was something I needed to see, something about you. They were with me in the hall when I found you there. Together," he gritted his teeth at the word.

Then he cursed loudly and banged his fists on the wall by my head, making me squeak in surprise, before backing away from me.

I couldn't believe how angry he was, and at me no less. I thought really hard about what could be going on. I moved a little closer, seeing his face twisted in anger and hurt, wanting to comfort him. He stepped back.

"Don't. Don't, Sherry. You think I'll just cave under your kisses? I guess I always do when it comes to you, but not tonight. How could you do this to me? You know how much I love you, what I would do for you. Anything. So why?"

He said the last words so softly that it was almost worse than his yelling. He was just hurt now. Hurt and feeling betrayed. I wished that I could do or say something to just make this go away. I stayed put but spoke evenly and quietly.

"Merrick, look at me. You're right, after all we've been through why would I do this? Why would I do this after I've spent so much time and effort in pushing away what everyone thought of me, of us, for being together just to throw all that away and be with a human after all. Why would I?"

"I saw you."

"I know you did." I forged on quickly so he wouldn't think I was confessing. "At least you think you did, but I'm telling you, right here and now, I promise you, I didn't do this. I have no reason to. You're my life and I love you more than anything. Please, believe me."

Without another word, he turned around and walked out. My Merrick, the man who came to earth to find me and be with me left me shaking, scared, crying and standing alone in the kitchen with a hole the size of Atlanta in my chest where my heart should be.

Misery Loves Company
Chapter 18 - Cain

I woke up in the morning, at least I assumed it was morning, to a scratching on my arm. I turned to find Piper. She'd come into Lillian's room, where I still was, leaning against the wall sleeping.

"Piper?"

"Cain, you need to come with me. Sherry's really upset."

"What? What do you mean? Where's Merrick?" I drawled sleepily and yawned.

"I don't know but she looks like she really could use a friend. She's in the laundry room."

"Ok," I said reluctantly, wondering why in the world this woman I barely knew was coming to get me to console Sherry. "I'll go see her."

"Good." Then she got up and left, just like that.

I turned to see Lillian still asleep. I braced myself on the wall to drag myself up, stretching and squinting through the aches that would surely be there all day. Sitting on the concrete floor to sleep definitely did not do a body good.

As I walked through, I saw that people were out and bustling about so it must be morning. I had no idea what time I finally conked out, but it was well after four o'clock.

I pondered, as I shuffled my feet in a haze, the events of the previous night. I remembered feeling utterly torn while Sherry battled through her tears to tell Lillian about Mitchell. I had the hand I *needed* in mine and the one I *wanted* was just out of reach. I restrained myself. Sherry had Merrick, she always had Merrick and didn't need nor want me, but as soon as I turned to Lillian and saw her devastated and ripped up expression, it all fell away but her. I couldn't think of anything but making that pain go away, and there was nothing I could do about it but wrap her up and take her away from it all.

It was so confusing, all of it. Then later in the hall, when it was just Sherry and me, I couldn't stop myself from letting the worry I felt for her take over and come out.

Stupid.

Just stupid.

If she hadn't stopped me there was no telling what I'd have done. I knew what she smelled like, I dreamed about that smell an embarrassing amount but I let it overtake me in my relief and worry for her and grief for Lillian. She didn't act suspicious. Probably just thought I was drunk or something. I wish I had that excuse.

It was like I was two separate people. When I was with Sherry, I wanted her. When I was with Lillian, I wanted her. When I was with them both, I couldn't make up my frigging mind. How did this happen? How was it possible? You couldn't love/like two people at once, could you?

Light bulb. I had to stay away from Sherry. No matter how much it hurt, that was all there was to it. After whatever this was that was wrong with Sherry and we got this Lighter attack resolved, that was exactly what I was going to do.

It wasn't fair to Sherry.

It wasn't fair to Lillian.

And it sure as hell wasn't fair to me, to do that to myself.

I did find Sherry in the laundry room as Piper had said but I also saw something I didn't expect to find in the cold concrete room.

Sherry was lying on a pallet in the corner on the hard floor, using a folded towel as a pillow and an old afghan thrown over her. She was crying, as Piper had said, and looked liked she'd been crying a lot.

"Sherry?" When she looked up her face twisted into a new round of tears as she tried to sit up. "Sherry, what's the matter? What are you doing in here?" Then realization hit me as I looked at her makeshift bedding. "Sherry, did you sleep in here?" I asked and moved to kneel beside her.

"Yes. I had a fight with Merrick."

This shocked me. Those two never fought and definitely not over something that would grant her being kicked out of their room, or maybe she left. That didn't sound like her, she wasn't one of those petty girls. "What kind of fight?"

"He thinks we...he said he saw..."

She couldn't speak for sobbing and crying. I couldn't help it. I pulled her to my chest to hug her and ground her. Finally, she got out what she was trying to say.

"Merrick thinks he saw us kissing - more than kissing - last night. I don't know what's going on."

"What?"

"He said he saw us. Piper and Polly saw us too he said." She sniffed and continued to shudder her way through the words. "They came and got him, to discover us."

"But that's ludicrous. We didn't do-"

"I know!"

"Maybe they just thought we were, maybe they saw us hugging-"

"No, I already tried that defense. He said...we were wrapped around each other, pressed against the hall wall kissing and ready to...to do more. I don't think they could mistake that."

"Then what's going on here?"

"That's what I'd like to know," Merrick's voice said from behind me. I turned, unfortunately for us, with Sherry still damnable looking in my arms to see a very pissed off Merrick. "Piper comes to tell me that you're upset in here, that maybe I'd been too hard on you last night and I should come check on you. I should have known what I'd find."

"Merrick, this isn't what it looks like." Cursing myself over those cliché words, I extricated myself from Sherry, though it hurt to do so with her so upset and the one she wanted comfort from so unwilling to give it. "I was just-"

"I can see what you were *just* doing, Cain."

Wow. Merrick. Was. Pissed.

He was really hurt. I guessed if I had Sherry, and I was sure she had been with some other guy, I'd be, too.

"Merrick, come on, this is me. This is Sherry. We wouldn't do that to you, man."

I stood up and Merrick straightened, crossing his arms over his chest and looking fiercely like he wanted to cause me physical pain.

"I know, that's what makes all this so bad to begin with. You, Cain, of all people. You know how much I love her. You know how much she means to me. How much I-" He stopped and his anger faltered, for a second he looked like he could burst with hurt.

"Never, Merrick," Sherry pleaded, standing up too and took a step forward but didn't make a move to touch him. "I'd never do that to you. You know I love you! You give me everything I need. I wouldn't do this to you."

"I don't belong here. I'll let you two work this out," I said and tried to make a break for the door but Merrick put his finger in my chest to stop me.

"No, I suggest you stay and comfort Sherry. I'll leave," he snarled and then pushed his finger just a little bit before letting it fall back down to his side.

Every military muscle in my body twitched with a need to hit something. I stayed my ground because hitting Merrick would solve absolutely nothing. And it was obvious he believed what he thought he saw.

"Merrick, please," Sherry begged again desperately. I'd never seen her so distraught. "Please believe me. If you love, believe me. I didn't do this."

"Sherry, I don't think I can believe or forgive you. One day, maybe. I have nowhere to go anyway, it's not like I can leave. I want you to admit it. Admit what you did with Cain. I don't even know how long it's been going on." He shook his head as if in defeat. "If you didn't want to be with me anymore, you should have just said-"

Without warning Sherry lunged forward and grabbed his shirt front, snatching him towards her up on her toes and pulling him down to kiss him. Their lips met. He didn't pull away but he was shocked. He stood completely still for just a few seconds. I could tell, she was putting all her love, all her everything, into this kiss like everything rode on it.

It hurt to watch, but I couldn't look away.

His hands came out to his sides, but he didn't touch her. It was like he was waging an internal war, he wanted to touch her but couldn't. His fingers flexed and fist clenched and then loosened. Finally he touched her, but it was to push her away.

She almost fell back from the force behind it, and I had to stop myself from trying to catch her. I'm sure that would have gone over well.

"Stop, Sherry!" he yelled and even I flinched at the harshness in his voice. "You can't just kiss me and expect everything to be ok. What? You thought because I wasn't human that you could just betray me and then try to fix it with sex later and I'd just be all right with it all?" he said breathing heavy and I felt completely invisible, but utterly grateful for it.

"No! I didn't betray you. I didn't think that. I would never do that. I love you, I never stopped, and I wanted you to see that," she squeaked.

"Just stop it, Sherry. I need some time to...figure out what I'm supposed to do here. I know this isn't the first time. I know you've been together, I just don't know how long. I want nothing more than just to pretend this didn't happen, but I can't."

"Merrick-"

"Stop! It's over, Sherry. No more."

Her eyes went wide. "It's...over?" she croaked.

"Yes." He clenched his face and then softened. "No. I don't know what I'm saying. Maybe it's this body, I don't know, but I can't get the image of you two out of my head and it's making me crazy," he growled through clenched teeth and ran his hands through his hair and down his face like he was in physical pain.

"Merrick."

"I'm going to go lie down. It was a long night. Don't follow me, Sherry," he bit out.

He left and Sherry crumpled back down to her pallet in a heap of sobs. I didn't think it would be appropriate after everything that just happened to comfort her again. Though I wanted to, something awful.

"I'm sorry, Sherry. We'll figure this out. There's got to be an explanation. I'll...I'll leave you alone for a while, while I go think," I said and prayed she wouldn't ask me to stay.

She didn't.

As I was walking out of the room I saw Piper walk by and peek in, slowing down as she did so. Hmmm. Then when she found Sherry on the floor, crying and crumpled she looked satisfied, a little smile even came to her lips, and she kept walking down to the commons room.

At that point, I thought it odd, but could put no further effort to it. I was worried about Sherry. What in the heck was wrong with Merrick? It was like he was possessed. He thought of Sherry as something precious and fragile and never talked to her like that. He never would have pushed her. No, I understand he'd be angry if he *had* caught us, but his voice was what worried me. So...cold.

Sherry looked completely and utterly out of her mind with grief. We all had a long night with hardly any sleep, and no one had had breakfast yet. I was sure that didn't help the situation, but...something was going on. Something was not right.

I decided to go see if Lillian was up yet.

As I passed the commons room I saw Merrick sitting on the stairs, so naturally I avoided the stairs, but I saw Piper beside him. Her hands were rubbing his back and he had his face in his hands.

She looked happy, too happy to be consoling someone whose marriage may have been on the fritz. Once again, I was too agitated to think. I let the thought go as I saw her leaning forward to press her head to his and whisper. Merrick didn't seem thrilled by her comfort but wasn't pushing her away either. What was going on?

I made it to Lillian's room. She was lying there, but not asleep. I knocked softly to let her know I was coming in but waited for no answer. These rooms didn't have real doors like the other ones. They were just plywood pieces with wide gaps so there was plenty of light pouring in.

Plenty of light to see her face, calm and pale with tears streaming.

I wondered if any of us would make it through this day when half the females in the joint were either crying in hysterics, crying in guilt and grief or like Piper, happy in everyone else's misery.

Four's A Crowd
Chapter 19 - Merrick

The stair was digging into my thigh I had been there so long. Just sitting there. Wondering what I was going to do. How could she? How could he? WHY?

All the while, Piper's hand was on my back to soothe me, to calm me, but it was doing everything but. I all but bit her head off, and even did that, too, to get her to leave me alone since we found Sherry and Cain together last night. She followed me around, consoled me, spoken reassurances in my mind and rubbed my back constantly. I should be thankful that someone was willing to try to make me feel better but I wasn't. Anyone but her maybe, but I was tired of telling her to go away so I just sat and tolerated her, trying to process what was going on.

It must be the body, this human body because literally, the memory of them together would not leave my brain. Even when I physically forced it out and tried to think of something else, it remained and let no other thing in.

Cain had Sherry pressed against the wall, the crook of her knee hugged around his palm, her leg wrapped around his waist, her arms around his neck and their bodies smashed together. They looked comfortable, like they had done that before, more than once and more in depth.

She was kissing him like she has kissed me, passionately, deeply and intensely, and I stood there frozen and watched, unable to look away. When she leaned her head back to give him access to her throat and he trailed his tongue and mouth down her neck, she moaned-

It was too much. I couldn't say anything, couldn't do anything but get away immediately. Then I came into the commons room and saw so many people who needed my help...so much to do. So I dove in head first and pushed Piper off, more than once. 'Are you ok?', 'Let me help you', 'She was never meant to be with someone like you', Piper chimed constantly, over and over and touched me, petted my arm, patted my back, grabbed my hands.

It was too much as well. I was stunned by her actions but finally got her to leave and then Sherry walked in and acted like nothing happened. Like she wasn't betraying me and there was nothing wrong, like she wasn't just with my best friend in the most intimate way. I was stunned some more.

I thought back to her life and never saw this in her. Never saw that she could do this to another person. I thought long and hard and wanted to believe it was a trick. But the scene of them just kept playing, over and over and over.

Then when I asked her about it she flat denied it, but I'd seen it with my own eyes. Her denial and tears plus the image of her and Cain all mixing together and jumbling was too much and I snapped. I was angry *at* her, which I'd never been before, and it scared me as much as it fueled me. I yelled, I gritted my teeth, I fumed. She looked extremely stricken and frightened, making me even angrier because I felt justified.

I knew I was doing it, but couldn't stop. I went to talk calmly to her, confront her and get her confession and go from there, but her denial? No. That I couldn't handle, not with what I'd seen.

As I sat there spying Cain from the corner of my eye, ignoring me and heading back down the same hall I'd seen their transgression, I felt sick. I felt even sicker when the loop of them in my head got to the part of her moan. The moan that I had thought I was the only man to ever make her do.

I knew Sherry was back there alone, crying and hurt, but what could I do? Was I supposed to just pretend it didn't happen because it broke my heart to see her cry?

Did I really think a human woman could love me as a human man? Yes, I did. Sherry fooled me, but how? She can't lie? And yet, she lied so flawlessly last night when she was trying to banish my accusations.

Piper's hand rubbed an uncomfortable spot on my shoulder blade and I'd had enough.

"Stop, Piper." I rolled my shoulder to sling her hand off. "I've already told you. I...appreciate you trying to help me but I don't want it right now. Would you please just leave me by myself for a while?"

"Merrick, I just want to help you. I want you to know that when Sherry wasn't here for you, I was. Your own kind. Me."

"That is abundantly clear, Piper."

Too much. I got up and went to my room- our room, alone and shut the door. Immediately, I heard a knock and opened it, praying it wasn't Sherry.

It wasn't. It was Piper.

"Piper! Come on. You cannot be this dense," I yelled completely frustrated.

"Can I come in? I've been thinking about something. I want to run it by you, in private."

"Piper, not now," I growled.

"If you let me in, I'll leave you alone for the rest of the day, I promise."

I considered it and thought the price of a day of being left completely alone was just about worth anything. "Fine. Hurry, I'm tired."

"Thanks." She saddled passed me and brushed her chest with mine as she did it.

It was all I could do not to roll my eyes and grab her arm, throwing her out of the room in the process. "Ok, now what, Piper?"

"I think you should get back at her. I know that sounds so humanly juvenile, but you deserve more than this. She deserves to be hurt like you were. You've only ever been with one woman. Maybe you should try it with someone else to see what it's like."

This should have stunned me but it didn't. At this point, I expected no less from her.

"This is your big advice? To have sex with you?"

"Me? Well, I wouldn't stop you if that's what you mean," she said and trailed a finger down my chest.

I slapped it away, not gently, and grabbed her arm. "Out."

"Is it this body? Because it's only sixteen years old? Don't be fooled by it, Merrick. It's still me in here."

"I'm not fooled. I know exactly who's in there."

"Merrick, just think about it. I wonder if Keepers in human bodies are any different than real humans during the act. It'd be worth some research I think."

She glanced towards the door and back to me. Then pushed me against the wall before I could move and pressed herself to me. Then kissed me. I pushed her back just as I saw light.

Sherry.

Sherry was standing in the doorway, watching with wide betrayed eyes. At first I thought, how dare she be upset, but even in these situations, retaliation wasn't the way to handle it.

"Sherry," I said, her name just popped out.

I surveyed Piper and me, and saw what Sherry saw. Piper was in our room with me, our dark room, and she had me pinned to wall with her lips mere inches from mine still.

Sherry turned and walked slowly away without a word. I was so drained, just so done. I pushed Piper out with force to the hallway, amid her protest to let her stay.

I shut and locked the door and lay down determined not to see anyone or hear anything else for the rest of the day. I was exhausted and it didn't take long to start to drift. The only thing I couldn't shut off as I fell to sleep was the loop in my head of Sherry and Cain in the hall.

Their betrayal.

It's Complicated
Chapter 20 - Lillian

I woke up, still in my clothes from the day before, to Cain tapping softly on my door. I lifted my head and he was there, just like last night, a guilty, sorrowful and sorry face on.

I remembered what happened last night. I remembered everything. Mitchell was dead. I didn't remember crying much, not serious crying. I just remembered Cain and him taking me away from the crowd, where I didn't want to be, and staying with me for hours. My feet were in his lap and every now and then he would caress my leg reassuringly, as if to say 'I'm still here'.

Now, here he was again and I couldn't think of a single thing to say to him. I'd lost the last two men I cared about, within the same year. No, I wasn't in love with Mitchell but I still cared about him and it wasn't fair that I never got to explore that if that's what I had wanted. He was my best friend, ever in my life.

Cain sat down beside me and pulled my feet into his lap once more and closed his eyes. We sat there for who knew how long. A couple of hours dragged by. I knew because the glow from Cain's watch was the only thing there to focus on. I thought Cain slept but I couldn't anymore. Eventually he opened his eyes and looked over at me.

"Hey," he said softly.

"Hey," I said and was glad to see I'd found my voice.

"I'd ask how you slept, but I bet I can guess the answer."

"Surprisingly good for the circumstances. What does that say about me, huh?" I said and wiped the tears from my face.

"That you were exhausted and grieving."

"Yeah, I guess. How are you? You didn't sleep in here the whole night did you?"

"Uh...yeah."

"Did you at least lie down?"

"I slept sitting up. It's good for the joints."

I was so glad to see that Cain would still be his same jokey self around me. I needed that now more than anything else. "Uh huh. So what you're saying is, you thought I'd freak if I woke up and you were lying beside me."

"Yeah, pretty much."

I laughed. I astonished even myself. I immediately wiped the smile off my face and felt the first wave of true guilt since I'd woken up.

My face must have said as much because he leaned over beside me. "Hey." He rubbed my shoulder. "It's ok to laugh. You don't think he'd want you to be sitting here crying all day, do you?"

"No, he wouldn't. Cain, I feel so guilty. He really liked me and I...well I went out and had every intention of having fun with you." I confessed all, to clear my conscience. I wasn't catholic, but at this point, I felt it couldn't hurt to get it all out. "If that meant kissing you, then so be it. I was actually hoping you'd kiss me. I had made the decision to be over Michael, to be done with grieving and move on. It didn't have to be Mitchell, though I didn't feel the same I figured I might could try with him. I had no idea that you might feel something for me other than friendship until last night, unless last night was just party kisses." He started to interrupt, to contradict, but I held up my hand and then continued.

"But to be honest, the reason I feel so much guilt over the whole thing, wasn't because I felt like I betrayed him, it was because I didn't care enough about him. After kissing you last night, I had planned on telling Mitchell that I wasn't interested in him that way. And now...I'll never get to tell him. He died thinking I was out thinking about him and liking him as more than just a friend."

"Maybe it's better that way. He died happy."

"Maybe, but it doesn't make me feel any better. I miss him already. He was my best friend-" I choked and sniffled. "Before we came here I had no idea that Keepers...dated. I honestly thought he was just protective because that's what Keepers were. And then when we got here and I saw Merrick and Jeff, it made me wonder about his feelings for me and then he confirmed my suspicions. When he kissed me, it felt good, but it was because it'd been so long since anyone had shown me any real affection. Or so I thought. It was just so good to kiss someone again. Is that terrible?"

"No." He chuckled sadly and scooted over next to me on the floor, pulling me into his side. "No. I don't think that's terrible. I think you're human. We were made to love each other, weren't we? All you need is love and all that."

"Yeah, I guess so." I punched him lightly in his gut. "Worse Beatles song ever, by the way."

He laughed but I still felt terrible, inside and out. I felt terrible that I hadn't cried it out yet and felt on the verge of bursting. I felt terrible that Cain's warmth was seeping through my shirt and I wanted to just lay there with him all day and not move. I felt terrible that I needed a shower and that was what I was thinking about.

"Well, you want to get some breakfast? I haven't eaten yet this morning. We've had a little...drama going on."

"Do tell," I croaked trying to direct the conversation to something else.

"Maybe later, when I can process it. Sleep deprivation and starvation don't mix. Breakfast?"

"Do you mind if we just stay here for a while longer? You can lay down with me this time. Or-" I had a sudden revelation that he probably was tired of looking after me and was ready to go on with his day. "You know what? I'm sorry, you go. I'm going to just stay here for a little bit and I'll see you later, ok? Thank you for staying with me last night."

"Whoa," he said in defense and looked at me funny, "about face. What's wrong?"

"I'm sure you don't want to sit here with me all day."

"I make my own choices, always have."

"I don't want you to feel obligated or think that I'll fall apart if you leave me."

"I have no doubt you'd survive." He cocked his head. "Do you *want* me to go?" he asked and looked at me closely.

"No," I answered and it came out as barely a breath.

"Then I'm staying, because I want to."

"Ok. Come lie down with me then."

He let me pull him gladly. We lay down, only our hands touching, facing each other. His watch ticked on and I stopped counting.

Separation Anxiety
Chapter 21- Sherry

I awoke to the sound of banging. Pots, I thought. Someone was cooking breakfast or lunch maybe, but I did not care about anything. I felt like the rug had been pulled out from under me and I landed hard, on concrete, naked, at fifty miles per hour. It hurt. I hurt so bad I could barely breathe.

I'd never been dumped before, let alone by the one person I wanted more than anything. It was sudden, out of nowhere and unfounded and creepy. Nothing added up and I was so very confused.

And he kissed Piper. The spawn of all my insecurities about him, the one person who thought she could take him from me. He kissed her. To retaliate? For revenge? For kicks? Just because he could? I didn't know any of those answers, but it hurt so bad to think about it, but that's when you can't stop thinking about something, right?

I lay there on my blanket for at least half the day. I didn't want to run into Merrick. As mad as I was at him for the Piper thing, I was more upset about his sudden interest in ending what we had. I had no idea what I'd say if I saw him.

I knew I had to get up. Someone other than Cain was eventually going to come in and wonder what was going on. I wasn't in a big rush to tell anyone so I got up. I pulled up my pallet, put it off to the side and made a break for the bathroom to freshen up. I looked at myself in the mirror for a long time. Merrick wasn't a liar. He really did think he saw what he said he saw. So what happened?

I looked just...ugly. My eyes were swollen and red from crying all night and my hair was a disaster, butI couldn't make myself fix it. I pulled it back slackly and peeked out for my husband that no longer wanted me before making a break for the kitchen.

It was empty, thankfully.

The clock said it was almost two in the afternoon already so I made myself a cup of tea and ate some leftover cornbread on the stove. It was dry, and there was no butter, but it was food. I downed the crumbly, sweet, salty square and tried not to think. I peeked again in the commons room for Merrick and, not seeing him, made my way to Danny's room.

He was there with Celeste. Honestly, I wasn't surprised.

"Hey," he said drowsily and half sat up. "What's up?" He looked at me with squinted eyes. "What's wrong? You look like crap."

"Thanks," I said quietly.

"Just saying."

"I'm fine. I...I'm just upset about everything, you know?"

"Yeah. Celeste finally went to sleep this morning. She was up all night with her mom, who still hasn't come down."

"Well, that sucks."

"Yeah. So, what time is it?"

"Almost two."

"Frig. No wonder I'm starving."

"Want me to grab you something?"

"Would you?" He looked at Celeste and back to me. "I don't want to be gone if she wakes up."

"Yes, of course. That's very sweet, Danny."

"Yeah, yeah," he said but he was grinning.

"It is sweet," Celeste said, eyes still closed. "I've got to tell you, Sherry. I have the best beauty siestas with your brother here," she said groggily.

Danny and I both laughed silently. "That's good, be right back," I whispered.

I did my same secret operative procedure to go and get him some cornbread as I had before. Once I returned with it I sat with him while he ate and then when he started yawning I backed out with a wave.

I sat outside his door and tried to think where I could go where I wouldn't bump into Merrick. I wanted to see Lily, something awful, but her room was right next to ours and she was so perceptive. She'd know something was wrong with me, she always did. Plus, Marissa should already have her for school.

So I went over to the other hall, passed the stairs, and saw Ryan. He was sitting at the bench of the small piano there. Just sitting. I sat beside him.

"Hey, Ryan. How's the leg?"

"Better. It's tough being human and having all these limitations."

"You're preaching to the choir, pal," I joked.

He laughed and shook his head. "Sorry. It's just...I'm not like the others. I haven't had as much experience and earth time as they have. It's hard adjusting. I feel like I'm missing something."

"Like what?"

"I don't know. I can't put my finger on it, but it's there, hanging in front of me like cheese to a rat. I chase it, but can't reach it."

I was shocked. I'd never heard Ryan talk like this before, so open and forthcoming.

"Well, is there anything I can do? You are human now, Ryan. All humans go through things like that. Where we feel inadequate or without a purpose or with purpose but no direction. I know Merric-" I choked on his name and took a small breath. "Merrick, he has those problems sometimes too. Where he feels a little useless because there's so many of you together and we all just kind of exist together."

"Yes! Yes, that's it. That's how I feel; stuck and useless."

I inched quietly and slowly into my next question. "Would you go home if you could?"

"I don't know." He shrugged. "You would think the answer would be easy wouldn't you. Yes. I should want to go home, but...I'm not sure. I'm scared because I'm not sure."

"Don't be." I looped my arm though his to soothe him. "It's your life now. Calvin is safe and here. You can choose who you are now. I'm always here if you want to talk, you know that, right?"

"Yes, thank you. You are the kindest human I've ever had the privilege of meeting."

I laughed, a little shocked at his flattery. "Oh, well, uh. Thanks."

"I didn't mean to embarrass you."

"You didn't. I just...I never thought the word human would be attached to a compliment directed my way before."

"I'm sorry."

"Ryan," I said in mock exasperation. "You don't have to be sorry. Humans joke with each other. We laugh, we play, we bicker, we fight, we're sarcastic. We love, we hate, we have good and bad in all of us. You just have to decide what you want to be. You're kind of lucky if you think about it." I turned to look at him full on. "You get a clean slate, a completely fresh start. No one knows you and there is no past to chase you. You can be whoever you want to be down here."

"But what if I have no idea who I want to be?" he said sadly, his chin lowering as if in defeat.

"Be you. I've met you and I like you just fine," I crooned.

He smiled and rubbed my arm with his overly warm hand. "Thanks, Sherry."

"No problem. Now, you want to play something with me?" I motioned towards the piano keys in front of us.

"I don't know how to play."

"I wasn't under the impression that you did, Ryan," I joked. "I can teach you a little. Here."

I played the first few chords of Twinkle, Twinkle Little Star and then let him mimic me. He laughed when he got it right the first time. "Ha! Will you look at that."

"I told you. It's easy once you figure it out."

We did the next chords and he followed. We laughed as we kept playing and finally finished the song. Then we played it again.

"So," Ryan said and looked me right in the eye. "Was this a display of metaphor? You showing me how I can mimic you on the piano just like I should mimic the rest of human behavior? Do you think that would help me to adjust better?"

"Well..." I dragged out. "I hadn't thought of that, Ryan, but it sounds like you worked that all out on your own."

"Well, it's sound advice, I guess," he said seriously.

"I guess," I joked. "See, you didn't need my help after all," I said and bumped his shoulder with mine.

"Sure I did. Thank you, Sherry. I mean it. You have always been good to me."

"You think too little of yourself. You are worthy of my friendship, Ryan. You don't have to thank me every time I do something for you. That's what friends do."

"I've never had a friend before. I have no idea what that even means."

"Well, now you do. We're friends. You can ask me anything, talk to me about anything and I'll always tell you the truth. Ok?" I said and smiled.

"Ok," he said smiling back, and it was strange how uneasy it seemed. I realized he didn't smile too often. He had a good smile. "Now, play something for me, something more advanced than children's rhymes."

I smirked at him and turned back to the piano to play. It was almost supper time, as I could hear them banging around in the kitchen. I began to play and had only gotten about twenty seconds into it when I looked around and saw Merrick coming down our hallway to the commons room. I watched him as I played and saw he was still angry and sleepy looking as he gazed at nothing and no one. His face was drawn and tight and his eyes were dark with no sleep.

He found my gaze, like he subconsciously sought it, and we locked gazes. Mine was pleading and his was defiant. My breathing was suddenly erratic and my chest ached anew.

I saw that I wasn't going to get anywhere with him today and I didn't want him to see me burst into tears, so I tore my gaze away and murmured my goodbye to Ryan, spouting something about being tired, and made my way back to the laundry room briskly before collapsing on my pallet once more and pulling the blanket over my head. Wanting to see no one, hear from no one, speak to no one. Trying desperately to forget Merrick's kiss with Piper and the way he had been so, so angry at me. Pushed me, looked on me with disgust and rage. I'd actually been afraid of him and I never thought that would ever have been possible.

So I cried, big, fat, hurtful, wretched tears in the dark and prayed no one came looking for me. All the while, wondering what the in the world went wrong.

Got Breakfast?
Chapter 22- Lillian

"Breakfast now?" Cain asked as he rubbed my arm soothingly. "You've got to get up sometime. It's morning again, you need to eat something."

"Ok." I let him pull me up and we went.

He grabbed my hand as we walked, easily and casually, swinging our arms slightly. Strangely it felt more friendly than intimate, like he was trying to show me I still had a friend and he'd be my friend through all this until I was ready to be more. I wondered about Sherry, if he still felt crazy about her.

We entered the kitchen and he sat me down in a chair and got me some coffee, to which I murmured my thanks. It was horrid and lukewarm but I drank it because I needed it.

There were others in the kitchen with us; Piper and Polly, who were eyeing me but I tried to ignore them, Jeff and Marissa were sitting at the table with me eating a late breakfast together as well.

Cain set a bowl of oatmeal in front of me and one for him across from me. He sat down and smiled.

"Mmmm. Oatmeal," he said with fake enthusiasm.

I chuckled under my breath and smiled back. I was thankful for him at this moment. Otherwise I would have just sulked in my room, alone.

I felt someone behind me and turned to look. It was Piper.

"Good morning, Lillian."

"Morning, Piper," I said and felt odd about her speaking to me.

"So, Cain, how have you been?"

"Fine, Piper."

"Really? Are you sure about that?"

I turned to look at her. What was her problem? Why was she badgering Cain?

"Yes. Fine. Thank you for your concern," he all but spat out.

"What's going on? Is this the drama you were referring to?" I ask.

"Oh, he told you then?" Piper chimed almost happily, coming to stand beside the table beside us.

"Told me what?"

"That Merrick and I caught Cain and Sherry in the hall."

My heart stopped a couple beats and then picked back up violently. I heard other gasps to echo mine and looked over to see Marissa and Jeff just as stunned as I was.

"What?" I asked.

"Shut up, Piper. You don't know what you're talking about," Cain said and shoved his chair back, taking his bowl to the sink.

"Don't I?"

"What is she talking about, Cain?" I asked softly and hoped he answered me, that nothing happened.

"I'm talking about Cain and Sherry practically - what is it you humans say - 'getting it on' in the hall outside your room the night of the ambush. Merrick is so upset. He's even refused to let Sherry stay in their room with him."

"What?" Jeff said but nobody answered him.

What? My head spun. Merrick and Sherry fighting? Those two were like glue to each other.

"Shut up, Piper! If that's the case then why did you come get me, huh? When Sherry was crying, you came to Lillian's room, where I was all night, and woke me up to go to Sherry," Cain said and I could see his high color getting higher.

"Because you caused all this! That's why! I figured you should be the one to comfort her, though in my book, she doesn't deserve any," Piper said and walked out with Polly in tow.

Something was terribly wrong with Polly. She hadn't said a word the whole time and it wasn't like her to miss an opportunity for drama. She was so pale and her eyes were so cloudy and gray. She slinked behind Piper like she was tethered to her, and had not a care or a bit of strength.

"Cain, what is she talking about?" I asked him again.

"Yes, Cain. What the heck is going on?" Marissa asked after me, she looked almost angry.

Cain sat back down, turned to me and spoke.

"This is the drama I was telling you about. For some reason, Merrick and Piper claim they saw Sherry and me in the hall making out that night, outside of your room. Piper, I could see making all this up but Merrick? I don't know what's going on, but...he really believes he saw us, Lillian. It's weird. He was furious yesterday." He ran his hands over his head a few times then linked them behind his head and leaned back in his chair. "He yelled at Sherry and pushed her away. I've never seen him that way, especially with her."

Marissa and Jeff scooted their chairs back and left. Their sudden departure and silence spoke volumes.

I pondered what he was saying. Did he expect me to believe him? That he was caught making out with Sherry, whom he confessed to me earlier to having feelings for, but it was Merrick who was making it up? What was going on?

"So...you're saying Merrick didn't catch you?"

"I'm saying I didn't do it. I wouldn't do that to her or him."

"Cain." I gauged my words carefully and looked around for eavesdroppers, seeing none. "You told me you had feelings for Sherry."

His eyes went wide and then he refocused and spoke quietly.

"Yes, I did, but I would never act on it. She's married. Besides, I wouldn't have told you but you figured it out. I was trying to move on too, remember?" he said referring to me moving on, per our earlier conversation.

I couldn't disagree or judge him for that but the rest of his story was a little ridiculous.

"Ok, so you got a little carried away and got caught. Denying it isn't going to make it just go away," I said softly.

"I didn't do anything. What is wrong with everyone? Am I that untrustworthy that no one would believe me when I say I flat didn't do something? Sherry is the most loyal person in here and no one believes her either." He scooted his chair back too, loudly. "What is going on here?"

He left, leaving me feeling strangely guilty and weird and off kilter.

I went to find Sherry.

I found her a while later after searching everywhere. She was hunched over on a pallet in the utility room, perfectly still, eyes open, staring at the wall. I wondered how long she'd been in there.

"Sherry? Are you ok?"

As much as I liked Cain and didn't appreciate him kissing someone the same night he had kissed me - though I had kissed Mitchell a few nights before so how much room did I have to talk - Sherry was my friend and I hated to see her so broken down.

"Lillian, something is...happening. I'm going crazy or something."

"Why do you say that? Because you gave in to Cain and kissed him? He can be very charming."

"I didn't!" she yelled suddenly and sat up.

Oh, no, not this again. Not Sherry. She didn't seem the lie and weasel type to me. "Sherry, it's ok, just tell me what happened."

"Nothing. I went to check on you, but you were asleep so I sat in the hall with Cain outside your room and we talked. I hugged him but I always hug him, it was nothing new. Merrick has seen me hug him a hundred times. That was it. He went back in your room and I went back up the hall. Merrick said we were kissing, like really into it and there was no way he mistook it for hugging him. I have no idea what he's talking about."

"Sherry, it's me. You can tell me. It's ok, I won't judge you." She burst into a hysterical round of tears and I felt like the utter worst friend and consoler. "I'm sorry."

I tried to touch her shoulder, but she pushed my hand off.

"That's it. I can't take this anymore. Nobody believes me! I have to talk to him," she said breathlessly as she got up from her pallet.

"You mean Cain?"

"No! Merrick!"

She proceeded to make her way out of the room, into the hall and to the commons room with me following after her.

I saw Merrick there, looked like he was waiting for something but he didn't seem upset to me. He seemed his normal chipper self. I could only stop, pray for Sherry and stare at the train wreck about to happen.

As soon as he saw her his eyes lit up and he reached his arms out for her to walk into, but she stopped and stared like a deer in headlights. He spoke. "Honey, what's wrong?"

He made a step forward, concern etched all over his face. She stepped back again. "Merrick?" she asked softly.

"What's the matter, babe? Did something happen?" he asked and then reached for her again.

She stood perfectly still and let him wrap his arms around her and then he kissed her sweetly on her lips, cupping her jaw in one hand. She let him kiss her, but didn't participate and he pulled back. "Something's wrong, I can tell. Tell me what's the matter, sweetheart."

Wow. Three endearments in one minute's time.

"Merrick?" she asked again.

"Sherry, what's the matter?" he asked, getting more impatient.

"You...believe me?" she choked out through tears.

"About what?"

"About *what*? Is this a joke?" she asked and appeared more confused than ever.

I was right there with her and then I saw Cain come walking back down the hall. He stopped dead in his tracks and stared at them, too, in total confusion.

"What do you mean? What's going on?" Merrick asked.

"You don't remember? You...you thought you saw Cain and I..." she looked over at Cain for a second and he looked back at her astonished and shrugged "you thought you saw Cain and me kissing."

"What? What are you talking about?" Merrick asked incredulously and looking none too happy. "You kissed Cain?"

"No! You thought I did. You really don't remember?" she asked, breathing the words.

"No, I think I'd remember that." He scowled. "Did Cain kiss you?" he asked softly and looked back at Cain for a split second.

"No! No. No one kissed anyone." She thought for a moment and then. "What day is it, Merrick?"

"Uh...Friday."

"No, it's Sunday. You don't remember the past two nights at all, do you? The Lighters attacking us?"

"The Lighters attacked? How? What happened?" he asked in a rage. Sherry, Cain and I exchanged worried looks.

Then Piper walked in.

A Bad Case Of The Blues
Chapter 23 - Sherry

At first, I didn't see Piper standing there. I was too enthralled in the situation. Merrick accused me of something so against my morals and thoughts, so incomprehensible and degrading. He had yelled at me, gritted his teeth at me, pushed me, left me crying and confused and now claimed to not remember any of it.

I was more than relieved.

I hoped he forgot the whole thing completely, even though the question of his kiss with Piper was still lingering there, unanswered. Then I heard Piper grunt angrily.

"Well, well. Merrick, what's going on in here?" she asked and I wanted to run to her and introduce that little instigator to my fist.

"What do you mean? Will someone please tell me what's going on?" he spoke loudly now and there were others in the commons room watching us, that didn't know about Merrick and me fighting.

"You don't remember?" Piper asked and eyed evilly the arms still around my waist.

"I guess not since I have no idea what it is everyone is talking about. What did you mean 'what's going on here'? What should be going on?"

"Nothing." She looked confused and angry, then started to turn and walk back into the kitchen but Lillian - surprising the heck out of me - grabbed her arm to halt her.

"Um, I don't think you get to just walk out and pretend like you don't know what's going on," Lillian said, but Piper, being the Keeper she was, ripped free of her grasp easily and gave her a look that would melt butter.

Then Cain was there beside Lillian and yelled for Jeff, who was walking in from the kitchen with Marissa.

"Jeff, help me get her to sit down and chat."

Jeff scowled at Cain like he was the devil, but grabbed Piper's other arm and they escorted her to the couch. Merrick and I walked to the other one and we all sat or stood, facing each other in a silent circle for a minute.

"Ok, I'll start," Cain said finally. "I think our Piper here has been playing games. Somehow, she got Merrick to think he saw Sherry and me kissing, and then she gets me to go see Sherry, and then Merrick to go right after me and see me with her there too, in the laundry room. I didn't put it together then, but I should have when I saw you spying on us. Then, you confronted me about it in front of Lillian and Jeff, knowing they'd be furious about it."

I remembered something.

"And Polly. Polly came to get me to tell me Merrick wanted me. She said he was in our room but when I went back there..." I paused and felt a grimace that I couldn't stop before going on, "he was in there with Piper."

"What? What do mean I was in our room with Piper?" Merrick shouted unbelievingly.

I couldn't stop as the pieces all fell together. I spoke directly to Piper.

"You wanted me to catch you in our room with him. You wanted me to think he'd kissed you."

Piper sat there calmly and quietly and then she spoke and what came out was pure sarcastic hatred and garbage.

"Well, you caught me. You figured it all out. I did it. I wanted Merrick to see what life could be like without you and that he didn't need you to feel human," she spat out the words, especially 'human' like it was all so disgusting.

I shook my head in rage. Merrick was sputtering and shaking beside me but couldn't make any syllables audibly into words.

"You thought I'd just give up on him?" I said looking right at her. "You thought I'd see you trying to kiss him and assume it was him kissing you? You thought I'd see his anger at me and be scared and want no part in it anymore? You honestly thought this was some fling that you could break up with petty juvenile tactics? We are married," I bit out, "and you don't know me very well."

I lifted from my seat.

Merrick grabbed my arm gently to hold me in place and I saw that even Piper had backed herself into the couch a little. I realized I had practically growled the words at her but I meant every one.

Jeff spoke then and looked at me for the first time this morning. "So you didn't? You didn't have an affair with Cain?"

"No! I would never do that to Merrick." I felt like I'd said that statement five hundred times in the past twelve hours. Jeff sighed and I saw his relief. He believed it too, they all had. Believed that I would cheat on the love of my life, the person I fought for, the person I would risk everything for, the one who came light years to be with me.

I was devastated.

Did no one have any faith in me or Cain? I buried my face in my hands to hide my expression - of rage - I was sure. "How is it that not one person believed us?" I said softly and was met with guilty silence and avoiding gazes as I lifted my head.

"Sherry," Cain said this time, "it doesn't explain how she got Merrick to see us kissing. I mean, how she got him to think we did," he said hurriedly.

"No, it doesn't," Piper said happily and laughed.

"Wait, wait," Merrick finally found his voice, "ok. You are saying that I somehow thought I saw you and Cain kiss, but you didn't. And Piper somehow orchestrated all this?"

Well, when you put it like that...it did sound crazy, but it was true. I didn't get a chance to answer. Merrick suddenly grabbed his head and leaned forward groaning.

"Merrick?" I kneeled in front of him. "What is it?"

"My head. It feels like it's...splitting," he moaned.

Then he jerked, moaned louder and fell forward to the floor. His hands shook, and he jerked and grasped his head.

"Merrick!"

I tried to sit him up but he wouldn't, he just kept moaning and rocking back and forth. I was scared to say the least. Something was happening to him and I knew it had something to do with what had happened. A tumor? A blood clot? That didn't make sense. If it was that, Piper wouldn't have seen what Merrick saw in the hall. So what was going on?

I tried to soothe him, tell him I was there. Jeff sank to the floor with me beside him and even Piper seemed in an upheaval about Merrick's condition, though she had no right to be.

Then he stopped rocking, stopped moaning. His eyes opened and he let go of his head. He sat up and looked right at me. His breaths came out in loud blows. His big wide green eyes locked with mine. He was oblivious to all the others standing over us.

"Sherry. Baby," he pleaded breathlessly with his eyes, looking terrified and shameful. He grabbed my face gently in between his warm hands that I loved so much. "Oh, baby, I'm so sorry. I can't believe... I remember. I remember everything." He buried his face in my hair and wrapped his arms around me. "I can't believe you let me talk to you like that."

"I didn't exactly let you," I answered quietly and he pulled back and wrinkled his nose into a grimace.

"No, I guess not. Sherry, I love you so much. I would never hurt you, you know that, right? Those things I said, the things I did...honey, I didn't mean any of it. That wasn't me. I don't know what came over me."

"You do remember? All of it?"

"Yes." His jaw tightened and he swallowed before growling his words to me. "And don't you ever let me put my hands on you in anger again." I heard a gasp, but didn't look to see who it was. I hadn't told anyone that Merrick had grabbed me. "You scream, you run, you do something. Do you hear me? Don't just sit there and-" He stopped and then turned a rage filled gaze to Piper who swallowed and heaved a breath. He all but bellowed the words at her. "You. You did this. Why? How?"

She tried to get up, but Jeff held her in place with a hand on her shoulder. She stayed silent and looked nervous.

"What do you remember?" I asked him, still letting him pet my hair because I missed him so much that I refused to make him stop, and he seemed to really need to touch me.

"I remember seeing you, a vision of you and Cain," he winced, "kissing and- but I can see now it wasn't real. It was a compulsion." His eyes registered the word as it said it. He was figuring it all out. "It played over and over in my head, nonstop. I couldn't think about anything else. I just thought I was so upset by it that it was making me crazy. In fact, it *was* making me crazy. I felt like I was on the edge, I couldn't sleep, I was shaking, I haven't eaten, I couldn't think."

"That's why you were so...irritable," I suggested.

"Sweet, Sherry. That's a nice way of putting it. Gah, honey..." He shook his head and then started again. "I remember yelling at you, pushing-" He closed his eyes as if in agony. I ducked my head so as not to meet eyes with anyone. "Pushing you against the wall and grabbing your arms. Going to bed alone, but I couldn't sleep because of the vision. Then, in the morning, Piper told me to go check on you. That I'd been too hard on you and you were upset so I did and found you and Cain in the utility room. I was so furious. I thought there was no way I could forgive you. Then I went to take a nap, Piper followed me and then you walked in on her trying to...kiss me."

"That's when Polly had told me to go see you."

"It would seem. Then, after I woke up, I went to go find Lily but didn't see her anywhere and I saw you at the piano with Ryan. I remember thinking that you were probably screwing around with Ryan too." He shook his head at himself. "I watched you walk away and then I went back to bed. When I woke up this morning, I didn't remember anything. I remember thinking something was wrong because it was so late and you hadn't woke me. I hadn't remembered you coming to bed either. It's so clearly compulsion. I can't believe I fell for it. How Piper? How?"

We all turned and looked at Piper.

She promptly turned on the water works.

"I'm not sorry! I thought I could make you see reason." She sniffed. "You can't love her, Merrick. She's a vile, vain, selfish human and a vapor compared to us. You can't give up everything for *her*. I won't let you!"

He ignored everything she said and went forward with his question, not looking a bit sympathetic for her tears. "I asked *how*, Piper."

"It doesn't matter. It apparently didn't work as it should have. Only two day's worth? It worked a lot longer with the others."

"What does that mean? And again I say how? The only person we know who uses compulsion around here is Danny but his only works one task at a time, but he couldn't make me see the vision. And Marissa..." he trailed off.

I looked at her and she was practically cowered in the corner, waiting for blame to be placed on her for this. It looked like she had seen the blame coming every since the word 'vision' was mentioned.

Jeff gave Merrick a look.

"It couldn't be Marissa either. Again, she couldn't make me see a vision of something that didn't happened like that, could she?" Merrick asked.

"Yes, I could, but I didn't," Marissa said softly.

"It wasn't Marissa," I said quickly. I certainly didn't need any convincing on that front. "Who, Piper?"

"I don't have to tell *you* anything. You are so selfish! You have no idea what you're taking from him! I'm so done here!" She yelled and screeched and let her tears fall while she banged her fist on the couch cushions like a toddler. "I hate it here! I want to go home, back to my normal body and out of this puny, black haired, evil teenage vessel that is holding me hostage. I'm over six thousand years old. Not sixteen! I'm so done with all of it! I hate it here! Hate it!"

Marissa then crossed the room and touched Piper's arm. "Tell us who helped you do this to Merrick," she compelled.

"Polly," Piper said then gasped and covered her mouth then yelled loudly. "Stop it, Muse!"

"Where is Polly?" Merrick asked and Marissa went to look for her in her room.

In the mean time, while Piper sat stewing and crying loudly under Jeff's firm grip, Merrick returned back to me and his apologizing, pulling me to look at him with a hand on my cheek, still not caring who could hear him.

"I'm so sorry. I was terrible to you. Baby, you have to believe that I'd never hurt you-"

I cut him off with a kiss and this time I didn't expect him to push me away. He didn't. He pulled me closer, into his lap and caressed my cheek and jaw line with his fingertips while his lips worked magic to heal my sorrows.

My Merrick was back. I was more relieved than words could say. I tried to think back to what had happened and see his face so angry at me, but I couldn't.

All I saw was my always patient, always loving husband. I was happy to forget the other.

He broke away, barely, letting his lips graze my lips and face.

"I know you'd never hurt me," I said and I meant it.

"Can you forgive me?"

"I think I've more than forgiven you."

"I need to hear you say it. And if you can't, then don't. I understand the things I said, the way I looked at you, the way I acted, was unforgivable."

"You were under compulsion, Merrick."

"Does that make it all right? No," he answered for me.

"It makes it not your fault. But if you need to hear it, of course I forgive you, though you don't need my forgiveness."

"Sherry," he breathed my name in relief, "we can never fight again. That was unbearable. I missed you."

"Agreed," I said and smiled at him.

He looked even more relieved and I determined he was done with his plight and accepting my words. He kissed my mouth again, softly and steadily, and didn't stop until we heard his name.

Cain.

"Hey, uh," Cain cleared his throat, "Polly's coming."

We looked up to see her coming down the hall with Marissa. Wow. She looked terrible. While I was trying to figure out the newest puzzle piece, Merrick lifted me up with him and set me to my feet, keeping a firm warm hand in mine. He turned to Cain, who was still a couple feet away, near Piper, but definitely avoiding Merrick's gaze.

"Cain."

Cain looked up reluctantly. Even though everything had been resolved, I felt his pain. Everyone lost faith in us, blamed us for something heinous. No one believed us, not one person. That sucked.

"I'm so sorry, man," Merrick said vehemently.

"It's fine, Merrick."

"No, it's not." Merrick took a step closer to him and extended his hand to shake. "You're a good, honest man, my best friend, and I accused you of something terrible. I'm sorry."

Cain stared at Merrick's hand for a few seconds. Then he took it and finally looked up to Merrick's face.

"No harm done. I'm just glad we got it all worked out. You do have some wicked pointy fingers, bro." His eyes gleamed with amusement and he rubbed the phantom finger spot on his chest.

"I'm sorr-"

"I'm just joshing you." Cain hugged him, patting his back all manly like. "It's cool. If I thought someone had touched my woman, I'd be off the deep end too. I have been off the deep end before actually."

"Thanks. We're good?"

"Yeah, we're good."

Cain and I looked at each other then. I so wanted to hug him. Once again, we were victims together, but now, after everything, it felt awkward. Would people be watching Cain and I now like hawks, waiting to see if we'd get too close? Was Merrick always going to have suspicions?

He smiled ruefully and lifted his shoulders in an 'I have no idea what to do now' gesture.

Screw it. I reached out and hugged him.

He hugged me back and murmured in my ear. "Sorry about all this."

"You didn't do anything wrong," I said and let him go.

I glanced back at Merrick, and saw him watching us and wince again, looking away. No doubt the picture flashing of Cain and me in Merrick's mind that he would never be able to erase.

That was when I knew things would never be the same. I wouldn't torture Merrick with his memories. We'd just lay low for while. No more visits and talks in the hall for Cain and me. Not alone anyway.

I went back to Merrick and wrapped my arms around his neck to whisper in his ear. "I'm sorry. I won't do that anymore."

"What? Why?" he said, but the softness told me he knew what and why.

"I understand. I can see your face, you know. I love you and will do anything for you. Even not hug or touch someone because it's brings a bad memory for you."

"It wasn't real."

"But you thought it was. You can still see it and it looks real now, doesn't it?" He exhaled, pursing his lips and nodded slowly. "Then I won't do it anymore," I whispered firmly.

He hesitated, then nodded again gratefully.

I looked over to see Lillian standing by Cain. She was whispering in his ear and he was nodding. Then she pulled back and grabbed his hand, they both smiled at each other.

Well, well.

Then it was time to deal with Polly.

Kiss and Not Tell
Chapter 24 - Cain

"I'm sorry for the way I spoke to you earlier in the kitchen. I should have believed you but...you have to admit, it was pretty unbelievable," Lillian whispered and smiled a little smile to which I returned. "I'm sorry. Really sorry. So...can we just forget all of this, and say you and I work together? Hmm? You can help me with all this Mitchell stuff, help me grieve and let me cry like a girl," she smiled again, "and...I'll help you get over Sherry. Well, I'll try. I can be your friend."

She squinted cutely and then bit her bottom lip, waiting for my response.

"That sounds like a plan to me...lovely."

She smiled and tucked her hair behind her ear, ducking her head.

Yes!! I was back in the game!

"Good. So we get this...stuff settled and then go brief everybody on the things we got, what they talked about at the rally. With everything going on, I think they forgot we even went."

"Yeah, I think you're right. And yes, that sounds like a plan, too."

"Good, sweetie pie," she said with a smile, remembering our joke.

She slipped her hand into mine, her fingers still warm and soft, but long and skinny. Pleasant to touch, but not like Sherry's. I wondered how long it would be before I stopped comparing everything to Sherry. But hey, Lillian knew and we were going in with eyes completely wide open. No hidden secrets. We could be honest and help each other get over all that past crap.

I glanced at Sherry and she was watching us. She glanced at our intertwined hands and lifted her eyebrow, smiling. I realized she was happy about this new development. I should be. I was but...whew. This was so much harder than I ever imagined. Why did I have to love her? Why? And why did Merrick's vision of Sherry and me have to be so close to the fantasy I'd had a million times, just like it?

We turned our attention back to Jeff, who just started his interrogation of Polly, who looked horrendous. I didn't mean that in a hateful way. She really did look awful, like someone took the sick-and-pale stick and beat her senseless with it.

"I don't know what you're talking about," Polly said sluggishly, but she kept glancing at Piper the entire time, back and forth.

It felt strange to be interrogating two teenage girls like that. Technically, only one was a teenager, but still.

"I think you do. Are you sick or something?" Jeff asked.

"I just don't feel well. Now let me go back to bed."

"Ok then, answer my question and you can. What did you do to Merrick?"

"I didn't do anything."

"Oh, come on. Enough already." Marisa stepped up and placed a finger on Polly's hands, folded on her pulled up legs, and said, "What did you do to Merrick?"

Polly started to whimper, then groan, clutching her stomach. She doubled over onto the floor and starting screaming. I was puzzled. Was this an act? Was she really sick?

"Don't, Polly!" Marissa yelled, scolding.

"Polly, you know what you're doing. You are only making it worse for yourself," Sherry said softly and knelt in front of Polly, though I'm not sure Polly heard her.

"Don't listen to them, Polly!" Piper yelled over the screeching. "You keep your secrets. It's the only thing they can't take from you on this God forsaken hateful planet!"

"Shut up, Piper!" Marissa yelled and knelt down with Sherry. "Polly, stop fighting it. It won't hurt if you don't fight it."

"Polly, you're going to hurt yourself," Sherry said and reached out to help Polly sit up.

Polly swung her foot up so quickly I barely saw it before it was too late but not for Merrick. He blurred over to her and caught Polly's bare foot inches from Sherry's face.

Sherry went wide-eyed and exhaled, then let Merrick pull her back into his lap, a safe distance away on the couch. He seemed reluctant to not be touching her anyway, like he needed assurance.

"Polly." Marissa was back at it, but Polly wasn't giving up.

I was still puzzled as to what was going on. Then I heard Simon in my head. I looked up to see him standing at the edge of the commons room.

It's the Muse's Wrath. It's compulsion. She can make you do something or see something. She can even see things that haven't happened yet but it's pretty much haphazard visions. Unfortunately, not always useful. Anyway, if you fight the Muse's Wrath it hurts, bad. If you just follow through with whatever task she's

265

given you, you're fine. Looks like our friend here is fighting it.

I nodded a thank you for the explanation and he turned, apparently having seen enough. I kind of missed Simon. I hadn't really had the chance much to talk to him or spend much time with him since we'd been at the bunker.

He was a killer at chess. We'd play at the cabin sometimes when I got home from work. He claimed King Louis XIV of France had taught him, as he had been an avid chess player.

He'd told me all about his travels, he called them, his times that he came to earth. King Louis was the only real famous person he guarded, but I still thought that was pretty cool. He had spent nearly two months here with him, which Simon told me was almost unheard of for Keepers to do before all this business started with the Lighters being here.

I snapped back to attention when Polly finally sat up and started spouting all kinds of gibberish. Then she doubled over again and screamed, writhing on her side on the floor.

The warm soft hand in mine squeezed. I looked over and Lillian had her head turned and eyes closed. She didn't want to see this. It wasn't pretty, I would grant her that.

"Hey," I waited for her to look up at me, "you don't have to stay here. You've been through enough already. I can do this and you can go rest or grab a shower. I'll check on you later."

She smiled sweetly, then reached up and kissed me.

Yes, kissed me, in front of everyone.

I wondered if she was doing me a favor, trying to dispel any lingering rumors that anyone might have about me and Sherry, but the kiss was too quick, too soft, a peck really. She wasn't doing anything of the sort - well, maybe a little - and I fell in love with her a tiny bit right there for it. She wanted to tell me that she wasn't going anywhere, but thanks for caring about her.

She smiled up at me and I smiled back down at her. When I turned back to the drama I saw that everyone else saw us. And everyone was puzzled. No one knew anything about that little development but Sherry, whom I glanced at to see if she saw and got a sideways grin from her. I just grinned, too, and let everyone think what they wanted to.

Polly sat up again and this time, her voice was strong and clear.

"My gift is visual compulsion. I made Merrick see a vision of Sherry and Cain. I made him relive that vision in his mind on a continuous loop as instructed by Piper. Usually, my compulsion lasts for multiple days, but Merrick's only lasted two. Piper threatened me, said that if I didn't do what she wanted she'd do something to me to make you make me leave. She said, you'd believe her because she was a Keeper. I didn't want to be out there alone, so I did it."

Then she shook her head, breathed deep and looked ahead like she had no idea what to do or what she had done.

Everyone, once again, turned to look at Piper.

"Well," I said since everyone else was silent, "I say a good old fashion hanging is in order."

Hunk Of Burning Love
Chapter 25 - The Taker

The manor was just how I remembered it, or how Crandle remembered it rather. It was quant, though quite large for a house in these parts and in this time.

In my day, all there was were mansions and castles. That or squat. You were somebody or you were nobody. You lived or you didn't. I guessed, compared to the mediocre surrounding the manor, I was living.

They knew I was the old me. At least I thought they comprehended. It was so tiresome, dealing with the Lighters minds with their blind obedience, ignorance and not much else. Not like humans, at least they thought for themselves. Humans could process requests and commands and not have to be told, slowly and word for word, what the instructions were. And God forbid something went wrong, the Lighters had no idea what to do but pummel whatever was nearest to them.

In my day as a human I was practically a God. I was the King's nephew when the Lighters invaded England. Back then it wasn't world domination on the agenda. It was just kingdoms, one at a time.

Some say I was spoiled, but I called it pampered. There was a difference. I lived in the castle with the king. I wasn't his heir or anything but may as well have been. The king's son, my cousin, was a pompous idiot who took longer to get ready for functions than the queen herself did.

He was prissy and whiny and so shiny. He had more metal on his person than the Royal Guard; hat buckles, belt buckles, shoe buckles, cufflinks, rings, dainty charm bracelets. Anything that brat could get made of silver, he did. It was embarrassing to be in his presence when the sun was shining. He reflected light like a lighthouse.

The king loved me and I…well…didn't love him, but was happy where I was. I had no intentions of doing anything but being important. And it so worked for me. I had girls a plenty, sometimes two at once every night and at every event, I was the prize catch to go home with. Or upstairs I should say, as all worthy balls were held at the castle itself.

Many a girl lost her precious virtue to my charms. It was almost comical how easy it was to slip past those laced up knickers that they claimed were welded so tightly shut until a ring was placed on a certain finger.

Ha! Not for me!

I had no intentions of marrying, though I could have held on to my game. I just wasn't interested. Then I died in a freak buggy accident and was absorbed by a Lighter trying to enter my body and take it over. I remembered the darkness, the horrible pain of my life leaving my body as I floated, but I was stronger. I wouldn't give up and I won. I remembered the feeling of being invaded by others, more than one. I suddenly knew and understood everything all at once.

The Taker could only come into the world when someone worthy and strong enough to handle him could be embodied. I was the Taker for a few years, I lost track. Those were the best years of my life. Then, some fool got a stroke of luck and was able to set the castle on fire while I slept. I didn't make it and I remembered, as I sat in the corner and burned, knowing I was dying and the fun was over, how truly pissed I was. Dead forever this time, at eighteen.

And now, here we were, 21st century and America. What a dreary and ugly place. No rolling hills, no houses worthy of mention, no courts or balls or bath houses. Nothing of amusement. I blew out an exasperated bored breath and let my forehead rest against the cool window pane of the sitting room, let the memories of the Takers after and before me settle in.   We shall see what these times might have to offer me.

I waltzed into the master bedroom and looked around. The clothes in the closet as well as the ones on my body were disgusting, not just dirty but in fashion as well.

After I showered and put on some equally unfashionable attire from the closet, which I recognized now, everything was becoming clearer the more I relaxed and let the memories come in.

I headed downstairs to find my service men lined up in the den, waiting for me to address them. Waiting for the new course of action. I immediately began to lay down the law, letting them know I was no piddly Taker. I was *the* Taker.

"Out of my way, fool," I growled to the one idiot half way blocking the doorway, though I had plenty of room to get through. He scrambled with apologies but I slapped him across the face. Everyone stilled. "I don't want your sorrys, I want your obedience. A simple 'yes, sir' will do."

"Yes, sir."

"Good. Now." I turned to address the majority of them. "I am Malachi, your Taker and as far as you are concerned, there is no other. No past, no future, just me, here and now. I am back and I plan to stay. I know Crandle was very much interested in this human girl, this Sherry. I admire him, the man had taste. However, my plans do not include her unless she is to be my lunch or playmate. My plan is not to eliminate the humans. What purpose would that serve? My plan is to enslave them. They will work for us, do our bidding, become our brothers until every last Lighter has been given a new body, and to feed and entertain me. Other than that, they are not to be destroyed and needlessly killed. Is that understood?"

"Yes, sir," a gruff chorus rang out.

"Good. Now, don't get me wrong, I am in no way a human sympathizer. I don't want them killed because they are of use to me. You don't throw perfectly good...what are they called? Batteries? Yes, that's it. You wouldn't throw perfectly good batteries away now would you? No. And we won't throw perfectly good humans away either. Only the ones who, after heavy persuasion, can't be swayed will be eliminated. Now go. You know your jobs. We'll meet with the Enforcers tomorrow evening to hash out a further course of action."

"Yes, sir."

As they walked out, I grabbed a particularly tall one. "You. Where are the girls?"

"Excuse me, sir?"

"The ladies, the whores, the followers who want nothing more than to bang the Taker," I explained and watch him scramble.

"Uh...I'm-"

"Crandle didn't have ladies for his pleasure?" I explained more slowly so he could understand.

He squinted and shook his head until...Light bulb!

"No, sir. He spent most of his efforts to find the human girl, Sherry."

"What a waste and a disgrace. Then again, maybe I should meet this Sherry after all and see if she's worth all the trouble. Ok. You get me girls, now. At least three and they better be young and hot." I couldn't help it. I rubbed my hands together in anticipation. "It's been a bloody long time and I'm ready to play."

Restoration
Chapter 26 - Sherry

Polly and Piper were both taken down to their rooms and told to stay put. To emphasize that order we put someone there to watch the doors, as their rooms were across the hall from each other. Miguel was the first to pull watch duty, though he had no idea why. Most people didn't know what had happened and I was glad to keep it that way.

Everyone was told as we convened for lunch that Piper and Polly had used Polly's gifts on someone here to harm them and they were being held until it could be decided what to do with them. That was a good enough explanation for everyone.

Piper was also berated for a good long while about threatening her charge and a Special. Jeff and the others couldn't seem to fathom how she could do that. She stayed silent, cried her angry tears and refused to further address anyone, but Jeff didn't give up.

"You cannot harm, in any way, emotional, physical or otherwise anyone if this bunker or you will leave. Are we on the same page, Piper?" Jeff asked, not deflecting his tone.

"Who died and made you boss?"

"Piper," Jeff warned.

"Whatever," Piper muttered.

Then Jeff turned to Polly. "You will not use your gift on anyone in this bunker again or you will leave as well."

"So not fair! I shouldn't be held responsible-"

"Are we clear?"

"Crystal," Polly sneered and huffed.

She was upset too, but for different reasons. She thought she should get off the hook completely because Piper 'made' her do it. The Keepers explained to her that it was her choice to participate and she should have gone to someone else for help instead of letting Piper sway her choices. She squealed in protest, but eventually was taken back to her room by Miguel, and Piper was escorted by Ryan.

The Keepers were all about choice.

And Piper and Polly could no longer be considered friends. I heard them yelling all the way down the hall as they made their way to their rooms.

"Don't bump me," Polly growled.

"You bumped me!"

"Stop being a brat. It's not my fault you're stuck here. You got me into trouble!"

"You're the brat! And spoiled!"

"So!"

Afterwards, we finished lunch. Margo, who had finally come down sometime during all the drama, sullenly made the soup I had prepared and tonight I'd make ramen noodles. Mmm.

Merrick was still feeling guilty and walking around like he had something to apologize for. I assured him over and over that I was fine. He hadn't *really* hurt me.

Him pushing and grabbing me was where his biggest problem was. He had used physical force on me in anger, though he didn't really have any control over it.

I decided it was time to put an end to his misery and hash it out, once and for all. I made sure Lily was with Marissa and Jeff before I retreated. They were just coming back from the hall where their room is and we were walking hand in hand. I asked them if they minded watching her for a while as I had to try to help Merrick get over all this. They understood and Marissa apologized again for not believing me.

Lily went to them eagerly and they skipped off to the second room together.

I pulled Merrick to our room for a little R & R. Requite and Restoration. Requite for the love he'd always shown me and restoration of his feelings that I trusted him and loved him completely.

He came with me but reluctantly, he wanted to stay out where people could see us, didn't want to be alone with me, which I was some peeved about. He was afraid. If it had been so easy for Polly to do that before, she could do it again and make him hurt me for real he had said. But I knew he'd never hurt me.

"Sit," I ordered him and locked the door behind me.

He sat down and I kneeled in front of him.

I explained how I knew there was something wrong the entire time he was angry with me. That I never doubted that he really loved me. That I knew something had to happen, to be resolved and was happy when it did.

He explained his feelings during it all. How he couldn't believe how angry he was and felt guilty for yelling at me, but couldn't do anything about it at the time. It overtook him. He told me how he really and truly thought I could just leave him and move on because he wasn't human and wasn't good enough.

And that hurt me more than anything else he had to say or do.

"I can't believe after everything we've been through together, you'd think that."

"You're better than me, Sherry. I believed it because it was believable. It's not crazy to think that Cain could have had feelings for you. You're gorgeous and lovable, you're sweet and you take care of everyone. I just assumed that someone else showed interest and you finally decided to act on it, this time."

"That's crazy! I've told you time and time again that that isn't going to happen. I don't know any other way to say it, Merrick!"

I was crying by this point, which he couldn't stand. He was undone by my tears and his face fell. He started to wipe them away with his thumbs. "I'm sorry. Don't you want me to be truthful?"

"Yes, always, but I don't want you to think *that*."

"But that's how I feel," he confessed as he pressed his head to mine.

"Listen to me." I was upset, almost as upset as when he accused me to begin with because now he knew the truth and was still thinking that the day would come when I'd leave him for someone else. I pulled back. "If I wanted someone else I wouldn't be with you. There's so little time left to waste it on something your heart's not in. I love you and I swear if this doesn't stop I'll...I don't know, but I'm sick of it! There is no one else I want. How many times do we have to be together in this room? How many times do I have to tell you I love you? How many times do I have to marry you for that to be crystal clear?"

He seemed taken aback. I was yelling and he knew I was serious. I was scared too. Scared that I'd have to have this argument every month for the rest of my life, every time a semi cute new guy came into the bunker. I was not interested in that.

"I know you love me, but I just think that you didn't date enough before all this and you had a bad experience. You haven't experienced enough to see what's out there and you'll see something you didn't even know you wanted in someone else later and that'll be that."

"Never. That's the whole point in marriage, Merrick! You don't get married until you find something better, then get a divorce. You know, even if I did see something else I wanted, which I won't, I promise you that, I would never act on it. The whole point of this ring I'm wearing," I picked my hand up in front of him in the dark, knowing he could see it, "is to show people, 'Hey, I'm married, back off'. I would never do what you saw me doing with Cain in that vision. Not with him, not with anybody."

"I know you think that now, but you can't know what you'd do in the future."

"Then why did you marry me?" I countered.

"Because I love you."

"Then why can't that be my reason? Who's to say you won't see something you like in another woman and leave me, huh?"

He snorted like that was the dumbest thing he'd ever heard. It pushed me passed the boiling point. My heart rate and breathing were out of control and I snapped.

"Merrick! Stop it! I'm not the kind of person to do that to someone else," I fought it but I burst into a sobbing mess, "and for you to have so little faith in me, hurts worse than anything. I'd rather you'd pushed me into a hundred walls than to say that to me."

I got up to leave. Our first real fight, without compulsion, and I was walking out. I thought he was going to let me go, let me walk out and leave him there, but no. Just as I reached the door handle and wretched it open he grabbed my upper arm and swung me around, kicking the door back closed with his foot. He pulled me to him and kissed me fiercely until I could neither breathe nor think.

He moved me backwards to the wall and continued to kiss me so deeply I thought I'd suffocate if he didn't let up soon. But he didn't, and despite my feelings, I didn't die. He lifted me up and pressed me into the wall, his hand caressed my face, my arm, my hair, while his body held me in place. My legs instinctively wrapped around him. Then he pulled back enough to gasp out his words to me.

"I'm sorry," he murmured low into my hair and neck. "You're right. Here you are, the sweetest thing to walk this planet, and you're mine and I can't stop thinking about you *not* being mine. I'm sorry... It still just seems like a dream to me that you really want to be here with me. Maybe it's the way this body reacts... I don't know. It's just so hard to accept that I could be what you really want, especially being a Keeper, not to mention be worthy of you."

I pulled back so he could see my face in the dark and know I meant business.

"I understand that. I feel the same way about you, and I have never cared that you are a Keeper. Have I ever said or done anything to make you think that that bothered me?" I didn't give him time to answer. "I can't handle this anymore, Merrick. I can't handle you thinking I'm playing some kind of game with you. Not only is it insulting, but it's absolutely not true."

"I know it's not a game. You're right. I was being an idiot. You're just too good to be true sometimes. I promise I'm done, no more. I'm sorry, ok?"

I paused just a second and heard the truth ring out in his voice.

"Ok."

I heard him exhale, like he'd been holding his breath. I realized I'd been holding mine, too.

"I missed you so much," he breathed. He nuzzled my neck and kissed under my jaw.

"I missed you, too."

"I'm so sorry for everything," he said huskily as he continued to caress me.

"I know."

"Forgive me." I couldn't speak, he wouldn't let me as he seared me with more scorching kisses. "Say it. Say you forgive me, baby."

"I forgive you," I whispered against his chin.

"Say you want me."

"I want you. I'll always want you."

"Tell me you need me here with you."

"I do need you. I can't live without you now, Merrick. You're thoughtful and human and a great father to Lily and you drive me crazy in every good way. I love you."

He exhaled, because he knew I was telling the truth. "That's good enough for me."

"Promise me that you're done with this. Promise me that you understand that you are absolutely *not getting rid of me even if you wanted to* stuck with me."

"With all my heart, I promise."

"Good. Now please, stop making me talk."

And he loved me and I loved him until it was so late, it was useless to even get out of bed. I learned why that little phrase about make-up sex rang so beautifully true.

I feel someone rubbing my arm. I wake up, fully expecting to see... Who? Who was I expecting to see? I'm in the Rabbit after all. Nobody ever rides with me but Danny. Matt refused to ride with me in it. We always took his big, quad cab Ford everywhere. But I had a feeling like I should be somewhere else, with someone else.

I pull off the ridge but am surprised at how dark it is out. It should be the afternoon. It should be...wait. Who's that? A lady. Wait- I know her. Mrs. Trudy? I stop the car.

She waves to me and then she's there, in the seat next to me. How do I know her?

"Hello, sugar."

"Hey, how did you-"

"No questions, I just wanted to see how you were doing."

"I know you."

"Why of course you do. I'm only gone this world a few months and you already writing me off as a bad memory?" she asked playfully.

It all floods back. Everything. I remember her, her son, the bunker, her death. Merrick.

"Oh, Mrs. Trudy," my voice cracks with emotion.

"No tears, honey, got no time for that." She looks at me thoughtfully. "You are still just as pretty."

"Mrs. Trudy, I miss you so much."

"I miss you, too. But, darling, you gotta be strong, for my family. *Our* family. Be strong because things are coming. Bad, bad, and more bad things. You gotta be perseverant. Diligent. Careful. Understand?"

"Yes. No. I don't know, Mrs. Trudy, I don't know."

"Yes, you do. You can do this. Everything hangs in the balance. Everything. We gotta tip the scales, sugar. So eat up." She smiled. "Pack in all you got and be ready for whatever they got to throw at ya."

She started to wave, her image waved and moved like ripples of water, and I remembered this. This is a dream. This is how people leave my dreams, just like my dad did. Her body swayed, then the background.

The ridge in front of us started to bleed and run like paint thinner splashed on a portrait. The rabbit was the last thing to go and I looked once more at Mrs. Trudy and she touched my cheek easily.

"You were the daughter I never had. Bye, sugar."

"Bye," I said through tears.

I awoke instantly and felt Merrick's hand rubbing my arm, in his sleep. I took a deep steadying breath and wiped the tears from my cheeks. I didn't know if the dream had been real, it felt real, but I needed it nonetheless. I needed a boost of Mrs. Trudy's guidance and no nonsense encouragement. I needed the calm of my ridge for just a minute.

Later on in the morning, it was Sunday so there was no school lessons, no training lessons, no chores except kitchen duty, so I sat by the stairs with Merrick and Lily, Calvin and Lana, Jeff and Marissa, Lillian and Cain, and Danny and Celeste. We played Name That Tune, with me on the piano. Cain won, almost every round. He was pretty impressive.

Celeste had finally gotten her mom to come down during the night while everyone was sleeping but had now barricaded herself in her room. We just decided to give her time and leave her alone.

After a while Cain got out his guitar, which I didn't even know he had brought one with him. It was a yellow wood Gibson acoustic. He sat down on the stairs in front of us and tuned it. He looked around and smiled shyly. I thought he looked kind of nervous, which was weird for Cain. He looked at Lillian and they smiled comfortably at each other.

Then he began to strum Collective Soul's 'Run'. He started to sing the words and I froze in utter shock. He could sing. Seriously.

Pretty soon, people gathered around and he played a few more and sang with that easy mellow voice. I joined in on some with the piano if I knew them but mostly just listened. He then played Mat Kearney's 'Where We Gonna Go From Here' to honor Aaron and Mitchell since they were buried and we hadn't gotten to have a memorial yet.

It was sweet of him to think of that.

Lillian was smiling through her tears the whole song. It wasn't a popular song. With this group of people I figured only Cain and I had ever heard it but it was pretty and soothing. We cried, we sang and just remembered the ones we'd lost. There were so many now...

He played a few more tunes, including, by request from Josh, The Hollies version of "He Ain't Heavy, He's My Brother".

I thought about my dad, my mom, Mrs. Trudy.

After Cain was through, he put down his guitar to indicate that his concert was over and people started talking again. Mostly about the ones who had died, funny stories or crazy things they'd said or done. Josh was telling a particularly hilarious story about his father.

Cain and I glanced at each other, remembering that we'd seen Josh's father outside that night before the cave and we'd never said a word to anyone. Josh's father wasn't just dead like he thought. Josh's father was a Lighter.

Which was worse.

"So anyway, he took this board, right?" Josh was very animated in his telling. "Like a piece of plywood and placed it over the hole in the window, only we had no way to prop it up or make it stay so, my dad came up with this crazy idea to use the mop. So he propped the mop up outside to hold the wood in place propped against the tree and we went to bed. Well, we heard a thud and a big crash and went to check. I was behind him and when we turned the corner to the kitchen, all you could see was the mop standing there. The mop head looked like hair and the tree branches looked like arms. Upright it looked like some lady was just standing there in our broken bay window. My dad screamed just like a girl. I thought he was gonna pee his pants."

Calvin and Franklin literally rolled on the floor laughing and murmuring "pee his pants".

We traded stories for a while and then I saw Lily start to nod off in Merrick's lap. Then a quick look showed Merrick nodding off too. I remembered that we hadn't gotten much sleep the past couple of nights, what with all the drama and uh, other things going on at night. Ahem.

I gingerly took Lily, and it was a hefty task, from Merrick on the floor and urged him by scratching the top of his head to follow me to bed for a nap.

I put Lily down and then we went to bed ourselves. By then it was lunch but I could care less. There were too many things on my mind.

We lay there and I decided to grill him, even though we were beat, on all the things that could happen, were happening and what he thought we should do.

"So, the new Taker has all the old Takers memories?" I asked after he explained as much.

"Yes. It's like, the very first Taker and every one after him is kinda stuck in the new one. He has their memories, their thoughts so they know exactly what they were thinking about, what they wanted, what they had planned to do. It makes the new Taker all the more dangerous because he knows what worked and what didn't."

"Why can't Lighters and Takers be female?"

"We have no idea. For whatever reason, Lighters in Lighter form are all males. We can only come here in the same sex of the body we take. Human females can be absorbed, but that's it. They can't be used as vessels."

"How do they reproduce?"

He laughed.

"They don't, honey. Neither do we. We are a limited number. That's why it's so hard on us when a Keeper dies. Because unlike humans, there will never be another one to come along and replenish the numbers. Just like Lighters, when they are all dead, they're dead. Done."

"So, I know it's impossible, but if we somehow killed off the thousands of Lighters who made their way here, it would be over?"

"Yes."

"But would the moon's light return?"

"No. The moon would still be dark because the Lighters weren't there."

"Hmmm. I never understood that- wait. The glowing skin? They all just sat up there and glowed all night?"

He laughed again.

"You are so cute. Yeah, kind of. After everything you've seen, is that really so hard to believe?"

He left his arm there as my pillow, but shifted so he could be sideways to face me. I did the same.

"Yeah. It sounds so fake and weird. I always thought the moon's light was a reflection of the sun's light."

"It was the only way humans could explain it."

"Hmmm, I see. So, I'm not trying to be self centered or anything but...do you think I'll have to worry, about this new Taker, you know, trying to come and take me?"

"I hope not. Like we said, I've never seen a Taker do that before. The human who absorbed him must have had a very strong sense of family. Some of the human stuff sticks around, just like it does with us when we take a body. Us usually more than them, but the Taker is very susceptible to human emotions and the Lighters *really* are when he's here."

"Well, good."

"And besides, this Malachi is not new, he's from England, back in the sixteen or seventeen hundreds. I remember he was particularly ruthless. He doesn't like to kill humans, or at least he didn't back then. He wants to make them his mindless minions and slaves, basically. He just wants to be treated like a king. Make them his maids, cooks, chauffeurs, army, his, uh, entertainment."

He cleared his throat.

"What? You mean sex?" I whispered it like it was dirty, because I thought it was.

"Yeah."

"Takers have sex? So it wasn't just the last one who had an interest in it?"

"No, they are in human bodies. The body's physical needs are the same as any other human. He doesn't love them, he uses them and keeps them on staff specifically for that purpose."

"What?" I felt my face scrunch in disgust.

"It is what it is to them. Some human men are the same way."

"That's...gross."

Gross! Gross! Who would want to have sex with a Taker? I guess, to them he was like a rock star or the president or something. Eew. I was appalled also by, not just the devious nature of the Takers but how it mixed with the human stuff too. Humans had enough meanness in us without adding to it. I wondered if he hurt them or cared about them at all. If he was terrible to them and hurt them, wouldn't they just not go back?

Then I remember the Takers compulsion. Oh, no. They stay because they can't leave. My stomach tensed and I felt sick thinking of helpless girls, just trying to be loved and feel special, though going about it completely wrong and being turned into- for lack of a nicer word- whores for evil, against their will. I prayed that wasn't true. I prayed that he was gentle with them and they at least wanted to be there.

I refused to ask Merrick if that was how it was with the girls, because I was afraid of his answer.

"Yeah, but it's what the Takers do, most of them. I remember Malachi was extremely unruly about things like that. But the saddest part is the human women lined up willingly to be his next girl. Just to be put on the list, to be next because he won't keep the girls for very long, is such a privilege to them."

"Ok, can we stop talking about that? It's making me sick thinking about it," I whispered because I didn't trust my voice. Suddenly I felt as if I'd led a very sheltered life.

"I'm sorry." He kissed my nose. "Let's talk about something else."

I racked my brain for *anything* else. "So, he's a Taker who's done the job already, but with a free education of the last couple centuries."

"Yep."

"Sounds great," I said sarcastically, "just great. I don't know if I can handle much more of this. Things aren't even really bad yet and I already feel so defeated."

"That's what happens when you lose people, but we can't let that distract us. That's what they would use against us, to take advantage. We always have to be diligent in our watching and waiting and training." He pinched my ear gently when he said training. I couldn't see his face in the dark but I knew what he meant.

"I know, I know. I promise I'll make it to training lessons tomorrow. It's Susan and Kay's day to cook. I'll be all yours."

"Actually, you'll be all Miguel's. I'm just going to watch."

"Why can't you help teach me?"

"I don't like the idea of practicing hits on you. Even if I accidentally hurt you, I'd have a hard time with that. It'll be hard enough watching and not wanting to jump in to help you."

Considering yesterday's events, probably more so now than before.

"But...I want you to. I want it to be you. Miguel is so busy already and Kay will be cooking tomorrow so you can take her spot in training. With me." I smiled smugly.

"Hmmm." A pause. "We'll see. I'm not too thrilled about the idea. It goes against my whole nature to even think about placing a hit on you. It's bad enough watching someone else do it. "

"Well, I'm the one who needs to practice right? So I'll be doing most of the hitting. Right?"

"I guess."

"Please," I said and bit my lip, for his visual benefit in the dark.

"Alright, pouter," he laughed, "you win." He leaned close until our noses were almost touching and whispered. "But be gentle with me."

"Maybe I will, maybe I won't," I teased. "I guess it depends."

"On what?" he said and ran his palm down my arm.

"On...whether or not you take it easy on me. I'd rather, not."

"I know you wouldn't, but I think I'll make that call. Like I said, we move faster than you and are stronger. I don't want to hurt you by accident because I get caught up in the moment."

"But you let the other Keepers practice on everybody else. You're not worried about them getting caught up in the moment."

Sherry, you are not everybody else.

"Fine." Subject change needed. I wound a piece of hair around my finger and eased into the more stressful subject I'd been wondering about. "So...how would you go home, if you wanted to? And the Lighters? Just think home and click your heels three times?"

He of course didn't get my Wizard of Oz reference.

"Uh, sort of. We have to mentally shed the body. It's all about free will and personal decision. We have to mentally choose to shed the vessel and reclaim our true form, then decide to go home. It's a process. It can't be done accidentally and it won't happen unless we really want it. It's all very technical and precise."

"Uhuh, so...technically, you could go home right now?" I asked cautiously.

"Technically? Yes, if I wanted to, though there'd be no job for me there, and with my Special, and all the other Specials with deceased Keepers down here, running around with no guardian, my conscience would be buzzing like crazy. I wouldn't be able to stand it."

"Your conscience?"

"Yeah. When we are working, from where I'm from, when a Special is your charge or if a newborn Special needs a Keeper, we get a buzzing feeling in our head. A nagging at our inner conscience telling us that someone needs us and it wouldn't stop at all right now. You'd get no peace. It'd be painful, even, and when you are at where I'm from, it's different. We don't have all these human things to deal with, distractions, all you have to focus on is your charge. So, the nagging would literally drive us insane if we didn't go to our Special."

"What do you mean human things? You had emotions before you became human didn't you?"

How could he have loved me if he didn't?

"Yes. We had emotions, but on earth human emotions are so tied into your body and actions and reactions and bodily functions and whether you've had food or not and all kinds of things we never had to worry about before. To never feel pain, to never feel exhaustion or hunger or...jealousy. If your body was perfectly content, humans would be a lot more mellow."

"Yes, that is definitely true. I know I get cranky when I'm hungry."

"Yes, you do." He tweaked my nose. "So...why are you asking me about all this?"

"Curiosity?"

"Is that a question or an answer?"

Just admit it, Sherry. "Ok, I was thinking about Piper."

"Piper?" he said and I could hear the annoyance and shock in his voice.

That Keeper certainly ruined any chance she might have ever had to be close to Merrick.

"If she's so unhappy here, why not just let her go home if that is what she wants? But I see why not, now."

"Why are you worried about Piper? You can't think I'd ever be interested. Not now-"

"No, I don't think that."

He sat silently for a few seconds, and then blew out a long telling breath. "You feel sorry for her?" he asked incredulously.

I didn't even have to think about it. "Yes."

"Don't you remember what she did to us? I say she deserves a little bodily prison after what she put us through, Sherry."

"I know, and I'm angry at her, too, but that doesn't mean that I want to watch her suffer. Especially if there was something we could do to help her, short of divorcing that is."

I snorted at my lame joke, but he stayed serious. "Sherry," he breathed and cupped my cheek. "Why? Why after everything that has happened to you can you still be so sweet and forgiving?"

He asked me softly, he wasn't mocking, he just genuinely wanted to know.

"Well, I choose to be, Keeper. Just like you choose your actions, so do I. Though I do worry sometimes that I'm getting bitter. That one day I'll snap and be epically bitter and nasty and mean and unlovable."

"Won't happen." He pulled me closer into the warmth of his chest.

"I won't be unlovable?"

"Well no, you won't, but you won't be bitter either."

"Why do you say that?"

"Because I just remembered that...I know you. If there was ever a reason to be bitter, it was at your parents for leaving you, it was for losing Mrs. Trudy, it would have been for what Phillip almost did to you and Marissa's Muse vision on you and to the Lighters for everything else that has happened in the past almost two years. If that won't make you bitter, nothing will, honey."

I thought about it and he was right. I hated the Lighters and I hated to use that word, but I did. Would I want to sit and watch one suffer? Would I enjoy that? Absolutely not.

I thought about the Lighter we interrogated and remembered how I covered my face and flinched at Miguel's tactics for information extraction.

"You're right," I conceded.

"I know," he chuckled. "Sometimes it works out that I'm right."

"You're right a lot of the time. But mostly..." I teased him again.

"You, of course." He smiled against my forehead, then snuggled me closer and rubbed his scratchy chin on my hair as I tangled our legs together. "Now close those gorgeous brown eyes and let's get a few minutes of sleep before Lily gets up."

"Yes, sir," I teased.

"I love you, honey."

"I know."

And we dozed off for a few minutes, me feeling a little bit better about my personal damnation.

Beck and Call
Chapter 27 - Lillian

Taking Cain and my clothes off the drying racks in the laundry/ utility room, I remembered the last time I was in this room. Mitchell confessed his feelings for me and kissed me.

I missed him, something fierce. His was my best friend, but I had no doubt that someone was looking out for me, other than Keepers and guardians. God placed me with my parents after I was abandoned at a hospital when I was three days old, then with Michael right before my parents moved to Guatemala for a ten year mission trip, then into Mitchell's care when I lost Michael, then Cain came along right before Mitchell died.

I'd always been taken care of and loved by someone, even when I didn't deserve it. But...this was making me wonder. I was starting to wonder if Cain would be next in the line of Lillian's collateral damage. If by loving me or protecting me you were somehow destined to leave this earth too soon.

Maybe I shouldn't get so close to him. Maybe we should just stay casual friends, maybe that would be safest for him. I wasn't usually so superstitious, but the evidence spoke for itself, no matter how much I'd miss the kissing.

I was so confused and hurt, but thankful. Was that weird? Probably but it was how I felt.

And Cain, he had definitely been good to me. It had been one whole week since the fight where we lost Mitchell. It took me a couple days to muster up the grief I needed to let go. And when I did, it flooded me. I balled and sobbed and cried and ached inside. I felt guilty on more than one level and missed Michael, Mitchell and my parents, and wondered why everything bad that every happened to me happened.

You know how those go. Those pity party sessions. Those indefinite feeling, long drug-out cry phases.

Well, I had a particularly bad one last night, which, to be honest, was my last. I'd gotten it all out and it was all thanks to Cain. He sat in my room every night this week and held me while I cried and talked and remembered. And last night, while I sobbed loudly and stained his shirt with my tears, was the worst one yet. And like I said, it was the last.

He was so sweet, gentle and careful with me. He let me talk, asked me questions about Michael and Mitchell and seemed genuinely interested, not jealous. And I knew he had to be tired, he'd just gotten off work but he still came every night and let me blubber on.

"I'm sorry this happened to you, but I'm here, whenever you need me," he said one night. Then he said, "Don't be silly. I'm honored that you trust me with all this," another night when I apologized for crying yet again.

I wouldn't make Cain sit through one more tear of me crying for another guy or anything else. It was gone, they were gone. It was time to move on and just remember them sweetly, but what to do about Cain?

Our days were spent laughing and goofing off together and the nights were spent with me a sobbing mess. It was a strange arrangement, but one I desperately needed. While he was at work, I missed him. It was weird. I barely know him but he had affected my life so thoroughly in these past couple weeks with his concern and gentle handling of me.

He hadn't made any moves on me since I kissed him that day in the commons room either, just sat with me, checked on me and watched me intently. We ate lunch together every day and joked before he went to work, and then when he got home from work, he came to my room and checked on me again. Then I'd pull him down to lay with me. It was so sweet how he never insisted or assumed that I wanted him to stay until I made the move to do so.

Heck, he could stay with me every night for all I cared but I doubted he would. He only stayed because I asked him to and I needed him to. With my new found revelation on the bad luck of being with me, I wasn't sure I should do that anymore.

Of course, I could be jumping to conclusions. Maybe, like Mitchell, he just felt like I had no one else and wanted to protect me or something. Maybe, that was all he felt. Maybe that was why he hadn't kissed me since that night of the rally.

I took all my neatly folded clothes back to my room and stacked them in the corner. I made my pathetic pallet and brushed my hair out. Then I took Cain's pile to his room. I started doing Cain's laundry this week as a thank you for him putting up with my neediness. I bit my lip as I held up a pair of black boxers and tried to imagine what he'd look like in them. Then I mentally chided myself for doing such a thing. If only I was certain of how he felt about me.

I then walked up the hall to the commons room. It was a Wednesday.

Since Polly and Piper's little stunt, they have been watched every minute of every day. We couldn't very well make them stay locked up in their room forever, though most of us kinda wanted to.

We had a meeting. It was explained to everyone what they both had done, to a small degree to let Merrick keep his dignity, and why they were being watched carefully. We couldn't use our gifts on each other, it was unacceptable. So... they stated that anyone else caught doing so, other than practice and training, would be removed from the bunker, including Piper and Polly, to fend for themselves. The good of the many has to outweigh the few. Now, whether they would actually kick someone out was left to be seen.

I seriously doubted it. I thought they were just hoping they never had to test it, though Jeff looked pretty serious to me. I learned in the past few days that you didn't mess with Sherry or Merrick, or you dealt with Jeff.

So this is the first day those two have been completely left to their own devices. Polly accepted the cleaning duty with as much grace as a self absorbed priss could.

I watched her as she comically tried to dust the lights and sconces. Her nose was scrunched in disgust and she flicked the feather duster over the glass in her fingers and coughed and sputtered, shivering like it was painful to do so. It was just a little dust, jeez.

I kept moving. Piper and Cain should be outside checking on the garden. Poor Cain got stuck with Piper for help. Oh, well, if anyone could handle her crap, it would be him.

I walked by and startled, seeing Ryan sitting on the stairs where I hadn't seen him before.

"Hey there, Lillian," he said and smiled, straightening.

Ryan was so very sweet and cute. I'd only talked to him one other time and that was for him to show me how to work the energy saver water thing in the shower down the hall. We got to talking after that and wound up talking for almost an hour. He told me all about Calvin, his charge, and answered all my Keeper questions. He asked me a dozen questions about being a preacher's daughter and being married and living in the mountains.

I thoroughly enjoyed it. He didn't make any passes at me, just talked. He too was definitely fond of these people, Sherry in particular, and told me a few stories about her that made me laugh. He explained to me about how he objected to Merrick and Sherry in the beginning because he thought Merrick would be missing so much from home. Because he didn't think humans and Keepers could have real relationships, that he didn't understand it, but eventually, after getting to know Sherry, came to be happy for them. I swore, everyone loved that girl.

"Hey, Ryan. What are you doing over here all by yourself?"

"Just sitting. Thinking."

"You ok?" I asked.

He seemed to be acting a little strange. "Oh, yeah. I'm fine. I'm really just guarding the stairs, though I'm not supposed to be. I'm still not very trusting of a certain Special." He nodded toward Polly who was shaking a dust bunny off her sweat pant leg like it was a tarantula.

"I see. I can understand that." I went to sit by him on the stairs. "After what they did, I can definitely understand."

"I still can't believe Piper. You just don't do that to humans, let alone your charge. I just can't see how she could do it."

"Well, teenage girls are finicky and emotional. I remember being sixteen. It wasn't all fun."

"Yes, but she's different. We all, Keepers I mean, deal with the accordance with our vessels, our bodies, but you can't let the chemical emotions control you. We still have our thoughts, our morals, ourselves."

"Is that why you objected to Merrick and Sherry? You think love is a chemical emotion?" I asked and watched his face to see how he answered.

"Yes, at first, I thought that. But I've seen enough to know that's not true anymore. Piper should be able to control herself. I've never seen a Keeper behave this way before. It's a little...disconcerting. It doesn't give the rest of us much hope of overcoming whatever we might be going through ourselves."

I watched him as he watched his hands in his lap. "What are you having problems with, Ryan?"

He finally looked up to me, seemingly startled by my question. "Nothing in particular. It's not so bad, being human, just different. I'm really liking it here. If things weren't so messed up, I think I'd enjoy it. See, I've only ever been here twice before and only for a couple hours. Most of the others have been here more often or for longer lengths of time."

"What's it like? Where you're from?"

"It's...there's no way to describe it to you, Lillian. No human words to use. Maybe, one day, when we have lots of time to kill, I'll try."

"Deal, it's a date," I said cheerily and he snorted.

"And how would Cain feel about that?"

"What do you mean? Cain and I aren't together. He isn't even interested in that, I don't think."

"You think wrong. Simon is very talkative about his charge. And Cain isn't exactly trying to hide anything. When he looks at you, you can see it, as plain as if I was reading his mind. I've seen it in others."

I felt a little uncomfortable, talking about Cain without him here, and with a Keeper who has a direct line to Cain's Keeper's mind no less. It felt like eavesdropping.

"Well, it was nice talking to you, Ryan. I'm going to hold you to that talk, now. I want to know all about it."

He smiled and looked at me like he didn't believe it. "Sure thing, Lillian."

"Ryan." I paused and collected my thoughts. "You can come talk to me anytime, about anything. I may not know what you're going through, but I can listen."

"Thanks, I really appreciate that."

I nodded to him and waved over my shoulder as I turned to leave and headed into the kitchen

"Hey, Sherry."

Sherry was sitting on the counter in the kitchen.

"Hey, how are you feeling? Cain said you had a rough night."

He did, did he? When did Cain see Sherry? Seemed to me like he'd been avoiding her.

"I guess. It's ok. He helped me through it."

"Good, I'm glad. I'm glad he's here for you. He's a really sweet guy to have around."

"Yes, he is. So when did you see him? I thought he was in the garden."

"Oh, he is. I took them up a glass of tea. I always do in the mid-mornings and afternoons, it's so hot right now. Anyway, Piper is giving him heck for sure. When I walked up, she was complaining because her arms were getting more tan and red than the rest of her. I've never heard a Keeper with so much negative chatter."

She jumped down off the counter, walked to the refrigerator and grabbed a pitcher of cold water out and made us both a glass.

"Thanks," I said as I took it.

"You're welcome."

"How can you be so cool about Piper after what she did?"

"I'm not cool about Piper. I'm fiery hot about her... but what am I supposed to do? Ignore her? Berate her?" She shook her head. I could tell she was angry, but was tamping it down. "I just think, it's not *completely* her fault, as much as I want to blame her. It sucks what she did and I can't imagine even a human doing that, but I have no idea what it's like to be trapped in a body that I don't want to be in so, who am I judge."

Wow. Sherry really was a selfless, altruistic martyr. I repeat, no wonder everybody loved her. Jeez, and she was so cute and unknowing of it and pranced around acting like she owed some kind of debt to everyone and was working double time to pay it back. Cain didn't stand a chance around her.

"I guess. It's just so weird to be holed up with criminals."

"It is weird. I think everyone's a little edgy but they are steering clear of me and I'm trying to... I don't know. I don't want to rile them, but I feel like maybe they just need someone to show them that we're here for each other no matter what. I mean, Polly didn't say anything about Piper's threat because she didn't trust any of us."

"With good reason. She hasn't exactly been very *kind* to any of *us*."

"True, and you know better than anyone that Polly is not exactly BFF material either, but we've all got to learn to get along if we're going to be stuck down here together. Maybe they can change or at least cope. That's what I'm hoping."

"Yeah, you're right. It's hard though, forgiving isn't the hardest part, it's the forgetting," I said, thinking back to my daddy's umpteenth sermon on forgiveness.

"Actually Lillian, I don't think we're supposed to forget. Then how do we learn any lessons? Forgive, but don't forget. Remember but don't dwell. Face facts but don't forget the mystery." She stopped and looked a little embarrassed. "Wow, I totally sound like a Hallmark card right now."

"It's ok," I laughed, "I'm used to it." Wow, I missed my dad right then.

"So now, tell me about your night out with Cain. I haven't had a chance to talk to you about it."

"Not much to tell. Didn't learn anything crucial, I don't think anyway."

"Really? Cain said you guys had a good time. That you danced and you were a lot of fun... He also said you kissed," she said smirking and wiping her hands on the dish towel.

"He told you that?"

That shocked me. I thought he wouldn't want Sherry of all people to know we'd kissed. I mean, yeah, I kissed him and she saw it, but I kind of thought he might be upset with me about that. A little. Maybe not. If he would tell her that himself, then he must really be trying to move on, to forget his feelings for her. Hmmm. Or he was just trying to make her jealous...

"Yeah, he did. He seemed a little...oh, I don't know, bashful about it, too. Not at all like Cain. What in the world have you done to him, Lillian?"

"What do you mean?" I said horrified by what she might have meant by it.

"I'm joking, honey." She grabbed my hands and I was surprised at how small they were. "I mean you've got him all tied in knots. I've never seen him like this before. I mean, I haven't knowm him that long, but... It's a good thing. He really likes you, I can tell. I'm a human lie detector, remember?"

"Oh, yes, well, I like him, too. I do. He's...really sweet."

"Good, I'm happy if you're happy." She smiled widely and then turned to start chopping something. Looked like onions. "Can you help cook dinner tonight? If I don't make the training session tonight, Merrick and Miguel are gonna have my behind."

"Sure, of course."

"Thank you. You know you should start lessons soon too. We all take them, just in case. They're in the last room, down the hall by the stairs. They start at about 4:30 or so."

"Yeah, I will. I always wanted to take a self defense class, just never got around to it."

"Good, they'll love a new recruit to pound on." She winked at me over her shoulder. "Now, I made some sugar cookies with the last of the flour before our next run. If you want one, they are fresh out of the oven, right there in that cupboard." She pointed to a high shelf above the freezer. "I have to hide them 'til dinner time or they'd never make it. And sadly, it's not the children I have to worry about."

"Uh, how on earth did you get them way up there, shorty?"

She just smiled, patted my arm and left me there. I thought about how long it'd been since I had a cookie. I was getting thinner, as was everyone over the past months. I wasn't sickly thin, just thinner. I wasn't too happy about that though. Michael had always loved my curves.

I decided to try for the cookies.

I grabbed a chair and still couldn't fathom how she finagled the cookies up there because I could still barely reach over the freezer top to reach the cabinet. I pushed my arms further and the chair slipped sideways from my one foot leaning on it that way.

Instantly I was airborne and on my way down to the hard tile. I braced myself for impact, but instead of hard floor, I felt hard arms. I looked up to amused eyes the color of the sea.

Cain.

"And what would you have done had I not chose this moment to come into the kitchen, hmm?"

"Hurt all over?"

"I think you're right," he said laughing and put me back to my feet.

"Thanks. I'm so playing the cliché girl in distress role right now, aren't I?"

"Kind of, yeah." He laughed. "Can I ask what you were doing up there?"

"I have it on good authority that there are cookies up there."

"Aha! So, that's where the wench hides them! She thinks she can fool Ryan, Danny and me, but now, with your help of course, I have the I Spy cookie mystery solved. However can I repay you?" he said and took my hands, bowing before me playfully.

"Well, I can think of a few things, but right now, cookies will do."

"You got it, gorgeous," he said, winking and making my heart jump.

It always jumped with him around.

He grabbed my chair, righting it as it was tipped over, and hopped up on it with gracefulness. He reached the cabinet with ease and brought the heavenly smelling clear container down.

We got a couple cookies each and he replaced the container in the cabinet. We escaped the kitchen, the crime scene as far as cookies were concerned, and ran to the second room. He put on a CD, something by Switchfoot.

We sat on the bed together, leaning our backs on the wall and stretched our legs out. He must have come in and showered because he smelled clean, like Irish Springs soap. And divine.

"So, what have you been doing today?" he said through a mouthful of cookie.

"Mm." I swallowed. "Not much. Laundry, so exciting. I talked to Ryan for a little bit and Sherry."

He nodded and ate his second cookie in one bite.

"I've got to work later. Only three more days until the need warehouses open and I'm unemployed." He sighed sadly.

"Yeah, well, I'm kind of ready for you to be. It sucks worrying about you while you're out at night. I can't believe you've still been doing it all this time anyway," I said, fidgeting with my frayed shirt hem.

"Worried about me? What on earth for?" he said it softly and I looked up at him to see him eyeing me with the strangest look on his face, like he didn't deserve someone's worry.

"What do you mean what for? It's kind of crazy dangerous out there if you hadn't noticed."

"Yeah, but I've been just fine. No one messes with me 'cause I have such a pretty face," he joked, but he still look bewildered.

"Well, that's true," I said and felt that familiar ping in my gut for flirting.

"Lillian, don't worry about me. There's no need to. I'm immune to the Lighter speak and besides, I'll be useless soon enough."

"You mean like the rest of us?"

"No, I didn't mean it like that."

"I know. It doesn't mean you're useless though. Everyone has a job here right? The garden is pretty important."

"Yeah, I guess," he conceded grudgingly.

"Well, you could always join the enforcers," I said sarcastically.

That had been Crandle's big idea of helping the ones who lost their job at the grocery stores and restaurants instead of going on unemployment, to give them jobs in the enforcement unit. One more curse disguised as a blessing.

"I should."

"What? I was joking," I said, wondering how he could have taken me seriously.

"Yeah, but I could. Think about it. It would be great for spying and getting information and it would give me something to do."

"No, Cain!" I yelled but then realized it and tried to tone it down. "I mean...I'm sorry, I shouldn't have yelled, it's just such a crazy idea, don't you think? I mean, it's bad enough what you do already, risking yourself every day. Right?" I exhaled, frustrated.

He reached over and grabbed my hand.

"What's the matter, Lillian?"

"Nothing."

"Tell me."

"It's stupid. And girly." I suddenly felt very, very stupid.

"Tell me," he repeated.

"Cain, just don't, ok. I'm don't want-"

He scooted over so that our legs were touching and then pulled me to look at him with a warm palm on my cheek, his thumbs rubbing caresses. "Tell me," he whispered the command and his breath moved the hairs around my face because he was so close.

"It's just...I have this theory."

I told him the whole bit. About God watching over me, about how every person who ever tried to protect me died or left. I procession down the line of deaths and abandonment's to further my point. Then, as much as it pained me, I had to tell him and I explained that we should remain friends, though I had no idea how he really felt about me. It was for the best because I didn't want him to die, too. The more I talked, the crazier I sounded, I knew.

He stared at me with contemplation and weariness for a bit, like he wasn't sure how to handle me, then he spoke.

"Lillian, you are not to blame for anyone's death. There is a God in the universe, yes, but he isn't out to watch you play musical chairs with all your boyfriends and family members, ok? You've just had a run of bad luck and bad timing. And...look, I know that our short time together hasn't been glamorous. It's been very strained and emotional but despite that, I love spending time with you. I *really* like you, a lot. A lot more than I ever have anybody else in just a couple weeks time." He moved a little closer and kissed the end of my nose so sweetly my breath caught. "Don't push me away or forbid me to see you before we even really have a chance to see if this can work or not, not because you're scared for me. Please, I want nothing more right now than to get to know you even more."

It took me a minute to catch my breath. When I did I blinked and tried to find words. He watched my lips fighting breath in and out and then moved in to kiss me. I couldn't let him.

"Please, don't," I said breathlessly. "It's hard enough already, Cain. Look, if

I lost you too, after all this..."

"You can't just not live because you're worried you'll lose people. If that's the case why would you get close to anyone, huh?"

"It's different, there's a pattern-"

"Screw the pattern, Lillian. I'm not gonna die because I'm interested in you. God is not out to get me or you. There is no agenda in the universe to curse Lillian. Bad things just happen sometimes and if you let it run you, you'll have nothing in the end."

"I know, Cain, ok, I know it's silly and stupid." I wanted to cry but his hands were still on me and I couldn't do it. Not now. "I would be pretty selfish if I just made the decision to be with you, knowing what I know, and then something happened to you. I'd never forgive myself."

"Then I'll make the decision for you."

He pulled me to him and pressed his lips to mine and though it devastated my senses to do it, I pulled back quickly.

"Cain! Please, I can't even think with your hands on me," I gasped, which I ultimately knew then that was a mistake.

One hand traveled to the back of my neck - his control tactic, I knew. "Look, if you're not ready or don't want me to, that's one thing, but being scared for me is another. If you're not ready...stop me and I won't try again, I promise."

My brain told me to rebel, to push him away for his own good, but my body was being disobedient. He waited just a few seconds, his blue green eyes like grass in the sea, looking straight into mine. Then he pulled me closer and I closed my eyes in blind anticipation. Knowing he wouldn't try again made me want to kiss him this time, made me realize that I did want him to, despite my protests.

Our lips met gently. He eased me into a slow sweet easy kiss. I couldn't take it so I wrapped my arms around his neck and heard a low grunt or mutter, but didn't hear the words as he opened my mouth with his and kissed me deeper. He continued to kiss me until I was witless. There was no frisky roaming hands, no tugging on my clothes, no ploys to reach for private skin. Just kissing - intense, vital to life kissing. It was extremely nice and exactly what I needed and wanted.

My heart beat a mile a minute just like his against my chest, out of sync with mine, making me feel like it was beating triple time. My breathing was terrifyingly loud, but I couldn't seem to stop.

Then we heard someone shuffle in and stop, speaking quickly. "Oh...sorry," a low, easy voice said.

It was Merrick stopped just in the doorway. We both pulled back and I tried to get up from the bed to flee in embarrassment, but Cain held me in place by a hand on my leg.

"It's ok, Merrick." Cain cleared his throat. "Did you get the drain fixed in the hall bathroom?"

"Yeah, Pap's pretty handy actually with stuff like that," Merrick said and I could tell he was trying not to stare and it even looked like he was holding in a laugh.

"Good, I can't do plumbing but I figured Pap could. He's kind of a jack of all trades."

"He is, thanks. I think he liked being useful. I only heard one negative thing from his mouth the whole time and that was that you were being lazy and weren't helping us. Though...now I see why." He smiled, clearly amused. "Hi, Lillian."

"Hey, Merrick. We stole cookies." I just blurted it out, anything to get him to stop smiling at me like that. No doubt Cain and Merrick would converse and plunder of the whys of that grin later anyway.

"Lillian! He's the enemy!" Cain said incredulously.

"What?"

"He's the cookie maker's husband," he stage whispered extra loudly.

"Oh! I see. Well, we could always bribe him with cookies."

"He won't be bought, I've tried." Cain smiled at me and then turned to Merrick. "Don't betray us and tell the little wife."

"She's little, but she's vicious. You are putting me in a very difficult position," Merrick said with arms crossed and a mock shake of disappointment to his head.

I stared at him, puzzled. I was mesmerized at his ability and *want* to joke and goof off. None of the other Keepers I'd seen had ever done that. I didn't even know they could. It was fun to watch. No wonder Sherry and Cain loved Merrick so much. He was so...human.

"Oh, I have no doubt you can take little old Sherry."

"For your sake, I won't tell her you said that."

We all laughed.

"Aren't you late for work, slacker?" Merrick asked, looking at his watch.

"Nah, they cut my hours this week since we only have a few days left. Hardly anybody comes in the shop anymore anyway. It's a sad day when the world can live without coffee."

"Do you think you can swipe some creamer on your way home? Tell your boss you'll take his supply off his hands?"

"Yeah. Actually, I already talked to him about it. He said I could take the creamer and coffee grounds. He hasn't placed an order for more in a long time, not much left anyway."

"Great, thanks. Sherry will flip to have real creamer in the house."

"Yep, no problem."

"Alright. I'm sorry I interrupted," Merrick said and smirked, shooting a quick glance at me. "I'll, uh, let you get back to it."

Cain picked up a throw pillow, tossing it at him and Merrick laughed as he dodged it and left.

"Sorry, he's just playing around," Cain explained.

"I know. I can't believe how..."

"How normal he is?"

"Yeah. I've never seen a Keeper act so human like that before. I mean, they do act human, but not joking and laughing like that. They are always so serious."

"Danny and Sherry really brought him, and really all the Keepers here, out of their shells by treating them like humans. Most people don't. You treat them like they're aliens just here to help us and that's what they'll act like. I know you've talked to Ryan some, but he can be such a hoot. And Jeff. He's just crazy, don't get him started and you'll be fine. And Merrick, he's the best friend I've ever had. It's strange."

"Why strange?"

"Because, I always had friends, but they weren't real. None of it was real. They'd stab me in the back for a hot girl in a second, but Merrick, he's not even from this planet, but I know I can trust him and he's always got my back. I can joke with him and he knows it. I can fight Lighters with him and know I have nothing to worry about."

I wondered if that was why he refused to give in to his feelings for Sherry, because it wouldn't be fair to Merrick.

"Well, whatever it is about him, it's nice. I always wondered what kind of relationship Sherry could have with a Keeper."

"Yeah, they are really awesome together."

I looked at him to see if he was upset or maybe wistful thinking about Sherry with Merrick but he wasn't. He was looking at me with amusement and something else. Something nice.

"Well, that's great for them."

"So...are we good? I'm sorry if I was pushy earlier," he asked and half smiled not looking a bit sorry.

"Yeah, we're good. Believe me, if I hadn't wanted you to, I would have stopped you."

"So, you admit you wanted me to?" he said and leaned forward a little bit to see my face, smiling. I smiled too and tucked my hair behind my ear. He reached up to trace the path I took to do it. "I love it when you do that."

"Why?" I asked but felt my lips curving up again.

"Because it tells me what you won't. That you're shy and loveable and unsure about yourself. Though I'm not sure why you're unsure, I've kissed you three times now, that should tell you something about how I feel about you."

"So, you get all that from me pushing my hair around?" I teased, loving that I could tease him and he completely got it.

"Yep." Oh, I loved his cockiness, his playfulness, his eagerness. "Hmm."

"Ok." He slapped his palms down on his legs. "I really do have to go to work now or I will be late."

"Well, have a good night and don't forget Sherry's creamer."

He got up and pulled me from the bed by my hands, scooting me to the edge then lifting me to stand very close in front of him. He grabbed my hands at our sides.

"You're not still worried about that, are you?" he asked softly and I knew exactly what he was talking about.

About his feelings for Sherry.

"Not really."

"Not really, or not at all?"

"Not really," I answered truthfully.

He sighed. "Lillian, you've got to get some self worth. Go look in a mirror, go watch the other guys in the bunker watch you, go listen to what everyone says about how sweet you are. You have no idea how great you are." He nuzzled my nose with his. "I think you could make me forget just about anything. I'm really enjoying this," he said softly, dragging out each word slowly like they were each important.

He did the most extraordinary things. Sweet one minute, cocky the next, teasing, then kissing, then talking about Keepers, then rubbing noses? It was fascinating.

"I am, too. I just don't want you to think that I would think that you'd be over her in a week. I can be realistic and patient. In fact, I still feel confused about Mitchell myself so…"

"You do?"

"Yes." Seeing his frown I hurried to explain. "No, not like that. I just still really feel bad about, you know, him thinking like he did. It scares me a little bit. I did like him, but..." I steeled my courage, "not the same as I feel for you. Not even close."

"I don't think you have to worry about Sherry anymore," he whispered firmly.

He bent down and kissed me again, his hands immediately came up to my face. We kissed for only a moment and then he reluctantly released me, keeping his face close.

"I really do have to go."

"I know. Go," I said and laughed at his pained expression. "I'll be here when you get home."

He laughed too, which was my intention. Where exactly would I go?

"I'll come check on you when I get home...but I'm not so sure it's a good idea for me to sleep in your room anymore," he said looking pensive, but happy, and I smiled up at him.

"Why? Worried about my self control?" I teased.

"Nuhuh, I'm worried about mine."

He pressed one last quick, soft kiss to my stunned upturned lips and turned to go, smiling smugly.

I walked into the kitchen in a daze to start supper wondering how in the world I could have had such an array of feelings for someone after such a short time.

Easy Does It
Chapter 28 - Merrick

"Good of you to join us, slow poke," Sherry goaded as I walked in, well after everyone else had started the training lessons.

She was sparring with Miguel. Well, I wouldn't actually call it sparring, more like dodging, because Sherry refused to take a hit, insistent that she didn't want to hurt anyone. No one had the heart to tell her she couldn't actually hurt any of us, even if she wanted to.

"I was talking to Cain...and Lillian."

"Really. Well, I'm sure Miguel is tired of doing basics with me when there are plenty of others who need his help, so I'm glad you're here." She smiled, walked over to me and pulled me down to kiss me. "Now, are you ready to hurt?"

I laughed and shook my head at her. "Sure. Let's go over here." We walked over and I tried to explain as I went. "Ok. Now, when someone is coming at your head with their arm, duck down." I corrected because she bent down at the waist instead. "No, not duck, bad word. Squat. Then you punch his groin. See."

I demonstrated the move.

"Oookay, but for the record, I'm not really thrilled about punching some Lighter's junk."

"Junk?"

Her eyes glanced meaningfully down to below to my belt and I got it. I laughed and had to chide her. We'd never get any work done like this. "Honey, I need you to focus. Be serious, ok. We're going to practice this move and I'm going to swing at you slow first, then fast. I want you to squat and punch each time, ok? Punch my leg for practice."

"Ok."

I admit, it was a little hard for her to squat with a walking cast on, but we still needed to try. We took a stance in front of each other and I swung slow motion. She squatted and punched like I told her to but she hit air, not my thigh.

"What's the matter?"

"I just want to practice like this. I don't want to hit you."

"You won't hurt me. I want you to know what hitting feels like. You'll hurt yourself in a real fight if you've never hit anything before. Now hit me."

We went again. She barely tapped me.

"Honey."

"Merrick."

"Come on. These sessions are pointless if you're not going to try."

"I am trying! I'll remember everything like this. I just don't want to hit you." I sighed and she came up to me and hugged me around my midsection. "We talked about this. I know I can't hurt you, I'm not stupid, but I don't want to hit you. I don't like how it makes me feel. Please. Let's just practice."

I scrubbed my face with my hands and sighed again.

"Fine. Let's practice this a few more times, then we'll practice kicks with the pillows."

"Ooh. I love the pillows," she said and smiled, taking her defensive stance again.

I smiled, too, rolling my eyes at her, and we set off. Then punching practice pillows. Then she did some maneuvering with getting out of holds with Miguel as I worked with Lily on her gift.

Whoa. That choking thing was no walk in the park. She didn't even concentrate, just thinks of it, touches you anywhere and instantly you start to feel it. I wasn't sure I wanted to do that with her again. Besides, she seemed to have it down anyway and she was extremely cute asking me if I was ok. Apparently, she couldn't stop it. It had to just run its course.

I turned back to watch Sherry. She was working with Ryan and Miguel, trying to knock their feet out from under them. Again, refusing to make any real contact. Then Ryan grabbed her around her neck and shoulders. She wiggled and squirmed, tried to turn, tried to jerk away and push at him, but to no avail, so she gave up, letting her arms go slack to her sides and pouting slightly, all disappointed in herself. Then Ryan whispered something in her ear from behind and tickled her side with his free hand, sending her into a giggling fit.

I laughed and just kept watching. Everyone loved her. Everyone loved each other and most put their differences aside to be able to coexist, even though it was not easy. It's the most human I've ever seen people act.

When I came here before during crisis, no matter what decade or century, the humans were always the same; self centered, reckless and greedy. There were always good ones too, but in a majority of people, those were the traits that come out in times of trouble. The gift of free will let them choose to be pitiless and callous but this group was different. This crisis is different.

Now Miguel and Ryan were coming from both sides with Celeste and Sherry in the middle. Celeste's gift was all in her mind so she needed just as much physical training as Sherry did. Miguel grabbed Sherry's neck and I winced at the memory of the Lighter in Phillip's body doing that to her. She slammed the inside of his elbow with the heel of her palm hard, like he showed her before. He was testing her and she passed.

That loosened his grip enough for her to twist and duck under his arm and kick him in the back of the knee with her heel from behind, forcing it to buckle. He fell forwards down on the floor and she looked horrified. She ran over and fussed over him, like she actually hurt him.

"Oh! Miguel! I'm so sorry," she said patting him and turning him over.

"Don't be, love, I'm fine, that's what I wanted you to do. It was awesome." He saw me walk up behind her. "This is one tough Sheila you got here. She just kicked my arse."

"I saw." I helped him up with a hand out. "It was highly entertaining."

"Miguel, I'm so sorry. See! This is why I don't like hitting for real!"

Sherry still looked stricken at actually having put down Miguel. If she would just look up to my face and stop freaking out she'd see how proud I was of her.

"This is training. I wanted to see what you could do. I want you to hit me, kick me, push me, whatever. Make me look like a fabulous teacher. And you, trying to look all innocent walking in here. You're a real conch at this, aren't ya?"

"Did you just insult me, Miguel?" Sherry asked, putting her hands on her hips, but she looked on the verge of laughing.

"No, love, it means smart." He grinned at her. "Ok, now let's go do some more holds. You can practice on Danny next. We all know he could use a good kick in the rear."

I saw Lily chasing Celeste around the punching pillows and when I looked back, Sherry was being thrown over Danny's shoulder in a blatant show of machismo. She squirmed and was doing that little girly scream. You know, half scream, half giggle. Miguel, Ryan and Celeste, holding Lily, were laughing. Even Lily was giggling at the show.

I walked over and decided to help the once again in distress Sherry.

"Hey! Put her down, boy, or there might be trouble," I yelled playfully.

"Make me, grandpa!" Danny stopped and yelled back.

"Don't take that, Merrick! Make him pay," Calvin yelled and ran over like he was about to join into the fray.

"Yeah," Franklin joined in, "rip his arms off!"

"Ouch. That's harsh. I give," Danny said laughing and put Sherry's feet back on the floor.

"My heroes!" she yelled in a southern belle accent and chased to kiss Calvin and Frank.

They bolted, running circles in the room.

300

"No! Toxic kisses! Run for your lives!" Calvin yelled and they ran from the room.

We laughed. Calvin and Frank were pretty funny. And Sherry had the ability to put anyone in any age group at ease.

"Eleven year olds," she scoffed. "Most guys don't run from my kisses," Sherry teased and sidled up to me in the corner as everyone else followed them out.

"I know *I* don't," I whispered in her ear and picked her up. She wrapped her legs around my waist and her arms around my neck. "You're doing so well with the training. I'm really proud of you."

"Really?"

"Really," I said firmly and her mouth quirked, fighting a smile. "Now, kiss me, wife."

"Yes, sir," she said, letting the smile come.

She kissed me. She always did. It surprised me actually. I'd had plenty of years of watching women and the strange things they did. I'd heard all kinds of excuses that girls gave to spurn men's advances. They were tired, they just ate, not in the mood, not now, not yet, I'm watching my show, I have a headache.

Not Sherry. I thought back to our short life together so far and Sherry has never, not once, given me an excuse. If I wanted her to kiss me, she did so willingly and smiled about it. If I wanted her, she practically ran ahead of me to make it happen. Man, I loved her so much. She was the anti-girl girl.

We started to smell rice, onions and pork and made our way out to the kitchen to form our usual line to proceed through and fill our plate. Sherry and I took ours to the wall beside the record player with Lily.

We ate our supper and laughed at Lily telling us about how she beat Calvin and Marissa in tic-tac-toe after her school lessons.

Then Jeff turned on the news and we all sat in stunned silence. Malachi was there. Right there on the screen for all to see, as pompous and dangerously cunning as ever. He was young and handsome, making him all the more treacherous.

Jeff shhed everyone and turned it up as the new Taker stepped up to the wood podium and began his speech, with flashbulbs clicking and lighting in ecstatic fashion.

"Hello and welcome, friends. At least, I hope all who are present are friends today. We have among us, in our cities and streets and homes, traitors. Not just traitors to me, but traitors to us all. Traitors to our beliefs, our families, our needs and lives. Our freedom.

"I want you all to take a walk with me. A walk in our minds and think

about where we are, where our lives are headed. I see independence from the government. I see freedom from persecution from Keepers and other factions that come against us to destroy us. I see a way to live our lives to the fullest.

"Hear me when I say that the Keepers day will come. I make it my vow and solemn oath that as long as I am a member of the human race, I will not stand by and watch you suffer. Keepers, if you can even call them that. I call them terrorists, because that's what they are. The definition of terrorists is simply this - the use of violence and threats to intimidate or coerce. They want to terrorize you into believing them and giving them your lands, your homes, your jobs, your lives, but we won't stand by any longer. We have a new way to protect ourselves. The enforcers.

"Who is capable enough to be an enforcer you ask? All people. Anyone who wants to shield others from injustice. We won't let them take the only thing that is completely free in the world to us. Our lives. We won't have it. Who's with me? Who else is willing to stand with me against the injustice of our people? Our mothers, fathers, brothers, sisters, our children.

"Come! Join us in the fight. Join us in the battle. Join us in this melee of sabotage! Together we can beat this enemy! And to make sure that it gets done with haste and due diligence, I am offering a reward. $1000.00 for anyone who brings me a Keeper or someone who is associated with one. $1000.00 for each one you bring me. Now go and make me proud."

And the crowd went wild. Great.

"Not good, Merrick," Jeff bellowed and had already started pacing. "Not good."

"Jeffrey, calm down. We knew it could come to this eventually. The need warehouses are starting, we won't be going out that often anymore anyway, and we've got the garden. It'll be alright."

"I know that, but this will only create a different set of problems. People will start hunting us instead of just being cautious of us. There will be people snooping around here now. Going through every abandoned place and home. They will find the others who are hiding and they will find them quickly, and there's not a thing we can do about it."

"We can find another way to reach the others," I answered but had no idea how.

I knew he was right. We were lucky to have the set up we did. Most of the others probably didn't have TVs, or something to even know what was going on.

"Well," Miguel cut in, "we could always do our own hunting. There are a few of us I'm sure who would be willing to track down the others hiding and bring them here. I'm not sure how many we'd find in this town, but we could look. We ain't got a Buckley's chance if we don't at least try. I'd go."

"I'd go. I know Cain would go, too," Ryan chimed.

Simon stiffened. "Ryan, now that's not fair. Don't volunteer my charge when yours isn't even capable of going," Simon said, but he wasn't angry, he was just worried.

"I'm sorry, Simon, but you know Cain. He won't sit here while we go, you know that," Ryan urged.

"I know," Simon conceded unhappily.

"Ok, ok, hold it. Just hold it. I'm not so keen on sending people out anymore. I'm thinking no more people out at all and you all are trying to send people out more often?" Jeff said and sank back down into the sofa, Marissa rubbing his leg to soothe him.

"We've got to do what has to be done. Right? We can't just not alert the others who may not even know that the hunters are coming for them," Miguel stood up and resumed Jeff's pacing path.

"I agree," I said and heard Sherry's little gasp beside me. "It wouldn't be fair to let them sit out there like ducks on a pond."

"Merrick," Sherry breathed my name but I knew I was the only one who heard her.

I took her hand in mine and squeezed it.

"It wouldn't be feasible to do it often," Jeff conceded looking less than happy. "We'd definitely get caught that way. Maybe once a month or so? Do a sweep of the town and maybe the outskirt homes, as much as we could do in one night. It'll do no one any good for us to get caught."

"Yeah, we can't do it all, but...it's our responsibility to do something," I answered and Ryan and Miguel nodded emphatically.

"I'll go, too. Don't look at me, Merrick, you could use my gift for this and you all know it," Danny said, never looking at me, only at Jeff.

I felt the ping in my gut and my conscience buzzed in my head. My fingers twitched with wanting to shove him back down to the sofa and tell him to keep quiet. But no more. Danny was an adult, a Special, but we could no longer keep them holed up and secure. We needed them. We needed their gifts.

He looked to Sherry, then me, to see if we'd contradict him. He knew I was still fiercely protective of him, though I'd tried to break the habit. It was almost as bad as if Sherry had stood up and said she was going. Well, not quite. Danny's determined brown eyes locked with mine and I felt my grimace but nodded once to him. He relaxed and nodded gratefully back. It didn't really matter anyway. I'd be going with him and I wouldn't let him out of my sight.

"Count me in, too," Max said.

"Ok," Jeff started, "we'll call a meeting and discuss it all, see who wants to help make a plan. This isn't something to do halfway. Simon, if we're going to do this, I'm afraid we'll need Cain in on this one. He's got the most strategic planning experience."

"Yes," Simon chimed sadly but proudly. "He was a sergeant in the Marines. You'll need him, which means I'm coming, too."

"That's good. That's saying he'll even really want to help. We might all just be speculating on his want to go with us."

"Oh, he'll want to. He served his country before all this started. He's won't stop now," Simon said confidently.

"Ok, it's settled. His last day of work is in two days, Friday. We'll have a meeting Saturday evening, once everyone gets done with everything. Lillian, when he comes in tonight can you tell him so he doesn't plan anything with his work, just in case they ask him to help clean or move things?"

She flushed a thick pink that was bright against her paleness.

"Uh, I don't think I'll see him tonight. I can tell him in the morning for you, though," she answered softly.

"Great," Jeff said, moving on, not even realizing he'd embarrassed her by implying that Cain would sleep in her room.

Everyone knew Cain got in past one a.m.

But not everyone knew what was going on with her and Cain.

I understood that, but didn't know that Cain had been sleeping in her room. Hmmm. Jeff knew because he bunked across from her room. Interesting.

The others started to disperse. Lana stood up and started walking out. She'd started to learn to read lips. She never learned because her mother home schooled her and wrote everything down. In fact, I was told by Sherry, who found out from Calvin, her mother forced her to wear a sign and pen around her neck at all times in the house so she could write her questions and her mother could write her answers because she didn't want to learn sign language.

Lana glanced at Sherry, the only person she could talk to, and signed what I could only assume was good night. Sherry returned the sign and smiled, but looked back to me and the smile vanished. She took a deep shuddering breath and I waited. Prepared for the pleading for me not to go, the tears, the worrying.

Instead she surprised me.

"Ok, um, I know you need to do this and I know that Danny is gonna go too and you're going to let him, not like you can really stop Danny anyway. And I know you're going to make me stay. But please, just promise me one thing. Please stay together and watch out for each other. Don't let them split you up. I know you'll both work to keep the other alive and that's what I want. If you'll do that, then I promise not to nag or cry and freak out about this whole thing. You're right. It's selfish to sit here, safe, while the others are out there struggling and in danger. I know that. Please, just promise me," she choked out the last words.

She was trying so hard not to cry, her bottom lip quivering, trying to be brave. Almost everything she just said was a lie. Well, the part about her not crying and worrying anyway. She would cry and freak out and worry and pace the entire time we were gone, but it couldn't be helped. It'd be doubly bad with Danny gone too, not just me. Not to mention Ryan, Cain and Jeff, all who she'd grown fiercely fond of, but she was trying. What more could I ask for?

I reached for her and drew her into my lap. She discreetly wiped her eye with the side of her hand and sniffed, not looking at me.

"Honey, everything is going to be ok. You'll see. We'll bring a pile of people in here and then you'll be happy as ever with all the new recruits for kitchen duty." I rubbed circles into her back as she lay against me. "I know you're trying. I also know you're a rotten liar. It's ok to worry, honey, though I hate it when you do. It's part of who you are. I accept that. What I don't like is your lack of faith. I told you before. I will always come back to you. And with Danny out with me, I'll be extra cautious. Too cautious we won't even be that much help at all in fact, cause I'll be so careful."

She elbowed me playfully and I felt her small chuckle.

"I know, I believe you. I'm sorry if I drive you crazy with my worrying and nag-"

"You don't apologize to me. When are you going to learn that, sweetheart? I told you, it's ok to worry a little, just don't worry so much that you think I won't be coming back through that door."

"Ok, I got it."

She nuzzled her face into my neck and wiggled her body closer then took a long soothing deep breath. I smiled and put my arms around her.

"That's my girl." I could smell her hair and rubbed my chin on it, stirring the scents and inhaled. Vanilla. "Ready for bed?"

"Always."

A Blaze Of Glory
Chapter 29 - Cain

This wouldn't get me fired, I knew. My boss had always liked me but with only two working days left, he would probably not be too thrilled with my being late.

The oscillating yellow and green lights in my rear view mirror were definitely getting my attention. That was what I got for kissing Lillian. Once I started it was so hard to stop. I was already running late and because I sped, I was gonna get a ticket.

But it was so freaking worth it.

I wasn't lying to her. I really and truly did believe that I was so close to being over Sherry. I couldn't stop thinking about Lillian. All this week, the distance I'd put between Sherry and me helped. I hadn't realized how much worse I was making things by following her around, by letting her consume my thoughts. But now, all day and night, Lillian was in my mind instead. I only really thought about Sherry when I saw her. So, I'd been continuing to steer clear.

Of course I couldn't completely avoid her, especially with her sweet self bringing me drinks and checking on me all the time. It was getting a little easier though.

Like I was a drug addict and was weaning myself off.

Even though I knew he was coming, I still jumped when the officer tapped the window with his flashlight, lost in my thoughts. I rolled it down and squinted as he pointed the light directly in my eyes.

"License. Registration. Reason for speeding. Reason for being this far away from town."

"In that order?" I asked and immediately regretted it. Stupid. "Sorry, just joking. Um, here you go." I handed him my documents fished from the glove compartment. "And, uh, I'm heading to work at the coffee shop in town, The Moody Brew. And I live out here, sir, with my grandparents."

"Uhuh."

He stayed busy, going over and over the two papers I gave him and still refused to let me see his face. He was wearing a uniform but the glare didn't let me see the color or detail. Then he placed the flashlight under his arm to steady it while he examined the documents again and I got to see him. I hadn't realized that this wasn't a cop. The lights on his car should have tipped me off. Yellow and green meant enforcer.

Crap.

"So, son, what are you going to do when they close up shop? Got another job lined up?"

"No, sir."

Dang it. I should have said yes. I knew what was coming next.

"Well, you should apply for the enforcers." He pulled the flashlight back and looked me and the truck over. Why was an enforcer pulling me over for speeding? He wasn't, I realized. He wanted to know why I was out here. Dang. "We've got plenty of positions, because there's lots of work to do. You can even get transferred to another city if you like."

"Well, I'll think about it. Sounds like a good opportunity. It would make my grandpa proud, that's for sure."

"You do that. It'll be good for you, son. Now, procedure calls. Step out of the vehicle."

"I'm sorry? Is there a problem? I'm already late for work," I asked, even as I stepped out of the truck.

"Nope, no problem. Just protocol. We have to search every vehicle and passenger that we pull over out past the city limits. This'll be good training for you, kid. You're gonna have to do this too, ya know. The key is to be friendly, but firm."

I stood to the side while he searched the truck and then he snorted when he found Lillian's lip gloss under the seat. He held it up for me to see.

"Not really your color is it, son?"

I laughed and tried to make it sound casual.

"Not really. My girl must've dropped it last night."

"That right? Where does she work?"

"She doesn't. She's..." think idiot "...been kind of sick lately. Got some kinda flu. She quit her job early since she was gonna have to stop working anyway. I hope it's not swine flu," I said dripping with concern.

He stepped back with haste.

"You know how contagious that stuff is?" he asked the rhetorical question and his voice jumped an octave.

"Is it? Never really thought about it, but after that big stink they made about it on the news you're probably right."

"Ok. Here." He leaned far forward without taking a step and held his breath as he handed me back my papers. "Come see us at headquarters when you're ready to sign up. And, you really shouldn't be out and about with that contagious stuff, you know that? You'll make everyone sick."

"Solid advice. Thank you, sir. I'll come see you tomorrow."

"No! I mean, give it a few days. You know, just take care of your girl a bit, and then come see me."

Bingo! Poor sap.

"Ok. Sounds good. Nice to meet you..."

"Enforcer Billings."

"Enforcer Billings. Have a nice night."

And then I heard a terrible screech, like a dying animal. We were both still standing in the street and hadn't moved to our vehicles yet. I felt my heart slam down in my chest. I knew that sound.

When Sherry and I had been chased to the caves.

A Marker.

The man was muttering something about 'what was that crazy owl' and looking around the darkness like he could see anything. The flashlight went up and I knew it in a split second, just in time, that I needed to move.

I grabbed his shirt back as he turned and jerked him to the ground. He groaned and complained and then started cursing me. I told him to shut up, to be quiet, as we lay on the warm asphalt. He apparently hadn't seen what I'd seen in that flashlight beam. The Marker made a swoop for him and was just waiting for his next chance.

The idiot was still squirming to get up. How could I explain what was after us?

"Shut up," I hissed. "There's something after us. You didn't see it?"

"No! Get off me!" he yelled making me want to just let the Marker have him.

"Shhh! Idiot!" I whispered.

Then we heard the screech again and the idiot went still.

"What is that? Sounds like a..."

"I know what it is, but trust me, you wouldn't believe me. If you want to make it, just stay quiet and do what I tell you. Hear me?"

"What are you talking about?"

I decided. I was probably already going to die or jump in my truck and hope that was good enough to save me. No point in letting him die too - without the truth. "Listen," I whispered quickly, "and listen good. Your friends, your savior, the dark haired guys all around; they are not your friends. That thing in the sky is not your friend either, he's theirs. Keepers are not the enemy. We have a bunker not far from here with a butt load of people in it. The dark haired guys are called Lighters. They are here to take over, not help us."

It was still pitch black, except for his flashlight beam, pointed the other way on the asphalt a little ways away from us. I couldn't see his face, but I heard his still breaths and the silence spoke volumes.

"Ok, son. So what you're telling me is that you are confessing to being a part of the resistance?"

"Of everything I just said, that's the part you want to fight about? I hate that word by the way, resistance. It makes us sound so hokey," I spouted sarcastically and was stunned when he actually answered me.

"The official enforcer word is traitor."

"Much better," I said with sarcastic enthusiasm and waited for his next move.

We heard the screech and I knew it was close, it swooped and I screamed for him to roll. Anywhere just roll. We did but I felt the wind from the beast as he fanned by and missed me with his wing by mere inches. Missed *me* anyway. I said the enforcer's name to see if he was still with me or not.

"Billings?"

"I'm here."

"We gotta move. These things don't give up. Listen, they're fast and usually come with more than one. We've got to grab that flashlight fast and see about making a getaway in our cars. I don't *think* he can hurt you in there anyway."

"Ok, I'm ready. Why don't you jump in my car with me? It'll be faster that way," he said and I knew.

"So you can take me downtown faster you mean?"

"Well, you did just confess to being a traitor."

"No, I confessed to knowing the truth. Why don't you come with me and I'll show you the rest of it. You can see it all firsthand and hear what's really been going on. There's a lot to know."

"Hmm. Ok, sure."

Too easy. Dang. Why did I think he would listen to me in the first place?

"Ha, you almost had me," I said wryly. "Looks like we're splitting ways after all." I remembered he'd seen my face and knew my name. There went my in-town cover. "Ok, go. Quickly and quietly. Do not stand up."

I heard the shuffling of him crawling towards the flashlight. I had no idea which way my vehicle was or how far because we were all turned around. I realized he was probably still going to try to play cop and arrest me even with the thing after us or at least not help me get in my truck. Why had I turned the lights off?

I saw the light picked up and turned my way. It stayed on me for a few seconds, memorizing my face probably for future line ups, and then started to sweep the area for our vehicles. He must have found them because I heard a grunt. I turned to follow the light and saw that they were a little ways away. We had crossed the four lane road somehow and were almost in the other side ditch.

Crap.

I started to move that way, then a multitude of screeching ensued and beating of wings. It sounded like chopper blades. Way more than one Marker. Crap!!

I yelled for Billings to stay down and go fast. I started moving but the flashlight beam jumped so much I couldn't see the truck anymore. We bumped into each other and he yelped.

"It's me. Listen, we gotta-"

Then an explosion lit up the sky and when we looked up I saw the beast for my first time. My first real look of what they look like instead of just hearing them and seeing glimpses. They were hideous. Half man, half bird, with a smidge of dragon. No faces, big bright yellow eyes with black bodies and wings, but feet and legs and claws. And like I thought, there was a ton of them. They were close and they were everywhere.

Billings began to whimper and when I looked over, he was scared stiff looking at them. The fire blaze gave us enough light to look around a little. My truck!

"My truck!" I repeated out loud. "What the hell happened to my truck"

It was in blazes and pieces and so, unfortunately, was Billings piece of crap car. They both exploded. What the...

"I tagged it," he answered solemnly. "I knew that story was fake so I got you to get out of the car and painted it. I was going to arrest you and they were going to destroy your truck. We were supposed to be long gone by now."

"You painted it? With a tracker? Why? Why destroy the truck?" I fumed not following his logic.

Painted meant marking it with a laser or tracker for a missile to follow so it knew exactly where to hit. So if I had somehow taken off in my truck, it would still have gotten me. I couldn't have gotten away. I was almost thankful for the Markers now. He failed to mention the part where he was trying to kill me and he didn't know I was in the Marines. Wow, the enforcers were not playing around.

"Well, it's a tactic we use. If you're missing, we hope they'll come out to find you. So we destroy the vehicles so the rest of the rebels won't see it somewhere and know we have you locked up. Plus, it would have killed you and the truck if you had somehow evaded me," he said calmly.

"That is some crazy logic, you know that? You idiots got the military involved?"

"Of course. Where do you think our base of operations is?"

Dang it.

"Look at what you did! You blew up your car too, idiot!" I yelled over the screeches. "Now we're gonna die! There's nowhere to go way out here! Do you understand that? Your military won't save you." I let out an exasperated breath. "Did you see them?"

"Yes," he answered quietly, "I saw them. I...can't believe it. I...I have a feeling you weren't lying about knowing what they were. I thought it was an owl and you were trying to scare me with your story."

"An owl?" I blew another exasperated breath in utter disbelief that they could recruit this fool and arm him with weapons. "Give me the light," I barked.

He did. I, while still lying on my stomach, tried to survey the land beyond what the blaze was illuminating.

"Roll! Roll!" I heard Billings yell.

I rolled into him as we both rolled inward toward each other and felt the cold air of wings across my face. It was freakish that they were such cold things when it was so hot outside, especially with the blaze of the cars going.

"That's it. We've got to get away from the fire before it explodes."

"They already did."

"No, idiot! They're on fire. The gas tanks haven't lit yet," I said and continued to look around and wonder what we were going to do. I started crawling away and he followed. We went into the ditch further away and I lay on my back and thought. Thought hard, pulling from training and ops and years of playing predator in the woods behind me house with the neighbor kids. It was only about six o'clock at night by then. We had a long wait until the light of morning.

I thought as fast as my brain would let me about how in the heck we were going to get out of this.

Surprise, surprise!
Chapter 30 - Sherry

"Surprise!" we all yelled and Calvin looked liked he had just seen a ghost.

"Aw, you guys," he crooned and blushed redder than a fire hydrant.

Lana signed to Calvin 'Are you surprised?' He signed back 'Yes!' and he let her hug him, in front of all of us. Such a sweet guy.

We'd planned that night after supper to lure him into the training room for 'extra training'. It was pretty comical how Ryan had insisted that Calvin go and you could tell Calvin was trying his hardest not to be peeved because it was Ryan and it was impossible to be mad at him, but he really didn't want to do any extra training.

I made cupcakes with no icing because we didn't have any. So they were muffins really. We had no presents except things people made and came up with. Lana sewed him a cloth sign for his door out of scrap pieces of fabric and old clothes laying around, patchwork and needlework that said 'Calvin and Frank's Base of Ops.' It was cute and he made a huge fuss over it.

Miguel gifted Calvin with a gun shooting lesson and to my utter shock, Lana was thrilled about it. Even though guns didn't kill the Lighters, it appeared we had a new enemy, the enforcers. Humans. She didn't want him to be helpless, didn't want him to be under anyone's thumb, didn't want him to not know how to defend himself and those he loved. I understood that completely.

After a while, we, well I, cleaned up and he thanked everyone for the little things we were able to scrounge up to give him.

I had just carried all the dishes to the quiet deserted kitchen and was putting them in the deep sink when I felt hands on my waist. I gasped, immediately bristled and swung around expecting nothing else but Phillip himself ready to attack me once more.

It was Calvin.

"Sorry, Sherry, I didn't mean to scare you."

"Oh, Calvin, it's ok." I glanced over to see Merrick leaning on the counter and watching me, lips pursed. "I'm ok, just tired. What's up, birthday man?"

"Um, my mom told me that most of this was your idea. I just wanted to say thanks. It was fun. The muffins were really good."

"Your mom helped me. We all did it together."

"Sure, Sherry. Sure."

I laughed out loud at him and his sarcasm. He was growing up way too fast for my taste. "I'm glad you had fun. Next year, we'll have real cake."

"You don't have to lie to me, Sherry. I know things aren't going to get better. It's ok though. It's the thought that counts, right?" he said and his tone wasn't bitter, he was just stating facts.

"Yes, that's right."

He hugged me tightly around my shoulders because he was taller than I was and still growing. Ugh. I was as short as a twelve year old.

He left, hopping away happily. Merrick walked over to stand right in front of me, looking down on me like the tower he was. "Are you ok?"

"Yeah."

"Why are you so jumpy?"

"I'm not."

"Liar."

"No, I'm fine."

"You're not going to tell me?"

"What?"

"Why you got so freaked out?"

"I didn't."

"Liar."

"I'm not!"

"Are."

"Merrick."

"Sherry."

I blew out a loud fast breath. "I just had a little flashback from Phillip, that's all. It was silly and I overreacted."

He grabbed my hands. "It wasn't silly. Why didn't you just tell me that when I asked you? Why do I have to play twenty questions with you? You remember I told you once you didn't have to be a stone around me, I still mean that. When I ask you something, I want the truth. Don't play coy with me when I know there's something going on. I know you, remember? Plus, you are an appalling liar. You know all this," he chided, trying to be half playful, half serious.

"Ok, ok, sorry. I just don't want you to add anything to that very long list of things you worry about for me."

He twisted his lips and looked contemplative. "It *is* a long list."

I poked his ribs and he bent over slightly laughing and grabbed me around my waist as I tried to bolt from the tickle fest I knew I was about to be a victim of. He swung me around in a circle, a tight grip on my waist from behind.

"Come on now. If you run away, you can't have your present," he said in a sing-song voice.

That stopped me. "Present?"

"Sherry Elizabeth. Did you really think after all these years I'd forget your birthday?"

Dang it. "No, but I hoped," I thought.

"What was that?" he said cracking a smile.

"Did I say that out loud?"

He laughed. "Yeah, honey, that was out loud. What? You thought you could make Calvin's party be on your birthday and work out this whole plot because we needed to surprise Calvin and the rest of us would be too busy to notice that you were trying to escape your own birthday?"

I couldn't lie, I was bad at it. It was proved to me over and over. Plus he knew me and he knew I hated to be celebrated and called attention to. "Yes."

He smiled wider and shook his head, amused and pulled a box out of his pocket. He held it up to me wordlessly.

I blinked, and then blinked some more. He wasn't joking. He bought me a present. How? What? I took it from him slowly and looked at it. He wrapped it in a magazine page. Captain Jack Sparrow peeked out at me from one of the seams of the ad he used as wrapping paper and tied to together with a hair ribbon.

I looked up to his face. He was watching and waiting. He wasn't anxious or bubbling like he thought I'd be excited about whatever was in that little box. He just watched me, knowing me, waiting patiently. Always about me, never about him. Always.

"What do you get a girl who already has everything she wants?" I asked, and he smiled shyly.

I thought about what it could be and wanted to cry before I even put my finger under the crease to ease the paper away. It tore easily and what I saw inside did bring tears. Big fat grateful loving tears.

It was a silver heart charm. I immediately knew that it would fit around the charm already on my necklace. That his charm would surround the other two silver hearts around my neck and they would all fit together. He meant it to be that way. It was perfect.

"How?" I asked looking down at it in awe and felt him swipe at a tear on my chin with his finger.

"Cain and Pap helped me make and solder it. I made it out of a soda can." He chuckled sadly, like he should be ashamed of that fact. "We melted it down and shaped it and...anyway, I had no idea what to do for you. Once again I feel the need to apologize for my inability to buy you real jewelry-"

I cut him off with a kiss. I'm talking about *a kiss*. I kissed him like there was not another second left to live. I couldn't believe him. How did he come up with that idea? He was just so...gosh darn sweet. I was shocked at my ability to still be surprised and also at Merrick's ability to always be thoughtful. Always planning, always thinking about me.

He broke away from the kiss and laughed breathlessly, placing his forehead against mine. "I take it you like it then?"

"I love it. You couldn't have gotten me anything else to make me happier."

"I just wanted you to have something that went along with what you already are. You love that necklace and I'm not trying to impose on it-"

I cut him off again, this time with my fingers on his lips. "No, Merrick, you belong here." I grabbed my necklace and rubbed it between my fingers with my free hand. "This is all I have left of my family. You're my family now. I love it," I reiterated firmly.

He kissed my fingers and hugged me, picking me up off the floor as I held the box in my hand over our heads where my arms rested, like the precious object it was.

"Thank you," I whispered in his ear.

"You're welcome, baby. I'm glad you like it."

I pulled back to look at him. "So, *you* remembered, but at least Danny didn't."

He grimaced. "Don't count on it," he muttered.

Ugh.

Danny, in fact, kept his part mellow and low key.

Birthdays were always the weirdest things in my family, the things that we always made a big deal about. Always at the lake, rain or shine, always under the willow tree, always useless odd gifts, always organic cake bought from the completely vegan organic place on the other side of town, way out of the way, but they were in the same book club as my mom. Hippie book club.

The reading list was Dharma Bums by Jack Kerouac, A New Model of the Universe by P. D. Ouspensky, Awakening the Buddha Within by Lama Surya Das, The Politics of Ecstasy by Timothy Leary.

Needless to say, I steered clear of the book club.

I never understood why school wasn't important to them, not in a real sense anyway. My mom read her books like they held secrets, but frowned upon the idea of college and was practically dragged to our high school graduations.

"How can I endorse a public school education when they teach our kids to be mindless sheep of the political agendas and thoughts of the world that had been established through greed and the rape of our earth, our minds and our choices," she'd say like a true spoken left wing.

Harsh is what it was. We were her kids and she thought there were things more important than watching us graduate? Or missing it just to make a point? Didn't she *send* us to the public school? If it was that important to her, why didn't she just homeschool us?

My dad had to go to college to become a dentist, but mom always hated that fact. She didn't even finish high school.

They'd met at a party. Some type of save-the-animals rally thing. The only way to get admission was to be wearing some type of faux fur with red paint on it. Then, once everyone was high or drunk and exhausted from dancing and who knows what else, they'd walk the night life streets of Chicago and make a statement.

My parents had told me this story I couldn't even count how many times, not even leaving out all the drug parts and unprotected 'free love' to which Danny and I would beg them to stop. They talked about how this was the peak of their lives. They were the freest they'd ever been, the most influential, and the happiest.

I wanted to say, 'Wouldn't now, having us and being parents be their happiest?'

I'd counter 'Mom, it's not the sixties. People don't refer to it as 'free love' anymore. Now it's called sleeping around. And how do you find these people? The ideas of living that way are dead, not to mention dangerous.'

She'd counter 'Being free is always dangerous and there's a community of free believers, or hippies as you call them, anywhere where you are willing to put forth an effort to find them.'

I'd roll my eyes, she'd call me a sullen brainwashed teenager and we'd call it even. Good times...

So Danny and Celeste had turned on the stereo in the second room. Andrew Belle was playing and I wondered where in the world they had gotten a CD of his from. Surely Phillip's collection didn't consist of it. Lillian was in there with them too as Merrick towed me in. They whispered 'Surprise!' when I walked in. I laughed at them and looked around at the setting.

Danny had laid out a picnic pallet of cookies with a lit candle in the middle on a saucer and there were a couple gifts on the blanket, wrapped in more magazine paper, and Danny's looked like it was wrapped in toilet paper. Hmm.

The lights were off so it was only the soft glow of the candle, but I could still see their faces. Celeste grabbed me from Merrick's grasp and hugged me tightly before pulling me down to the pallet beside her.

"Danny told me all about your parents. About how they used to take you on picnics so we thought you might like this. It was all Danny's idea though." She looked up at him smiling. "Your brother is so sweet."

"Come on. You helped," Danny said settling down beside her and Merrick nestled himself behind me, pulling me against him for support. "Besides, I wasn't sure if you'd like it or not. I mean, our parents haven't exactly won any awards for parental guidance or thoughtfulness, especially lately."

"It's great, Danny. Thank you," I said and realized I was still holding the box with Merrick's heart in it.

I pulled it out and handed it to Merrick over my shoulder.

"Please?"

He smiled and moved my hair over to reach the clasp. After a few seconds he replaced it, trailing his fingers along the chain down my neck and collarbone a little longer than needed, making me shiver. I looked down to see it just as I had pictured it. All three hearts nestled together perfectly.

"It turned out good," Danny said and I looked at him sharply.

"You knew about this?" I asked, rubbing the charm with my fingers, getting a feel for the newness of it.

"Of course I did," he said proudly, at having known the secret before me. "Merrick asked me if he thought- ow!"

Merrick kicked Danny's leg and was glaring at him comically.

"Shut it, Special," Merrick rumbled. Celeste was covering her mouth trying not to laugh. "I gotta have some secrets," he said and kicked Danny again, more gently this time, to drive home his threat.

Celeste burst out laughing.

"Hey!" Danny said, pulling her into his lap. "You're supposed to be on my side."

Celeste just giggled, looking up at him affectionately and then snuggled happily back against him. I realized, I was sitting in between Merrick's legs and Celeste was sitting on Danny's lap and Lillian was just sitting there alone and quiet.

"Hey, Lillian."

"Hey," she smiled. "Happy Birthday. Here- oh, wait." She turned to Danny. "You want to go first? I'm sorry."

"No, it's ok. Mine's lame anyway. Go ahead."

She handed a little soft bag to me that wasn't wrapped. It was a little purple mesh purse\bag with a short handle. It was very cute and very Lillian.

"Aw, thanks, Lillian. It's pretty," I said and reached out to touch her hand but didn't leave Merrick's lap.

"I know you don't have a lot of use for something like that now, but it's all I had left from my stuff. I certainly don't need it anymore. Besides, Michael's mom gave it to me."

"Lillian." I felt punched in the chest. "I can't take this. This is special to you-"

"No, no, it's not. Michael's mom hated me. She especially knew I hated the color purple. Guess what color everything she ever gave me was?" she said and laughed.

"You're sure?"

"Positive."

"Thank you. This is perfect for a bath caddy. I always drop shampoo or something on the way to the bathroom. Thanks."

"You're welcome."

"Me next!" Celeste chimed and squirmed to reach in her pocket.

"Ok." I closed my eyes and held my hands out in front of her. "Lay it on me."

I was completely giddy and happy by then. I hated being celebrated but this was nice. It felt so easy going to just sit and be with the people I loved and not have silly balloons and false sentiments, and songs and nasty cake. Plus, being reminded of how much everyone cared about you, even though it could be the end of the world and it was not like they could go out and buy me anything, really made me feel awesome.

Celeste put something extremely light and soft in my hand. I opened my eyes and stared at it. It was a bracelet; a crocheted yarn bracelet. It had all the colors, but it wasn't rainbow tacky. It looked good like that and she had woven little designs that looked like circles with lines through it. I gasped.

The Keepers tattoo! She crocheted the Keepers symbol onto the bracelet for me. And something else that brought tears to my eyes. Crochet. She learned how to crochet from Mrs. Trudy.

"I've been working on it for a week, every since Danny brought up that your birthday was coming. I know it's a lame silly bracelet, but...Mrs. Trudy..." She choked back a sob. Danny squeezed her and then I hugged her to me.

"I know. Mrs. Trudy taught you to do this, I remember. Celeste, this is..." I pulled back to look at it again. "This is so fantastic. Thank you so much."

"No problem. Here." She helped me put it on. It was a little stretchy so I could glide it on and off easily.

"How did you know if it would fit?" I asked.

"Easy, I took my wrist size and split it in half."

Everyone laughed and I pushed her shoulder playfully. I looked at Danny expectantly with raised eyebrows. "What?" he asked me smiling. "You think I got you something?"

"Give it," I said and smiled.

"All right, but I guarantee you, it's lame. I'm not that crafty."

He handed me the two boxes wrapped in magazine paper and the one in toilet paper.

"Three?"

"Three," he said amusedly.

I opened the toilet paper first. It was a folded picture of us as kids on Halloween, him as the white Power Ranger and me as the Tooth Fairy. Mom had always told us there was no tooth fairy, and me being the disgruntled 'brainwashed' daughter I was, I wanted to prove her wrong. In the picture, we were standing with our arm around the other's shoulder and holding our lantern buckets in the other hand with missing teeth and big smiles.

"Danny, you kept this?" I asked and he nodded.

"It's been in my wallet this whole time. I found it a few years ago right after you moved out. Mom was throwing all your stuff out, the stuff you left in your room, and this got mixed in with it." He shrugged. "I snagged it."

"I can't believe you had this." I leaned back to show it to Merrick. "Remember?" I asked him and he smiled.

"Of course."

"Of course." I smiled, too. "Thanks, Danny. I don't have one picture. I never did. Mom wouldn't let me take any when I left."

"I know. That's why I want you to have it."

I was about to cry so I moved on, clearing my throat. "Ok, next."

The other two boxes weren't significant, just silly stuff he'd rounded up and fiddled with. Paperclips shaped into a running man and a big slotted wooden spoon. He'd burned the words "Sherry's Kitchen" on the handle with a wood burning pen from Phillip's workshop.

"Guys, this is so great. Thank you. I can't believe you guys did all this."

They murmured the usual "It's fine", "We wanted to" and "No problem".

"Well, I'm going to head to bed," Lillian said and yawned. "I hate staying up when- well never mind. Good night, guys."

"Wait," I called after her and scrambled to catch her in the door. "What's the matter?"

"Nothing...ok, fine. I remember, lie detector." She shifted on her feet uncomfortably. "I just worry the whole time Cain is gone. So, I usually go to sleep early. I'm not good at waiting anymore. I always think the worst..."

"It's ok, Lillian, I understand. I didn't realize things were going so good with you guys. Moving along, you know."

"Merrick didn't tell you?"

"Tell me what?"

She cleared her throat and glanced at Merrick, but he was talking to Danny.

"He caught Cain and me in this room earlier today."

"Caught you what?" I whispered and felt my eyes widen.

"Just kissing."

"Ahh." I giggled. "No, he didn't tell me. That's why he was late to practice," I realized.

"Yeah. Cain checks on me when he comes in at night, too. I mean, we're not like official or anything. I just really, really like him. He...seems to like me. He says he does... Gah, I'm so out of practice," she said all flustered and tucked her hair behind her ears furiously.

"Calm down, Lillian." I couldn't help but smile and tried to stifle a laugh. "Trust me, Cain doesn't exactly beat around the bush. He's pretty blunt. If he's said something along those lines, you can trust that it's true. And he's not going to waste his time on something either."

"If you say so. I'm just trying not to make a huge deal out of it, but I'm freaking out a little bit. I just can't- I just can't believe how much I feel for him. We barely know each other. And I'm so scared when he's gone. I can't put my finger on it, but it's really...unnerving."

"Well, you've lost two people recently. I don't think you have to look far for an explanation."

"Yeah. Alright, well, happy birthday. Goodnight."

I hugged her tight. "Thanks. And don't worry. He'll be fine. He knows what he's doing. Night."

When I turned back to go sit in the lap of my awesome husband and eat cookies with some other really important people to me, I almost forgot all about Lillian and her troubles. I was solely focused on my little family and my haphazardly perfect little life.

Protective Ways
Chapter 31 - Lillian

It was late. I had no idea what time, but I had a bad feeling that it was really late. Cain hadn't come home yet. Well, at least I thought he hadn't. He didn't check on me or maybe he did. He said he wasn't going to sleep with me anymore, but surely he would have woken me to say hi before heading off, right?

I got up and shifted out my door two doors down to Cain's room. It was dark and quiet in the hall. I knocked easily and opened the door but his sleeping bag was empty.

I groped through the house, checking the clock in the living room first, 2:05 a.m. He was an hour late. I checked all the rooms that I could imagine him being in and then the ones I was sure he wouldn't be in and then I started to panic. I had a horrible feeling. It was not a coincidence. It was all coming true, the theory I had about me and the people I get close to.

Cain was in trouble because of me.

He laughed at me and told me I was nuts for thinking it and now look.

I ran to Merrick and Sherry's room, knocking slightly as I pushed open the door. They were wrapped up together pretty good. Her head was on his chest with his arm around her shoulder, her legs and his were intertwined. I hated to disturb them, but I knew something was wrong.

"Merrick," I whispered but realized that was not gonna cut it so I shook his foot too. "Merrick."

He jolted groggily and looked around, his shirtless arms immediately wrapping themselves tighter around Sherry to protect her from whatever may be lurking. Wow, dude was built. Then he saw me and squinted just as Sherry started to stir.

"Lillian? Is everything ok? What's the matter?" he asked in a flurry of slurred hushed words.

"It's Cain, he's still not here. He's an hour late. Something's wrong," I explained.

"Um." He scratched his head as Sherry sat up. He shhed her and pulled her back to him to lull her back to sleep, rubbing his hand up and down her arm. "I'm sure he's fine," he whispered. "He's not always very punctual. He's probably out doing something with his boss or something."

"I feel like something's wrong, Merrick. He hasn't been late not once since I've been here."

He sighed and looked at me. Not like he was annoyed but like he was thinking which I appreciated.

"Alright, if he's not here in an hour, come get me and I'll get a couple of the guys to go with me to look for him, ok? Is that good?"

"Ok."

"I'm sure he's fine. Cain's just upset about his job and all. He probably didn't think you'd even notice him being late but come get me and we'll go in one hour."

"Ok. Sorry I bothered you."

"You didn't," he said and smiled lazily, he could barely hold open his eyes. "Don't worry, get some sleep."

I slid back out the door and immediately knew what I had to do. Number one, I couldn't wait one hour for help when I knew something was wrong right then. Number two, I couldn't put all those people in danger to go look for him when - even though I was sure - what if I was wrong and he was just out with his friends. I had to do this myself.

I ran to my room, pulling off my pajamas and grabbing jeans and a t-shirt and snagging my tennis shoes all in a blur. I ran silently down the hall through the commons room to the stairs, still forcing on the last sneaker. I grabbed a flashlight and then a set of keys.

The tag above them was labeled 'Jeep' so I unlocked the latch door and knew it would creak but kept going and didn't stop until I was through the stock room and at the back door of the store.

I was shaking scared. I could hear my teeth chattering and it took me a few tries to get the deadbolt unlocked with my shaky hands.

I didn't want to go out into the dark at all let alone by myself but there I was, doing it to by myself and on purpose. I had to get to Cain. My mind ran rampant with all the things that could be wrong. I just knew...

I tried to push all that aside as I eased the door open to peer into the pitch black night. I flipped the switch on the flashlight and looked again. The light beam was shaking along with my hand but I didn't see anything other than dirt so I shut and locked the door behind me and ran for the Jeep.

It was eerie how quiet it was. The Jeep door shutting sounded like a gunshot it was so loud in the silent dark. I fumbled with the keys and put in into reverse. Stinking stick! I stalled once and then got it into first gear and started on my way, absolutely no idea where I was going or what I'd find, but I had to try.

I knew which way town was so I headed east. It took a while, before I reached anything other than darkness.

I could see it before I reached the big blazing ball of fire and smoke. A sane person probably would have slowed down but I sped up, knowing this is where I'd find Cain. Once I stopped the Jeep, in the middle of the road, I jumped out and searched all around the cars. There were two burning and though it was totally trashed and burnt, I could make one of the out as a truck. Cain's truck.

"Cain!" I yelled because I didn't know what else to do.

I continued to look around the blaze, shining my flashlight around but couldn't see much. The fire was producing a lot of light itself.

"Cain!"

Then I heard a flapping and felt wind on my back. I was knocked to the asphalt by something and felt the keys slide from my grasp. I rolled over quickly, thinking I knew exactly what it was that hit me and as I raised the flashlight, it was the first good look I'd ever gotten at a Marker. I expected nothing less. It looked like pure evil right out of a Hollywood movie.

Its wing brushed my face as it swooped by. I screamed and scrambled to my feet once it was gone and was immediately brought down by another object.

Except this one had arms and fingers and they wrapped around my mouth to quiet my scream. And it was lying on top of me to pin me down.

"Shh," someone whispered in my ear from behind and removed his hand from my lips.

"Cain," I whispered in relief.

He turned me quickly with a look of horror on his face. "Lillian? What the hell are you doing here?"

I hugged him around his neck, pulling me to him as close as I could get. He smelled like smoke and was filthy. And I was *so* happy to see him.

"I had to come find you."

He pulled back to glare at me. "What? How? What are-"

"I knew something was wrong. Didn't I tell you I was cursed? When you were late getting home, I knew. So, here I am."

"So, you snuck out of the bunker, stole the Jeep and drove the thirty minutes to get here in the dark by yourself and unprotected, on a hunch that I might be in trouble instead of just hanging out somewhere?" he guessed angrily.

"Well, you're here aren't-"

I was cut off by another a loud metallic screech. He rolled off me and grabbed my flashlight, shining it around to see. "Keys?" he asked briskly.

"Around here somewhere."

"Never mind."

323

We were clear. He grabbed my hand, yanking me up and pulling me fast behind him to the ditch. Once inside, we lay down in the dirt and mud beside each other and he turned the light off.

"I can't believe you did this," he growled beside me in the dark.

"What? I knew you were in trouble. I couldn't just go back to sleep and act like there was nothing wrong."

"You should have sent someone else."

"Merrick said he'd go in a little bit if you didn't turn up, but I didn't want to wait and I didn't want to put him in danger either."

"Oh, but yourself, that's ok?"

I bristled at his tone and his words. "What is wrong with you? I thought you'd be happy to see me."

"This isn't a date, Lillian. No, I'm not happy to see you. You should never have tried to do this-"

"Hey! What is your problem? I came out here to help you!"

"But you're not helping, are you? I had to run over and save your cute butt once already, remember?"

"If we can just find the keys, we can leave-"

"And die while we're looking around up there? There are Markers everywhere. I've been here for hours, Lillian, they aren't going anywhere. We'll have to wait until daylight and now, I've got to worry about keeping you alive, too, not just me."

I couldn't hold it in any longer. I thought I'd burst with anger. I'd spent the last two hours going crazy with worry and instead of being grateful that I tried to help him he was angry at me? It was the strangest feeling of complete anger and complete relief. He was ok, but he was ticking me off.

I embarrassingly burst into tears.

"Ah, come on now," he said still sounding way to angry, "none of that."

I kept crying, quietly of course, he couldn't hear me, but must have felt the shaking of my body. It was ladylike, it wasn't like I was snotting all over the place, but still, it was embarrassing. I covered my face with my hands and turned away from him, though I knew he couldn't see me. I bumped into something else. Something warm and hard.

A body. I screamed.

A warm hand covered my mouth again and I felt Cain's body pressed against my back.

"Shh. It's ok," Cain whispered again and took his hand away.

"Hey," a new voice said, "sorry. I didn't mean to scare you. I just didn't want to interrupt your fighting."

"This is enforcer Billings. Billings, this is Lillian."

Cain sounded a little calmer, but I was still trying to tamp down on my own anger. For some reason, when I got really angry, I cried.

It had always been extremely embarrassing on the playground with the mean girls at school. The only fist fight I'd ever been in was in middle school, and I cried the entire time.

"Is this lip gloss girl?" Billings asked.

"Yeah, this is her," Cain answered with a sigh.

"Lip gloss girl?" I asked.

"Yeah, your boy Cain here has been telling me all about you."

"He has?" I asked surprised.

"Yeah."

"Can I ask who you are?"

"I'm an enforcer. I pulled Cain over and was arresting him when we were attacked."

He spoke so nonchalantly and Cain didn't say anything. It was very strange.

"Ok. And why are an enforcer and a rebel being friendly?"

"Have you seen those things?" Billings asked me emphatically. "You don't come back the same after seeing something like that. Cain told me all about them and the Lighters and I gotta say I believe it."

"Well," Cain said, "like I said, we've been here for hours. I wouldn't have told him anything about you, had I'd known you'd show up like this," Cain muttered.

Anger flared red hot and sticky once again. "You jerk. You are such a jerk! How dare you yell at me when I've been worried sick about you! I come out all the way out here-"

He cut me off by grabbing my arms and twisting me to face him. I started again.

"I was so worried-"

He kissed me - really kissed me. His hand locked behind my neck and his lips moved against mine so hard and yet so in sync. He kissed me deeper and I didn't try to stop him as my anger flitted away to nothing like salt in the wind. It was amazing how much he seemed to just take away all my troubles. I didn't understand why he was kissing me when I thought he was angry, but I wasn't going to question it, right then.

I was just happy he was alive to do it.

The kiss went deeper and deeper, harder then softer. His hand began to wander away from my neck, down my back to my hip. He pulled me closer with it there then it traveled to the back of my thigh. That got my breathing so out of control that I had to pull back.

He immediately started talking through his ragged breaths, still close enough to fan my face with his breathing.

"Don't you understand why I was so angry? Any idea? Here I thought some random person had pulled up on the scene and when I finally see your face, it's you! The one person in the world I want to keep away from this mess the most. You. Scared. Me." He exhaled loudly and ran his fingers down my cheek. "You don't risk yourself. Not for me, not for anyone. I see now why Merrick acts so crazy like he does over Sherry. It really sucks worrying about you. When I saw you, a million ways you could get hurt, or worse, flashed before my eyes." He shook his head and I felt the movement. "Lillian, nothing can happen to you. I won't let anything happen to you."

"I'm sorry. I didn't mean to cause trouble, I just knew I had to do something. I couldn't let you die because of me," I said through a new round of tears.

He exhaled again, his hand rested on my cheek. "Please don't cry anymore." His thumbs moved under my eyes to swipe tears away. "I'm sorry I yelled, sweetheart, I shouldn't have, but I've never been that scared in all my life."

"Not even with-" I bit my lip, but it was too late.

"No, not even with Sherry in the caves," he answered softly. "This is not your fault. This isn't the curse, it's the enemy. I don't want to hear any more curse talk. Right now, let's just rest while we think about what to do."

"Well, Merrick knows I knew you were missing. He'll come soon if you or I don't show up."

"You're probably right."

"I'm glad you're ok," I whispered. "I was so scared I was going to get to you when it was too late."

"They can't hurt me. I'm a-okay, lovely," he said and chuckled.

Once again I marveled at his way of being witty in all situations and completely in awe of his mood swings. Then I didn't at marvel at anything but lips.

His. They brushed my cheek, then my jaw, searching. When he found what he was looking for, he fastened his lips to mine again. This time, I was happy instead of just relieved and I pulled myself up to hover over him, straddling him in the muddy dirt and twigs. He kissed me fiercely, his hands roaming once again to nowhere that wasn't decent. I lost all reason and sense of time and propriety. I kissed him like my life depended on it and he had the answer to survival. He seemed equally eager and his grip got tighter and tighter on my hips. I heard a noise, a groan or whimper, then realized it came from me. Then I heard another noise.

"Um, I'm still here. I let you have your little reunion kiss, but I'm not going to lay here silently through anything else," Billings said quickly.

Screeching brakes to a halt. Crap, I'd forgotten he was even there. I pulled back, glad for the dark to hide the fire engine red blush over me. However, Cain laughed into my hair.

"Sorry, got carried away. If you could see this girl, you'd understand."

"Cain!" I whispered to him in the dark, but I knew Billings could hear me and I couldn't help but smirk a little.

Cain laughed again as did Billings. He kissed my lips gently once more then pulled me back down in the dirt, bunching me into his warm dirty side and wrapping his arms around me. "Not too uncomfortable? This ok?"

"Better than ok for the circumstances. I'm sorry, Cain. I know I have no business acting like I'm some kind of hero. I just ran to get here, I didn't think about much after that."

"It's ok." He squeezed me. "I told you, I overreacted, but that isn't a license to risk yourself. I still think you shouldn't have come at all, let alone by yourself, but we'll get out of this. Don't wrinkle that pretty little nose with worry. I won't let anything happen to you."

"It's not just me I'm worried about."

"Ahh," Billings said sarcastically, "I didn't know you cared."

"Eat it, Billings," Cain said and I could tell from his tone he was playing and they both chuckled.

It appeared Cain had made a new friend. A very important friend. An enforcer. Now if we could just get out of there alive.

I fell asleep. I woke up wanting to curse, but didn't believe in it.

It was still dark and everything was quiet. I assumed Cain was still asleep. I was beginning to wonder what time it was as I lay there. How much longer could the night last? It seemed like the longest night of my life.

I whispered to see if Cain was awake. "Cain? You awake, sweetie?"

"No, but I am, baby," a voice said low in my ear and it wasn't Billings, he was on Cain's other side.

Before I had a chance to move or think he snatched me up from Cain's grasp and dragged me by my arm up the incline of the ditch to the road.

I heard Cain yelling for me, cursing about not finding the flashlight. The fire of the vehicles had finally burned out and it was all pitch black. All I could see was nothing. All I could hear was Cain's yelling. All I could feel was the stranger's cool breath on my face as he pulled me closer.

I saw the light in my peripheral, Cain must have found the flashlight and I heard Billings calling to him as they made their way up to the road to meet us. The man held me in front of him like a shield. To my astonishment, he started to glow, illuminating. Between him and Cain's flashlight, I could make out my surroundings.

Cain ran up and stopped short at the sight of us. The man was behind me. I couldn't see what Cain saw, but I had no doubt it was a Lighter by the sheer fear in his eyes. Billings stopped next to Cain but straightened up and tried in vain to wipe at his uniform.

"Enforcer?" the Lighter asked. "What are you doing holed up here with rebels?"

"Sir, I was arresting this man when we were attacked. By these...things, sir. We escaped and I have been anxiously awaiting backup."

Explanation To Come Later
Chapter 32 - Merrick

It was morning, I thought. I remembered clearly Lillian coming into our room last night. She never came to get me so Cain must've come home. Little jerk, worrying Lillian.

I knew he was just hanging out with someone. This was his last chance to after all, but Lillian was seriously scared. Hmm. I should go check on her just to make sure he made it in safely.

After, of course...

"Morning, beautiful," I whispered in her ear.

I could tell the second she woke up. I know everything about her, even the way her breathing changed even though she hadn't moved a muscle. The way her fingers went from lax to tense without moving.

"Good morning. I think... It's still early isn't it? What are you doing up?" she asked through a yawn and snuggled back up against me like she already had the answer and the answer was that it was too early.

"I've got to go take care of something real quick. Just rest."

"What's the matter?"

"Nothing, honey. Just go back to sleep."

I knew she'd know I wasn't completely telling the truth so I kissed her, which always seemed to take her mind off everything. It worked.

"Hurry back," she said against my lips making me *really* want to stay.

"Anything for you," I joked as I got up and she giggled sleepily, rolling over to my side of the pallet, folding herself further into the covers and throwing one leg out.

I pulled on some jeans and realized Sherry was wearing my shirt again. Hmm, one more reason to stay. Luckily, I still had a couple in the corner pile of clean ones. I snagged one without looking at it and headed out the door quietly.

The halls were empty so it must still be early. Commons room clock said 5:45 a.m. Yeah, too early. I walked barefoot through the commons room to Cain's room. His bedroll was empty but messed up, however, that told me nothing because I didn't see Cain as a guy who was into making the bed.

I went down to Lillian's room, at least I thought it was. It was Miguel's and he was sprawled out in a broad manner, arms and legs spread wide, filling almost every corner and inch of the small room and his mouth was open.

I went one door down and saw another empty bed and knew right then, I was about to be upset.

I peeked in a few other rooms to be sure and found exactly what I expected. I went to the stairs and saw keys missing. The Jeep.

I shut my eyes for a second and tried to calm myself. I pinched the bridge of my nose and took a deep breath. I knew that if I had been out there by myself and was late, Sherry would have done the same thing. I knew this, but I also knew how furious I would have been with her and how furious I was with Lillian.

These dang women, always trying to get themselves killed for someone. If they weren't playing martyr, they were playing hero. Ah!

I ran to Jeff's room and tapped on the door and waited, knowing it was locked. I heard nothing so I called him in my mind.

Jeff... JEFF!

What?

Lillian and Cain are missing. Get your butt up and let's get going.

What?

You heard me. Explanation later.

Jeez... I'm coming.

Now the hard part. Simon.

I knew he was gonna freak royally because he was Cain's Keeper and would be equally hurt that Lillian came to me instead of him for her Cain problem, but as far as I knew, Lillian had never even spoken to Simon and she knew me.

Simon.

Yeah?

330

I cracked open his door and looked at him. He was awake and watching with a steely look of anticipation and readiness.

"Cain's missing. So is Lillian. Come on, let's go."

"Again?" He sighed, remembering the last time I told him his charge was missing, when he and Sherry were in the cave. "That boy... I'm coming, I'm coming."

He got up hurriedly and I turned so as not to see him in his boxers, but it was a little too late.

Simon's body was one of the oldest that the Keepers were in. Mostly, we tried for the younger ones if we could get them so we didn't have to worry about health issues and elderly limitations, but he didn't really have a choice on this one. None of us did, as evidence as to why I was in Sherry's ex-boyfriends body.

We blurred down the hall and found Jeff waiting by the stairs looking at the same key hook I'd seen.

"They took the Jeep?" Jeff asked so I showed them both in their minds what Lillian had said to me and my assumption of what happened.

"Oh. Well, ok. Let's go," Jeff said and Simon just sighed again.

"Hold it. I've got to tell Sherry where I'm going."

"Alright. I guess I should tell Marissa. You probably saved me a chewing out just now."

"Marissa? Chew you out?"

"Hey, that woman is passionate about everything. Even violence. She could probably take me if I was caught off guard."

"That I'd like to see."

"Brothers, please," Simon said exasperatingly. "We must go."

"You're right. Sorry," I said and blurred to Sherry's room.

I bent down and pushed the hair from her face.

"Sherry. Honey, wake up, listen."

"Hmm?"

"I'm leaving. Cain was late getting home last night and Lillian left to go look for him."

"What?" she said almost head bumping me when she sat up.

"No freaking out." I grabbed her chin with my fingers. "We're going to go look for them. We'll find them, don't worry."

"I suppose you won't let me come," she phrased it as a statement because she knew my answer.

"Absolutely not."

She bit her lip and sighed. "Ok," she conceded surprisingly easy. "Hurry, go, and make sure you come back." She grabbed my arm tight. "Please be careful."

"Always."

I kissed her quickly and touched her cheek for just a second, feeling her skin. It always seemed like the thing I wanted to remember most when I was in danger; the exact way her skin felt, so I found myself doing it every time I left her.

Love ya, honey.

"I love you, too," she answered softly.

I blurred to the stairs just as Jeff got there and we set off up the stairs and toward the carport/shed. The van was the Crandle fanatics van that they abandoned at the bridge when Calvin showed up with his fire fingers. It would be dangerous to take it, because if someone recognized us in it, but Cain had his truck and Lillian had the Jeep. Phillip stole Sherry's Rabbit, Bobby's van was in the river and Phillip's El Camino only held two people so...we were running out of options.

The Gremlin it was.

Miguel and his crew came in that car, all five of them crammed and packed in together. We hopped in, I drove and Jeff rode shotgun while frail Simon lounged sullenly in the backseat.

"We'll find them Simon," I said.

"I know. I just wish Cain would say something to me about this stuff. I didn't even know for sure anything was going on with Lillian and him, just speculation. And she went to you instead of me but she knew I was Cain's Keeper." He shook his head. "I'm old. He doesn't relate to me and doesn't need or want my help. He doesn't tell me anything anymore."

"Simon, come on. She just knows me is all because of Sherry, and I know it's strange, but things are different. We're all trying to pull back from our charges some. They don't need us as much, not individually. We need to treat them all like our charges."

"I know, I know all that, but it doesn't make the buzzing go away now does it," he snapped.

"I'm sorry, Simon. We're all dealing, I know. It doesn't feel right. It feels completely wrong to not watch our Specials like a hawk all day and night but we have to pull through that, find a distraction."

"Not all of us were lucky enough to jump into young handsome bodies. I'm sorry if I can't have your enthusiasm," he said almost bitterly.

I broke my own rule as I drove along the highway. I pushed into his mind. I knew he could tell right off because he would feel the fuzziness but he didn't say a word.

He was genuinely worried about Cain, that didn't surprise me, but he felt resentful, that surprised me. Resentful of me, Jeff, Kay, even Ryan, us more than any other Keepers.

We were all close, all had something he didn't, all had something to offer Cain that he didn't and were attached to humans here and he wasn't and didn't want to be. He just wanted to go home and he hated the fact that he knew we wanted to stay. That we had *reasons* to stay.

I looked at him in the mirror and didn't see anger. I saw shame. He let me peek at his thoughts, knowing what I'd see but wanted me to know how he felt. I gave him a knowing nod and glanced at Jeff. He'd seen too. He looked guilty and a little sick. I spoke forcefully in Jeff's mind.

Hey, you didn't do anything wrong. We're all different just like humans are. We get to choose how we cope, how we handle things, how we live. He's not judging you. He'll be fine. He's just worried and homesick.

He nodded. Then I spoke to Simon.

We can talk anytime you want but I've spoken to Danny about this. About how hard it is for me to tamp down on my freak outs about him. He understood and tries to work with me on it. Cain would too if you'd talk to him. As for the rest, I'm sorry. I'm not trying to flaunt anything to you. I think you should try to enjoy what you can, while you can. We may not be going home at all, brother. You know this. Content, remember? Be content.

I didn't bother to tell him I had no intentions of going home at all now and doubted Jeff's as well. His nod to me looked sincere. I focused back solely on the road and thought about all the ways I wanted to kick Cain's rear for putting Lillian and me through this crap.

And Lillian, sweet Lillian, wasn't much higher up on my crap list.

Who Your Friends Are
Chapter 33 - Lillian

Cain looked at Billings sharply.

"Is that right, Billings? You've been playing me?"

Billings didn't even look at him. He marched closer to the Lighter and me, looking right passed me to him.

"The girl, too. She came later looking for him. She said there were others coming to help them. This could be that big cell we've been looking for out here, sir."

"Billings! What- Why?" I asked, wanting to cry or hit him but was too exhausted even try.

"I'm doing my job. I was always doing my job. I can act with the best of them to do what needs to be done. What? You thought you'd befriended an enforcer?" He chuckled to himself. "Now, why would I do that? I am not a rebel, I'm a patriot. Sir, what should we do with the traitors?"

"We'll handle them here."

Billings jolted still.

"But sir, per the amendment to the patriot act, we are to escort all rebels and anyone related to their activities into the nearest enforcement facility or law office for further processing."

"And then what do they do with them, enforcer?" the Lighter asked menacingly.

"Well, after questioning, they are terminated, sir."

"Ok. So we are only skipping a step. I assure you, you will be commended for your actions today, enforcer, not punished. You take him and I'll take this...pretty little creature to our new leader I think. He's been on the lookout for fresh young things, although she is a bit dingy. Or maybe not. Maybe I'll have a little fun with her first." He moved my hair aside and brushed his cold fingers down my neck and I shuddered.

"You keep your hands off her or I swear to all I believe in I will kill you slowly," Cain growled and took a step towards us.

I looked at him, trying to look brave. Shaking my head, begging him not to do anything stupid. He looked the most scary I'd ever seen him, every inch the Marine I'd heard about. I believed every word he bit out too. He would kill or get himself killed trying to save me. I couldn't live with that. I did the only thing I could think of.

"Yes," I said. "Take me to him."

"What?" I heard more than one, but wasn't sure who said it.

"I said take-"

"I heard you, human. What it this trickery?"

"No tricks. I'll trade myself for Cain and I'll go willingly if you'll let him go, right now."

"I don't need you to trade. I can force you just as easily," the Lighter said and I could feel his cold sweet breath on my neck.

"Yes, but I'll do whatever you want and I won't tell anyone. You can have your way with me and then send me to the Taker and I'll keep quiet. I promise, just let him go."

"Taker?" Billings asked. "What's that?"

No one answered him. I knew I'd piqued the Lighter's interest. I wondered if Lighters were interested in sex. I guess I had my answer. I knew the Taker wouldn't stand for him messing with his girls before he got to them, at least I'd hoped not. And now it seemed I had my answer to that too, because this Lighter was considering my offer. And I wanted to vomit.

"Lillian, what are you doing?" Cain ground out in a growl, not sounding too happy with my proposition.

"Saving you, but this time, I actually get to."

"Don't," he pleaded, looking into my eyes.

"I have to. You can help the others, I can't. I'm useless."

"Shut up! No more chatter!" the Lighter yelled and turned me to look at him.

I looked into his eyes wondering what he was going to do. The Keepers had said that the Lighters compulsion didn't work on us anymore. Only the Takers direct compulsion worked anymore on those of us who knew what they were. He searched my face, his eyes moving frantically and thoroughly.

"No tricks?" he asked.

I wanted to have a bluff up my sleeve, a plan of some sort but I was winging it and seemed to have placed myself somewhere I couldn't back down from. I shook my head reluctantly. He got the strangest look on his face. Almost like affection, and then he leaned forward and smelled my hair. I could hear Cain grunt and growl angrily behind me.

335

"I remember," the Lighter said softly. "I remember that smell- this body remembers. Jasmine? That right?" He looked at me expectantly and I nodded again. "Mmm, this body has missed smelling a woman," he said thoughtfully, like it surprised him.

I was speechless. I'd never heard a Lighter talk more than a sentence let alone have a conversation with one. Let alone talking about the smells of a woman. Freaky.

I couldn't help but notice as he stared down into my eyes how young he was. His body was no more than twenty five. He had black hair, of course, and cut close. He had a little scar right above his left eye, on his forehead. Under different circumstances, I would have thought him really handsome.

"You remember what the last person in that body remembered?" I asked not being able to stop myself.

To my utter shock, he answered me calmly.

"Yes. Well, the body does. It reacts to your shampoo. Someone used to wear that scent and the body remembers smelling that smell, and liking it. And your eyes, I've seen that color somewhere before. Also," he touched my hair gently and I gasped slightly as his fingers smoothed away the strays at my temple, "your hair. The body loves your hair."

What the-

He wasn't even talking like, sexually, anymore. He was just talking calmly, like it was meaningful and surprising. I had no idea what to do. Cain must have been just as freaked because he stayed silent. The Lighter looked into my eyes and though they were still black and dark, I swear I could see emotion. Not just emotion, but regret.

I bit my lip. I did not want to feel sorry for a Lighter. He spoke again, holding my gaze.

"I don't know what's happening to me. I feel like...like I couldn't hurt you, even if I wanted to. I feel like I don't want to. I don't understand."

He looked so stricken I knew he wasn't faking. I remembered Merrick and Jeff talking about this. About how the Taker makes them weak because he's human and it compiles on top of the human emotions they are already fighting because of the human bodies they are in. I remembered Piper going off the deep end because of her human emotions. What if...

What if they could be saved? Changed?

"What's your name? Do you have one?"

"Lillian," Cain hissed at me, I ignored him.

"I am called Daniel. You are Lillian?" he asked softly and seemed surprised by my question as much as Cain was.

He still had his cold hands on my upper arms, holding me in place but his grip was loose.

"Yes. What are you going to do with us, Daniel?"

"I-"

He was interrupted by a loud noise behind him. I realized I hadn't heard any Markers since we'd been up there. I wondered if the Lighters could control them but I didn't ponder that long. Daniel turned with me still with him and paled, more than a Lighter could already with their pale skin.

He didn't turn me around, but I glanced over my shoulder to see what he saw; another Lighter, standing on one of the burnt car hoods and watching Daniel and the rest of us with dark, careful eyes.

"Need any help?" he asked happily.

"No, the enforcer and I have everything under control," Daniel answered briskly.

Billings stepped up beside us.

"Yes, sir. We've got it," he said though after everything that just happened he didn't seem so sure.

"What? Hogging all the fun for yourselves? That's not nice. We haven't had any bust in a few days now. Come on, let me take the girl. You two can take the man."

I heard crunching and squeaking. He was climbing down the car hood and then a thud as he jumped into the dirt behind me.

Daniel pulled me behind him, leaving his arm around me to make me stay and I gasped at the notion. He was trying to protect me? I looked back at Cain.

He was grimacing and shook his head at me, looking way too strung and wired, meaning he had no idea what was going on either.

"What's going on here?" the new Lighter asked with an accusing tone. "What are you doing out here with these rebels?"

"Sir, we told you-" Billings started.

"Silence. I'm talking to you." He pointed at Daniel. "Are you...are you attempting to keep her from me?" He laughed as he spoke the words.

"Just go."

"How can you do this? What's happened to you?"

"Just leave us, we'll handle this," Daniel commanded calmly.

"Not. A. Chance."

I peeked over Daniel's shoulder again to see the new Lighter smiling and looking very much like he had found the fun he was looking for. What was Daniel going to do? What was Billings going do, turn Daniel in for growing a minutes worth of conscience?

"All right then. I'll give you your fight," Daniel said and turned quickly pushing me towards Billings. "Run!"

Billings caught me as I stumbled just as I heard the smack of skin on skin and turned to see Daniel locked in a blur of a fight with the other Lighter. I looked up at Billings and he looked shocked, watching the scene with me, then he shrugged.

"Take your miracles where you find 'em, kid."

He towed me over to Cain, who met us halfway and snatched me from Billings like he was a viper. And, in a way, he was. I'd almost forgotten Billings had betrayed us. Cain pulled me behind him and started to back away, to where I didn't know.

"Hey now. I'm still on your side," Billings said with hands raised in surrender.

"Oh, yeah? It didn't look that way to me."

"What was I supposed to do? I was trying to think, buy us some time. I had on my uniform. It's not like he wouldn't wonder what I was doing with you."

"I don't buy it."

"Neither do I," the new Lighter said as he picked up Billings from behind and threw him like a sack of dirty laundry towards the ditch.

Billings rolled down into it and we couldn't see him anymore. I glanced around and didn't see Daniel anywhere. He caught us, then tried to save me, then deserted us? I was so confused.

"Now, give me the girl and I'll let you die quickly."

"Yeah? That's what you *all* say," Cain answered.

I could hear Billings grunting as he tried to climb back out of the ditch. I grabbed Cain's hand and squeezed. If nothing else, it's the last thing I wanted to touch before I died. He squeezed back.

"Oooh. Smart-alec. You are going to be fun," the Lighter said and laughed, then lunged for us just as something blurred right in front of us, making the Lighter falter his steps.

"Hey!" Billings yelled as he chucked another piece of wood from the ditch at the Lighter, hitting him in the arm. "I'm an enforcer gone rogue, a rebel now. Wouldn't you love to take me downtown for questioning?"

"Fool. You have made a mistake like nothing you-"

He was cut off by another blur. Daniel punched him in the chest and when the Lighter landed in the dirt, skidding and sliding from the force, Daniel jumped high into the air, coming down in a cloud of dust as he knelt in a fluid motion and drove a blackened crowbar right through the chest of the other Lighter.

I felt the cold rush of wind and saw the bolt of lightning shoot into the sky from his chest. I screamed, having never been close enough to see one die before. Cain turned and hugged me to his chest, burying my face in the crook of his neck so I couldn't see as the Lighter turned to nothing. Which I knew he would. No traces of anything would be left.

It was quiet for a few seconds, then I lifted my head to find Cain and Daniel with locked gazes, staring across the five feet of dirt between them.

I started to move toward him and Cain tightened his grip. Before he could speak I spoke. "He saved us, Cain. He saved me. Let go," I whispered.

He did, but looked none too pleased with the idea.

"Daniel, are you alright?" I asked as I inched forward

"I am fine. I feel..." He shook his head and let the crowbar fall to the dirt. "I shouldn't feel anything at all. I feel badly for killing my brother, but I couldn't let him hurt you." He looked around the cars and rubble then back to me. "You need to leave, others will come. I can't fight them all," he said in a rush.

I walked right up to stand in front of him.

"Why? Why didn't you want him to hurt me?"

He looked puzzled and conflicted. He thought for a second then took a breath.

"You made me feel. You make me want to be something different than what I am. I don't know if that's possible but I couldn't let him take that from me. And...I felt it would hurt me to watch you in pain."

"Come with us." I just blurted it out and heard Cain's aggravated noises behind me.

"Lillian, I don't think that's such a good idea," Cain said slowly.

"Cain he saved our lives! He says he wants to be different."

"Your Cain is right," Daniel said never taking his eyes off me. "I cannot come with you. First, this feeling may leave when you aren't here to produce the feelings for me."

"I don't believe that-"

"Second, your people will not accept me, no matter what I may want to be, I am what I am, that I cannot change."

He looked so sad I grabbed his hand in between us where Cain couldn't see. Daniel looked down at our hands and moved his thumb back and forth over my skin in an exploration more than a caress. He was frowning like he was trying to figure something out.

"I'll help you. I'll talk to them. We'll figure it out. What are you gonna do? Just go back to the Lighters and pretend none of this happened?"

"I do not know what I am to do. I suppose, no, I cannot go back after what I've done."

"Come with us. Trust me."

"I can't. That would put you in danger, upset the balance of your people." He moved an inch closer and spoke softly. "I am what I am, Lillian."

"Lillian," Cain called and when I looked back he nodded towards the sunrise. The sun had almost risen without me realizing it. "We have to go. Come on, baby. I know you want to help, but you can't make him come. He's right though. Can you imagine Merrick and Jeff if we brought a Lighter back with us?"

I could and it wasn't pretty. I turned back to Daniel. "You saved us. The Lighters will kill you." I bit my lip and just said it. "It feels wrong just leaving you like this."

He looked surprised and then leaned forward just a bit.

"It feels wrong just watching you go," he whispered softly and then quickly looked to the sky and his jaw clenched. "Go. They are coming. I'll hold him off. Go!"

"Lillian, let's go," Cain said pulling on my arm. He turned quickly back to Daniel. "Thanks. I don't know why you're doing this but thank you."

"It is I who should thank you." He looked back to me, directly into my eyes. "You taught me to feel. Now go. Be safe."

I couldn't think of a thing to say so I reluctantly ran with Cain's hand in mine, Billings scrambling to keep up with us. He had redeemed himself and showed us he was telling the truth. It was just implied he was going with us since he tossed wood at a Lighter that could have literally killed him in two seconds and would have had Daniel not come back.

Just as Cain scooped the keys up from the pavement, we heard a metallic loud crashing behind us. We turned to see another fight, blurring blacks, dark and then pale. Crashing into the blackened cars and rolling around on the dirt. Daniel was fighting another Lighter so we could get away.

Cain jerked me forward and we jumped in the Jeep. As he squealed the tires on the pavement doing a 180 towards home, I turned to look out the window. Daniel was standing there, still motionless, and alone so he must've killed another brother for us. I felt sick leaving him there but I understood what they both were saying. It didn't make it any easier though.

As I watched him get smaller and smaller out of the plastic back window, he lifted his hand in goodbye to me. I lifted mine in return.

Don't Call Me Hot
Chapter 34 - Cain

"I...cannot believe that just happened," I said in a rush of relief and astonishment.

"I know. Man, you can't get luckier than that," Billings agreed.

"You're telling me."

"I feel terrible," Lillian said quietly behind me from the back seat. "I can't believe...I mean, I know we couldn't bring him with us, but it's still not right. He saved our lives."

"Lillian," I said softly, trying not to seem like I'm reprimanding her. Though, I kinda wanted to. "He saved us, yes, but I don't know why. Maybe he was tricking us. Maybe he's following us right now." Hmmm. "I didn't think of that."

"He's not," she stated firmly. "I know he's not."

"How can we know for sure? Lighters aren't exactly known for their forthcoming truthful nature. He could have been lying that whole time. It could have been an act."

"It wasn't. He killed two Lighters."

"Maybe that was part of his plan, the Takers plan. Two to sacrifice to get the bigger cell of rebels found."

"No."

"Why? Because he was sweet on you? That doesn't mean anything, L. You are pretty cute, you know. Even evil can see that."

"Yeah." Billings turned in the front seat to look at her. Really look at her and I wanted to stop the Jeep and dump his ogling butt in the street. "Now that I can see you, even though you're all caked in mud, I'd have to agree. Pretty hot actually."

"Dude," I said feeling peeved, zero to sixty, and pushed him back into his seat.

"What?" He held his hands out like he was innocent. "It's true. You said it."

"She's mine. *I* can say it."

I thought for sure she was gonna call me on the 'she's mine' remark but she didn't.

"He wasn't sweet on me. He was scared," Lillian said loudly to cover up our banter and poked her head in between the front seats. "Don't worry about him. He's not coming after us. And you." She looked at Billings. "Don't call me hot." She wrapped her arms around my seat headrest, around my neck and put her mouth on my ear. "And I love it when you call me L."

She kissed the back of my neck and stayed there, closing her eyes and sighing long and relief filled. I could see her face in the rearview mirror. She was muddy, as all of us were. It reminded me of when I first saw her; all dingy and dirty from weeks of running and hiding. It made me think that I never wanted to see her like that again, that she deserved more than this. That I couldn't wait for us to be able to live somewhat normally and not always looking behind us and hiding out like fugitives.

I put my hand on her arm and we rode silently for a while. Billings closed his eyes too and slouched in his seat. Then...crap.

Another car was coming our way. I barely ever saw traffic out here and with our luck of last night it couldn't be good, but as I passed them I saw it was the pea soup green Gremlin and Merrick was driving.

I started to slow, but he did a quick 180 turn and got on my tail, following us home so I kept going.

As soon as we pulled into the parking lot, I swung back into the spot in the shed and he pulled in beside us. Billings was still asleep. I hopped out and helped Lillian out too. She kept hold of my hand after I shut the door and she stayed close like she was scared or worried. I wondered why.

Merrick came around the back of the Jeep to meet us, looking every bit the Keeper he was.

"Well, Cain, there are easier ways to piss me off you know, if that's what you're going for. Ways that don't include risking your life," he said easily and braced himself on the Jeep with a shoulder, crossing his arms while Simon and Jeff came to stand behind him, also crossing their arms and I suddenly felt this looked more like an interrogation than a rescue.

"Good to see you, too, man."

"What *the mess*, Cain."

"I'm so glad you're picking up the language, dude. It becomes you."

He chuckled reluctantly and rolled his eyes as he bumped my fist I held out for him. "I'm glad you're all right, Cain. We were worried," Simon said and I twinged with guilt at the look on his face. Like a disappointed, high strung father.

"No worries, Simon. Sorry, we have a lot to tell you."

"What in the worlds were you thinking, man? What happened? And you." Merrick looked at Lillian, but her head was still down. "You scared me, you know. Why did you come get me if you didn't plan to wait on me? You don't trust me?"

"I already raked her over the coals, man," I said and was a little surprised at the way he spoke to her, though I had already done much worse.

"I'm sure that you did, but that's not what I'm trying to do. I understand, I do. Sherry would have done the same thing and I would have yelled at her for it, too, but I told you I'd help you."

"I didn't want to put anyone else in danger," she said softly.

"She has this theory-" I started, but she interrupted me with a strange soft voice.

"Don't make fun of me, Cain."

I stopped. Because that was exactly what I was about to do. Not intentionally, but outing her fears to this group of guys, standing around... She really believed it, no matter how silly it was.

"I'm not," I said softly and waited for her to look at me. When she did, I gave her a crooked smile that I knew she couldn't resist. She smiled, too. I looked back to Merrick. "We'll tell you all about it. There's a whole lot to tell, but first, I need to get this girl inside, clean up and get some breakfast. Ok?"

"Yeah. Definitely, sorry. You both look terrible. I'm sure it'll be an interesting story."

"You don't know the half of it. L here is about to blow your mind, Keeper." He looked between us wearily. "Oh and by the way? Why don't you wake up that enforcement officer in the front seat and bring him in, too. He's good people."

And I walked off, holding Lillian's hand, wanting to laugh as I could actually hear their jaws drop behind us.

We were met by Sherry, of course, at the stairs. She was fretting - Sherry style - pacing an oval in the floor at the bottom of the stairs, rubbing her necklace charm in between her fingers and biting her lip.

She seemed disappointed for just a sliver of a second at the sight of us, but then it vanished to happiness and I knew why. We weren't Merrick, but for the first time in months, that didn't upset me as much. I wanted to point to the sky and thank the big guy right there. Jump up and down. Something.

It seemed the Sherry train was leaving the station.

Instead I just took the gleeful hug she offered and looked at Lillian over Sherry's head. Her face was slightly amused but also careful. It pained me to know that she still thought I was hung up on Sherry. I was going to have to try harder to prove her wrong on that one.

She hugged Lillian next.

"Where's Merrick? He found you guys right?" Sherry asked in a panic.

"Sort of. He's outside. He'll be down in just a minute."

She started asking for details and whys? I immediately took over because I knew sweet Lillian would just sit there and answer question after question no matter how hungry, tired and muddy she was. "Later, Sherry, ok? It's been a rough night."

"Oh! Of course. I left you guys some breakfast on the stove. You want to eat first or shower?"

Lillian and I looked at each other and said at the same time, "Shower."

"Ok, you do that. I'll start some fresh coffee," Sherry said and fluttered off to the kitchen.

I took the shower down the hall and Lillian went to the one by the laundry room. I tried not to think about it, actually.

Once I was clean and changed my clothes, I made my way down the hall and heard yelling. I knew instantly what it was about. I wanted to smack myself for my stupidity but instead, I took off running.

"Miguel! Stop!" I yelled as I rounded the corner and saw what I had predicted.

"This is an enforcer, mate, in case you didn't notice. You just brought an enforcer into our house!"

Miguel had Billings by the shirt collar and there was a crowd around him who seemed to be egging him on. Merrick and Jeff looked to be trying to diffuse but didn't really have any explanations because I hadn't given them any yet.

"I know. Listen. I have a very good reason for doing that, but right now, you have a pretty important ally by the shirt collar and he doesn't look like he enjoys being manhandled."

In fact, Billings looked redder than I'd ever seen a man get.

Miguel let him go slowly and eyed him the whole time. Then Billings jerked away from him and moved around to my side a bit.

"Sorry, man. I didn't think to say anything to anyone," I said, knowing how lame it sounded.

"Whatever. Just fix it because I'm stuck here with you. It's not like I can just go back out there after what I did," Billings said loudly, but seemed to be getting back under control.

"And, just what is it that you did?" Jeff asked as Marissa came up to stand beside him, rubbing his arm to calm him, always Jeff's regulator.

"I hit a Lighter to save your friend here."

Silence. Wide eyes. Everything I expected.

"Like I said," I interjected before anyone else could start, "everyone just sit down and I'll tell you the whole story. You are not going to believe what happened."

I sat down and started telling my part, about how Billings pulled me over and was searching the truck and about to arrest me, and then the Markers came.

Lillian brought a plate of biscuits and gravy and coffee to me and Billings, who was standing affronted on the back wall. She was holding everything on her arms in true waitress fashion and I could see her doing that before all this. I smiled gratefully at her and took it as she went and grabbed one for herself and returned to sit next to me on the couch.

Just about everyone had come out to listen to what had happened to us. It was a packed room as everyone stood or sat tightly wound together. Nobody asked questions, everybody just listened intently.

Once Lillian and I finished our food, I pulled her into my lap and patted her spot on the couch for Margo to sit. I was pretending to be courteous to an old lady when really, I just wanted Lillian to sit on my lap. She came willingly, tucking her hair behind her ear and watching me talk with...admiration?

We got to the part where Lillian got there in the Jeep and I heard Merrick grunt. When I looked he had an eyebrow raised, but he was smiling a little smile. One that said 'Jeez these women'. He looked down at Sherry, who'd come in and wound herself up in his arms, and then back up at me, still smiling.

By that point, nobody was convinced about Billings any more than they were at the beginning. Miguel was glaring at him. We'd talked about this before. People looked at the enforcers as the worst type of traitor because they were humans, who weren't marked, and were working directly for the Lighters to weed us out of their own free will. Other humans. Even after the story, they might take some time to warm up to Billings.

Lillian had been quiet the whole time. I didn't know if she wanted to talk about the Lighter or not but she didn't seem to want to.

"So, the Lighter had Lillian and just stopped. He was looking at her, right down in her face. Then he told her he remembered the way she smelled, her perfume. Then he said he didn't know what was happening to him and then he said...that he didn't want to hurt her."

"Excuse me?" Jeff spouted incredulously and came a few steps closer.

"Jeff, I know, ok. I know, just listen. I wouldn't have believed it if I hadn't heard it with my own ears but he said it."

"It was a trick," Merrick said shaking his head anxiously.

"I thought that too, but then he..." I looked at Lillian. She shrugged. She understood like me how hard it was gonna be to explain it all. "He protected Lillian. He pulled her behind him and killed another Lighter that came up while all this was going on. He killed two Lighters in fact. He told us to run and to be safe. He thanked us, well, he thanked L for...helping him to feel.

"Impossible," Max heaved the words out.

"Whoa, this is heavy," Miguel said, the enforcer behind us all but forgotten.

"Not possible," Jeff said. "That's not possible."

"Oh, it's possible. It happened. He told her his name was Daniel," I explained.

"They have names?" Margo asked, but everyone ignored the question.

"He was sad," Lillian finally spoke up. "He said he was sad that we had to go but he wanted us to be safe. He said he felt bad for having to kill his brother. You didn't see his eyes. They were so...human."

"It had to be a trick. They could've followed us here," Simon spoke up from the kitchen doorway.

I looked at Lillian because I'd said that same thing. She just looked tired and so ready to be done with this.

"I thought that, too, but you guys weren't there." Lillian looked up sharply at me, thinking I was going to agree with them as I had before. What better way to show a girl you lov- whoa. Like. A girl you *like* that you trust her. "He was serious. I don't think he could've faked that and he did kill them, I saw it. It was like a flipped switch. He just...changed."

I went on to talk about how Billings had helped and all, trying to sway the subject. Didn't work. People were freaked, upset, joyous, but mostly freaked. They all started talking at once. So Merrick shouted over the shouting.

"Ok! Ok. The important thing is that we have a new addition. A very useful new addition."

"Thanks for that," Billings muttered sarcastically.

"I'm sorry, I'm not trying to downplay what you did and I'm not implying you're going to be some spy for us. I just wanted to introduce you and welcome you. So... Why don't we all tell, uh, Billings our names and uses around here. My name is Merrick, this is my wife Sherry. And I'm a... Keeper."

Billings sucked in a long, steady, loud breath and his eyes got as round as half dollars. Don't blow it Billings. Don't blow it with crazy Keepers-are-evil talk.

"What?" he asked softly. "Like, a real one? I thought that was some made up junk they told us to keep everybody in line. Like the boogieman in a kid's story."

"Not even close," I answered.

"So, you have a Keeper living with you. That must come in handy. So, what exactly are they good for?"

"Billings. Dude," I said trying to save him from himself.

"What? I can't ask what they do? I didn't even know Lighters could do anything until I saw it back there. I didn't even know you called them that. And Takers? And Markers? I had no idea about anything. Nothing. So I have no idea about Keepers either. I've been kept in the dark about everything I've done for months now. Who knows how many innocents I put away- I think I deserve a little truth," Billings spouted in a fury.

"Ok. Yes, you're right. Merrick is a Keeper, but they are not like the Lighters. They can blur really fast, talk in your mind and have a constant fever but that's about it. Nothing crazy. So, don't worry about them, ok. Everything you ever heard about them was a lie. Alright?"

"Ok."

"Don't freak out."

He snorted, but still looked scared and like he'd made a huge mistake coming here. "After you told me you have a Keeper here? Why would I freak out?"

"Because we're just getting started."

"What- What do you mean?" Billings said and pushed himself even further into the wall.

"Keepers? Cool? Can I just out this thing and get it over with?" I got about a hundred yeses in my head at the same time and thought I was gonna have an aneurism. It frigging hurt. "Jeez! Guys, come on," I said holding my head.

"Sorry," Jeff said and had the decency to look sorry as did others. "Go ahead. You're right, it's easier this way."

"Wait! Did you say Keepers? Like Keepers, plural?" Billings squeaked.

"Yeah, ok, like pulling off a band-aid. Billings I'd like you to meet Merrick, Jeff, Simon, Max, Ryan, Kay..." I pointed and went down the whole procession of every Keeper present and then ended with outing Marissa as a Muse, because she was a fancy one too.

We also introduced him to the Specials and demonstrated some gifts when he didn't believe us. If he was red a minute ago, he was ghost white now. He looked ill. Seriously like he wanted to run away and never look back.

"S-so, this is what they were keeping from us?" Billings said in a small voice.

"Dude, there's a lot to tell you, ok? We haven't always had these gifts. This is a recent thing and the Keepers aren't bad. Well, not all," I joked, but Billings looked up quickly. "Joke, man. Listen, we've been up all night. That's not helping things, let's get some rest. You'll have your own room. We built a lot down here so we have room for new people when they come along. Just rest and let things sink in. We'll answer all your questions later, but if I don't shut my eyes they are going to shut for me."

"Ok. All right, fine," Billings answered and looked around like he didn't know where to begin or what to do.

I set Lillian in my spot where Margo was tittering on about something and went to help Billings get settled. Sherry got there first.

"Hey," Sherry said coming to stand with him and she brought Lily with her.

"This is Lily. Lily, this is...uh... Do you want us to just call you Billings?"

"Uh," Billings' eyes were glued to Lily, and then he shook his head and spoke up, "yeah, Billings is what I've been called for months. I'm used to it now."

"Ok, Lily, this is Mr. Billings. He's going to be staying here with us."

"Hi," Lily said brightly.

"Hi," Billings said softly with a full on Lily trance.

I almost felt sorry for him. Sherry knew when to pull the Lily card. It worked every time.

"There's an empty room beside Mig- um, Calvin and Frank, if you want to put him in there, Cain. I'm Sherry by the way. Merrick is my husband."

He took her offered hand and looked at her a little wearily.

"Yes, I heard him say that. So you married a Keeper?"

"Yes."

"You look a little...young to be a wife and mother, if you don't mind me saying so."

Sherry did mind, I knew it. It drove her crazy when people said anything about her being young and being married to a Keeper. Her take on it all was that things were different. The world was different and the same rules and social standards no longer applied. We should all be here for each other, one big happy family. But she kept her sweet smile in place.

"Probably, but we found Lily. She was brought into the family just like you were, from outside. Lily, do you want to go see Merrick for a little bit?"

"Uhuh! Bye!"

"Bye," Billings called after her and then Sherry went on.

"They found her in the city and brought her back here after the Lighters turned her family into lunatics who abused her. We've had a lot of people join us since we started. Miguel, Josh, Racine. A lot of others. We've lost a lot of people too." She took a deep breath and wrapped a curl around a finger, twirling it round and round. I wondered if she even realized she was doing it. "I know you're not very trusting of us and I understand that, but I promise you, we are not what you have to worry about. If you need anything, let me know. We've got extra clothes and soap and things like that. You can get cleaned up and then take a nap for a while, and then I'll have lunch ready in a bit. Ok?"

"Ok." Billings seemed a little more relaxed now.

Sherry had that effect on people. I knew she was trying to calm him down, for one, so he wouldn't bolt while we weren't looking, but also, because he looked positively green with fright.

"Don't worry, once everyone gets to know you, you'll be fine here. The Keepers are pretty human, you couldn't even tell until we told you." She raised her eyebrow and smiled to challenge him. "I'm glad you're here and thank you for saving Cain and Lillian. I'm serious, you need anything, let me know."

"Ok, Sherry, thank you."

She smiled at him, then at me and walked back over to Merrick with Billings watching in odd fascination. At first I thought he was checking her out and then when I looked back, I saw Merrick picking up Sherry in a hug with her feet off the floor and kissing her. Kissing her good. I remembered that he had been out looking for me and Sherry had been fretting. They'd be pretty lovey dovey for the rest of the day then. I looked back to Billings.

"Wow," Billings muttered, "that Keeper gets more action than I do."

"Dude, we are gonna get along just fine," I said with a knowledge that it would be so as I slapped him on the back.

Billings was thirties. Blonde hair and except for a little pudge around the middle was in pretty good shape. He was probably in the military before this.

Cain, I'll take Billings so you can rest.

I nodded thanks to Simon and then pointed Billings towards him.

"He'll show you the extra clothes and stuff and give you the short tour. He's cool."

Billings walked off with a wave and I turned back to see Lillian conked out on the couch where I'd left her, no Margo. She was so exhausted. I scooped her up and took her down the hall. She snuggled against me, sighing softly. Like she felt totally safe, warm and comfortable.

I pushed her door open and laid her in the sleeping bag, taking off her shoes and pulling the covers over her. She grabbed my arm.

"Stay."

Ehhhhh, jeez. "I can't," I admitted and was surprised at how gruff my voice sounded.

"Yes, you can," she said sleepily. "I give you permission."

"Um, no, I can't. No matter how exhausted I am, I'm... not sure I can just sleep in here with you."

"Why?"

"Lillian," I groaned, "you're making me insane."

"I trust you."

"L, I want to do this right with you. I've got to come at this with a whole new approach. I know I sound like a walking cliché, but I can't help it. And I can't stay."

"Sure you can, because I'm not giving you permission to do anything but sleep." I laughed at her and she giggled cutely, her eyes still closed. "Please? I'm so cold," she said and did a fake shiver.

"You little liar," I said through a smile. She had a point. I had to keep my hands to myself if she wouldn't let me do anything else, right? "Ok, just sleep. No hanky panky, not even a little."

"None. I promise not to ravish you."

"Good. Cause it's you I'm worried about," I said sarcastically.

She smiled and pulled me down next to her. I figured she'd roll over but she snuggled right up against me and burrowed in like a little kitten, her eyes closed the whole time.

It was odd how much she trusted me. Completely and utterly.

I pulled my arm around her and felt her breaths get slower and slower until she was out again. I just laid there for a while, rubbing my hand up and down her soft arm, thinking about everything that had happened.

Billings, the Lighter, Lillian. Jeez, Lillian braved the dark and Lighters and whatever else that can come out to come save me, not even knowing where or what. It still shocked me to see how much I felt for her in just a few weeks. She was so...something. Like what Merrick said that day about Sherry. That he felt like she was made for him, like she was a creature right out of his dreams. Yeah. That was what it felt like.

"Thanks for coming to save me, lovely," I whispered.

I knew she was asleep and didn't hear me, but I still needed to say it. Then-

"Anytime, sweetie pie, but let's not make this a habit, ok?" she whispered amused and drowsy.

"You got it," I answered with a chuckle, kissed her forehead and closed my eyes smiling.

Thinking about how I'd almost thought the word 'love' today. I've never said that word to anyone. Not even my fiancé. She never said it, so neither did I. My parents weren't the type to say it so, I've never used it...except with Sherry but only in my head.

But now, looking back and comparing it to Lillian, I didn't know. Sherry was the first person to be utterly real with me. No games or lying or agendas and I think that' was why I fell so hard. And she was so sweet and caring and always thoughtful, mindful of what you needed and that was real too. I'd never been in love before so, I guess I needed to see what it was like.

It sucked, royally, because I couldn't have her but now... I have to say, I was happy about that. I was just getting myself ready for Lillian.

And now, I was.

I Just Became My Mother
Chapter 35 - Sherry

＇

"Come on," I told Lily. "I know this is all so exciting, but it's nap time."

"But-"

"Lily. Honey," I reprimanded her softly and then stiffened.

Holy cow! I just became my mother!

"Ok. I need to tell Mewwick goodnight."

"Ok. Come on."

I towed her to the other side of the commons room, her little, cold, soft hand latched to my fingers. Her long golden locks brushing my arm and I walked and she skipped.

"Goodnight, Fwankwin," Lily chimed as we passed him sitting next to Eli, his dad, on the floor playing checkers, and he waved to her.

"Lily bug," Merrick crooned and grabbed her up. "Nap time already?"

"Uhuh. I had to come say goodnight."

"Well, goodnight, sweetheart."

"Goodnight. Can I still call you daddy? You said I could."

He sucked in a breath. We'd had this conversation already, but she never said it to him or anything else about it since. "Of course you can. Anything you want."

She hugged him tight around his neck. "Goodnight, Daddy."

His smile over her shoulder was blinding. "Goodnight, baby."

Then she kissed him on the cheek and reached for me to take her. I did and we stood there for a second as I looked up at Merrick. I needed to make sure he wouldn't pass out or anything. He didn't. Just looked at her like she was the precious thing she was.

"Ok. Let's go, bug," I said.

"Wait. What can I call you Shawwy? Mother?"

I wanted to laugh at the formal title but held my breath. I never dreamed she'd say those words to me. I hoped but never thought. Was this real? Was I dreaming again? That would make more sense.

Honey, breathe.

I looked up to him and took a deep breath.

"Well..." I started, but had to clear my throat. "Probably mommy would be easier. But you don't have to call me that if you don't want to."

"I want to, I wike it."

"Ok. That's fine. Ready?"

"I gotta go potty fiwst."

"Well, let's go."

"Ok, Mommy."

Ahhh. She said it.

I didn't think I could make it any further, not one step. I knew I was only just barely twenty, ok. I knew, but you have to understand what was it was like to think you'd never have kids. To never hear certain words directed at you, never tuck someone who fits in your arms into bed. I'd done lots of those things I'd never dreamed and it didn't matter one bit that she didn't come from me and Merrick. She was mine and his, all the way.

I realized, I still hadn't moved, stuck in a trance or something. Cain always joked that people got stuck in the Lily trance. I guessed he was right.

Honey...Hold on, not yet. Do you want me to take her?

I looked up and saw that familiar sympathetic face, but this time with a twinge of amusement mixed in. Then I felt the tears on my cheeks that I hadn't even felt before. Oh! He was telling me to hold it together until I got her in bed. I must have looked like I was about to lose it, so I wiped my face and took a deep breath pulling her along with me to the back hall.

We skipped our way, she did her business and we skipped back down the hall to her little room. I helped her change into her night shirt and laid her in the pink frayed covers.

"Sing to me?" she asked and then yawned cutely, turning sideways on the pillow.

"What do you want to hear?"

"Um...that song that says 'angels'."

"Ok. You know I love you, bug, right?"

"Uhuh. I wuv you too Sh- Mommy."

I pressed my lips together to dam back the tears for just another minute. I wondered if I'd ever get use to the jolt in my heart when I heard that word. Mommy.

I sang happily, though it was hard to sing through a smile, but not impossible.

Sleepyhead, close your eyes, I am right here beside you.

I'll protect you from harm. You will always be in my arms.

Guardian angels are near, so sleep on with no fear.

Guardian angels are near, so sleep on with no fear.

If Lily only knew how true Brahms lullaby really was. Guardian angels were near, right in the other room in fact. She was the safest she could be in this world right now.

And...she was out. I knew it would take no time at all. I crept out of her door backwards and bumped into Merrick, there waiting for me. I didn't say anything. I just turned and let him pull me into the circle of his arms. I pressed my face into his warm chest as we stood there in the hall. He smoothed my hair, wrapping his fingers in it, massaging and twirling the curls.

You're a mommy.

I nodded against his chest and smiled. I felt his shirt damp under my face. I didn't care because they were tears of happiness.

"And you're a daddy." I pulled back to look at his face. "Did you ever imagine that?"

"No, I never thought to." He smiled. "Come lay down with me for a while, Mommy."

I laughed and followed him to the next door down to our room. I lay down in the sleeping bag and felt him climb in behind me. He wrapped his arms around me, his heavy forearm over my waist and kissed my neck from behind.

When he spoke, his breath tickled my neck and ear. "I'm a selfish bastard."

I stiffened. That was the absolute last thing I would have thought he would say at a time like that. "What are you talking about?"

He sighed and waited before he spoke. When he did it was careful and low like he was ashamed, like he was confessing. "I'm happy. I'm *so* happy that you've got Lily and I've got you. But none of this would have happened if the Lighters hadn't come. If they hadn't messed up everything on earth. I'm selfish because I'm...almost glad they did. I shouldn't be this happy about circumstances that have hurt so many people. Have killed innocents, killed Keepers, devastated the balance of things. It's just...wrong."

"I know how you feel. It's strange to feel like you got everything you ever wanted, but at the expense of so much. There are people out there suffering, but for me, I feel like it's Christmas. But it's not wrong to try to make something good out of something bad. That's what we should do. That's what we're doing. Lily needs parents, right?"

"Yes."

"So what's wrong with taking the role of it and being happy about it?"

"Nothing's wrong with that, but I just...I don't know. It's hard to explain, Sherry. I've spent my whole existence content and comfortable. I never knew what happy was. I saw it but never experienced it and didn't know what I was missing. Until you. I guess I just don't know how to be happy."

"Well, you better start learning, pal."

He chuckled and I could feel the vibrations all through me. "Mmhmm. I guess I better."

"That's more like it. Now, tell me what happened today. I heard what Cain said, but how did you know that something was wrong?"

"Lillian came and woke me up last night. Said Cain was late and wanted me to help her go after him. I told her I would if he didn't show up in an hour but she went ahead and left without me."

"Hmm. Well, people do crazy things sometimes. I'm sure she thought she had a good reason."

"Oh yeah? She was afraid I'd get hurt. That was her reason," he said incredulously.

"Really?"

"Yeah, you girls and your need to protect everyone. That's our job, you know, which some of you are working overtime to put us out of work. There are plenty of Keepers here to look after everyone. You don't have to fret so much."

It was kind of funny how worked up he was getting.

"Well, I'm just glad they're back and nothing bad happened- well, nothing too bad. They must be more serious than I thought or she wouldn't have freaked out like that. Right?"

"I guess. I found them- what do you call it- making out, in the second room, once. Lillian was incredibly embarrassed. It was pretty funny, actually."

"Yeah, she told me. I can't believe *you* didn't tell me!"

"It wasn't my news to tell."

"Well, I know you're an alien and all," he smacked me on the thigh and I yelped but kept going, "so I'll educate you a little about human girls. All girls like to hear about sweet romantic things, even if it's none of our business. So, in the future, just so you know, I want to know things about other people kissing. It's a girl thing."

"I see. So you're nosy, that's what you're telling me?"

"If that's the way you want to see it, then yes. As long as I get the scoop, you can call me whatever you want. I need some entertainment around here."

"I'm not entertainment enough for you?" he said huskily and kissed the side of my neck.

"You are pretty entertaining. Yes."

"Hmm. I'm not sure if you're complimenting me or not."

"Well, I'll leave that for your interpretation." I rolled over to face him as he laughed. "So, nothing exciting happened? You didn't have to fight any Lighters and you didn't meet this Daniel character?"

"Nope. I passed Cain on the highway and we just followed them home. The fun stuff had already happened."

"Fun stuff," I repeated and shook my head. "You think fighting Lighters is fun?"

"Well, fun's a strong word. Exciting?"

"Exciting," I repeated flatly.

"Well, I am a guy. It's get the blood pumping. Male Keepers and humans both love to beat on things. It's ingrained apparently."

I laughed and rolled my eyes. "Wow, you really *are* a guy," I said and he grinned against my cheek.

"And I'm hungry."

"One more reason. Hungry for food?"

He clucked his tongue at me. "Are you trying to seduce me?"

"Never! I am a lady," I said sweetly and twirled a curl around my finger."

"Oh, that I know for certain," he murmured against my throat making me giggle.

I heard a pound on the door. "Oh, come on, you two. It's the middle of the day for crying out loud!" Danny yelled and banged again. "Come on, Sherry. You said you would make spaghetti for lunch. Merrick can wait."

"Is that so? Can you wait?" I asked Merrick, lifting my eyebrows.

"If I have to, but I am pretty hungry," he said apologetically.

"Fine," I muttered and then yelled louder to Danny. "Fine! I'm coming!"

"You better be. It's not just me you're starving, you know."

"I said I'm coming, brat!"

I turned to Merrick before he could get up and kissed his neck, the scratchy shadowed part under his chin. He let out a strangled breath and bunched my curls easily in his fist as I went lower to the hollow of his neck and pulled his shirt collar down an inch. Then, I pulled back quickly.

"Well, I guess I better go get some lunch ready," I said chipper.

He grunted, frustrated. "That's not funny. You better be glad you're cute and a good cook."

"That's all you keep me around for! Shock value to your human taste buds."

"Mmhmm, among other things."

"What things?"

"These," he whispered and ran his thumb over my bottom lip. "These." He picked up my hand and kissed my fingers. "These, your little elf ears."

"Hey!" I protested.

"This," he ran a finger down the length of my nose and then tapped the end. "And this, this is my favorite." He made a little circle over my heart, on top of my t-shirt.

"Merrick," I sighed and bit my lip. "I'm never gonna leave with you talking like that."

"Well, now that I think about it, starving to death sounds easy in comparison. Starve with me, Sherry," he whispered humorously in my ear and bit my earlobe gently.

"You are gonna be in so much trouble with your Special."

"It'd be worth it." He started to pull me on top of him, but I held my hands out against his chest, like that could stop him. Willpower on his part is what stopped him, not my brute strength. "I think you are seriously overestimating my self control," he grunted.

"I better go make lunch, for real. Come on, Keeper."

He growled and blurred to his feet, then helped me up by pulling my hands. "If you're doing this to me to keep me interested, trust me, it's working," he said sullenly.

"Aww, I'm sorry, poor Merrick." I rubbed his chin with my knuckles. "I'll make it up to you later."

"You better," he commanded huskily and wrapped his arms around my waist, pressing his forehead to mine. He took a deep breath and let it out slow. "Do you know how happy I am?"

"Do you know how happy *I* am?" I countered.

"Oh, come on, already!" Danny said from the other side of the door and banged his fist again. "Yes, yes, we're all happy. Now let's get cracking with some lunch. Pleeeease."

"I'm gonna kill your Special," I told Merrick.

"Not before I do," he said and bent his head to kiss me.

Then he opened the door behind him and blurred to grab Danny in a head lock. Noogie involved. "Is that any way to talk to your sister?" Merrick said as he rubbed his knuckles over Danny's head.

"Dude! I'm starving. You can violate my sister another time when it doesn't mean that my stomach has to growl because of it."

"You have two hands," I chimed coolly as I walked passed them in the hall, both of them still wrestling.

I looked back and watched them for a second as they laughed and grunted, twisting each other's arms and trying to knock their feet out from under the other. Calvin and Frank caught wind of the excitement and made a break for the fray.

"Pile up!" Calvin yelled and jumped on top of Merrick's back, who was over Danny and they all fell in a heap. Then Franklin came running up behind Calvin.

"Oh, yeah! I'm the cherry on this loser sundae!" he screamed and then belly flopped on top of the pile.

Poor Danny on the bottom was groaning and wiggling, but it was no use. Eventually Merrick pried the two boys off and they were whole heartedly attacked by Merrick and Danny. Pay back.

I smiled and giggled at them. I saw Ryan about to fall off his chair laughing and Jeff and Marissa were clapping and egging the boys on to keep on retaliating. Then I turned to fix the all important lunch. Spaghetti and...Piper? Yikes.

"Hey, Sherry. What are you up to?" she asked me with a big fake smile.

"What do you want, Piper?"

I was in no mood to play nice with her. I hadn't spoken a word to her since the incident. When I took her and Cain drinks at the garden, I always talked to Cain and she didn't speak to me either, so I wondered what she was up to.

"A truce. I'm stuck down here with you it seems and as much as I hate you," she practically spat out the words, "and I do, we might as well try to have some semblance of peace. For Merrick's sake if nothing else," she crooned sweetly.

I rubbed my necklace charm, now even better with Merrick's gift lovingly attached, in between my fingers to steel myself.

"That was in no way an apology."

"Nope. It wasn't and you're not gonna get one from me, because I'm not sorry. It's wrong for you two to play house. I know it, you know it and Merrick knows it. He just can't let his pride go and say I was right."

"You are ridiculous. You know absolutely nothing about humans because you don't want to. That's fine. I'm all about a truce, ok. Great. The terms of the truce are this; you stay away from me and stay the farthest you can from Merrick. Other than that, I have no interest in talking to, seeing or even being in the same room as you," I spouted as I felt that old fire rise up just thinking about what she did to us.

I started chopping the onions, taking it out on them instead.

"Harsh, Sherry. You haven't got me fooled, you know. You are not sweet and innocent."

"I never said I was." I stopped chopping and looked up at her. "I'm willing to coexist with you, like you said, we're stuck together but I'm not going to do this with you every day. Get over it, stay away from us. I mean it."

"Oooh, she's got a knife," she said feigning fright and putting her hand on her heart, then straightened up and took a step forward. "You don't scare me, Sherry."

"Good, I don't want to. I don't need to. I got the guy, remember?"

"Whatever. We'll see how long it lasts. I live forever, how about you?"

"Not in that body you don't," I said it, kinda wanting to take it back - just a smidge - but figured she deserved it.

She fumed, her eyes bugging, fist clenching and shaking and then she stomped out in her ridiculous half-calf leather boots that she insisted on wearing around the bunker like she was going somewhere. Even Celeste wasn't that bad. Well, not anymore.

I finished the lunch, with the help of Kay and Katie, and rang the dinner bell. i.e., the oven dinged, and everyone started piling in to fill their plates with pasta and sauce, no meat, but the homemade garlic bread was tasty.

Merrick came to sit with me after he made a huge plate on the back wall.

"I was going to come rescue you, but I figured you two needed to just get it all out."

"You heard?" I said turning sharply to him.

"Yeah," he said and smiled guiltily.

I felt a flush coming. I disliked having to be anything but nice to people. It just wasn't natural to me and I hated that Merrick had witnessed me taking her bait and giving it back to her.

"Well, I'm sorry. I know I was harsh to her, but I just-"

"Hey. No, she needs to know she can't push you around. I'm proud of you."

"Really?" I said stunned, thinking surely he was trying to softly reprimand me for bickering with her.

"Really."

"Ok. But I still kind of feel bad. I hate confrontation."

"I know you do, honey," he said sweetly and pulled me to him to kiss my temple. "Just one more thing I love about you. You did good. You were truthful, not hateful. That's the difference between you two."

"If you say so."

"I do."

I smiled. "I saw you get your butt kicked."

"You did? And you didn't come save me? Those boys are vicious. All elbows and knees."

I laughed and took a bite of my noodles, muffling my next words. "I remember Danny that way. He always fought dirty."

"I remember." He smiled and took his thumb, wiped at the corner of my mouth, then stuck it in his mouth and sucked the red off. "You and your extra sauce."

He leaned down to kiss me and he tasted like sweet tea and basil. And Merrick.

Do You Speak English?
Chapter 36 - The Taker

"I know what I told you, but you have to understand, I've not been in this world for many years. Ok? I don't understand all these gadgets. The last Taker had no interest in television."

"Yes, sir. I understand and apologize, but they are ready and waiting. And I know you are wary of the makeup but they assure me it's necessary," one of the minions said.

I didn't bother to learn their names. No attachments, no endearments, no niceties. That was the only way to rule.

"Makeup is for sissies. This isn't my first broadcast you know. Now leave me."

"Yes sir," he said and walked out leaving me to my thoughts, which at the moment were irritated.

I never knew being the leader was so tedious. I didn't remember it being this not-fun before. Of course, we didn't have all this technology then. A nuisance, really. What was it good for but to zone yourself out from your life? If your life was so dull you must escape it and pretend to be someone else vicariously through a group of characters in a box on a table, you should do something about that.

I mean theater, which we always had, was entertaining somewhat, but I would never had traded my life for someone else's in it.

Ah, this is the second television appearance and I was already so done with it. But I agreed, for my plan to work I needed the humans to understand the ramifications of siding with *them*. Not with me was against me. There was no neutral anymore. No stand bys, no sit-this-one-outs. It was all or nothing. Live or die.

Everything was moving along rather nicely. The enforcement brigade was shaping up in numbers. Laughable effort, but numbers nonetheless. Humans were pitiful as they let their eyes judge and rule their bodies and actions.

Who cared if there were a hundred humans to one Lighter? It was all about presentation, skill, usefulness and craftiness. All of those things humans seem to lack. Except gullibility. They had that in droves.

But the human girls...were everything I remembered and more. The girls of this century were incredibly easy and willing. I rarely even had to use my compulsion on any of them. It was entertaining how easy it was this time around. How utterly, devastatingly quick this all would be.

The current girl was slipping her fingers in my collar as I sat and thought. She had no idea what I was and didn't care, only that I was in a position of power and girls wanted to be in her place. That was all it took.

I heard them knocking once more and I swatted her hand away. She sulked off to sit on the settee by the mirror. She knew the drill.

"Come in," I barked.

Waiting was never my strong suit but I must play my part for the humans.

"Everything is squared away. The newscasters have been given a list of the questions to ask you. This taping will be forwarded to all broadcast networks all over the United States within the week."

"Excellent. Water?"

"Certainly, sir." He picked up a bottle from the little refrigerator box under the counter and handed it to me. "Anything else, sir, before you go on?"

"Just get me in front of the camera. I'll do the rest."

Something's Just Not Right
Chapter 37 - Lillian

I woke. I felt a bit weird. Something...there was a button in my mouth. I pulled back and realized...oh. Cain's button. His shirt button, because my face was pressed to his shirt front. I pulled back further to look at him. I could barely see him with the sliver of light from the crack in the door. But it was enough.

He murmured my name in his sleep and my breath caught. I panicked, just a little bit. He was dreaming about me? Already? Was that bad? Good? Weird? I didn't know.

He felt me pulling away from his arms a bit and tightened them around me, murmuring my name again. He kissed my forehead, still asleep. I delighted at the novelty of it.

I had always loved that. The forehead kiss was a telltale kiss, I'd always thought. I mean, there was no tongue involved. It didn't get you hot and bothered. It was just sweet. When a guy started to give you forehead kisses, that was when you knew things had gone past his initial physical attraction to you. There was more there to ponder. Chaste kisses were the foundation for sweet and lovely things to come and he just did it. Granted, he was asleep, but on some subconscious level... right?

I maneuvered out of his arms finally and left him to finish his nap. He was up longer than me last night. Plus he was a guy and the unspoken rule; guys sleep anywhere, anytime, under any circumstances and would gladly do so. So, being sleep deprived must be doubly bad for them.

I inched out into the hall and straightened my clothes from being sleep bunched to find Miguel in the hall, sitting on the floor with his legs crossed, whittling of all things.

"Hello, there," he said easily.

"Hey, Miguel."

"Better?"

"Hmm?"

"Nap. Do you feel better now? You kind of passed out earlier."

"Yeah...I do, thank you. Long night."

"I heard."

I looked at him curiously.

"You whittle?"

"Is that what this is called? Then, no. Absolutely not. But I pretend."

I laughed and he got up, folding his knife in his pocket and holding the somewhat carved wooden piece in his hand.

"So, you and Cain?" He nodded to my door, knowing he was still in there, in my room.

"Um." I thought about what Cain would say. Would he want everyone to know we were official? Were we official? I was so bad at judging these things. So I just answered what I hoped was the truth. "Yeah."

He nodded like he once again already knew the answer. He looked a little disappointed.

"He's a good guy."

"Yeah, he is."

Awkward silence followed. "You don't happen to have a hot sister stashed in there somewhere, do you?"

I laughed at him, thankful for his break in the silence and his humor. "I'm afraid not."

"You've been through hell. You deserve a break from all this. And I don't just mean just today." He looked at me poignantly. "You've had it rough for while. I hope you're happy with him. Cain deserves a little bit of happy, too. We all do."

"Yeah."

I knew Miguel had had a little crush, or something, on me. I felt bad now.

"Well, I'm going to grab a cup of coffee. Want to come with?"

"Sure, I could use it, in an I.V. preferably."

He chuckled as he swung his arm for me to lead the way. "I'll see if I can rig that up."

We walked down the hall and I saw some people eating and some sitting. There were hardly any people in the commons room and things were relatively quiet. It smelled like pasta and my stomach growled, loudly.

"Let's get you some spaghetti to go with that coffee," Miguel said laughing.

"Thanks," I said and ducked my head, embarrassed by my body's inability to control its functions. "I only ate a couple hours ago, but I'm starving."

"Sherry's cooking will do that. That girl can sure whip it up for someone so young. But she learned from the best, I guess," he said sadly and smiled like he was remembering something.

"Trudy? I've heard Sherry talk about her."

"Yep. Mrs. Trudy was fierce."

"Hey!" Sherry yelled over the table in the kitchen and came to hug me. "Are

364

you doing ok? Hungry?"

"Starved." I looked knowingly at Miguel and he winked at me. "Don't, Sherry, I'll get it." I grabbed her arm to keep her from heading toward the stove. "Everybody worries just a little bit too much about me around here. Why is that?"

"We love you," Sherry said sweetly.

She meant it and I felt a pang in my ribs. My heart clenched. "Thanks, Sherry. I love you, too."

"*And* I'm outta here," Miguel said raising his arms, backing away like we were dangerous.

"Miguel?" Sherry asked playfully.

"Girl talk comes out, I hit the road. I can't deal with tears. Literally. I'm allergic."

"Well then you'd better run-"

He took off running and then turned at the door to wink at us before walking out.

"He's crazy."

"He's sweet."

"That, too," Sherry said laughing then sobered. "So, how's Cain?"

I stiffened and immediately felt guilty. He'd assured me he was over her. I shouldn't react this way. They were friends long before I came along and we all lived together. I had to get over this.

"He's ok, I'm letting him sleep. He's just tired."

"Speak for yourself, cutie." Cain walked in behind us and didn't stop until he was flush in front of me, our toes touching. "I don't know about you, but I feel great."

He reached for me, his arm going around my waist, his hand to the back of my neck. He smiled and bent his head down to mine. His lips pressed gently. It was an easy kiss, I think that's what he meant for it to be, but I felt him hesitate. Then he pressed harder and his lips parted.

I felt all restraint drain from me like water through my fingers. My hands squeezed his shirt hem in my hands and he kept kissing me. Sherry and I had been in the kitchen alone and I distantly heard a little giggle and a girly cleared throat before footsteps retreating.

Cain had somehow walked us back to the wall. I hadn't felt myself move but I felt the wall stop my back. Once again, I could tell he was being tentative with me. Gentle. I could also tell this wasn't the end of his list of wants, but he was attempting to rein it in. I remembered we hadn't had any kisses since we'd been home. Not any 'we're safe, we made it home, I'm so glad' kisses. That must be what this was.

I moved my hand to his chin, his cheek, then around to the back of his head to rub and scratch his barely-there hair and he groaned and pressed me further into the wall.

Hmm. I think he liked it.

I did it again and he groaned - half growled - again then broke off and looked at me, touching his tongue ring to his lip like he needed to figure something out.

"What?" I ask breathlessly and thoroughly amused.

"You're not gonna make this whole 'being a gentleman thing' easy on me, are you?"

"I thought you didn't want to pollute my ears with filth talk? That's practically an innuendo, mister."

He laughed and nuzzled my nose with his. "You are just so amazing. I hope you know that," he said softly, his blue green gaze on my blues.

I just smiled.

Then Danny walked in.

"Oh, for Pete's sake! Can I go in any room in the place and not see the Nature Channel?" Danny said with his hands on his head like he was in pain.

"*Please*! You and Celeste are twice as bad as anybody in here," Cain said through a laugh.

"Not the point. It's like the Love Boat up in-" Danny was cut off as he turned back around to go in to the commons room.

We burst out laughing. Once we settled, Cain smoothed my hair back, tucking it behind my ear. "If Danny is complaining, it must be bad."

"Terribly bad. Aren't you concerned?" I said mockingly.

"Not a bit." He kissed me once more before licking his lips and grinning then he sniffed. "Is that spaghetti I smell?"

Sherry, Baby.
Chapter 38 - Sherry

"Ok. Um, that's fine, I guess. I've just never worked the store before," I answered Margo not really understanding why she was insisting I learn to operate the store.

"I know. That's why I think it's important for you to learn." Something was definitely going on. She hadn't looked me in the eye since we'd been talking. "I know there's a lot of people here, but what if something happened to all of us who do know how to work it? I think everyone should take a crash course, at least one night, just in case."

Her words were on the verge of a lie. It was the truth but not all of it. I couldn't really figure it out, but...

"Well, you have a point. But the need warehouses are coming soon so we won't need it anymore," I argued.

"But maybe we can sell something else other than food. We are the only place for miles around. What about emergency stops and things like that?"

"But you know Merrick, he's not going to like this and he'll probably insist on helping me."

"Uh..." She looked unsure. What was with her? "That's ok. He can stay with you if he wants."

She seemed to be wording things carefully.

"Ok. Well, Lillian, Danny and Celeste have kitchen duty tonight so I'm free. This afternoon then?"

"Yes. Great, meet me up there in an hour and we'll get started."

"Ok."

She walked away stiffly. Margo hadn't been the same since that day she was tricked by the Lighters to ring the bell, causing us to investigate outside and some of us died. I understood her guilt but I wished she would ease up a little. It was depressing to watch her be so depressed.

I marched out of the kitchen to the commons room to find Merrick sitting with Lily on his lap in the corner. They looked to be conspiring. I quirked my brow and watched them with intense fascination. I heard Merrick humming and saw him swaying.

Merrick? Humming?

Then I heard his voice stretch together in long baritone notes that sounded strangely like singing.

Merrick? Singing?

I inched closer, trying to look inconspicuous but failing miserably as I stubbed my toe on the record player console.

"Hi!" Lily said cheerily.

"Hi," I answered and took a seat beside them on the floor. "You two look busy."

"We are. Daddy's teaching me a song."

Daddy...Ahh.

"Really? What song?" I asked then looked at Merrick. "I wasn't aware you knew any songs."

"Well, Cain kind of taught me one, on one of our trips to town."

He cleared his throat, like he was uncomfortable.

"Uhuh. And what song is that?"

Lily took over and belted out the lyrics sweetly and I was pleasantly surprised. The kid could actually stay on key.

"Aww, Lily, thank you. That was so great."

"I wuv that song! I can't believe you have a song with youw name in it!" she said amazed.

"I know," I said, tweaking her nose. "Pretty neat, huh?"

"Do I have a song with my name in it?"

"Well," I thought racking my brain, "there is a song by the Pink Martinis called Lily, but I'm not sure it's age appropriate."

"What's age appwopwiate?"

Merrick and I laughed.

"It means not for you. You want a snack?"

"Yes, pwease."

"I see Marissa in the kitchen. Why don't you run and ask her for some crackers."

"Ok."

She skipped away. We needed to change her nickname from Bug to Skippy.

I turned to Merrick. "Margo wants me to work the store tonight. She thinks we should all learn to run it, just in case. Something about opening the store for a new venue other than food since the need warehouses are coming soon. I don't know what else we'd sell. Tires?" I asked sarcastically.

"Hmm. Well...I see her point. I'll come with you."

I laughed, knowing he would.

"I figured. We've got about forty five minutes until we need to head up. Got any ideas of what we could do?" I bit my lip and he smiled.

"Oh, I have some ideas, but they aren't what you're thinking."

"Are you sure? I'm pretty sure it's the same." I climbed onto his lap.

"Mine involves you lying on your back."

I felt my eyes bulge. "Merrick!" I chided.

"In the practice room."

"What? I don't think we should-"

"You'd be on your back because that's where I'd put you. After I kicked your cute butt."

"What-" It dawned on me and I looked up to see his teasing smile. "You want to practice. Like, for real practice? My idea was way better," I grumbled.

"Well, we've got to get some training in some time and with us in the store tonight, we may as well use this time for it."

"Ok," I conceded grudgingly, "fine, but if anybody is lying on their back, it's gonna be you, pal." I poked his chest as we stood up together.

"Says the girl who won't even take a swing."

"Ah! Well, I may have to change that rule. Like, right now."

"Bring it, gorgeous. I'm ready."

"Ok. Just don't use your alien mojo on me," I said backing up like I was scared.

He grinned widely. "Oooh, you are in so much trouble now," he rumbled and made an advance towards me.

I took off running. He could have beaten me and overtook me in a second, but he didn't. We ran all the way, him on my heels to the practice room in the back and then he grabbed me, turning me towards him. He knocked my feet out from under me, catching me under my back and legs before I hit the ground. Then he laid me gently to the floor.

"You were saying," he taunted before pulling me up to my feet.

We practiced the holds and the breaking maneuvers. I still refused to punch him until we were using the practice pillows. I kicked and punched and blocked and felt pretty good when we were done. But sweaty, as predicted.

We took a quick shower and I pulled my wet hair up into a loose bun to keep from having to fix it. I followed Merrick upstairs. I hardly recognized the place.

For one, most of the shelves were empty. We hadn't been able to get deliveries for a long time. The Taker knew people would avoid going to the big stores and just do that so he kyboshed the whole thing. So we had been adding items for the store to our normal shopping trips but it was hard to stock a store that way.

Besides, the need warehouses were about to end all that.

We found Margo behind the counter, wiping. I envisioned her up here, hour after hour, wiping. She didn't seem like the type to just sit and relax.

She looked up and saw us, he gaze focused on Merrick and not me. Again, she looked uneasy. She swallowed and put on a fake smile.

"Great, you're both here. Let's get started."

She showed us how to work the cash register, an older one. I got it in no time, but Merrick was another story. She walked us through and told us what all the switches and buttons were for. How to lock and unlock the doors. Emergency procedures for gas pump issues. Gas being the only thing that could still be delivered, she also showed us the paper and procedure for that.

After an hour, my brain was exhausted and I felt like a gooey overfull sponge.

"Ok, Margo. I'm not sure I can remember much more, tonight. We're here. Let us run things while you go take it easy."

She still refused to look at me so I thought maybe she just needed a break.

"Uh, well, if you're sure."

I looked around at the store. Dead and not a single customer had come in the whole time I'd been up here.

"I'm sure."

"Well, be careful." She hugged me. It felt awkward and desperate. I was starting to think something was wrong that she wasn't telling us about. "I'll leave you to it then."

She left and Merrick looked at me questioningly. "You noticed that, too?" I asked.

"Yeah," he answered.

"She's still freaked. I'm sure it's fine. Ok, what to do now?"

"Shelve chips?"

"Sure. Sounds exciting," I said with mock enthusiasm.

We shelved chip bags for a few minutes, then Margo stuck her head around the corner.

"Merrick? Can you come downstairs for a minute?"

"Sure. What do you need?"

"I- Can you just come down. Hurry."

She took off the other way. Merrick followed her quickly, thinking the worst I'm sure. He turned to me before reaching the corner.

"Stay inside, ok? I'll be right back."

I nodded.

Not a minute later I heard the door ding to alert me that a customer had entered the store. I shot up from where I was and smoothed the dirt from my pant legs for the floor, making my way to the counter.

"Can I help you?" I asked.

I looked up half way to the counter to see three Lighters standing there watching me. They didn't look like they were there to buy anything. The last traces of the sun were disappearing behind the afternoon horizon and it cast an eerie glow over the three like angels. They were *anything* but angels.

I tried to slow my pulse that had shot up to loud levels in my ears. I smiled and cocked my head slightly when they didn't answer me. I tried to be flirty or ditsy or something, anything but myself so they wouldn't suspect anything.

"Looking for anything specific?"

"Yes. And we've found it." The middle one blurred to me and grabbed me my upper arm. "You. Let's go."

He started to tug me away. I wondered if they still had memories of me from the previous Taker. They didn't say my name. Was the new Taker after me? Was that what they were doing?

"I can't just leave. I'm working," I tried to reason.

"Not anymore you're not."

He stopped me and looked me dead in the eye. His black eyes widened, focused and darkened even more, if possible.

"You will come with us and there will be no fussing. Understand me?"

I realized he was trying to compel me. Well, Lighters didn't really compel but persuaded with their Lighter speak. Merrick had explained it all. Takers compel but it was apparent I was still supposed to feel some kind of pull and do what he said. He sat there looking at me close and expectantly. It was then I got it. They had no idea who I was or they'd know I was a rebel and immune to the Lighter speak. They didn't remember me.

So what were they doing with me?

I did the only thing I could think of, pretend. If I didn't go along with them or if I tried to run, they would catch me and they'd find the others. It'd be an ambush, a surprise attack. And they'd know we were here if they got away and could come back to finish the job.

I begged silently for Merrick to come back but I could stall no longer. There was no way to alert Merrick without letting the Lighters know others were here.

"Ok. Yes, I understand. I'll come with you. Can I leave my boss a note?"

"No. Move."

I moved, his freezing hand was still on my arm as he led me out of the store front. I tried to keep my face impassive and blank. I wanted to scream. Every vein and muscle in my body rebelled, making me shake but the Lighter didn't seem to notice. The other two Lighters flanked us as we headed to a small black BMW. It was ironic, my only chance to ever ride in a BMW was with Lighters and I couldn't even enjoy it.

"In," the Lighter commanded tersely and pushed my head to get me inside quickly and not gently. "Seat belt. Wouldn't want anything to happen to you. Yet."

I put it on as the other two Lighters sat with me in the back and the other one started the car. I looked back at the store once, searching for Merrick's face in the window, looking for me. Nothing. We drove away and I could hear the gravel crunching under the tires. It was the saddest sound I'd ever heard.

I knew they'd have no way to find me, no way of knowing where I was. I also knew, they'd never stop looking. Merrick would never stop, even if it killed him.

We drove for a while, the only light around us were the cars headlights on the road in front of us. No one said a word and the radio wasn't on. Silence. I was getting antsy, I could see we were heading to town, but other than that, I hadn't been here enough to remember anything significant about the place. Once I saw lights up ahead, street lights, I leaned forward to see better. The Lighter beside me pushed me back into my seat and then spoke.

"Now?" he asked.

The one driving met my eyes in the mirror.

"Now."

I saw the elbow coming from my right before I felt it, but it was too late to do anything about it. My head and face smashed into the window on my left.

And then nothing.

I woke with a gasp and felt a burning sensation on my face. That's wasn't all I felt. My eye was swollen and my ear and temple hurt. I blinked hard in the too bright harsh light. I finally focused and saw I was lying on a rough concrete floor. White floor, white walls, white ceiling and nothing else.

I was alone as I looked around. I tried to sit up, but immediately regretted that. My stomach heaved and wretched but nothing came up. I wondered how many times I'd thrown up already to have an empty stomach. I could see stars dancing in front of my eyes and my head pounded like someone was squeezing it between their hands to the tune of my heartbeat.

It was so hot, I was sweating and my shirt was stuck to my body. I pushed back against the wall, as far from the door as I could get. It took me a minute to understand the gravity of the situation. My vision blurred and my stomach still felt queasy. I had a concussion, I knew that much. I remembered the Lighter hitting me, I remembered leaving the store. I remembered everything.

Well, I thought I remembered everything up until he hit me. Who knew what had happened since then. How long had I been there?

I wrapped my arms around my knees to press on my stomach. Anything to make the nausea go away. I leaned my head back against the wall, taking deep breaths and tried desperately not to think about Merrick. Danny. Lily.

I felt tears come just thinking their names and the very idea of never seeing them again.

Oh, God. Merrick had to know I was gone by now. Had to. He would be frantic, setting up a search party. I hoped not. Maybe Jeff could talk him down, talk him into sense. They didn't have a chance in finding me. They'd just risk everyone else. I hoped Merrick realized that.

What was I doing here? Why hadn't someone come in yet?

I suddenly realized something and pushed all thoughts away. Could they read my thoughts through the door? If so, I wasn't going to just keep feeding them information. Instead, I ran through all the words to every Beatles song I knew.

Hours passed. Silent, except for my whispering words, hours. Long, painful, hungry, thirsty, hot, gut wrenching hours. I had no idea what time it was or how long I'd been barely humming when I ran out of the Beatles songs I knew. There had to be a reason for this. They wanted something from me or they wouldn't have brought me here.

Some of my hair had escaped the bun and was matted to my forehead and neck. My clothes were dirty and sweaty, it looked like they had dragged me through the dirt and I was missing a shoe. It was so hot. It wasn't just hot, like naturally, it was blazing warm air as if they were pumping heat in the small room...on purpose. I'd thrown up but didn't know where, I didn't smell great and my breath was rancid. I could've drank five gallons of water and eaten who knows how many plates of lasagna.

I decided to see if my theory was correct, if they were listening. I cleared my mind of everything but one thought.

'What do you want with me?'

I waited and repeated in my mind and waited and repeated. I stared an angry hole in the door just willing someone to come through it. Nothing.

I slipped into a pre-sleep state. I didn't close my eyes, but just zoned out. I was a little worried. You weren't supposed to go to sleep after a concussion were you but I had been asleep already. I kept my eyes open and focused on the lines between the white bricks of the walls.

I moved on to 80's rock ballads to hum mindlessly, then random annoying pop songs, then commercial jingles. I sang the Toys-R-Us jingle more the twenty times, thinking that would drive anyone insane and they would surely come stop me. But, no. I had to think of something else, something productive, but couldn't risk them seeing it.

The hours stretched even longer, and soon, I became so exhausted than I couldn't not fall asleep. It had to have been more than a day. Had to be. The last thing I remembered was sliding down the wall to the hard floor. My rear and back numb, pulsing and aching from sitting so long. My head hurt so bad that I didn't think I could take it another second without screaming, then...sleep found me, unwanted as it was.

I woke with another gasp, having no idea if it had been seconds or hours since I'd fallen asleep. It felt like déjà vu. I blinked at the lights still on and bright. I laid back and pushed down the heaving of my stomach, tried to balance out the stars and blurs in my vision with actual sight.

Then I realized someone was in the room with me. I could hear his breathing. I rolled slowly over, trying desperately not to let the screams of agony from my head hurting and body cramping vocalize. I sat up to face the door to see a Lighter leaning his back on it. It was shut but he was just standing there, arms crossed, looking menacing and pensive.

He pushed off the door and came to squat in front of me. He had on a big long black jacket and black pants. His boots were almost touching my feet he was so close. He watched me carefully with his black eyes and I couldn't do much but stare back and wait.

He reached inside his jacket pocket and pulled out a bottle of water. He didn't wait for me to take it or taunt me with it. He twisted off the cap and reached out, took my shaky hand in his ice cold one and put the water bottle in it. I put it to my lips, trying to savor it, save it, but no good. I was thirsting to death, literally, and without even meaning to I guzzled the whole bottle in seconds.

He almost smiled - smiled? - and pulled out another one. Setting it off to the side near me. Then he pulled a granola bar out and unwrapped it for me. He pushed it towards me and I took it. I bit into it and closed my eyes at the pain of my stomach growling. I swallowed with barely chewing and bit again.

He sat the whole time right in front of me with fascination all over his face. Then he spoke as I took the last bite.

"Better?" he asked, his voice soft.

I swallowed hard and cleared my throat.

"Yes."

He nodded and pulled another bar out for me, setting it beside the water bottle. I was tempted to grab that one, too, as I was still hungry, but something told me that might be my only meal for later. Then he held his hand out for me. I tentatively put my hand under his and he dropped two white, oblong pills into my palm.

I should have been wary about the pills I guess, but if they wanted to hurt me, and they already had, I knew they could. They wouldn't drug me, wouldn't do it the easy way. I grabbed the water bottle and took one sip to swallow the pills, then saved the rest.

My stomach was not happy with the sudden intake of food after being so empty and I felt like I wanted to be sick again, but I took deep breaths to stave it off.

"How's your head?" he asked quietly.

"Hurts," I answered just as softly.

"I'm sorry about that."

"You didn't do it," I said, clearly remembering the Lighter who had sucker punched me.

He smiled and looked like he wanted to laugh at my joke.

"The medicine should help."

"Thank you," I said quietly and nodded once.

"Do you know why you're here?" I shook my head. "You know what I am." It was not a question but I nodded anyway. "How?"

I silently rehearsed the Pledge of Allegiance in my mind instead of answering.

He chuckled softly. "You know, because of you, I've gained an extensive knowledge of earthly American musical history." Aha! So they were listening. Thank God I thought to sing instead of pining for a rescue from certain individuals. "You're smart, that's good. You are going to need to be." He shifted and got closer to me, completely blocking the door's view from me. "You are going to need to be strong and disciplined and patient if you want to make it out of this."

I looked at him blankly. I was very confused. He was strange and unlike any Lighter I'd met before, which unfortunately had been a few.

He whispered his words to me, like it was a secret. "I've been assigned to your door for now. I know you won't believe me, but I'm blocking you, meaning-no one can read your thoughts but me. When I'm in this room with you, I'll do that, but when I'm not don't trust anyone or anything. Keep your mind blank. Use your songs, whatever it takes."

I felt my brow furrow and he sighed softly.

"You'll have to stay here. I can't just walk out with you, not right now. We'll have to wait for the right time. You'll have to tough it out for a while. I know it's not fun and they will be in later to interrogate you. And that...definitely won't be fun but I'll help any way I can. Be strong."

He got up to leave, my mouth wide open in confusion and wondering. He was tricking me, trying to get me to let my guard down around him.

He turned back around to look at me.

"I'm not, like I said, I knew you wouldn't believe me, but at this point, it doesn't matter. I can't change anything. You're here and most humans don't leave this place."

"Where am I?" I croaked out.

"You're at an enforcement containment facility for rebels. This cell is an interrogation room. The last room most humans see before..."

He didn't need to finish. I knew exactly what he was going to say. Before they die.

"Why are you telling me this? Trying to scare me into confessing something?"

"I won't have to scare you," he said sadly. "You'll be scared plenty enough without my help, but...I'm working on something, just tough it out until then." He turned to go, but stopped at the door, turned one last time and gave me a sad smile. "By the way, my name is Daniel."

Useless Measures
Chapter 39 - Merrick

I practically blurred to keep up with Margo as she ran down the hall. All the way down, passed all the new rooms, passed the new bathroom. All the way down to where the rooms ended and the new construction began.

I couldn't help but wonder what kind of problem there could be way down there. Then she stopped and turned around. She just stood there, looking at me. I stared at her expectantly.

"Margo, you said there was a problem, didn't you?"

"No, Merrick. I didn't."

"No you-" She was right. I assumed. "You told me to come, to hurry. What is it?"

"Just wait."

"For what?"

"Just wait!"

I sighed and looked around. I watched her for any sign of something. She just continued to stand there. "Ok, Margo, I'm sorry, but I don't like Sherry being up there alone. I'm going to go back up if there isn't anything you need."

"Just wait!" she yelled and grabbed my arm to stop me.

"For what?"

"Something's going to happen."

"What do you mean?" I said as chills ran up my arms.

"Just wait for it. We must wait."

I tried to pull my arm, but she tightened her grip and I didn't want to hurt her. "Let go, Margo."

"Almost time." She looked all around at the walls and ceiling. Her eyes were glazed over. "Just wait. Almost. See, I had to be careful. Sherry can tell if I lie. She can tell, so I had to watch my words. Be careful, they told me. Don't look at the ones eyes who had been marked by the Markers before, they'll know, they said. Make sure you do this, they said. Don't mess up."

I jolted and felt my heart skip. I grabbed her shoulders and made her look at me. I knew that look. I pulled her shirt up and there it was. She didn't even try to stop me.

NO! No, not Margo.

The shiny red circular patch was right over her ribs on the right side and she was under the compulsion. Oh no. With the patch, they could see through the person's eyes, anytime they wanted. They had seen everything. The bunker, us, the store. Who knew how long she had it on. It must not have been too long or they would have been here already to storm us, right?

"Margo, what did they tell you to do?"

"They said to get one that was important and small, fragile and easy. One that the rest of us would come after if she was taken. One that would draw us out of hiding. One that we would try to rescue."

Sherry. No!

I took off running. I blurred all the way up to the commons room, up the stairs to the store and saw it was empty.

Sherry! Answer me!

I ran outside. It was dark and I didn't see any lights anywhere. I ran into the street and looked both ways. Nothing. I blurred back into the store and searched every closet, every room, and every cabinet.

Sherry!

It was useless. They used Margo to lure Sherry there and she lured me away so they could take her. Oh, God, no. They took her. It was hard to breathe. No! No stopping. We had to go, move quickly if we were going to get her back.

I blurred back downstairs, straight to Margo. She was still leaning on the wall down the hall where I left her.

"When did they put this on you?"

I pulled up her shirt again and pointed to the patch but didn't touch it.

"This morning. They wouldn't take me. I'm not important they said. I'm old they said. They didn't want me."

"Margo," I chose my words carefully, "they can't make you take the patch."

"No. No, they said they'd make me a Lighter if I didn't put it on. They said I'd be one of them and turn against you. They said she'd be safe it I took it."

"Who'd be safe? Sherry?"

"Celeste."

Of course. They saw Celeste in her mind and used it against her. I didn't bother to contradict her that females couldn't be Lighters and they were lying to her. It didn't matter anymore. This was all about to get very ugly.

"Do they know about us? Why didn't they attack us?"

"They don't know. I only thought of Celeste. I couldn't help it. I didn't think of any of you down here. I was smart, was good. Only Celeste. They put patches on everyone along this highway. They are looking for us. They want us all to look *for* them, be their eyes. They are looking for *us*."

So they were just spreading out. The store wasn't pinpointed.

"What else did they say? Why take Sherry, then?"

"They are taking people to torture them for information and then put them out as bait for a rescue. That's how they think they'll find us. You'll rescue her and they'll find you. Poor Sherry. Tortured."

"Enough, Margo! Enough!" I barked.

I couldn't listen to her say another word about Sherry and the things I had no doubt they'd do to her. Were we not prepared to do just that and more to the Lighter we captured when they took the kids?

I took off my button up shirt and tied it around her eyes, leaving me with a white undershirt.

Jeff! Max! Ryan! Kay!

I called them all in my mind, pulling Margo behind me we swiftly made our way down the hall. I banged on doors the whole way. I heard people come out of their rooms behind me.

"Commons room. Now!"

Get everyone in the commons room. Now!

We got there. I was so mad I was shaking furiously. I felt like I could literally kill someone. This was worse than the caves. There'd be no hideout for Sherry this time.

It wasn't Margo's fault, I knew that, and now, she was going to die for being naive. Once the patch was removed, she'd die and there wasn't anything we could do to stop that.

We assembled. It looked like a lot of people, but no way to remember everyone to tell if we were all there or not. I was going to start without waiting any longer but Jeff interrupted.

"What's up, Merrick?"

What did Margo do?

"Mom? What's the matter?" Celeste asked.

I ignored her, for now.

"Everyone, lift your shirts." They all just looked at me like I was insane. I was too mad to hold my anger in. "Now!" I bellowed.

They did, reluctantly, and I searched. I saw Jeff searching, too, knowing what I was looking for.

"We'll need to search everyone further, just to make sure."

"Why are you looking for patches on us? Why would one of us have one?" Cain asked.

I lifted Margo's shirt in answer and heard the gasps, a scream I knew was attached to Celeste, the cries of outrage. Most everyone knew you had to accept it, it couldn't be forced on you. Celeste ran forward and started to remove the shirt I had tied around Margo's eyes.

Kay got to her before I could grab her. "No, Celeste. We can't, honey, you know that. She'll see, which means they'll see. She's not herself right now."

I knew from the look on Celeste's face she knew what that meant. She'd been there when we had to deal with Bobby. When he attacked us and then when the patch was removed. She knew her mother was going to die.

She cringed back up against Kay and buried her face in her neck as Kay wrapped her arms around her. She looked back at me and shook her head in anger and resentment at what would have to be done. There was no easy way to do this.

And they didn't even know about Sherry yet.

"Max? Will you take Margo to a room somewhere? We'll have to...deal with that later." I took a deep painful breath. "They took Sherry," I blurted out and felt a hot sear of pain through my chest at speaking the words out loud. I laid a hand on the wall to steady myself.

I couldn't even recount or recall the explosion of emotion and words and movements that happened after that. I did remember the pressure and fuzz of so many Keepers probing my brain at once to get the full story.

"Oh, no," I heard Jeff mutter beside me as he saw what I knew, Marissa pressing him for details quietly.

Danny came bounding through the line and stood beside me, taking Celeste from Kay. He was torn between comforting his girl and rescuing his sister. He petted her head and I was proud, for just a second, I let myself be proud, let the rage go and saw him. He was doing what needed to be done. He couldn't just let Celeste stand there broken and he couldn't forget Sherry needed us.

He was fierce. He looked me in the eye. I knew what he was doing. He was waiting on instructions, on plans to go and get his sister. In his mind, there was nothing else to think about.

"Wait, wait!" Piper yelled. "Now, they set this trap and don't even look at me, Merrick. I saw it all in your mind. They took her on purpose, knowing you'd all run after her like a bunch of naïve idiots. You cannot go after her and risk everyone else."

"Oh, this is just your dream come true isn't it, Piper!" Celeste yelled, pulling her face up from Danny's shoulder to look at her. "Sherry out of the picture. Everyone knows you hate her!"

"I do, but that has nothing to do with it. They told Margo it was a trap for us. It would be dumb to just go after her."

"True," Jeff said and looked at me. "But since when do we do the smart thing? I'm with you, brother, all the way. Say the word."

Everyone seemed to be torn. This was Sherry we were talking about. We had to get her back but it *was* a trap. What *were* we going to do?

"Uh, Merrick?" Cain spoke up and detangled himself gently from Lillian, who was clearly stricken at Sherry's ordeal, stepped forward. "I know a way." He glanced over at Billings. "Billings? I still got that job offer?"

Billings looked puzzled, then brightened and nodded his head.

"It could work. They hire people every day on the spot. That Lighter, Daniel, killed all the Lighters who saw me help you so I shouldn't be compromised. I could go with you, be your mentor. We could start in the morning."

"Wait. What are you talking about?" Danny asked.

"They'd take her to an enforcement facility containment building. There's a big one in Effingham. I'd bet my last paycheck they took her there. And, *hello*, I'm an enforcer. Guess who can get in and guess who gets a nice fat bonus for bringing in a new recruit."

"So, you're saying you and Cain are gonna just go in there and walk out with Sherry?"

"What else we got?"

Danny hung his head. Celeste rubbed his back and whispered something in his ear.

I tried not to look at him. I tried not to think. I knew all the things they'd be doing to her. I couldn't imagine waiting around until morning to go after her. I felt nauseous. I felt ill and green and devastated all at once. I needed to do something. I needed to jump in the first vehicle I could find and go after her now, the fact that I'd be killed in the process didn't matter, only the fact that she would too was stopping me.

I didn't know how much longer I could just sit here though, chatting about what to do about it.

"Wait, wait, wait," Piper chimed in again. "This is all a little coincidental, isn't it? Billing comes here the day before Sherry is taken? Seems a little too much of a coincidence for me to accept."

"Hey. Now hold on a minute-" Billings said, looking defensive, but it was too late.

I could already see the wheels turning all around me. People were wondering if she could be right. In fact, for a second, I entertained the idea myself, but then I remembered a certain Muse with a knack for figuring out these things.

"Marissa?" I said and when she looked, I nodded my head toward Billings.

She knew what I wanted. She started to cross the room towards him. He of course was wide eyed, not knowing what we were doing, but Marissa looked harmless enough. If he only knew.

"No way!" Piper yelled when Marissa was almost to Billings. "You made the rules. No using our gifts on each other, remember? So she can't touch him or else she has to leave. Your rules!"

"Shut up, Piper! This is different and you know it," Jeff yelled taking a couple steps forward toward Marissa. "Go ahead, babe. No one's going to touch you."

She looked to me. I nodded and then she looked at Danny.

"Please," he said softly.

She nodded and started towards him again.

"Nuhuh! I won't stand here while you change the rules to fit the situation! I do it and you throw me to the wolves but you'll let- Hey! Put me down!" she yelled and squealed.

Miguel picked her up and threw her over his shoulder, fireman style. He looked back at us and yelled over her screaming.

"Go on then. I'll take this one and find a nice, quiet, *locked* place for her," he said and then carried her screaming and beating his back down the hall yelling. I heard her say Neanderthal and barbarian but I blocked her out.

Jeff moved forward and spoke loudly at Marissa's side.

"Everyone understands the situation right? Anyone object to Marissa using her gift on Billings to get the truth?"

No one raised their hand and he urged her on with a hand on her back.

"Go ahead, sweetie. All clear."

She stepped in front of Billings.

"This won't hurt, just let it happen. Ok?" He nodded, reluctantly, and she touched his arm. "Are you telling the truth about wanting to help us?"

"Yes," he answered flatly.

She touched his arm again.

"Do you still work for the Lighters, the enforcers?"

"No."

Once more she touched his arm.

"Will you betray us to them, turn us in?"

"No."

"Good enough for me. Let's get cracking," Danny said and crossed his arms, ready for battle.

Cain spoke next, just as fierce and determined.

"Ok, now that we got that out of the way, let's get this all worked out. Billings, you and me got to get ready. We head out to work for evil, first thing in the morning."

THE END FOR NOW...

Be on the lookout for other books available in Kindle, E-book and paperback for the Collide series and other series by Shelly Crane.

Thank you to my God first of all and my family for supporting me through my endeavors of writing. It was a whim one day that has turned into this thing that I love. Thank you all who have helped me and to the ones who purchase my books, I hope you enjoy reading it as much as I enjoyed writing it.

Thank you.

You can find Shelly at many avenues. She would be thrilled to answer your questions or take your comments, good or bad.

http://www.facebook.com/shellycranefanpage

http://twitter.com/#!/AuthShellyCrane

http://shellycrane.blogspot.com/

Shelly is a bestselling YA author from a small town in Georgia and loves everything about the south. She is wife to a fantastical husband and stay at home mom to two boisterous and mischievous boys who keep her on her toes. They currently reside in everywhere USA as they happily travel all over with her husband's job. She loves to spend time with her family, binge on candy corn, go out to eat at new restaurants, buy paperbacks at little bookstores, site see in the new areas they travel to, listen to music everywhere and also LOVES to read.

Her own books happen by accident and she revels in the writing and imagination process. She doesn't go anywhere without her notepad for fear of an idea creeping up and not being able to write it down immediately, even in the middle of the night, where her best ideas are born.

Shelly's website:

www.shellycrane.blogspot.com

11157527R00218

Made in the USA
San Bernardino, CA
07 May 2014